D1234702

WANTED
BOOK ONE IN THE WANTED SERIES

FROM *NEW YORK TIMES* AND *USA TODAY* BESTSELLING AUTHOR
Kelly Elliott

Wanted

Published by Kelly Elliott

Copyright © 2012 by Kelly Elliott

ISBN 978-0-988-7074-2-9

http://authorkellyelliott.blogspot.com/

Cover photo: Rutheah Rodehorst with Blue House Fotos www.bluehousefotos.com

Cover designer: Sarah Hansen with Okaycreations.net

Thank you Sarah for the beautiful cover!

Editor: Debra Zupancic

Interior Designer: Jovana Shirley, Unforeseen Editing, www.unforeseenediting.com

Other books by Kelly Elliott

Wanted Series

WANTED

Saved

faithful

Believe
a novella

Cherished

Full-length novels in the WANTED series
are also available in audio.

Broken Series

BROKEN

 Dedication

This book is dedicated to my husband Darrin and my daughter Lauren.

Contents

Seven Years Old

I stood crying against the wall. Mommy was acting weird again and it was scaring me. This is how she acts when she drinks the bad stuff that Jefferson calls beer. I just want to run and get away before she sees me again and yells. She said she was going to make me cookies and that we would go to the park to swing on the swings. I was so happy thinking about how much fun we would have.

Mommy had been mad ever since her friend called. She told me we were not going to the park today because she was feeling sad and needed a drink.

"You would not have fun at the park Ellie anyway." But I knew I would especially because I loved the swings at school. I wish Jefferson was home; my tummy hurts so bad, and I'm so hungry.

Then she screamed out my name…. "Ellie!"

I jumped and quickly wiped the tears away. If she saw me crying she would just get mad at me again. I walked up to her very slowly.

She was sitting at the kitchen table with her face in her hands. "Y-yes Mommy?" She looked up at me and frowned. I know who she is thinking of when she looks at me that way. She tells me all the time I have his eyes. Jefferson says my eyes are blue like the sky.

Mommy has pretty dark brown hair. My hair is much lighter than mommy's. Jefferson likes to brush my hair and always tells me how pretty I am and that I am a princess. He said some day my prince will come and save me and take me away from this bad place. Mommy never tells me I am pretty, she just tells me I look like my daddy. She hates my daddy.

"Ellie, Ellie, Ellie." She said her l's really funny, like she was having a hard time saying them.

"Do you know that you will *never* be wanted? No one will ever love you, just like I have never been loved. No man will ever really want you. You need to know that now. I wish someone would have told me that; fuck it would have saved me a lot of pain."

Mommy was still talking funny. Did she not want me anymore?

"Mommy, I'm sorry for whatever I did. *Please* don't be mad at me. *Please* want me mommy!" I cried out. She just started to laugh and then she put her head back in her hands and told me to get out of her sight. I had a funny feeling in my chest and my tummy. Why was it so hard for me to breathe? I walked over to the corner in the kitchen and sat down.

When will Jefferson get home? I just want Jefferson......I need Jefferson.

"You will never be wanted by anyone......remember that Ellie darlin', remember that"......

Nine Years Later

Bryce had brought me to my favorite pizza shop for my sixteenth birthday, and I was so excited. We'd been dating for four months now and he was just so sweet, he only ever kissed me and never tried to take it further which was so nice. He said he loved how innocent I was.

While we waited for our pizza I excused myself and went to the restroom. I was standing at the sink when a girl with beautiful blonde hair walked in. I instantly recognized her from school. I was pretty sure she was in eleventh grade like Bryce.

I smiled as she walked up to me. She returned my smile with a sad smile and seemed nervous.

"Ellie Johnson right?"

"Yes, I'm sorry, I recognize you but I can't place your name."

"That's okay; I wouldn't really expect you to know who I am Ellie. My name is Denise Watkins."

Oh, I've heard of this girl. Ari said she was easy and that every guy with a working penis had fucked her.

"Ellie, I really like you. I mean I like how sweet and kind you are to everyone. I wish I could be more like you."

WHAT? Where the hell did that coming from?

"Um, thank you Denise, that's very sweet of you to say that."

"Ellie, I'm going to cut to the chase here. Do you know where Bryce was last night? I only ask because I think you deserve the truth."

I shook my head yes. I had a very bad feeling about where this was going.

My mother's words popped into my head.

You will never be wanted by anyone……..

"Yes, he was um, he was at a study group at Melissa's house last night."

Denise looked sad. Her eyes filled with tears and she looked away from me.

"No he wasn't Ellie."

"How do you know that?"

She lowered her head, and I could see the tears falling from her eyes. Oh holy hell.

"I know because he was fucking me in the backseat of his car last night."

I just stood there….stunned. I couldn't believe it. This was not happening to me. I thought he was different!

Oh my God……I felt like I was going to be sick.

"Why are you telling me this?"

"I didn't want to tell you but I really like you and you're so innocent and that fucker does *not* deserve to have you on his arm like some trophy

3

while he is going behind your back and fucking everything with a pussy. I'm sorry Ellie. I didn't mean to hurt you. I hope that you can forgive me some day."

I shook my head to clear my thoughts. I looked her right in the eyes and I could see how embarrassed and disgraced she was.

"Thank you Denise for telling me, I really do appreciate you being honest with me."

I tried to get composed before I turned and walked out of the bathroom. As I walked back up the table where Bryce was sitting, he had the nerve to smile and wink at me. He must have seen Denise come out of the bathroom behind me because his face fell for a second.

I walked up to him and gave him my best smile.

"Hey Ellie, is something, um, wrong?"

"Nope….I just realized something though Bryce."

He looked around as if he was looking for Denise….or maybe he was looking for a way out.

"Ahhh, what's that Ells?"

I reached down and picked up a piece of pizza and took a bite of it and then looked at his nice white t-shirt and smiled.

"I realized that you're nothing but a cheating bastard!" I slammed the pizza right into his chest and then picked up his root beer and dumped it over his head.

As I walked away from Bryce I made a mental note to have Jefferson kick his ass.

I was never going to date again!

1 Ellie

Two Years Later

Two days before I was set to graduate, here I stood against my locker in a state of shock. People were walking by and going to class, not knowing the hell I was going through or at least not caring.

Memories of what my mother said to me when I was seven had to come back to me right at that moment.

My whole body started to shake.

Why? I wanted to just scream out as loud as I could WHY?

Maybe my mother was right; no man would ever want me or would ever truly love me. I needed to just give up on men for good.

I just wanted Jefferson, when would he get here? I had to tell him what happened or he will know something is wrong the moment he sees my teary red eyes. Jefferson will know what to do to take away this pain before I have to go home and face my mother. I can never let her know what happened. She will never let me forget this, just like she always brings up Bryce. God, I was having a problem getting air in my lungs. I just needed Jefferson.

Jefferson is my older brother by three years. He has been the only person in my life to be there for me. He was going to the University of Texas and studying Architectural Engineering. He worked his ass off in school to get perfect grades and of course he kicked ass on the football field as well. He received a scholarship to play football at the University of Texas. He could have gone anywhere, but he stayed in Austin to help take care of my mother and me.

He would not leave me all alone to deal with her. He is all I have in this world.

My father left when I was three. He came back to see us only once after he left. It was right after Jefferson got his scholarship to UT. He showed up on our doorstep acting like a proud father. I thought Jefferson was going to beat the shit out of him. He only stayed long enough to give Jefferson and me part of an inheritance from a grandmother neither of us remembered. He also caused our mother to go into another drunken fest and lose another job.

Jefferson made me put the money away for college and he bought his truck and paid off what was owed on our mother's house. My mother is nothing but a drunk who half the time does not even know she has two kids. I'm nothing but a reminder of the man who left her alone and unwanted. She told me how much I looked like him when I was younger. Her hatred for him drives her to drink away her problems, or at least she attempts to drink them away.

Jefferson is another reminder of our father but my mother pretty much just ignores him more than she does me. As long as he puts money in her account each month for her alcohol she is happy. Jefferson has worked since he was fourteen to help keep food on our table. I stopped counting how many jobs my mother has had in the last ten years. Sometimes she would be gone for days at a time which was fine by us. How Jefferson managed to work, study and get to football practice all the while taking care of his baby sister I will never know.

I love my brother so much for all that he does, even for our mom. Jefferson is the only person in my life who has been there for me.

I only needed two people in my life……..Jefferson and Ryan…….
Well shit……at least up until thirty minutes ago I thought the only two people I needed in my life were Jefferson and Ryan. Ryan has been my boyfriend for the last eight months; pretty much all of my senior year has been spent with him…….. what a fucking waste.

I guess I should say he was my boyfriend. That fucker! My body started to shake again as the image came back into my mind. I felt the tears threaten to come again. No! I wasn't going to cry over him anymore.

I had gotten a text message from Ryan asking me to meet him in the auditorium during sixth period. I was an office monitor and it was not uncommon for me to meet him during sixth period before he left campus for the day. I could've sworn he told me he was leaving right after fifth.

Today something was different and I knew it the moment I walked through the door of the auditorium. I heard moans coming from behind the stage. I slowly walked up and found Ryan behind the stage having sex with Jessica Harris. I thought I was going to throw up. I stood there like an idiot watching them for probably a good minute before my brain started to work again.

I finally was able to turn myself away from one of the worst moments in my life only to walk into a prop for the stupid *Wizard of Oz* play the drama class was putting on tonight. It made a loud crash as it hit the floor and I turned just in time to see Ryan look up at me with a stunned look on his face and to see Jessica give me the most evil smile I'd ever seen. I mean really…that bitch could throw daggers at her mother while singing a Disney song. At that moment I knew this was all her doing, she set it up for me to be here and see this.

I turned and jumped over the prop to run out the door. All I knew was that I could hardly breathe and I really needed to get out of there and fast. I heard the bastard calling out for me.

"Let me explain! Ellie! *PLEASE* let me explain!" he kept yelling out. Really…how could he possibly explain why he was having sex with the one girl in school who hated my guts?

Ever since Ryan asked me to the fall dance Jessica has made it her mission in life to hate me and take Ryan away. With her perfect blonde hair, blue eyes and daddy's money, she wanted for nothing and got almost everything she wanted. I guess she accomplished her mission of taking Ryan from me.

After I spent the last twenty minutes in the girl's bathroom ugly crying with my best friend Arianna standing outside the bathroom stall begging me to tell her what was wrong, I was ready to go beat the shit out of Jessica Fucking Harris.

I was finally able to somewhat speak to Ari once the sobs settled a bit.

"Ohhh, my gawd, Ari that fucker….that no good for nothing"…..and there it was…another round of endless sobs.

"Please Ellie, you are really scaring me. Please tell me who and what the hell you are talking about before I scale this fucking door and beat it out of you," Ari screamed over my loud cries.

"It's ….it's Ryan. I saw him having sex with….with….Je…Jess…Jessi…."

I can't breathe……OH MY GOD! Why?

"I just saw Ryan fucking Jessica Harris behind the stage!" I screamed out with such a force even I was waiting for someone to come in and see what the hell was going on in the girl's bathroom down in C hall.

For a few minutes I thought Ari had left me in my misery alone. I was alone, sitting in the girl's bathroom crying over some jerk, crying all alone.

I would always end up alone.

How stupid was I to think that Ryan would wait to be with me until I was ready. I just never felt like Ryan was 'the one' I was saving myself for. We had barely even kissed and he never really tried to go any further. My mother told me the first and last time she met Ryan that I was only arm candy for him.

I'm always going to be alone. I shook my head…. That's not true….. I had Jefferson. I would always have Jefferson.

"Holy hells bells…..Jesus, Mary and Joseph… that dirty rotten son of a bitch cock-sucking mother fucker! I'm going to cut his balls off and…"

God I loved this girl. Arianna had been my best friend since we were ten. She was beautiful, funny and smart as hell. She was graduating as Valedictorian of our class. She was the same height as me, 5'5 and we both weighed around 120. That made it nice since I loved to borrow her clothes.

She had beautiful medium brown hair that fell just below her shoulders. She had hauntingly beautiful green eyes. Her only downfall....she didn't know when to stop talking. The girl could rattle on all day if you let her. Get her pissed off and you would be shocked at the string of curse words she could rattle off.

"Ari please, if anyone is going to cut his balls off it sure as shit is going to be me and not you. But thank you for the love," I said as I walked out of the stall more composed than I really should have been.

Somehow in the last sixty seconds it hit me. I was not meant to be happy or find love. Just like my mother told me when I was younger.

I will never be wanted.

Not by anyone, let alone by one of the most popular boys in the senior class. What a fool I had been. Argh, I just needed my brother to get here. He would take me away from this disaster, just like he always has.

Once Ari made sure I was okay she hightailed it out of the bathroom before the bell rang to let Mrs. Johnson know I was not feeling well. She was planning on telling our science teacher I was having terrible cramps and was in the girl's bathroom.

She was right in a way...I was in terrible pain but it had nothing to do with cramps. It was my heart breaking and nothing more. Mrs. Johnson would not care. It was the last day for seniors anyway and all we were doing was playing stupid ass games.

I had sent Jefferson a text message right when I walked into the bathroom and locked myself behind the stall, asking if he could come and pick me up early. Ari had seen me running from the auditorium and came after me. I had managed to avoid Ryan by hiding out on the other end of the school for the last few minutes. I was silently hoping he just left school once he could not find me. It was now between classes, and I was just praying my phone would chirp with 'I'm here honey' and I could just get the hell out of dodge and into the safety of Jefferson's truck. If I can manage that and not see Ryan, I should be okay.

"Ells....please let me talk to you."

FUCK a duck....yep... it was true........my life will *never* go like I wish for it to. Holy hell!

"Go away R-Ryan". Oh hells bells; keep it together Ellie, keep it together. DO NOT cry in front of him!

"Please Ells, I made a terrible mistake. Jessica was saying all this shit about how she heard you telling Ari you had no plans of getting closer to me and how you were going to break up with me before summer...and...well shit! Ellie I just was not thinking straight honey. I've been trying to be patient with you Ellie but for fucks sake, all we ever do is kiss and well...I just broke. A guy has needs and well um.... She just broke me Ellie with her bullshit and I had a small moment of weakness. I promise you it will never happen again. I promise. I. Will. NEVER betray you again Ellie. I promise you honey. Let's just forget about this okay? Move on; we can move on, right Ellie?"

Oh my God, I think I just threw up in my mouth. A guy has needs? Is he insane! He had a *small* moment of weakness? You have got to be fucking kidding me! Did he really just say that?

I got the courage from somewhere deep inside and turned to face him.

"You have got to be kidding me right? THAT is your reason for fucking Jessica? Because I was hoping you were going to at least make it worth my while Ryan." I managed to spit that all out even with the tears I was holding back and the anger that was growing.

"Make what worth your while? Ellie I'll do anything!" Ryan pleaded.

At that moment I summoned all the deep down empowering woman bullshit Ari's mother is always preaching to us. "Girls, you are stronger than you know…. If you don't like being treated like a doormat then get the fuck off the floor." Oh and my all time favorite…. 'If you obey all the rules, you miss all the fun'. That one was a quote by Katharine Hepburn. Ari's mother adored Katharine Hepburn and I swear she has made us watch every one of her movies.

Yep! Once I had all that empowering shit boiled up in my small 5'5" one hundred eighteen pound body, I balled my fist up and hit that mother fucker as hard as I could in the face. Okay, I'm not going to lie and say it did not hurt. It hurt like a son of a bitch, and I'm pretty sure I let out a scream of sheer pain once I made contact with his jaw but….to see Ryan's head snap back and everyone stop and stare. Jesus it was worth it!

Even if I did think I just broke my hand. SHIT!

"For making that worth my while you asshole, SHIT!" I yelled at Ryan. For just one second I felt so good, until I felt my hand start to throb harder.

Ohhh shit……

"Ellie what the hell is going on?" It was Jefferson. I was pulled out of the daze I was in as I stood there and looked at my ever increasing swollen hand.

"I got your text honey, WHAT is going on?"

Jefferson looked at me then down to my hand and then over to Ryan who was now nursing his jaw and it must have all clicked in that moment. Jefferson had Ryan pinned up against the lockers in two seconds flat.

"What the fuck did you do to my sister you asshole? I will *kill* you if you have hurt her!" Jefferson hissed between his teeth.

I walked over and tried to grab Jefferson off of Ryan before he hurt him or worse, got in trouble for beating the shit out of a high school student. I forgot about my hand, and I lurched back in pain and let out a small gasp when I grabbed at his shirt. Just then I felt warm strong hands on my shoulders and my whole body started to tingle and feel warm inside.

What the hell? What was going on?

"Stand back here Ellie so you don't get hurt sweetheart." I looked up and was looking into the most beautiful blue eyes I'd ever seen. I had never seen a guy as good looking as the guy who was standing in front of me. He must have been at least 6'2" 230 pounds. I know this because Jefferson was 6'1" and 220 pounds.

My eyes traveled up and down his body quickly. Holy shit this guy was built! I always thought my brother Jefferson was the most handsome man I'd ever seen. Jefferson had light brown hair and emerald green eyes. He worked out every day for as long as I could remember. He said it was his way to release his stress. We could not go anywhere ever without every girl tripping over herself to get his attention. The thing I love most about my brother is that he is clueless to all of it. Just take my brother to the lake and have him take off his shirt and BAM...girls everywhere. He had a beautiful body and had part of his chest and upper arms covered in ink. He had a Texas flag tattoo on his upper left arm and a tribal tattoo on his right chest and shoulder that went down a little ways onto his back. He and a few friends went last summer and got tribal tattoos.

But this guy standing in front of me was breathtaking.......I couldn't tear my eyes away from him.....

I heard a small laugh escape from his beautiful mouth and noticed he was still holding onto my shoulders. I snapped out of yet *another* daze.

He smiled down at me and at that moment everything sounded muffled. I barely heard Jefferson yelling at Ryan, or Mr. Watson screaming and asking Jefferson why he was on campus and to let Ryan go. I only saw the most magnificent smile looking down at me. My whole body felt weak, and I had to really think about breathing. I managed to look around him to see what was going on with Jefferson.

He gave my shoulders a small squeeze and a moment later he turned and grabbed Jefferson off of Ryan.

"Jeff, take it easy man. Calm the hell down dude; he's not worth going to jail for!" He said in a soft and calm voice.

Yep, I'd never heard a voice so sweet in my life. Can your body physically melt from a voice? What the hell was going on with me?

"I'm going to kill that fucker if he hurt her in anyway Gunner, I.Will.Kill.Him!" Jefferson shouted as he looked at Ryan.

So, this was Gunner huh? My brother's best friend from college. Jefferson talked about Gunner all the time but I had yet to meet him. I had seen him plenty of times on the football field though. They played football together for UT and were both majoring in Architectural Engineering.

Gunner let out a laugh that moved through my whole body like a warm blanket. What was happening to me? I just stood there staring, I couldn't move. What was it about this guy that had my insides just melting? I mean,

I just saw my boyfriend screwing someone else and I was NEVER…let me repeat myself…I was NEVER going to fall in love again. All men were pure scum. Evil bastards that just wanted to get one thing from you. SEX. Let them know you are a virgin, and I guess they will invest months of their lives to say that they took that away from you.

Bastards……

I looked at Gunner again. There was something about him. I was shocked by my immediate intense feelings for him especially after what had just happened. I looked his body up and down as I licked my lips after my mouth went dry in an instant. I tried to tear my eyes away from him but couldn't. He was built just a bit bigger than Jefferson. He had brown hair that had that perfect messy look only a guy this hot could pull off. I looked up to his eyes…. holy shit…those beautiful blue eyes. I could see myself getting so lost in those eyes. I dragged my eyes down away from his face and they went right to his large muscular chest. He had a tattoo, YUM. I could see part of it on his arm, just sticking out from under his tight white t-shirt. You could almost see his black tribal tattoo under his shirt if you looked hard enough and I sure as hell was looking hard. It appeared to start on his chest and moved up his shoulder and back down onto his arm. What I wouldn't do to get a peek of that and run my fingers along…….

OKAY! Wait….. Hold the fucking fort Ellie! Good God what am I doing? I had to shake my head to clear my thoughts. I was practically undressing my brother's best friend in my mind.

No! I will never let myself be hurt again by another man. My mother was right; no one would ever want me, and Ryan was proof of that. I was never going to let another man into my life to hurt me ever again.

Just then I was brought back to the real world by Ari asking me to let her see my hand. When she got there I have no clue.

"OH FUCK….. ELLS! Jeff! We need to get Ellie to the hospital like RIGHT NOW!" Ari was screaming trying to get Jefferson's attention.

"Dude, listen to me; your sister is hurt. We need to get her to the doctor. Don't worry about this fuckwad Jeff. We can take care of him later." Gunner said as he gave Ryan a look that oozed out hate and disgust. If I had not known better I would've thought he wanted to kill Ryan more than Jefferson did.

Jefferson's body relaxed in an instant. I've never seen anyone calm my brother down that fast. Jefferson walked over to Ryan and leaned in close enough so that Mr. Watson did not hear but I sure as hell heard it.

"I'll be back for you bastard,"Jefferson hissed.

"Let's go Jeff," Gunner said as he guided Jefferson away from what Ari was now calling 'the crime scene.'

We started to walk down the hall to go outside when Ari started her famous rattling ways.

"They are for sure not going to let you walk now Ells…oh my God, what the hell were you thinking hitting him and doing it right here in school in FRONT of everyone? I mean, I know you're third in the class but they might not let you walk! I can't be up there giving a speech knowing my best friend is not going to be walking with me on the same stage. Have I not taught you a damn thing?! I mean, you needed to wait….."

"Arianna! *Please*, shut the fuck up will you?" Jefferson shouted.

Even though my hand was so swollen and hurt like hell, I had to giggle. Jefferson and Ari had a love/hate relationship. Ari loved Jefferson and Jefferson seemed to hate Ari. It was not always like that though.

When I was ten years old Ari became my best friend after she moved from Dallas to Austin. Jefferson was thirteen and used to play with us and tease the shit out of Ari. Then something changed when we were in ninth grade and he was a senior. He would barely look at Ari. He never wanted to be around her, and that made life a bit difficult for me. I know he cares for her like a sister though. When Brad Roberts bragged that he was going to take Ari out to her parents' lake house one weekend and take her virginity, Jefferson found out about it and beat the shit out of Brad. Ari of course took that as a sign of his undying love for her.

I took it as he was protecting his little sister's best friend because Jefferson just does things like that. That is why I needed him so much and would be lost without him.

Ari and Jefferson continued to bicker back and forth all the way out to Jefferson's truck; I just tuned them out because my hand was hurting so much, otherwise I would have been annoyed with their bickering.

Jefferson helped me up into the back seat of his Ford F250. Gunner ran up behind him and handed me a bag full of ice. HUH? Where and when did he get that?

"Thank you ah, um, Gunner," I stuttered out.

Jesus what was wrong with me? I couldn't even talk right. Why did he give me such weird feelings? Just when I thought it could not get any worse he smiled at me.

Fuck me….those beautiful sky blue eyes and perfect white straight teeth to round out the most beautiful smile I've ever seen.

"No problem Ellie. Try to keep it up above your heart sweetheart and here, take these Advil." He handed me Advil and water.

Gulp, I couldn't even speak. Ari leaned over and whispered in my ear, "Breathe Ells, breathe." I sucked in a long breath and managed to thank him for the ice, bottled water and Advil.

"Hey, I'm Ari by the way, Ellie's best friend," Ari said.

Gunner gave her the sweetest smile then leaned in a bit closer to me.

12

"Let's get you to the doctor, what do you say?" Gunner whispered against my ear. The feel of his hot breath against my face caused my body to start to shake.

"Ahhh, yep okay, doctor sounds good, yep let's go, let's roll, let's *do* this thing."

Okay. Why was my mouth still talking when clearly my brain had checked out the moment he smiled at me? He shut the door and jumped into the front passenger seat. Jefferson started his truck and of course, Tim McGraw's "Truck Yeah" started up. I swear to God if I had to hear that song one more time I was going to hurl.

I looked over to Ari who had a shit eating grin on her face. She leaned over and said low enough to where only I would hear her. "Okay *that* boy wants in your panties!!!"

I just gave her my best SHUT THE HELL UP look and said "PESH…You're crazy! Have I told you lately you seriously need therapy? Seriously….. you do Arianna…I'm beginning to get scared for you," I bit back at her.

Ari threw her head back and laughed. "Bitch, you can't tell me I'm wrong on this one. Matter of fact, I would bet you that Coach purse you've been eyeing the last three months, that that boy wants you."

I had to let out a laugh which caused my hand to start throbbing even more and my heart to break.

You will never be wanted by anyone……….

"Even if I could afford to take you up on that, I know for a fact you are dead wrong on this one," I stated just a little too loudly

"Ari is dead wrong on what Ellie?" Jefferson asked while pulling out of the school parking lot.

"Nothing Jefferson, she is just delusional that's all. She is seeing things that are clearly NOT there," I said as I narrowed my eyes towards Ari.

"Well, whatever crazy shit Ari is going on about I don't care. I want to know right now what the fuck happened between you and Ryan!"

Ari shot Jefferson a look and rolled her eyes at him. I'm pretty sure I heard dickwad come out of her mouth also.

Shit….here we go. I have to tell Jefferson what happened and pray to God that he does not kill Ryan. I mean, I truly did not care what the hell happened to Ryan anymore. I would rather like to see someone kick his ass but not Jefferson. Jefferson had to think about his scholarship and his future. Not about what some asswipe had just done to his sister who probably deserved it. Gunner turned around and gave me a smile that melted my heart, not to mention my panties. It was almost like he was giving me the courage to start talking. I gave him a small smile back, and my body actually felt like it was humming. I thought I was going to start having trouble breathing again but his smile seemed to make me forget about it.

What the hell?! I have never had a guy affect me the way this guy did. What was going on with me? I needed to focus here. I shook my head again to get these crazy thoughts out.

"Well, it all started when I got a text from Ryan to meet him in the auditorium…….."

2 Gunner

Senior Year of High School

The moment he walked into the principal's office the air turned cold. If the look that he shot me was any indication of how pissed he was, I was in for a good, long lecture. He always started out with "What you need is ROTC," or "Maybe I should just send your ass to military school, make something out of the worthless piece of shit you are." I'd love to be able to tell him not to pull that drill instructor shit on me, but he would probably knock the shit out of me and I would end up in military school anyway.

My father joined the military straight out of high school. He wanted nothing more than to get away from his father's ranch in Mason, Texas. I'm pretty sure when he dies, he will still be in the Army. He is good at what he does, if he would only leave it at the front door when he got home. He worked long hours and was often in a piss poor mood.

I looked up as I heard the door open to Mr. Deets' office. My father stepped out dressed in his Class A uniform and carrying his Campaign cover in his hand. Shit. He looked even more pissed than when he first walked in.

"Mr. Mathews, if Gunn…errr, um, Drew gets in one more fight, I am afraid we are going to have to suspend him from the football team. That is the last thing we want to do. We need you, Drew, to win State," Mr. Deets' said as he shook my father's hand and winked at me. My father replied with a "humph" and turned to walk away.

My father hates the idea of me playing football. My grandfather and mother practically had to beg him to let me play when I was seven. Once I stepped out on the field I knew I found where I belonged. Football is all I have. I care more about football than I do girls….or the Army.

I stood up to leave and shook Mr. Deets' hand before I turned to follow my father out the door. I knew he would remain silent until we got to his truck.

Shit! I don't know why I hit Brad Jennings. Okay, well, I do know why. I saw the fucker behind the school push his girlfriend up against a wall, and it looked like he was about to hit her. No fucking way I was going to let some douche-bag asshole hit a girl.

So, I got involved.

There really was no use in trying to explain it to him. He wouldn't understand. Even if he did he would still be pissed. It was the third fight I'd been in since school started two months ago. This latest fight was the last straw with Mr. Deets' saying I might get cut from the team.

Get cut from the team? Football was all I had. I had to get my shit together and get my head on straight. It was the first time in my life I ever felt accepted and needed…..the feeling was fucking great. The only other place I felt needed was at Gramp's ranch.

Ever since my father got transferred to Fort Sill when I was just entering eighth grade, I had come to depend on football as my escape from my drill instructor father. That man lives to tell me I need to focus on my grades and go in the Army like he did. There is no way in hell I was going in the Army.

My plan was to take the football scholarship I was offered at the University of Texas and get back to my grandfather and the ranch. Some of my best childhood memories are from his ranch. Man I love that place. I could practically smell my Gram's chicken and dumplings.

I told my grandfather that my dream was football and to get into architectural engineering. He is, of course, one hundred percent supportive which I think pisses my father off even more.

The minute the door shut to his F150 black truck I knew the shit was about to hit the fan.

"What the *FUCK* do you think you are doing getting into *ANOTHER* fight Drew? Your mother is going to be devastated by this!"

Sure, bring my mom into it you asshole. "It's Gunner, I like to be called Gunner." I shot back at him a little too pissed off. I was mad that he was trying to bring my mom into this and guilt me yet again.

"The last time I looked on your birth certificate it clearly stated your name was Drew Garrett Mathews. Not fucking *Gunner*. Where the fuck did you come up with that name?" My father hissed at me through gritted teeth.

"Coach was telling the rest of the team how to hustle and used me as an example on the punt special team. He said I played the gunner position better than anyone, and I always made it down the field the fastest and made the most tackles. He started to call me Gunner and so did the guys. It just stuck."

"Is that so? Think you are a hot shot 'cause you are some high school football star player? Bullshit! You are never going to make anything out of your life playing goddamn *football!* Nothing! Where could you possibly go in your life? You think football is going to get you anywhere?" My father said with so much hatred I cringed.

I had yet to tell him about my scholarship and made my mother and grandfather promise not to tell him. I was going to wait until after football season, but fuck it.

"Sir, I got accepted into The University of Texas. I got my letter this summer. I intend on going."

My father let out a laugh that just about made my stomach drop. "How the hell you think you're going to pay for college? I'm not helping I can tell you that right now."

"I got a *football* scholarship sir; and Gramps said he would help out with a place to stay in Austin," I said with as much strength in my voice as I could muster. He didn't need to know Gramps already said he would cover any other expenses my scholarship lacked.

"Is that so? Well, just to let *you* know. Do not call me when you fail. Which you will, I guarantee it. Do not call me when you need help. Do not call me when your little football plan does not work out. As of right now, I am done with you."

Four Years Later

"Dude, I cannot believe we only have one more year of college!" My best friend Jeff shouted over Tim McGraw's "Truck Yeah" song. Shit, if he played that song one more time I might have to knock the shit out of him.

"No doubt! I'm just glad school is done. Man this year has been kicking my ass!" I shouted back over the damn song. Just then Jeff's phone vibrated and lit up. We were at a stop light so he picked it up to read it.

"I'm getting a text from Ellie; that's weird," Jeff said as he turned the music down.

Jeff's little sister Ellie was a senior in high school and was about to graduate in two days. I'd never personally met her face to face but sure knew enough about her to feel like she was my little sister as well. He was throwing her a graduation party Saturday night. She had turned 18 in November and he had been putting off having her come to any of our parties until she was out of high school.

No one on the team was to meet her until then and even then, she was pretty much off limits. He was very protective of his little sister.

I was an only child so I didn't get the whole tighter-than-tight sibling thing. I did know that Jefferson and his sister where pretty damn close though. They grew up with a mother who was almost always drunk, and Jeff pretty much raised his sister.

"Ahhh shit, we need to swing by and pick up my sister. Something must be wrong if she wants to leave school early," Jeff said as he made a quick U-turn.

"Holy shit........you are actually going to allow me to meet your baby sister?! HOLY FUCK.... Let me write this shit down! I get to me meet the ever-baby sister of Jefferson Johnson!" I said as I let out a laugh.

"Shut the fuck up douche bag!" Jeff said as he punched me on my left arm. "Hey, I'm sorry, I know you wanted to stop by McBride's and look at that gun."

"I can take a look at it later today or tomorrow. No worries." I had my eye on a Remington Model 870 12 gauge pump action for a few months now. I could always head over to McBride's gun shop another time.

Jeff and I were planning on going out to my grandfather's ranch in Mason in a few weeks to catch up with the old man and help out with some things he needed done around the place. Nothing made me happier than hanging out with my Gramps and helping out on the ranch. Most of the happy memories from my childhood are thanks to my grandfather and grandmother. There is nothing that I would not do for them. Nothing.

"What do you think is going on? I mean, she never asks you to pick her up early," I said to Jeff as I looked at my watch. His sister had to have at least another hour of school left.

"Shit I don't know. I know she was happy the other day knowing everything was set for her scholarship to UT. She has worked her ass off in school. The money from our grandmother should help cover the additional costs that her scholarship won't. I had it invested, and it's done really well," Jeff said as he sped towards Ellie's school.

From what I gathered from hearing Jeff talk about his sister was that she was pretty damn smart. She was third in her class. Worked her ass off in high school taking every Pre-AP class she could get into and even took some Community College classes to get a jump start on her college classes. She already had enough college credits to enter UT as a sophomore. Jefferson was pretty damn proud of her and bragged about her all the time.

"Hey man, do me a favor....send her a text from my phone giving our ETA of five minutes will ya?" Jeff asked as he sped even faster towards her school. To say that he was over protective of his baby sister was putting it lightly.

For some reason my hands started to shake when I was punching in his message to Ellie. What the hell? I mean, I got a little bit excited at the idea of finally getting to meet Ellie face to face but come on? Maybe it was just my shoulder acting up. I hurt it during spring training and now I carry a bottle of Advil in my pocket everywhere I go.

Yeah, surely that was it. I mean come on; it is just Ellie, Jeff's sister for Christ's sake. She had been over to our place a few times but Jeff always made sure I was never home when she was over. From what I can remember she looked like she was cute, and I could tell she had a rocking body. I've seen her from afar plenty of times. She was really into yoga and even got Jeff hooked on it for a little while. Bastard kept trying to get me to go to some yoga place downtown. Fuck that. The yoga shit coach makes us do is enough for me thank you very much.

We had been sitting out in the parking lot for a few minutes and no Ellie. Jeff sent her another message but nothing.

"Shit. I have a bad feeling," Jeff said as he strained his neck to watch a side entrance for his sister.

"Come on, let's just go in and see what is taking her so long," Jeff said as he jumped out of his truck.

"Dude, do you think this is a good idea going into a high school? I mean, don't you have to do the whole check in shit so you don't freak people out?" I said as I practically ran to keep up with him.

"Nah, I know where her locker is. They never keep this side door locked. I sometimes bring Ellie stuff to eat during her off period."

It must have been between classes because kids were fucking everywhere. Holy fuck; you couldn't give me a million bucks to go back to high school. Just walking down the hall gave me memories I wanted to just push back down, way....way.... far down.

I noticed Jeff tense up next to me and I looked down the hall to see what he was looking at.

"What the fuck?" Jeff whispered. I followed his eyes.

What the hell? My stomach did a total dive when I looked and saw a girl standing with her side facing towards us. I knew in an instant….this was Ellie.

"Ellie what the hell is going on? I got your text honey, WHAT is going on?" I barely heard Jeff say to his sister. Ellie turned to look at Jeff and my breath caught in my throat when I saw her. She was the most beautiful thing I had ever laid my eyes on. Her beautiful blue eyes were red and bloodshot and she had a dazed and confused look on her face. I looked down and saw her holding her hand, and it appeared to be hurt. I immediately balled my hands into fists. The anger that built up inside me knowing someone had hurt her shocked the shit out of me.

"What the fuck did you do to my sister you asshole? I will KILL you if you have hurt her!" Is all I heard before I tore my eyes away from Ellie. Jeff had some douche bag kid pinned up against the lockers. I've seen Jeff mad but I have *never* seen him lose his temper like this.

Just then Ellie walked up and tried to pull Jeff off of the kid, but she jumped back and let out a cry like she was in pain. No way was she going to get anymore hurt. I walked up and placed my hands on her shoulders to get her out of the way. The moment my hands made contact with her body I felt a jolt go from my finger tips to my toes.

What the fuck was that?

"Stand back here Ellie so you don't get hurt sweetheart," I said as I brought her a few feet away from where Jeff was going insane on some high school kid. Ellie turned and looked up at me. Her eyes widened in surprise. My god she had the most *beautiful* blue eyes. Her hair was a beautiful light brown and was wavy and just past her shoulders a few inches. All I wanted to do was run my hands through her hair. I couldn't even form the next words in my head.

By the way she was looking back at me, she felt the same way. She was staring at me like I was trying to take her soul. I felt her shudder under my touch, and I let out a small laugh. She narrowed her eyes at me and looked over my shoulder at the commotion going on behind me.

There was some guy now yelling at Jefferson. I needed to get him out of here before we both got our asses put in jail.

I gave Ellie a reassuring squeeze, smiled down at her and then turned my attention to Jeff.

"Jeff, take it easy man. Calm the hell down dude; he's not worth going to jail for!" I said to Jeff in a calm voice. I knew he was upset and I needed to bring him down.

"I'm going to kill that fucker if he hurt her in any way Gunner, I.Will.Kill.Him!" Jeff shouted as he looked over at the douche bag.

Just then I heard another girl shout out; "OH FUCK….. ELLS! Jeff! We need to get Ellie to the hospital like RIGHT NOW!"

I looked over and saw Ellie's hand swelling pretty quickly. The anger that started to build up inside me once again scared the shit out of me. I had not had this much anger since my senior year of high school where I took it out on a few guys by way of fighting. This fucker did something to hurt Ellie and all I wanted to do was smash his head on the floor.

"Dude, listen to me; your sister is hurt. We need to get her to the doctor right now. Don't worry about this fuckwad Jeff. We can take care of him later," I said to Jeff as I looked over at the mother fucker who hurt Ellie somehow. I wanted to kill him right there.

"I'll be back for you, bastard," Jeff hissed through gritted teeth. I pulled on Jeff's arm to get him moving, "Let's go Jeff."

Jeff and Ellie and the other girl started to make their way out of the school and to Jeff's truck. I had seen that we passed the cafeteria on the way in so I ran in and quickly bought a bottle of water and asked the lady for a small bag of ice for Ellie. By the time I got back outside I was jogging back to Jeff's truck. I heard Jeff and the other girl bickering about something. I thought I heard Jeff call her Arianna at one point.

Once Ellie was in the back seat I reached in and gave her the ice.

"Thank you ah, um, Gunner." Ellie barely got out her words. Dammit she must be in a lot of pain. Poor girl can barely talk.

"No problem Ellie. Try to keep it up above your heart sweetheart, and here, take these Advil," I said as I handed her the water and a few Advil from my pocket stash and tried to give her a reassuring smile. My god she was beautiful. Her friend leaned over and told her to breathe.

"Hey, I'm Ari by the way. Ellie's best friend." I gave Ari a smile and looked back to Ellie.

"Thank you," Ellie said as she took the Advil. As soon as her fingers brushed against my hand I felt jumpage in my pants. Holy fuck this girl was affecting me in ways I had never known was possible.

"Let's get you to the doctor, what do you say?" I said as I leaned in close to her ear. I know I should not have done that, but dammit I had to know how she smelled.

Daisies….She smelled like the daisies Grams grows in her garden. It was a pure sweet innocent smell. She shivered with the feel of my hot breath against her face.

I. Am. So. Fucked.

"Ahh, yep okay, doctor sounds good, yep let's go, let's roll, let's do this thing," Ellie said in the sweetest voice I had ever heard. God, she was cute as a button when she stammered on her words.

21

I shut the door, quickly adjusted my problem in my pants and jumped into the front seat. Jeff started his truck and yep…sure enough…it was still on "Truck Yeah." I swear I'm going to delete that song on his iPod the first chance I get.

"Ari is dead wrong on what Ellie?" Jeff asked while pulling out of the parking lot. I just couldn't wait to get the hell out of there. I was still worried they would call the cops. The sooner we got out of there the better.

"Nothing Jefferson, she is just delusional that's all. She is seeing things that are clearly NOT there."

"Well, whatever crazy shit Ari is going on about I don't care. I want to know right now what the fuck happened between you and Ryan!"

I was pretty sure I had heard Ari just call Jeff a dickwad. What was up with Jeff? He never would be so rude to someone. In the last five minutes I've heard him to tell this poor girl to shut up, bicker with her like a married couple, and he pretty much just called her crazy. Huh? Wonder what was up with that. I'm going to have to ask him about this Ari chick later.

"Well, it all started when I got a text from Ryan to meet him in the auditorium…….."

3 Ellie

Two and a Half Hours Later

I was getting tired of waiting for the doctor to come back into my room with my pain medicine prescription. By the time I finished telling Jefferson and Gunner what happened, I just wanted someone to shoot me. They both looked like they were ready to leave and go kick Ryan's ass. A small part of me wanted them to. My hand hurt so bad I just wanted to cry. Thank God it was not broken. The urgent care doctor said it was a Grade 2 sprain. No torn ligaments but I needed to do something called R.I.C.E. Ari of course wrote down what RICE stood for. I couldn't think let alone try to remember some acronym.

Gunner had been leaning up against the wall just opposite of me the whole time. I tried to keep my eyes either on Jefferson, Ari, the doctor or the floor. Every time I looked up at him he smiled, and I felt butterflies in my stomach. I would smile back politely and then look away.

No one has ever had this kind of effect on me before, not even Ryan. It *always* bothered me that I never got those butterfly moments with Ryan that all my friends talked about. I knew deep down inside Ryan and I were never meant to be. I mean, I'm not even feeling upset anymore about what happened.

Of course it could be the incredibly hot guy standing across the room who was burning holes into me with his eyes. His beautiful sky blue eyes that just melted my heart and for the first time in my life, made my body tighten with anticipation…down there.

Oh holy hell….what is going on with me?

I shook my head to clear my thoughts again. I could not let this guy get under my skin no matter how freaking hot he was. I looked up at him again and this time I felt the heat rise up and flush my face. Gunner let out a small laugh that made his whole body tighten. I licked my lips as I watched his body respond to his laughter. My god this guy had a nice body. All I wanted to do was inspect every square inch of it.

Wait…..That fucking bastard just laughed at me! This is why I'm never going to have anything to do with men again. I will die a virgin and be proud of it.

"Sooo, what are the plans for Saturday night?" Ari asked while looking at Jefferson I'm sure the same way I had been looking at Gunner.

"I know what my plans are, not sure about yours squirt," Jefferson responded back to Ari.

"Oh.My.God! Can you *please* not call me that! I'm eighteen years old and not a child you asshole," Ari hissed.

"Well you sure as hell act like a child squirt," Jefferson stated matter of factly

"I thought we were having a party at the house to celebrate Ellie's graduation," Gunner said as he looked back and forth between Ari and Jefferson. He seemed just as confused about what was going on between them as I was. I would swear they were in a staring contest with the way they were looking at each other.

"Wait.....wait just one damn minute. You're having a party.....at your house? For us? Oh. My. God...this is awesome!" Ari jumped up and nearly knocked over the sharps container that was to her right.

"Um, no squirt, I'm having a party at my house for Ellie. Not you." Jefferson said as he turned to look up at me. I smiled my biggest 'I love the shit out of you' smile as I looked at him.

"Are you for real? I mean I finally get to meet all of your friends and go to a college party!" I was about to act like a total fool myself and jump up and down. If Gunner had not been in the room, I so would've done it.

"You bet I am Ells. You only graduate from high school once. It's one of my presents to you!" Jefferson said as he got up to come and hug me!

I was so excited I could hardly contain myself. When I looked over Jefferson's shoulder there was that drop my panties smile again. This time I didn't mind it so much. I smiled back at him just as big as he was smiling at me. I have to admit I think I was more excited knowing I was going to be at a party where I knew for a fact Gunner would be. I had been to their house before, but Jefferson always made sure Gunner was never home.

They lived in a two bedroom house that belonged to Gunner's grandfather. He bought the house when Gunner moved to Austin to attend UT. Jefferson and Gunner hit it off within days of meeting each other and Gunner asked him if he wanted to bunk with him at his house. That was a no brainer. Jefferson would do anything to get out of our house with our drunken mother. I spent most of my days at Ari's house anyway. Mansion I should say. Her dad was a big shot lawyer but you would never know they had money by the way Ari acted. That was one of the things I just loved about her.

"Am I at least invited to my best friend's graduation party dickwad?" Ari asked with so much sarcasm it was dripping off of her.

"If she wants you there squirt, that's fine by me." Jefferson said as he rubbed the top of Ari's head like she was five years old.

"Fucker!" Ari said as she pushed his hand away. Jefferson and Gunner both laughed.

OH. MY. GOD……..that laugh of his. Like his smile, or his touch, or his massive chest was not enough to be my undoing. His laugh about dropped me to the ground. A feeling ran through my whole body every time I heard this guy laugh. What the hell?!

The doctor came back in right at the exact moment I thought I was going to combust from the look Gunner was giving me. He gave me my prescription, another round of how to take care of my hand and out the door we went. Thank God. Between Ari and Jefferson going back and forth with each other and Gunner standing across from me sending me looks that about had me wanting to rip his clothes off…I was more than ready to get the hell out of dodge.

"Hey dickwad, can you swing back by the school so I can pick up my jeep?" Ari shouted over Maroon 5 blasting out of the stereo.

"Ellie and I both have our last shift tonight." Ari and I both worked part time at Flipnotics. It was a little coffee shop near downtown Austin.

"Oh *fuck no* is Ellie going to work tonight. She has to rest her hand and she is on pain meds. Are you fucking insane Ari. Thinking Ellie is going to work tonight," Jefferson shouted back to Ari.

"Yeah, that is not a good idea going in to work tonight Ellie. You need to keep your hand and wrist elevated to keep the swelling down." Gunner said to me as he turned around and looked at me.

WOW, he really looked like he was worried about me. My heart started to beat faster and I felt the blush creep up into my face.

NO! Wait…I needed to stop this right now. I could not let Gunner Mathews get into my heart. No. It was closed for business. Shut down, never to be opened up to any hurt again.

You will never be wanted by anyone…..Would I ever be able to get my mother's voice out of my head?

Ari sat there and looked stunned. She just kept looking between Jefferson and Gunner and finally just laughed.

"What? Are you both her freaking mother? No, I think not. Ells can do whatever she damn well pleases and you two asswipes have no say in it what so ever. If she wants to go to work or not go to work that is *her* decision to make. I can't believe you two…my god." Ari said in a harsh tone directed more at Jefferson than Gunner.

Gunner gave me a small smile and turned back around and looked out the side window. For a brief second I was pissed at Ari for hurting his feelings. He was only worried about me. Just the thought of it had me thinking things I should not have been thinking about Gunner.

Holy shit……I started to blush just thinking about what his touch would feel like. Jefferson brought me out of my wayward thoughts.

"You know what squirt, you're right, I'm not her mother but I am her brother. Ells I don't think it is a good idea honey. Plus you are taking pain meds and you really cannot use your hand."

Maybe Jefferson was right. It had been such a long day and I was so tired. My hand was killing me and all I really wanted to do was curl up somewhere and go to sleep and forget this whole day even happened. Well, maybe not the whole day. If Ryan had not cheated on me I wouldn't have been graced with the presence of Gunner all afternoon.

Gunner....even when I think about him my stomach takes a dive. Does that really even happen to people? According to my mother all men are evil bastards. Jefferson isn't an evil bastard. He would never purposely hurt anyone. Although he does seem to be doing a good job at getting Ari all fired up today. They are currently going back and forth about what is better for me again. If I didn't know any better....

OH MY GOD! OH. MY. GOD. Jefferson likes Arianna! Holy fuck, how did I not see this? The way he keeps looking at her and talking to her. The time he beat up Brad Roberts. Once Ari started high school and *really* started looking more like a girl than his little sister's....*squirt friend.* OMG! Jefferson pretty much dumped us both and no longer hung out with us right after that.

How could I forget he used to call her squirt? WOW....this was something I would have to think on later. Right now trying to deal with my hand and these crazy intense feelings for Gunner was enough to handle.

"Oh my god will you two *PLEASE* shut the hell up!"

Ari and Jefferson immediately stopped talking and Ari looked over and took my good hand.

"Ari, I hate to admit this but I really am so tired and my hand is killing me. Maybe I should rest a bit. Today has been such a long day and I'm ready for it to just be over," I said as I looked up to Jefferson who turned around quickly to give me a smile.

"You're right sweets, I'm sorry. I will let them know what happened and why you can't come in. Tonight was our last day anyway," Ari said as she leaned over to give me a hug.

"Thanks Ari, you're the best!" I noticed Jefferson's body tense up right at that moment. He must have thought of something.

"Ells maybe you should plan on staying the night at my place. If mom is home she's going to ask you a million questions, and I'm not sure if you want to talk to her about that douche bag Ryan. You always keep a bag of clothes and stuff in Ari's jeep right?" Jefferson asked as he pulled into the high school parking lot.

"Oh, hum, yeah I didn't even think about mom or anything. Last thing I need is to hear her saying I told you so." I practically whispered as I thought about my mother and how I'll never hear the end of it when she finds out about Ryan.

Jefferson wants me to stay at his house…..Gunner's house……..

Oh holy hell…..this is going to be bad. Please, please, pleeeease say that Gunner is going out all night or has some big thing he has to leave town for. *Please* don't let him say he is going to be there. I mean Jefferson has never even let me *meet* any of his college friends, even his BEST friend, and now he is wanting me to spend the night in the same house with the guy who practically just has to look at me and I'm ready to jump him.

Shit! Shit! Shit!

"I mean if that's okay with you Gunner? Ellie can take my room and I'll sleep on the sofa," Jefferson said has he jumped out of his truck to help get my things.

"Of course, it's cool with me! Ellie can stay over *anytime* she likes. Our place is her place as far as I'm concerned," Gunner said as he turned back and looked over at me, winked and then gave me that freaking ass panty melting smile.

Bastard! He knew what he was doing. He can't fool me any. He knows he has an effect on me, and I'm probably nothing more than a game to him. HUMPH. I'll show him!

Giving him back a *very* seductive smile, well at least very seductive for me anyway, I purred back in a very lovingly sisterly way.

"Ahhh, Gunner how very *sweet* of you. Now I feel like I have *two* big brothers looking out for me. You are such a good *friend.*" His smiled faded quicker than a Texas sunset.

HAH! Take that you bastard. I'm sure that just threw about a gallon of cold water on his libido. Huh…made me feel pretty damn good too! I had to smile at my small victory and do a little mind fist pumping.

Jefferson had opened my door and was waiting for me to get out of the truck. He looked between Gunner and me and frowned slightly as he helped me out.

Ari came up behind me and whispered in my ear, "I am SO looking forward to that Coach purse." I quickly turned to look at her and gave her the most angry look I could manage.

"NEVER, going to happen' Arianna….EVER!" I hissed through my teeth at her. Ari just threw her head back, laughed and handed Jefferson my overnight bag I kept in her jeep.

"Whatever you say sweets."

"When you two are done talking in riddles can we get going? Gunner has some place he needs to be." Jefferson said as he walked over to his truck and threw my bag in the backseat. Gunner gave Jefferson a strange look.

"Have fun Ells! I'll give you a call later tonight to see how your night went!" Ari said with a laugh as she got into her Jeep ready to head off to work. She had the top off of her jeep and she was throwing her hair in a pony tail. She truly was beautiful. Hard to believe she didn't have a boyfriend. I looked over at Jefferson who was staring at her before he seemed to get his wits about him and started to walk over to the driver's side of his truck. Ari honked her horn, and all I saw was her pink spare tire cover as she drove off.

I stood there and watched my bitch of a best friend drive off and leave me to fend for myself. Pesh, I will remember this. I turned and headed to climb into the back seat and Gunner took my arm. My breath instantly caught, and if I didn't know better I would have thought he had the same reaction.

"Why don't you sit up front with your *brother* Ellie. I'll sit back here."

Boy did he stress brother! Ooops, wonder if I made him mad. The thought of making him mad or upset seemed to unsettle me. My stomach started to feel sick. What the fuck? Maybe it was just my hand hurting.

"Oh, okay, um thanks. I mean, I'm sorry if I kept you from something you had to do this afternoon. Thank you for all your help by the way. I really do appreciate it." Good lord, I somehow managed to get that all out without sounding like an idiot.

"It was no problem at all Ellie. Besides the fact you have a hurt hand, I've rather enjoyed my afternoon," Gunner said with the sweetest smile. Okay, this guy really knew how to confuse me already.

I looked down to where he still had his hand on my arm. He quickly dropped his hand and opened the truck door for me. I turned to smile at him right as he was shutting my door. Once Gunner was in, Jefferson fired up his truck and started to head to their place. He reached over and messed around looking for a song and then "Truck Yeah" started up again.

"NOOO!" Gunner and I shouted at the same time. Jefferson just threw his head back and laughed. He looked over at me and gave me a wink and pulled out onto the main road.

I am *so going* to delete that song from his iPod the first chance I get!

My heart was pounding and I felt like I was fighting for every breath. What was wrong with me? I had been to Jefferson's place plenty of times. It was a cute house and I loved going there. The house was a two bedroom house with a huge backyard in Hyde Park. It was a white house with blue trim. The front porch had a porch swing on it and I always thought how nice it would be to just sit on that swing and read a book. I'm sure Gunner's grandfather paid a small fortune for it but Jefferson said it was a good investment.

Gunner has never once asked for rent from Jefferson. They just split the rest of the bills. The only problem with this place was.....it was for sure a bachelor's pad. The few times I had been there I noticed all the football and architectural stuff everywhere. I'm still amazed that both Gunner and Jefferson had decided to major in the same field. It's no wonder they became best friends. They both loved football and architecture and FOOTBALL.

We turned down Avenue F and my heart started to pound so loud and fast I was sure Jefferson and Gunner could hear it. Jefferson pulled up and parked next to what I'm guessing was Gunner's truck. It was an older model F250 beige truck. What was it with Texas boys and their trucks?

"Is that your truck Gunner?" Regretting it the minute it came out of my mouth. I mean come on Ellie, who else's truck would it be?

"Yep! That's my girl! My Gramps gave her to me when I got accepted into UT. She's a 1998 F250 that was used on the ranch but, she has never failed me yet," Gunner said jumping out of the truck and opening my door for me.

Hmm, manners, good looking and a rocking body. Yeah, this guy is too good to be true. I would do good to keep telling myself that.

"You refer to your truck as a girl?" I looked over at the truck and back at Gunner. OHHH mistake…there was that damn smile again. Wait? When did it go crooked? Maybe it was just the way he was smiling right now. I don't think I would have missed that….would I? My head was spinning and my hand was throbbing. Good lord I'm so fucked with this guy.

Gunner let out another one of those laughs that made me go all Jello on the inside. SHIT! I should have just taken my chances with my mother.

"Yes Ellie, I refer to her as my girl. This way I know the only way my heart will ever get broken is if she breaks down on the side of the road and leaves me stranded," he said as he gave me a wink.

Holy hell this guy was killing me, what a flirt! Okay….I can play this game! I dug down deep and pulled out my sexiest voice……

"Well…… I'm sure your heart is safe then….aren't Fords pretty reliable? I mean, I would hate to think of your heart being broken. It would just make me all sad," I said as I looked up at him through my eye lashes. His crooked smile got even bigger and for a moment he looked like he wanted to kiss me.

My heart started to pound even harder…holy fuck…was eighteen too young to be having a heart attack? I mean what the hell else was this?!

"Gunner!" Jefferson called out and snapped me out of my moment of weakness and I spun around to look at my brother who was holding my overnight bag and giving both of us a curious look.

"Dude, can I talk to you for a minute?"

OH. MY. GOD…what was I doing? I just flirted with my brother's best friend, in *front* of my brother and now he was going to chew his ass out. Or worse….beat the shit out of him.

Oh great! There goes my party Saturday night. FUCK ME!

"Hey Ells, you mind heading in and I'll bring your bag to my bedroom?" Jefferson asked as I slowly started to walk towards him.

"Umm, yeah sure no problem but, um is everything okay?"

"Of course it is honey; I just need to ask Gunner to do me a favor," Jefferson said as he pushed me up the stairs of the front porch. I turned back around and watched as Gunner ran his hands through his beautiful messy hair while he walked up to Jefferson. Oh how I would love to run my hands through his hair. He took one look up at me and smiled. I felt my lower lip going numb and realized I was biting the shit out of it.

I turned back towards the door and opened it. As soon as I walked in I had to smile. It smelled just like Jefferson in here. And it smelled just like… Gunner…oh yeah…

I was fucked for sure.

4 Gunner

The moment Jeff had asked Ellie to go inside I knew something was up. FUCK! I needed to be more careful around her, especially in front of Jeff. In just the short amount of time I'd been around her today I wanted to know so much more about her. What were her favorite flowers, her favorite restaurant, band, and movie?

Holy fuck, what the hell was going on with me? I had this incredible urge to just be around her. I mean I've been with girls, plenty of girls, but none of them have ever affected me the way Ellie has. Just touching her alone causes me to get a semi. What the fuck is that about? She's my best friend's sister who just broke up with her douche bag boyfriend this morning.

Gunner man…..chill the fuck out.

Well, let's get this over with. I walked over to Jeff but not before I looked up and saw Ellie looking down at me biting her lip. I'm pretty sure it took all my strength not to let a moan out from just the sight of her chewing on that lip. I knew she was worried about what Jeff was about to say to me, especially since she just attempted to flirt with me for the first time today. God she was cute as a button, but holy shit she was so innocent and yet, so seductive at the same time.

She gave me a weak smile and turned to walk into the house. I let out a big sigh and walked up to Jeff.

"What's up dude? Is everything okay?" I asked getting ready for the first punch to be thrown.

"Yeah dude its all good. Listen, I totally forgot I had a date tonight with Rebecca. I've been putting this off for weeks now. If I call her now and cancel……" Jefferson said as he looked back at the house.

"Gunner, I hate to ask this of you but, can you stay home tonight and take care of Ellie? I don't want to leave her alone. She has never taken these kinds of meds before. I mean I know I'm asking a lot out of you to sit and watch my sister. I think she would okay with it. Actually, I kind of think she might like you dude."

I just stood there stunned into silence and I looked around for a second. Where the fuck was my best friend Jeff? The one who refused to let any of his friends meet his baby sister until after she was out of high school.

The Jeff who actually threatened us with bodily harm if we ever laid a hand on her.

This day just keeps getting more and more fucking weird.

"Umm, no I don't mind at all," I said to Jeff as I looked at him with a stunned expression on my face.

"Jeff, man can I just ask you a question?"

"You know you can Gun...shoot."

I ran my hands through my hair again trying to decide how you tell your best friend you are attracted to his baby sister you literally just met hours ago, and now he was about to leave you alone with her for who knows how many hours.

"Jeff, umm, I mean I don't mind at all staying home tonight, I didn't have any plans but dude. You've never let any one of your friends around your sister, matter of fact you threatened us with bodily harm if we ever laid a finger on her. So, now you're just going to leave her here with me, alone when you use to make me leave anytime she would come over? I mean I think she is beautiful and, umm, I kind of...um, well I.......*fuck*.....I don't really know what I'm trying to say here Jeff I'm confused as hell," I said as I looked back up towards the house and then back at Jeff who was just standing there smiling.

Jeff let out a laugh that caught me by surprise.

"What the fuck is so funny?" I asked looking at him like he had lost his mind.

"Dude, you got it bad. So fucking bad you can't even talk straight!" Jeff said as he laughed his ass off, and I just stood there in stunned silence.

"You don't think I didn't notice the two of you staring at each other all afternoon? Or the fact that Ellie was devastated by what that fucker did to her but five minutes after she saw you she was pretty much like, Ryan who?" Jefferson said as he let out another laugh.

"Wait, I'm so fucking confused because Ellie has always been off limits. Dude you told me once you would cut off my balls if I ever so much as looked wrong at her. Are you trying to set me up for something here? I mean, if you want a fight we can just head to the gym and duke it out Jeff. Fuck man don't play around with me like this," I practically begged him. Yeah.....something was not right here. I don't fucking beg anyone for anything.

"Listen Gunner, you're my best friend. You're like a brother to me. I would lay my life down for you and I know you would do the same for me. If I was ever going to trust anyone with my sister it would be you dude," Jeff said as he put his hand on my shoulder.

Just fucking great....here was my best friend trusting me with his sister and all I was trying to do was calm the erection I got every time I was around her.

"Umm…. Jeff I need to be honest with you. I think I'm attracted to your sister. I mean I would *never* disrespect you or Ellie in anyway. If you tell me right now to back off and never look at her again, dude I'll do it. It would be hard because I'm pretty sure your sister has me tied up in knots, and I'm a bit confused by this entire thing but, I would do it for you Jeff," I said as I ran my hands through my hair waiting for Jeff's reaction to my admission of being attracted to his little sister.

"Gunner, Ellie had a pretty fucked up childhood thanks to my mom. She pretty much told her she was useless just like she did me. In Ellie's mind she will never be good enough for anyone. I only ask that you give her time. If she ends up having feelings for you then just see where it goes. Just keep in mind that she is innocent, *very innocent* and best friend or not, you hurt her, then I hurt you," Jeff said as he gave my shoulder a much harder squeeze.

"Jeff you know I would rather die than disappoint you man. I promise you that. I promise to take care of her whether it turns out we are just friends or it becomes more than that. Always dude."

Jeff gave me a hard ass slap on the back and we started for the door.

"Good to know Gun…..good to know! I'd hate to have to beat the shit out of my best friend. Now, let's go see how she is settling in shall we?" Jeff said as he turned to head into the house.

My heart started to beat faster and I wasn't sure if I was more anxious to see Ellie in my house or by the fact that I pretty much just got Jeff's blessings. Man, this day just keeps more interesting as it goes on. What the hell else could happen?

As we walked into the house Jeff called out for Ellie. She came from down the hallway and had her hair pulled up in a pony tail and had changed into a pair of Jeff's sweats and a UT t-shirt. I'd never seen anyone so goddamn sexy in my life. I had to walk to the kitchen to adjust the damn hard on I was getting…again! I think my dick has gotten hard more just this afternoon then it has all fucking year.

"Hey honey, how're you feeling?" Jefferson asked as he walked up to Ellie.

"I guess I'm okay. I think the meds are kicking in 'cause I'm really tired." Ellie said with a yawn.

"Let me go put this in my room and grab a few things. I really hope you don't mind Ellie but I had plans for tonight, and I've blown this girl off three times already. I can't back out again. Gunner offered to stay home and help out if you need anything," Jeff said has he walked back to his bedroom.

"Oh, umm, yeah that is totally fine Jefferson. I don't need to be babysat though," Ellie said as she watched Jeff go to his room and grab a change of clothes then head to the shower. I heard Jeff tell Ellie he knew she didn't need a baby sitter then he hollered down the hall he was taking a quick shower.

I was still in the kitchen so I grabbed a beer out of the fridge. "Gunner listen, please don't stay home on my account. I'm really fine. I think I just need to eat something and lie down and rest for a while. I'm sure I will fall asleep really fast," Ellie said as she looked everywhere except at me. She really was innocent and damn she was beautiful.

"Don't be ridiculous Ellie; I have no plans for this evening. I was planning on just chilling and watching a movie or two. Are you hungry? We haven't been to the store but I can run and get you something. You probably should eat since you are taking the pain medicine sweetheart."

She looked at me for the first time since she came out of the bedroom and her face instantly went red. My breath caught in my throat. Her eyes just held mine for what seemed like forever before she finally talked.

"I *am* kind of hungry. Oh gosh though, I hate to even ask you I'm so embarrassed. Um, I'm sure Jefferson has time to run and get me something." She said as she was about to turn and go ask him through the bathroom door.

"NO! Really I'll go get it. I'm hungry myself and I haven't eaten since breakfast. Let me run and grab it and I'll be back in no time. Just let Jeff know I ran out to get us something to eat," I yelled as I raced out the door.

I knew exactly what I would get her. I remember Jeff saying one time if she had her pick of anywhere to eat this would be the place. As I jumped in my truck and fired it up I could not help but smile. There was just something about that girl........

Holy shit! I'd never seen a guy rush out the door as fast as Gunner did. The moment he heard me say I was hungry he practically jumped over the bar and offered to go get food! I had to giggle. There was just something about him.......what was it?

I mean this morning I woke up with a boyfriend and tonight I'm having fantasies about my brother's best friend. What the hell was wrong with this picture? Maybe it's because I know he is Jefferson's friend. I've always been kept away from them so maybe it's just the fact that Jefferson is okay with it that has me attracted to the guy. Who knows.

I walked up to a book shelf and saw a picture of both Jefferson and Gunner. Funny, I've never seen this picture before. They were both in their swimsuits and it looked like they were at the coast. I was going to have to wipe the drool from my mouth if I kept staring at Gunner like this. Hot damn he had a nice body. His tribal tattoo was gorgeous. Hmmm? Wonder if I'll ever get to see it in person? I started to feel a dull ache between my legs and had to press them together to make it stop.

"That picture was taken this past spring break in Port A," Jefferson said has he walked up behind me.

Startled that I'd just been caught staring at Gunner's picture; I quickly put it down and turned around and smiled. "You sure are one handsome fella Jefferson. I bet y'all had girls all over you down there," I said as a way to divert him from what I was doing.

Jefferson threw his head back and laughed. "Nope; well don't get me wrong, there were a few sluts that tried to make their way back to our condo. We couldn't be bothered with most of the girls down there though. Most of them are just hoes."

"Well gesh, thanks for that. If you haven't forgotten, Ari and I went to Port A for a few days during spring break so are you calling us hoes?" I raised my eyebrows up at him, waiting for his answer.

"Now come on Ells, I would never ever say you were like those girls. Ari now....she's another story," Jefferson said as he let out a laugh and walked into the kitchen and got out a beer.

"Hey! That's my best friend! She's not a slut. I'll have you know she has never even had….." I stopped myself suddenly before I just announced to my brother that Ari was still a virgin. With the way their relationship had been lately he didn't need any more to use against her. Jefferson stopped his beer at his lips and tilted his head. Oh shit.....a smile slowly came across his face.

"So, squirt is still a virgin is she? Huh. This is news. This could be very informative news indeed!" He let out a gruff laugh.

"Jefferson Michael Johnson, so help me God if you even hint to her that you know I will *never* talk to you again. EVER!" I said as I got up and started poking his massive chest.

He just laughed and rubbed the top of my head like I was a child. "Don't worry honey; her secret is safe with me!"

That reminded me..... I remembered Jefferson's and Ari's strange exchanges all day.

"Speaking of Ari, what was going on with you two today?" Jefferson stopped dead in his tracks and turned to look at me.

"What're you talking about? Nothing is going on between us. Why would you even ask that? I mean she is, well she's just Ari," Jefferson said to me with a shrug of his shoulders. The stricken look on his face was like I just asked him to solve the problem of world hunger.

"I didn't mean to imply there was something going on. It's just that you were bickering with her, and it seemed like you were trying to just piss her off on purpose. She is my best friend Jefferson and I'm tired of you always treating her like a spoiled child. She is not a bratty child. She is a grown adult woman and she deserves to be treated better than that. I would expect that from you of all people."

"Oh, believe me, it's not lost on me how much of an adult Ari is. I'm sorry Ells; I'll try not to argue with her as much. I need to get ready for my date," Jefferson said as he turned and walked away. He stopped and turned around and looked in Gunner's bedroom.

"Where's Gunner?"

"Oh...I just mentioned I was hungry and he pretty much darted out the door to go get food. He said he would be back in a few minutes." I said as I sat down on the sofa and turned on the TV.

"DAMN Ellie! You got that boy going every which way but loose!" Jefferson said with a laugh.

"What are you talking about? He said he was hungry too and was going to get some food. Gesh Jefferson, you act like he was jumping off a bridge for me or something," I said annoyed at where this was going. Jefferson turned back around to come and sit down next to me while he let out a small laugh.

"You really don't see do you Ells?" Jefferson asked as he bumped into my shoulder.

"See what? What're you going on about Jefferson?" I was really starting to get annoyed by him.

"Ellie, I've known Gunner for three years now. I've never seen him with the same girl more than a few times. He is so focused on football and school he pretty much has never given a girl more than five minutes of his attention. Don't get me wrong; he likes girls!" Jefferson said with a laugh and a shake of his head.

What the hell did that mean?

Was Gunner a player? Did he sleep around a lot? I mean he sure had the looks to get any girl he wanted. My head was starting to spin again and the thought of Gunner with another girl had me feeling angry inside.

What the hell?

"I can honestly say I've never seen Gunner run and fetch dinner for someone!" Jefferson laughed again. "Ellie honey, I know you just had this whole bullshit thing with Ryan the douche bag this morning, and you believe that bullshit mom fed you years ago but, Gunner is attracted to you princess. He's a good guy Ellie but…"

Jefferson cut off what he was saying and he looked down and away from me.

"But WHAT?" I asked, clearly anticipating Jefferson to tell me to stay clear of his best friend.

"Ells I want you to know I would trust my life and yours with Gunner. I trust him, but this is you we're talking about. I just don't want him to break your heart or hurt you Ellie. I really don't want you to jump into something you're not ready for honey. Just promise me you'll be careful," Jefferson said as he took my good hand and brought it up to his mouth and kissed the back of my hand.

I busted out laughing and Jefferson just looked at me.

"What's so funny Ells?"

I just could not stop laughing…. "Oh my gosh! You're what's so funny! I mean come on Jefferson! I hardly think that Gunner is interested in *me* of all people! I'm sure he is only being nice to me because of you!" I said in between laughs.

Jefferson dropped my hand and stood up. He looked down at me and sighed heavily. "Ellie, you're beautiful, inside and out. You're very desirable princess, and trust me when I say this, Gunner is interested. He's a great guy, just be careful that's all I ask. I have to get going or I'm going to be late, and the wrath of Rebecca will be upon me!"

My heart was pounding and I felt like I was going to be sick. No…I would not let this happen. Gunner was not interested in me! Was he? If he was, it was probably only for sex. No matter if Jefferson was his best friend or not, men were all the same. I was not going to have anything to do with it. I just had to make sure I kept it to the 'friends' level with this guy.

I looked over at his picture with Jefferson on the beach and sighed. Jesus, this was going to be hard. The guy was beyond good looking and his body…..I had to squeeze my legs together to ease the throbbing again.

Yep, this was going to be hard. Very, very hard. A second later the front door flew open and Gunner came in holding bags from my favorite sandwich place, Schlotzky's.

"Hey you! Glad you're still awake. I remembered Jeff said your favorite sandwich was the Turkey breast on Rye from Schlotsky's. I hope you're hungry sweetheart. I got you two," Gunner said with that crooked smile on his face and those blue eyes sparkling down at me.

I let out a laugh as he sat down and set all the food on the coffee table. He started to take out 4 sandwiches, 5 bags of chips and two drinks. Good lord who was this all for?

"I wasn't sure what kind of chips you liked so I just grabbed a few of them. You like sweet tea right?" He asked as he started to spread out the feast before us.

"Ummm……WOW Gunner! Yes, I love sweet tea! I would've been happy with just the sandwich thank you. The cracked pepper chips are my favorite though," I said as I let out another laugh.

How in the world did he think I would eat two sandwiches? "I don't think I can eat both sandwiches though, I'm sorry," I said as I looked over at him. He was already taking a bite of his sandwich.

"No problem sweetheart! I'll eat what you don't want. We can just throw the chips in the pantry for later," he said as he unwrapped the other sandwich he had bought for me. I smiled at how much he reminded me of Jefferson. Jefferson could eat a cow I swear.

My god Gunner was so damn cute when he ate. Shit, he was just so damn cute period! No, he was beyond cute. He was handsome. I practically could feel the heat coming from his body. I needed to move away a bit before his leg touched mine. If it did I'm pretty sure I would fall apart.

I looked over at him just as he looked over at me.

"You okay sweetheart? Are you not feeling well? You need more medicine?"

I just smiled at him and shook my head no and took a bite of my sandwich. He smiled that big crooked smile, and just when I thought it couldn't get any worse, I noticed the goddamn dimple on his cheek.

Fuck me…..this was going to be *very* hard.

6 Gunner

Okay, I have seen plenty of girls eat before and I never thought twice about it. But when Ellie ate, my whole world about stopped. Who am I kidding; everything she did made my whole world stop. She ate all of her sandwich and finished off her chips and the brownie I bought her. Thank god she was not one of those girls who would only eat lettuce and snack on carrots. Jeff came out dressed and ready for his date.

"Alright I'm out of here. You sure you are okay with this Ellie?" Jeff asked as he bent down to give her a kiss goodbye.

"Yes. I said I was fine. Have fun tonight," Ellie called out as Jeff slapped me on the back and made his way out the door.

"Did you get enough to eat Ellie?" I asked her as I cleaned up the mess on the coffee table.

"Oh my gosh yes! I'm *so* full and *so* tired! Thank you so much Gunner for getting my favorite! I'm surprised you even knew that." She said as she looked up at me with those beautiful blue eyes that caught my breath every fucking time she looked at me.

"No problem sweetheart, it was my pleasure. I heard Jeff say enough times what he was bringing you for lunch so I put two and two together that this must be your favorite place.

"Do you mind if I watch a movie with you? I mean I'm tired but, I don't think I could fall asleep this early," Ellie called over her shoulder to me as I brought all the trash out to the kitchen. Holy hell, just her asking to watch a movie with me and BAM…..hard dick! I needed to get it together or it was going to be a long fucking night.

"Of course I don't mind! On the table next to the sofa are all of our movies if you want to pick one." I called back out to her. "You want something else to drink?"

"Um…just water please." She answered me with a smile so sweet my heart about dropped to my stomach. I would give anything to have that smile greet me each and every morning.

"Soooo, you really were planning on just staying home tonight and watching a movie? Seems to me you would have some hot date like Jefferson. A guy as good looking as you surely has a girlfriend." Ellie rattled off as I walked up to the sofa and set her bottle of water down along with another beer for me.

"Yes, I was really planning on watching a movie tonight and no, no hot date or girlfriend," I said back to her with a laugh. "Jefferson would laugh his ass off if he heard you say he was on a hot date!"

I sat down on the sofa and reached around the back and pulled up a blanket for her.

"Do you want me to get you a pillow?" I asked as she looked through the movies.

"Oh no…I can get it. You don't have to wait on me Gunner. I'm perfectly fine to get things on my own."

Good lord I could watch her lips move for hours. I tore my eyes away from her mouth and looked up to see her staring back at me. Yep, this was going to be a long night. We sat there for I don't know how long just staring at each other before I jumped up and walked into Jeff's bedroom to grab a pillow and another blanket. I needed to adjust my growing dick as I walked down the hall.

I walked into my bedroom and quickly changed into some sweat pants. If things kept going the way they were, my dick was going to be squished in my jeans all night if I didn't change. On the way back into the living room I stopped in the kitchen to get a bag of ice for Ellie's hand.

I sat back down on the sofa and handed her the pillow and the other blanket. I also grabbed the small sofa pillows for her to prop her hand up on.

"Thank you Gunner," she said in the sweetest voice I've ever heard. There goes my heart again for like the umpteenth time today.

"Sure, um…got to remember to keep this elevated. You find a movie you like?" She looked up at me with the most adorable smile. I couldn't help but smile back at her. The things this girl's smile did to me and in more than one place.

"YEP! I can't believe you have this! I *love* this movie." She said with such childlike excitement.

I looked over to the movie she was holding and it was *Cars*. No fucking way!

"You want to watch *Cars*?" I said with a laugh.

"Hells yeah! This is like my all-time favorite movie! Ari's little brother and I watch it all the time. You don't like *Cars*? I can't believe it. It's like…the BEST movie EVER. Why do you even have this movie if you don't like it?" She rattled off so fast I had to laugh at her.

"No! No! *Cars* is perfect Ellie. It actually is my favorite movie also. I love watching it and I'm not afraid to admit I bought it. I have a secret love of saying Ka-Chow when no one is listening." I said as I took the movie from her hand.

"*Cars* it is!"

I walked over and put the movie in the blue ray player. I turned back around and if I was not mistaken, I would say someone was just checking my ass out. I gave her a smile and a wink and watched that beautiful blush take over her cheeks.

"Are you comfortable sweetheart, need anything while I'm up?" I looked down at her poor hand. It was still pretty swollen but didn't look too bad. She was trying to adjust herself on the sofa with all the pillows and the blanket. I let out a small laugh and she looked up at me.

"Glad to know I'm amusing you. I can't do this with just one hand. ARGH! I feel so useless. Shit!"

She threw her head back against the sofa. Poor thing, I knew she was in pain and was trying to act like she wasn't.

"Here Ellie sweetheart, let me help you." I reached over and set the pillow on the end of the sofa. "Here, lie down."

I picked up her legs and the instant I touched her I felt a jolt of electricity go through my entire body. Good lord I can't even help her with the simplest of things without getting a reaction out of my betraying body.

"Really I'm okay sitting up Gunner. If I lie down you won't have anywhere to sit!" She practically jumped away from me.

"Don't be silly Ellie, lay down. *Please.*"

I smiled when I saw her relax. She lifted her legs onto the sofa and I adjusted the pillow for her. I took the smaller pillows and put them on the edge of the sofa so she could put her hand up. She took the ice, and I saw that she winced when she put it on her hand.

"Do you need more pain medicine?" I asked her as I moved the coffee table over to where she could at least reach over and grab her water if she needed it.

"No, I just took some not too long ago. Gunner really, you don't have to do all of this. I'll be fine. Besides the fact that I'm just feeling sleepy I'm okay, really."

I was now kneeling on the ground in front of the sofa adjusting her blanket.

I looked up at her and was stopped dead in my tracks. Her beautiful light brown hair was just past her shoulders and had a bit of a wave to it. Not curly but not straight either. Her blue eyes looked like the sky and her smile...... well damn, her smile would always be my undoing I decided at that very moment.

I smiled at her and for some reason I reached up and pushed her hair behind her ear. Every time I touched her I felt her heat move through my body. I wanted so badly to reach down and just brush her lips against mine. And then it hit me, I would do anything for her. I would lay down my life for this girl.

"I know you can take care of yourself sweetheart. I just want to help. Now let's watch this movie shall we?" I said as I stood back up and moved to the other end of the sofa.

I lifted up her legs, sat down and grabbed the last small pillow I purposely kept out to hide my hard on. I placed her legs on the pillow and hit play. It would take several minutes into *Cars* before my heart rate finally settled back down.

The moment he pushed my hair behind my ear I knew I was in trouble.

He was being so thoughtful and kind. For a second I really thought he was going to lean down and kiss me. I almost was willing him to do it in my mind. How silly am I being? I know he is only taking care of me because I'm Jefferson's sister. There is no way a guy like this would *ever* be interested in me. Jefferson was dead wrong. I'm so far out of Gunner's league it was unreal.

Gunner sat on the other end of the sofa and rested my legs on his lap. Well, not really because he put a pillow in-between him and my legs. I must admit I felt a tad bit disappointed when I saw him do that. Ryan *never* would have sat on the sofa like this. He said he could not take touching me because it only made him want me more. Maybe he just didn't want to touch me because I was never desirable for him. To be honest, I would never have been ready to do anything with Ryan. We barely ever kissed and that was all. I guess he felt the same way. He never really wanted me.

You will never be wanted by anyone............

"Hey, what are you frowning for over there? Do you want me to change the movie, *Cars* not doing it for you sweetheart?" Gunner asked as he started to stroke my legs.

OH. MY. GOD. He really needed to stop doing that. This boy must have magic in his fingertips....holy fuck! There goes that pressure in-between my legs again!

"No, it's fine I was just thinking about the whole thing with Ryan today. I'm sorry." I said as I tried to relax while he was sending jolts of electricity up and down my legs. Gunner's face immediately fell and he looked like he wanted to hurt someone. He stopped stroking my legs and pushed both his hands through his messy hair. I immediately missed his touch and regretted bringing up Ryan. As I watched him run his hands through his hair I licked my lips. What I wouldn't do to straddle him right now and run my fingers through that hair. I wonder if it was as soft as it looked.

Oh holy shit! I needed to stop this! I tried to clear my head of my thoughts and looked back up at Gunner who was now looking at me. This was starting to get awkward the way we kept staring at each other.

"Hey, um Gunner can I ask you something?" I said as I sat up a little to get a better look at him. My god he really was breathtaking. He smiled at me.

"Always…."

Yep, I would never forget that smile for as long as I lived. The feelings it sent through my body were like nothing I had ever experienced.

"Why do you keep calling me sweetheart?"

SHIT! As soon as I asked him that his smile faded just a little bit.

"I didn't realize I was saying it a lot, I'm sorry. If you want me to stop or it bothers you, I'll try to be more aware of it," Gunner said as he looked back at the TV.

Oh no….FUCK! I think I just hurt his feelings. FUCK! FUCK! FUCK A DUCK!

"No no, please don't stop. I mean, I like it. I mean, um, well…" Good lord what was I trying to say here?

"It's just that you called me that the first time you touched me, I mean when you pulled me back away from Jefferson and Ryan. I guess I was just surprised to hear anyone other than Jefferson use an endearing name for me. That's all," I said as I laid back down on the pillow. Gesh, now I felt like a complete bitch. Here this god of a guy was staying home tonight and waiting on me and I just insulted him. SHIT! I truly sucked at this stuff.

"Ryan never called you sweetheart or anything?" Gunner asked, his voice filled with surprise.

"HA! No….about the only thing he ever called me was Ell or Ells. That should have been another sign," I said the last sentence practically under my breath.

"Well I can tell you this Ellie, if you were my girlfriend, I would let you know every day how much you meant to me, through words…..and much more," Gunner said in a sexy ass voice.

I wanted to say *show me this much more* and show me now please*!*

Okay, that just woke up my whole body including my libido. WOW….no one has ever said anything like that to me before. Whoever snags this guy is going to be one hell of a lucky bitch.

"That is the nicest thing anyone has ever said to me. Thank you Gunner, so much. I'm sure you're going to make some girl a very happy woman someday," I said with as much of a smile as I could muster.

The thought of another girl in his arms drove me almost mad. What was wrong with me? God help me…..I turned my attention back to *Cars*.

Before I knew it he was stroking my legs again and I fell into a dream. I dreamt I was walking along a riverbank. It was me walking but I was also standing in the background watching it all play out. All I could see was my back walking away from me. Then to my side a man came running up and picked me up in his arms and spun me around. He gave me the most loving kiss. He whispered something in my ear, and I threw my head back and laughed. He turned and I could now see the front of his body....it was Gunner. He had white linen pants on that were rolled up so the water did not touch them and a grey shirt. He looked like heaven. His smile was that crooked smile that I instantly fell in love with and would do anything to see every day. Just then I turned along with Gunner to start walking back in the direction I was watching my dream.....something was different about me but I couldn't see what it was. I barely could see my face or my body. Everything got blurry. Gunner dropped my hand and started to walk away from me. Wait! Where was he going?! Why was he leaving? He looked so sad.

I heard someone talking to me. It was my mother...... *Wake up Ellie......you will never be wanted like this Ellie darlin'...... He does not want you Ellie, wake up......Does not want you......* NO! That was not true. I saw the way Gunner looked at me in my dream......he loved me.....he had to love me....

Ellie sweetheart wakeup.......

8 Gunner

I woke up with a startle. It took me a second to realize I was still on the sofa. Oh man….my neck was killing me! I must have fallen asleep watching the movie. The movie was over and it was just replaying the main menu over and over again.

Gunner?.......Gunner don't go!......NO! He does, you're wrong….. you're wrong! Gunnerrrrr!

What the hell?! I looked over and Ellie was dreaming, if you could call it that. She was calling out my name in her dream. Holy shit! She sounded scared to death. I jumped up careful not to knock her off the sofa. I pushed the coffee table a little out of the way, and I knelt down next to her and started to stroke her hair.

"Ellie sweetheart wakeup, Ellie wake up……sweetheart *please* wake up."

Fuck! My heart was pounding a mile a minute. What the fuck was she dreaming about and where the fuck was I going? I would *never* leave her….ever.

"Ellie sweetheart wakeup." Ellie's eyes opened suddenly and she looked right at me. Next thing I knew she started to cry and sat up and threw herself into my arms. She was crying hysterically and I was really fucking freaked out. I was going to kick my ass if I hurt her in a dream. I couldn't possibly fuck this up in a goddamn dream…….could I?

"OH MY GOD! Gunner……" Ellie cried out in-between sobs.

"Shhh, Ellie it's okay, everything is okay, I'm here sweetheart, and I'm not going anywhere. I promise." Just then Ellie pulled back and looked at me. Her eyes were filled with tears and she looked so goddamned confused. She shook her head no for a second and just stared at me.

"No one will ever want me Gunner, or stay with me…...ever." She whispered.

What the hell? My god, what did her mother do to her?

"Ellie sweetheart that's just not true."

I pushed a lock of her hair behind her ear. My god she was even beautiful when she was crying. The only thing I wanted to do at that moment was take away her fear and doubts. To show her how much she was wanted. I looked down to her soft tear soaked lips and licked my own lips. I started to lean in to kiss her and I heard the front door lock move.

Ellie must have heard it also because she quickly pulled out of my embrace and sat back just staring at me with this lost look on her face.

Jeff walked in and surveyed what he saw.

"What's going on? Ellie? Are you okay? Did you hurt your hand again?" Jeff said as he looked back and forth between the two of us.

"No....um...no," Ellie struggled to talk and was shaking her head as if trying to erase a memory. She quickly wiped away her tears and looked up at Jeff. He looked back at her and snapped his head over to me.

"What the fuck did you do to her Gunner?"

Wait......What?

I quickly stood up and turned to Jeff. "I didn't do a damn thing! We fell asleep watching a movie and she just woke up crying out from a dream. She literally just woke up crying."

I left out the part where she was crying out my name. I mean, I was not in the mood to get my ass kicked for hurting her in a fucking dream.

"Jefferson! Gunner has been nothing but a gentleman to me all day and night. I can't even believe you would think he would do something to make me cry." Ellie was sobbing even more now. Jeff looked at Ellie and back at me.

"Dude man, I know you would never, it's just I walked in here and she's crying and…..fuck," Jeff said as he knelt down at the edge of the sofa. I pushed the coffee table back out of the way.

"Ellie honey what is going on? Why are you so upset? Is this about Ryan?" Jeff asked as he moved to sit down next to Ellie on the sofa. Ellie's face flew up to meet mine. She looked so confused and upset. My stomach was in my throat and for some reason I felt like I was going to get sick. I needed to go outside and get some air.

"I'm going to step outside a minute and get some fresh air," I said as I moved to the front door.

"NO!" Ellie shouted and stopped me in my tracks.

"This is *NOT* about Ryan, I haven't even thought about him hardly all day. It was just, it was just…...I guess it was just a nightmare. I…..I….. really don't even remember. I just remember waking up being scared that I was all alone and I lost…..I lost…...." She looked back up to me again and her tears started to flow again.

"What did you lose honey?" Jeff asked as he held a sobbing Ellie in his arms.

She was looking at me with such sad eyes. What the fuck was going on in her head.

"I don't remember Jefferson. I just want to take a pain pill and go back to sleep. Maybe that's why I had the weird dream…it was the pain medicine," Ellie said as she settled down a bit.

"Gunner, can you grab her medicine in the kitchen?" Jeff asked as he looked up at me with a sad look on his face.

"Sure, no problem."

I walked over and grabbed the old bottle of water I had brought out earlier tonight. I looked up and saw Jeff walking Ellie back to his bedroom. He was saying something to her that I couldn't make out. She just kept nodding her head in agreement. I would give my life to know what they were talking about.

Holy fuck…...What the hell was she dreaming about? When I said I was going to step outside she just about freaked out. Do I ask her what the dream was about? Maybe I should. I mean she was calling out my name after all. What if I was a prick in the dream? Now *I* needed to shake my head to clear my thoughts. I walked over to the sofa and grabbed the pillow and blanket I had brought out earlier. I started to walk back towards Jeff's bedroom. I stopped at the door when I heard Jeff's voice talking slow and calm.

"Ellie, you *cannot* let something our mother said to you when you were little dictate your entire life honey. It was bullshit. She is a miserable person who just wants those around her to be just as miserable. You DO deserve happiness honey and you will find it. Trust me," Jefferson said as he leaned down to give Ellie a kiss on the forehead.

A surge of jealousy zipped through me. I would give anything to be the one who was comforting her right now. FUCK……I'm jealous of my own best friend? The pain I was feeling because she was hurting was killing me. I just didn't understand it. I just met this girl. How could I already feel so protective of her? Jeff got up and started to head out of the room but not before he stopped and gave me a slap on the back and a wink.

"Hey, here is your pain pill and a fresh bottle of water Ellie."

Ellie looked over at me and gave me a smile that just about brought me to my knees….again. Okay…when were these feelings going to stop taking over me like this?

"Thank you so much Gunner. I'm sorry; I don't know what came over me when I woke up. Um…… did I say anything while I was asleep?"

Shit, do I tell her what she called out or act like I didn't hear her calling out my name. "Yes, sweetheart you did. You kept calling out my name and something about someone being wrong but that's all you said."

I watched her face as I told her what she had said in her sleep. She frowned and looked away towards the window.

"Oh…...well, um…… I'm sure it was probably just because you had been so attentive this evening. I don't really even remember what I was dreaming about so…..." She looked back over at me and I swear I saw tears building in her eyes.

Bullshit. I knew damn well she remembered her dream. Why wouldn't she tell me? What the hell was she afraid of?

"Well, it doesn't matter Ellie. You need to get some rest sweetheart. Do you need something to prop up your hand? Or need anything else?" I asked her while I shuffled my feet back and forth like I was five years old again. She smiled at me and just shook her head no.

"Thank you again Gunner for everything but I think I'm fine. I really do appreciate it. I'm sorry to keep you up so late at night. I'm just going to try and get back to sleep. I'm so glad seniors have off tomorrow!" She said with a giggle.

I walked over and turned off the side light. "Well, um......good night Ellie."

I turned and started towards the door. I turned one last time to see her close her eyes and pull her blanket up and tuck it under her chin. She was so adorable......and I was so fucked.

I walked out and saw Jeff sitting on the sofa holding one beer up to his lips taking a long drink and another beer in his other hand.

"Must have been some date for you to bust out two of 'em." I said with a small laugh.

"This one is for you. I thought you might want one before heading off to bed."

I reached over and took the beer out of his hand and sank down in the sofa and took a drink.

"I have to ask you Jeff, what the *fuck* did your mother say to Ellie."

"I always thought it was her story to tell, Gunner, but I'm beginning to think it has affected her more than I thought. When she was seven my mom was really drunk one night. I wasn't home so Ellie was there to take the brunt of it. Funny thing was I was spending the night at a friend's house which I NEVER did. I just had to get away from her. I mean, I was always trying to get in between her and Ellie. Protect Ellie from our mom's hurtful words she lashed out all the fucking time. When I left she was sober......was not even drinking a drop of alcohol. I thought things would be okay. She talked about taking Ellie to the park even."

Jeff ran his hand through his hair and spoke something under his breath. I was pretty sure he had said fuck.

"When I got home the next morning, Ellie was sitting in the corner of the kitchen......asleep. Still wearing the clothes she had on the day before. My mother was passed out at the kitchen table. I ran up to Ellie and woke her up, she just started to crying as soon as she saw me. She started rambling off how our mother didn't want her anymore, how hungry she was, how mommy told her no one would ever love her.....ever."

Jeff stopped and put his head back on the sofa. His body started shaking.

"FUCK! If I had only just stayed home that night, it would have never have happened and Ellie wouldn't have this messed up idea in her head that she will never be good enough for a guy. She thinks her fate is to be alone. Like my mother."

Jeff took another swig of beer and looked at me. Tears filled his eyes and I was stunned. In the three years I had known this man I had never once saw him cry, even when he got hurt on the football field.

"Jeff, man, you cannot possibly blame yourself for what your mother did or said. You were ten years old for christ's sakes. That is *not* your fault. You couldn't save her from every little thing," I said as a part of me just wanted to go and have a few words with their mother.

"Gunner, be patient with her. I see how she looks at you and how you look at her. I think she is confused by what she is feeling for you. She told me tonight she is scared, she said she is having feelings for you she never felt for Ryan and she barely even knows you."

Holy shit my heart was pounding. She admitted to Jeff she had feelings for me? Okay, where do I go with this? I felt like I was about to get sick to my stomach so I took another drink of my beer.

"Gun, I see the panic on your face dude!" Jeff said with a small laugh.

"I'm so glad you think this is funny asshole," I took the last swig of my beer and set it on the coffee table. Shit…how do I even begin this with him?

"Jeff, I have these crazy feelings for Ellie. I mean shit; I have NEVER felt this way before in my life. First I thought it was just because, you know….it was your sister. You know….you want what you can't have and all. I mean, I literally wanted to beat the shit out of that boyfriend of hers five minutes after I met her. I kept thinking I would do anything to take away her pain while sitting in the urgent care room. I have this insane desire to take care of her. What the fuck is this?" I said as I sat back on the sofa and threw my hands into my hair.

Jeff let out a laugh. "Dude…..if I could tell you I would. I know that feeling of wanting something so bad……" Jeff just stopped and stared off into space.

"What's going on Jeff? Do you have feelings for Ari?"

"WHAT? What the fuck makes you think that? Ari is like a little sister to me. I mean, she is, she is…..um she is annoying as hell. She talks too fucking much and she drives me nuts. The only feelings I have for that girl are feelings of annoyance!" Jeff said as he got up and took the two empty bottles of beer to the kitchen garbage.

"Okay, 'cause I was a bit surprised at how much you two were going at each other all day. I just got the feeling there was some um…..tension there," I said as I wiggled my eyebrows up and down.

51

"Fuck you dude. I had a shitty night and I'm going to sleep," Jeff said as he headed to the bathroom.

"What? Was Rebecca not her normal bubbly cheerleader self tonight?" I called after him. All I got in return was a middle finger shot in my direction.

I woke up from a total dead sleep. I sat up confused for a few minutes. Where the hell was I? My heart started to beat rapidly. I looked around and realized I was in Jefferson's room. I looked down at my hand. I was surprised it didn't hurt nearly as much as it did yesterday. I pushed back the covers and walked out into the kitchen. I heard someone and my heart started to flutter. Was it Gunner?

"Hey there honey! Did you sleep well?" Jefferson said in a very chipper mood.

"You must have had a good night last night to be so happy first thing this morning," I replied back with a yawn. I was NOT a morning person. I sat down at the bar stool on the island.

Jefferson let out a laugh. "You never were a morning person Ells. And no, my night sucked. I couldn't wait to get home. Did you have any more nightmares?

"Nope I slept like a baby. Soooo, what's with this date last night? How come it sucked?" I asked as Jefferson handed me a plate of scrambled eggs and a Sunny D. He started to whip up more eggs as he looked over at me like he really didn't want to have this conversation.

"It sucked because the girl who I went out with is a cheerleader who cannot take no for an answer. I got tired of giving her excuses so I thought it would be easier to just get it over with it and go out with her."

"Hmmm, so there is no special girl in your heart Jefferson?" I asked as I took a bite of eggs. God I have missed his eggs! How crazy was that?

Jefferson let out a small laugh. It almost sounded like it was filled with sadness.

"Ells the only special girl I have in my heart is you honey. Always has been, always will be." I smiled up at him and my heart melted. I was starting to put two and two together. I really was beginning to think that Jefferson just might have feelings for Ari. Maybe I was way off here but something just was not right.

Speaking of things not being right.......

"Um, where's Gunner? Is he still sleeping?" I asked, trying not to sound like I cared too much where he was.

"Shit no that cowboy is not still sleeping. Even if he is out partying until three am he is up by six am and headed out to the gym for a workout,"

Jefferson said as he grabbed his plate and a bottle of Sunny D from the refrigerator. "He runs up to the gym, works out and runs back damn near almost every day. He puts my workouts to shame."

"Oh, wow. No wonder he looks…...." I shut my mouth before the next words came out. Good God, I needed to get a grip. This was just insane how this boy, no not boy, MAN……it was insane how this man affected me. I was starting to bounce my leg up and down hoping I would not miss him before I had to leave.

"Do you have to work today Jefferson? I mean if you do, I can give Ari a call to come and pick me up. I still have to go clean out my locker since I didn't do it yesterday. I guess I need to go home today also. Not that mom would even notice I didn't come home last night," I said as I got up to clean off my plate.

"Yeah honey I'm sorry. Gunner's last day was last week and today is mine. This internship has been great experience though. I'm kind of bummed out it's over. Gunner is excited because all he wants to do is head out to his grandparents' ranch," Jefferson said with a smile.

From what Jefferson has said around me about Gunner, he absolutely adores his grandparents. Any free time he gets he heads out to their ranch. God I want to go to the country!

"It's okay. I can just give Ari a call and see if she can come and pick me up. I know she was planning on working on her speech for tomorrow." Just the mention of Ari's name and I saw Jefferson tense up. YEP…..there was something there whether he wanted to admit or not.

I heard the front door open and I looked up.

Holy fucking hell I think I'm going to faint.

Gunner came walking into the kitchen, no shirt on, sweating……really sweating….looking……really H.O.T. I had to remind myself to breathe. Fuck me this guy was too good looking for his own good. Oh holy hell…… his tattoo was so sexy….and….he had two! My eyes traveled up and down his perfect body.

Jefferson walked up and took his finger and used it to close my lower jaw.

"Breathe sweet girl….breathe," Jefferson whispered in my ear. It snapped me out of my temporary moment of insanity. I mean really…no one deserves to have a body that fucking amazing.

"Hey, morning Ellie. How did you sleep? You need anything, pain pills or anything?" Gunner asked as he walked into the kitchen and grabbed a bottle of water from the refrigerator.

"You headed off to work Jeff?"

"Yep, leaving in a few minutes, can't believe this is my last day. Hey Gunner, Ellie needs a ride back up to the school to clean out her locker and then she needs to head home. You busy? Would you mind giving her a lift?" Jefferson asked as he looked at me with a shit eating-grin on his face. I knew exactly what he was doing. I can't believe my own brother was selling me out……..bastard.

Before Gunner could even answer I shot back, "No that's okay, I'll give Ari a call, she can come and pick me it's no big deal," I said as I gave Jefferson a dirty look and turned to look at Gunner. I had to quickly look away. Every time I looked at him I got a dull ache between my legs. Jesus, I needed to just get away.

"Nonsense Ellie, it would be my pleasure to give you a ride swee…..um….I can give you a ride to where ever you need to go," Gunner said with the sweetest smile. It was not lost on me how he was about to call me sweetheart and stopped.

SHIT! I can't believe I even said anything last night. Fuck!

"Yeah, besides, I thought you said Ari was working on her speech today for the graduation tomorrow," Jefferson said as he started to walk to his bedroom. I sure as hell hoped that he could feel the daggers I was throwing his way with my eyes.

"That is very sweet of you but, I need to go to the school, clean out my locker and then head home." I'm sure you have other things you need to do," I said as I turned to see him staring at me.

Gulp…..it was hard to swallow….hard to even think with him standing there with no fucking shirt on looking at me like that. Squeezing of legs….again……

"Nope…not a damn thing to do but take you to clean out your locker and then home, sounds like those are my plans for the day. Maybe we can even stop and get a coffee at Halcycon's after we clean out your locker," Gunner said as he started to walk past me. He stopped and pushed a piece of my hair behind my ear. He sure liked doing that……he brought his hand down and ran it lightly down my jaw line.

Oh.My.God. I literally felt a jolt of electricity run from where he touched me down to my toes. I was barely able to open my mouth let alone talk.

"Okay, um….yeah. I um, I've always wanted to go there," I said with a smile.

Oh shit, I felt the blush moving up my face. Gunner just laughed and tapped my nose with his finger. "Damn sweetheart, you're cute as a button when you blush. I'm going to go take a shower and get ready to leave. Give me a few minutes and then we can head out okay?"

"Sure, I still need to get ready myself. So….okay…meet ya back out here, so yeah, we can head out after that."

Holy hell I just needed to shut the hell up. At least he called me sweetheart again. My stomach got butterflies the moment he said it.

I got up to head back to Jefferson's bedroom to get ready to go. Oh my gosh, I sure as shit hope I had something decent to wear packed. Jefferson came walking down the hall dressed in dress pants and a button up shirt and a tie. WOW. I had to smile at how good looking my own brother was. He just grabbed me and spun me around!

"You have a good day today sis, okay?! I'll talk to you tonight and hey, invite whoever you want to the party tomorrow night. Talk to you later honey okay?" He leaned down and kissed me on my cheek.

Just then my I heard my cell phone ringing so I ran into the bedroom to grab it.

"Hello."

"Sooooo…..bitch, tell me how it went last night! I can't imagine much happened since Jeff was there the whole time." Ari didn't waste a minute just jumping right into it.

I just laughed. Never one to not just get right to the point…that was just Arianna.

"Well, actually Jefferson went out last night so Gunner and I ended up watching a movie." Silence……..

"Ari are you still there?"

"Oh yeah, sorry about that I'm still here Ells. I guess I was just shocked to hear that Jeff would have gone out and left you alone with Gunner. Wow. He must really trust this guy to leave him alone with his little sister." I had never heard so much disappointment in Ari's voice. It broke my heart that she was so stuck on Jefferson and he just would not give her the time of day.

I started to speak again when I saw Gunner walk out of his bedroom with a towel wrapped around his waist………he had walked into Jefferson's bathroom and came right back out with something in his hand. Then I heard his bedroom door shut. Next thing I knew I heard a loud thump on the floor. I tore my eyes away from the door and looked on the floor.

Oh holy shit I dropped my phone! "Ari???"

"Jesus H. Christ, what the fuck Ellie? I mean I was talking and then next thing I know I hear a loud noise." Ari was yelling in my ear.

"Can you be quiet just one second Ari…." I said as I got up and shut the bedroom door all the way.

"Holy shit Ari…..Gunner just walked out of his bedroom wearing nothing but a towel! I mean I thought the sight of him walking in shirtless and sweaty was enough to make me go into shock….this just fucking topped it all. This guy is KILLING ME! I've never had these feelings before Ari and I'm starting to get freaked out. I even had a dream about him last night." I whispered as I went back and started looking through my bag. SHIT! What was I going to wear? Just then I saw a short denim skirt and a light blue tank top.

"Ari did you put your outfit in my bag?"

Ari started to laugh. "I sure as shit did. I had it next to your bag so I threw it in there yesterday...you never know when you are going to need a cute little outfit."

"Oh my god you just saved me! Gunner is taking me to school to clean out my locker and then downtown to Halcyon's for coffee. I didn't have a thing to wear. You're my hero." I said as I stripped down to just my t-shirt.

"Of course I am....the only thanks I want are all the juicy details of this....coffee date....you're going on with hotty Gunner. How hot did he look with his t-shirt off 'cause yesterday he looked mighty fine with the t-shirt on, and if my ears just heard right, you have now seen him twice with no shirt on....once when he was all sweaty from doing just what?" Ari said as she laughed her ass off.

"First off, it is not a *date,* he's just doing me a favor by taking me to school and then home. Second, oh hell yeah he looked hotter than hot with his shirt off! He has a tribal tattoo just like Jefferson but it starts on the right side of his MASSIVE chest, goes over his shoulder and then down his arm a bit. He also has a tattoo on his abs.... I think it's the brand for his grandfather's ranch. It was an M inside a triangle," I said as I slowly opened the door back up and ran into Jefferson's bathroom.

"Oh holy hells bells.....Okay if that does not sound sexier than shit! Speaking of sexy, is Jeff dating someone now?" Ari asked trying to sound all casual but I knew damn well the moment I mentioned Jefferson and date in the same sentence her world stopped spinning.

"No, I guess it was some cheerleader who would not leave him alone until they went out. Listen, I really have to jump in the shower really quick. I'll call you when I get home! Get that speech written girl. Oh, Jefferson said we could invite a few friends over tomorrow night so if there is anyone you want to invite. Make sure Amanda and Heather know about it. Amanda will have fun at a party full of college guys! Just keep it to a few close friends of ours okay?" I started up the shower and took off my t-shirt, bra and panties.

"Alright girl, I'll get on it. Have fuuunnnnn! Don't do anything I wouldn't do! HA!" Ari said as she started to laugh.

"Bye Ari....."

Just as I was about to hop in the shower I realized I had forgotten my razor....if I was wearing a skirt I was doing a quick once over on my legs. I grabbed the towel off the rack and wrapped it around my body. I opened the door just a tad. Gunner's door was shut and it sounded like he was on the phone. Should be safe to make a quick run and grab my razor. I bolted out the door and into Jefferson's bedroom. I grabbed my razor out of my bag and turned back to run back into the bathroom. Gunner's bedroom door was literally almost directly across from Jefferson's bathroom. As soon as I made it out the door, Gunner came walking out his door, still on the phone and still in his fucking towel! I slammed right into him. I don't know who was more surprised or more embarrassed because he turned the shade of the red towel that was, thank God, still wrapped around me, and I am pretty damn sure my face was just as red if not more.

Gunner dropped his phone and I dropped my razor. Unfortunately we both bent down at the same time to pick up our stuff.

"FUCK!" We both shouted as our heads hit.

"Holy fuck Ellie....I thought you were in the shower!" Gunner said as his eyes took a sweep from the top of my body to the bottom. I was pretty sure he liked what he saw because he started to lick his lips and there went his goddamn hand through his hair! Oh holy shit.......now his hair was wet and it was even hotter.

Oh lord...I think my legs are about to go out from underneath me. I started to sway a little bit. Gunner reached out and grabbed me.

"Ellie, are you okay sweetheart? Does your head hurt? Do you need to sit down? Dammit did I hurt your hand?" Gunner's eyes were filled with so much worry and.........love? No....he was just worried that he hurt me that was all. I mean my God look at him. What could *he* possibly see in *me*?

"Um....Oh Shit! Shit! Shit!....Gunner I'm SO sorry. I thought it would be safe if I ran out and grabbed something. I'm so, so sorry. Um, no my head and my hand...they're fine really," I said as I looked down to where his hands were still holding onto both my arms. He followed my eyes and immediately dropped his hands.

"Good, good, I um, I'm glad you're not hurt," he said as he smiled down at me. Fuck. A. Duck.

I smiled and started to walk into the bathroom. As I was shutting the door, Gunner was just standing there....frozen. Once the bathroom door was all the way shut I had to lean against it for support. Damn....if only his towel had dropped. I had to giggle that I even thought that. Hey, I was human after all. The dull ache in-between my legs was starting to become a familiar thing when I was around this guy.

I jumped in the shower and tried to go as fast as I could. Just the thought of spending more time alone with Gunner gave me butterflies. I had to remember though; we could be nothing more than friends. A guy who was that good looking and had that much of a rockin' body, yeah, he would never waste his time on someone like me. I need to just keep telling myself that. Now if only my body would listen.

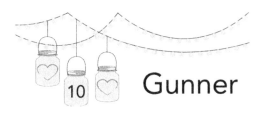

10 Gunner

I shut the door to my bedroom and leaned against it. Holy shit….down boy! I cannot believe I just fucking ran into Ellie, and she was wearing nothing but a fucking towel.

Good lord I can't catch my breath...breathe…in…out…shit!

Mother fucker! I cannot believe how much I wanted to just pull that damn thing off of her and take her right there against the wall. Yeah, Jefferson would sure as shit beat the fuck out of me for even thinking that. SHIT! I hope I can look at her today and not picture her naked.

I wish I had time for a cold shower but that was out of the question. I needed to get dressed and make a few more phone calls for tomorrow night. First thing was to call back Jake, the guy who was DJ'ing for Ellie's graduation party. Then I needed to order some food. Jeff had his last day of work today, and then after that he was going to get some stuff for the party.

I quickly threw on a pair of shorts and a shirt. My dick was still somewhat hard from seeing Ellie in that towel. Christ, the things that girl does to me. I couldn't believe how excited I was to just spend the day with her. Spending time with Ellie was now on my list of favorite things to do. Before the only two things I cared about were football and the ranch. Now there were three; Ellie, the ranch and football and they were in that order.

I heard the shower turn off and knew I only had a few minutes to get this shit taken care of. I picked up my phone and called Jake back. He was not too pleased I just hung up on his ass but what was I going to say. Sorry dude…the girl who makes me hard just by walking into a room was standing in front of me with nothing on but a towel. The next call was to order some food. The third call was to Grams. What the hell was I going to get Ellie? I had never in my life bought a girl a gift, let alone a girl who is this special to me.

Wait…where the fuck did that come from?

I knew I could honestly say I would do anything for Ellie. Anything to make her smile, hear her laugh or feel her touch. She was special to me.

Fuck…..I'm so fucked……

"Gunner?" I heard Ellie call from outside my door. I had just hung up with Grams and had the perfect gift in mind. Just the sound of her voice made my stomach do flips. Man….can I make it through this day without wanting to kiss her? I took a deep breath and opened the door.

FUCK ME….

Nope…I was never going to be able to make it through this day without kissing those sweet soft lips. She stood there staring up at me with such a sweet innocent smile that my heart just melted. I was ready to drop to my knees and tell her I would do whatever she wanted. My god ….was it possible she was getting more and more beautiful every time I looked at her?

She had on a short, but not too short, mini denim skirt along with a blue shirt that made her blue eyes just jump out at you. Her hair was pulled up in a ponytail and she had just a hint of makeup on. Her lips were tinted a light pink, and I couldn't stop staring at them. I wanted to know how soft they felt against my lips so fucking bad.

"Hey um, I'm ready if you are? I mean, I'm not in any kind of hurry or anything I just……" She trailed off as she looked me up and down and started chewing on her bottom lip. I reached over and tilted her head up towards me and pulled her lip out from her teeth.

"That lip is too soft and beautiful to be abused like that Sweetheart." I said as I smiled down at her. I was pretty sure I saw her whole body shake. A blush started to creep onto her cheeks. Damn, it was one of the sexiest things I'd ever seen.

"Right….um…so are you ready to go? I just need a bag or something to clean out my locker," Ellie said as she looked around at everything but me.

"WOW…your room is so…….clean."

"Why thank you Sweetheart. I'm sure my mom would appreciate knowing that all those years of bitching at me to keep my room neat paid off," I said with a laugh.

Ellie let out a giggle and looked up me.

Jesus….the moment her eyes met mine I swear I forgot how to breathe. I leaned down towards her only to have her look away and take a step back.

Shit.

"Um, okay well, let's find you a bag or something shall we?" I said as I moved passed her and headed down the hall to the kitchen. FUCK. I need to remember what Jeff said…..she needed time and here I was trying to fucking kiss her every chance I could. What the fuck was wrong with me? Christ….I need to think about something else…..football….nope that won't work…. football gives me a hard on…..puppies……dogs….I think I would like to get a dog…..what kind of dog? I wonder what kind of dogs Ellie likes.

Okay…I'll think of dogs every time I have the urge to kiss her.

Oh what the hell Gunner, you're losing your goddamn mind.

"You sure seem lost in thought."

I was now standing in the middle of the kitchen…just standing there thinking about fucking dogs. I shrugged my shoulders and started digging through the drawer where Jeff keeps all the extra bags.

"How big of a bag do you need?" Silence…….

"Ellie?" I stood up and she was standing there just staring at me.

"Ellie what's wrong? Hey….can you tell me what is wrong Sweetheart?" I squatted down so I could look in her face. She seemed so lost…what I wouldn't do to crawl in that brain and figure shit out for her.

"I….I don't know what's wrong Gunner!!I just had this panic come over me! What if I can't do this? What if I fail at this too? I mean….I'm soooo not sure that I'm ready to go to college, my mother keeps telling me…." Ellie turned and looked away the moment she mentioned her mother.

I placed my hands on her shoulders and turned her around to look at me. Oh Jesus H. Christ she was crying. My heart just took a nose dive right into my stomach. I reached up and wiped away the tears that were streaming down her beautiful face. She gave me a weak smile.

"Oh god I'm so sorry. You must think I'm a nut case….I'm so sorry Gunner." Then she just lost it. The sobs where taking over her whole body. I pulled her close to me and ran my hand through her soft hair.

She smelt like daisies again. I felt my dick getting hard just from having her up against my body.

Holy fuck…….what am I suppose to be thinking about again?

DOGS!…..Golden retrievers, Labs….yellow, black or brown? Big dog or little dog, German Shorthair Pointer??

"Ellie it's going to be okay Sweetheart, I promise you it will be okay. I know this is a scary time but you are smart girl and you can do anything you put your mind to. Please don't ever doubt yourself just because of something your mother said to you. I know what it feels like to have someone tell you that all you'll ever do is fail," I said as I took a deep breath and buried my nose in her hair. My god….daisies….all I could smell was daisies.

Ellie looked up at me confused. "What do you mean you know what it feels like to have someone tell you'll ever do is fail? Gunner you're amazing! The most amazing person I've ever met. I can't….I can't even believe anyone would think that about you."

I just laughed and gave her shoulders a squeeze. "Come on Ells, let's get this show on the road….we have a locker to clean out and a coffee shop to hit up!"

I reached down and grabbed a couple plastic grocery bags. Ellie walked back into Jeff's room and came out carrying her overnight bag and her backpack.

"Here, let's switch," I said as I took her bags from her and gave her the plastic bags.

"I got off pretty easy on this exchange!" Ellie said with a light laugh. Thank god…she was no longer upset. Gesh, how I would like to just knock some sense into that mother of hers, but from experience I knew it would do no good.

We headed out the door and made our way to my truck. I'm not sure why I was so excited to see her sitting next to me in my truck. I've had plenty of girls in my truck in the last three years but no girl was or would ever be like Ellie.

The moment his fingers touched my face and wiped away my tears, I felt the electricity zip through my whole body. His eyes showed so much worry in them that it made my stomach twist in knots. I know he is just concerned because I'm his best friend's sister but…..

No…I couldn't let myself think that way. Then he dropped the bomb shell on me! Who was it he was talking about? Who said Gunner would fail? I just couldn't believe it. I mean he was super smart from what Jefferson told me, smarter than Jefferson he said. He was an awesome football player. I had seen him play plenty of times when Ari and I went to see Jefferson play. He was super fucking handsome. Yeah…no way this guy would ever want to be with someone like me.

We headed out the door and started towards Gunner's truck. He had a huge smile on his face which caused me to smile. What was he so happy about? OHHH that's right…his truck is his "girl." Jesus…why did I just feel jealous of a damn truck?

He walked to the passenger side of the truck and opened the back door and put my bags in. Then he opened the front door and held my arm as he helped me in.

"Did you remember to get your pain pills Ells?" Gunner asked as he looked at my hand. It really felt a lot better today that was for sure. "Yep…took one this morning after breakfast and packed them in my bag *mom*." I said as he looked me up and down. He threw his head back and laughed. God his laugh moved right through my body and made me ache between my legs. I ever so slightly squeezed my legs together to ease the throbbing. Just then he looked at me with that damn crooked smile. He took his finger and tapped my nose.

"You're so goddamn cute you know that?!" He looked like he wanted to lean down and kiss me….YES!.....Come on!!!….A little more….more….just a little closer…..

"What's your favorite dog?" Gunner asked as he pulled back and stood away from the door.

"Um?" What the fuck? That just came out of nowhere. Holy shit! Here I thought he was thinking of kissing me and he was thinking of…….dogs?

"Think about it!" He said as he smiled and shut the door.

I watched him walk around the front of the truck and there went those hands through that beautiful hair. I'm pretty sure he does that when he is nervous or upset. God it's one of the sexiest things I've ever seen. What is he nervous about?

Dogs? I'm so confused by this guy.

Gunner jumped in and looked over at me. Oh holy shit....there was that beautiful smile and he was just staring at me.

"What is it? What's so funny?" I asked as I smiled back at him.

"Nothin', you just look damn good sitting in my truck Sweetheart that's all!" Gunner said with a laugh.

"Oh okay!"

Gunner started the truck and I was silently praying "Truck Yeah" would not start up....please god....*pleassseeeee*.......Just then Daughtry's "Every time You Turn Around" came screaming over the speakers. OH thank god!!

"You like Daughtry I'm guessing from the smile on your face," Gunner said before he started to back out of the driveway.

"Yes! I love them. Love this song too. But honestly...I was praying that "Truck Yeah" would not start up. I'm not sure what I would've done to you had you started that song," I said as I looked over at him. He jammed on his brakes and just stared at me.

"Oh thank *FUCK* I'm not the only one! Holy shit, I want to delete that song from Jeff's iPod. I'm *so* sick of it," Gunner said as he looked at me with the most serious look on his face. I had to start laughing.

"I've thought the same thing. I swear every time he starts it I just want to haul off and hit him," I looked down at my hand that was a bit still swollen.

"Great minds think alike Ells!" Gunner said with a laugh as he backed out and headed towards the school.

That was like the third time Gunner had called me Ells. Tons of people call me Ell or Ells. So why when he said it did I get butterflies in my stomach? The same way I did when he called me Sweetheart.

"Chocolate lab." I said when the silence in the truck was starting to get to me.

Gunner looked over at me with a confused look on his face. "What?"

"You asked me what my favorite dog was. I think it's a chocolate lab. I've never had a dog but if I ever got one.....I would want a chocolate lab I think," I said as I looked out the window, not sure why tears were starting to build in my eyes.

"Oh yeah, right the dog. You've never had a dog? WOW...boy or girl?" Gunner asked as he turned into the high school parking lot.

"I think I would want a boy. Yep....someone to watch over me and protect me and love me like there was no tomorrow," I said as I turned and looked at Gunner. He was just staring at me....again. He did that a lot. There went the hand through the hair.

Shit...why did that turn me on so damn much. I moved around in my seat to help with the ache.

"You know you don't need a dog for that Sweetheart. I'm pretty sure you could find someone who is more than willing to take on that job," he said with the sweetest smile. I so badly wanted to ask if he wanted to apply for the open position. HA! Yeah right. He couldn't even kiss me......

"What would you name him?" Gunner asked as he jumped out of his truck and ran around the front to open my door. Good 'ole Texas charm....I bet he has girls falling all over him. Well, I was not going to be one of them....or so I kept telling myself that.

"Um, let's see.....I think I would name him....Gus." I said with a smile on my face. Yes...I liked that. It was a good strong name for a dog. Gunner let out a laugh that caused me to stop and look at him.

"What the hell is wrong with Gus? That's a good strong country boy name for my country boy dog. I can't believe you are laughing at my name choice. Some friend you are Gunner Mathews!" I said as I hit him with my good hand.

After what seemed like FOREVER he stopped laughing.

"Gus? You want to name him Gus? How the hell did you come up with that name Ellie?" Gunner said as we started to walk towards the school. He reached down and took my left hand into his right hand. Did he realize he was holding my hand? My god...the butterflies were going crazy in my stomach.

"Well, if you *must* know....one time Jefferson took me on a drive out to Fredericksburg. Said we needed some country air. I saw the name on a mailbox, and I don't know, I just liked it," I said with a shrug of my shoulders.

"Do you like the country? I mean, would you ever want to live out in the country or are you a city girl?" he asked as he bumped his arm into my shoulder. Good god all this contact was driving my libido insane.

"No...I'm NOT a city girl. Well, I mean I am 'cause I grew up in Austin and all. I want nothing more than to get away from Austin and live in a small town with lots of land, and I would love to have a beautiful ranch style home and go outside every morning and feed the chickens. I want to hear nothing but nature. No cars, no horns, no freaking people blowing their damn cigarette smoke in my face. I want to be able to look up into the sky and see the millions of stars every night. I've never seen what a true night time sky looks like with all the stars. I would love that."

I stopped at the side door to the school and looked back at Gunner. He was standing there with a huge shit eating grin on his face. I tilted my head to look at him. What the hell was he thinking? He sure did seem happy.

Huh....I noticed as soon as I started talking about wanting to live in the country he dropped my hand.

Gunner cleared his throat and just shook his head. "Shall we get this over with Sweetheart?" he asked as he held the door open for me. I would NEVER get tired of this. Ryan never once held the door open for me or opened the car door for me.....nothing. Gunner was a complete 180 from Ryan.

"YES! One step closer to my new life as a college student," I said as we headed down the hallway.

Gunner

DOGS. Labs….Chocolate labs……Chocolate labs named Gus….OH holy shit this was not working anymore because all I could think about was the damn dog Ellie wanted…...my Ellie…….

I walked down the hall following her to her locker and tried to keep my dick from getting any harder but it was a fucking chore. I couldn't believe my ears when she started saying she wanted to live in the country. I felt all the air leave my lungs. I dropped her hand that I hadn't even realized I was holding and just stood there listening to her describe the life I wanted. The life I wanted with…...her. That was it. I know Jeff said I needed to give her time and be patient. Fuck that. It was on. I was going to do everything in my power to win Ellie's heart, starting right now.

I had to keep my eyes everywhere but on her. She kept leaning over and that fucking skirt kept creeping up further. Holy shit she had a nice body.

Okay…ceiling…look at the ceiling, look at the other lockers…dogs…Chocolate lab dogs named Gus running around the ranch with Ellie and a little brown haired girl chasing after it.

Wait! What? Where the fuck did that come from? Oh my god….what was happening to me? I'm standing in a damn high school day dreaming about the ranch and Ellie having my child and a fucking lab named Gus!

It's getting hot in here…….

"Gunner? Are you okay? You look like you feel sick. Are you feeling okay?" Ellie said as she took the lock off of the locker door and bent down to pick up the bag she packed.

"Um, yeah yeah…I feel fine Ells. Here let me take that. Is this it? Where are all of your books?"

Ellie handed me the bag filled with just a few notebooks, stuffed animals and a few odds and ends in it.

"Oh…Ari turned them all in for me earlier today when she turned in all of her books. She wanted to get here early so she could get it done and then work on her Valedictorian speech. I think she is pretty nervous about it. Are you sure you're okay?" Ellie asked as she looked me up and down.

I really wanted to tell her no, I was *soooo* not okay. I was day dreaming about uprooting her life, moving her out to the middle of nowhere and oh yeah….getting her pregnant with my kid.

Deep breaths Gunner….deep breaths.

"Sure yeah…..I'm okay! I think it's just really hot in here. Isn't it really hot in here to you? Alright if you're done let's blow this Popsicle stand what do ya' say?" I said as I tried to get some feeling in my legs again.

"YES! Let's get out of here!" Ellie said with a huge smile on her face.

Shit, there went my heart. We headed back out to my truck and I tossed her bag in the back seat with her other stuff. I opened the door for her and helped her get in. I would never get tired of seeing that blush creep up her cheeks every time I did this. She deserved nothing less than to be treated with the upmost respect.

I walked around my truck and saw Ellie answer her phone. Her smiled dropped and her eyes shot up and looked right at mine. I almost stopped dead in my tracks. My guess it was that douche bag Ryan. Should I stand outside the truck and give her privacy? Fuck that….I opened my door, climbed in and started the truck.

"No, it's none of your damn business…..I don't need to explain anything to you so please do not call me again," Ellie said as she ended the call. She immediately looked at me and there it was…that smile that freaking made my whole insides melt.

Damn……this girl was beautiful.

"Ryan?" I asked as I started to pull out. I can't even believe he had the nerve to be calling her; that douche bag.

"Um, yeah, I guess he stopped by my house and my mom told him I never came home last night so he was just trying to find out where I've been."

"Sweetheart you don't owe that damn fool an explanation of anything you do. Do you understand that? He lost that privilege when he slept with some other girl. Please don't let him ruin our day okay Ells? Tomorrow you graduate and then it is a whole new beginning for you," I said as I reached over and took her left hand. I was surprised when she pulled her hand out of mine.

"I know I don't owe him anything, believe me. I guess I'm more upset he went to my house and talked to my mother. Now she will no doubt be telling me how I fucked this up like I fuck up everything I touch. But anyway…..thanks Gunner, I appreciate you being such a good friend," Ellie said as she kept her eyes towards the road.

Well….that was a loud and clear message. So she was thanking me for being a good *friend* huh? Why does this girl think everything she touches she fucks up? Her mother no doubt.

"Well I don't believe that for a minute Ellie. You're beautiful, smart…third in your class….and you have a very bright future. Whatever your mother says to you is just bullshit."

Ellie let out a laugh. "So everyone keeps telling me but….anyway….I don't want to talk about my mother or Ryan. I can't wait to go to Halcyons! I've never been there but have always wanted to go."

I looked over at her. She really was an innocent lost little girl. So many things she had never gotten to experience. I want to be the one to share all of them with her for the first time.

We drove around for a few minutes looking for curbside parking. No such luck. I ended up just valet parking. It was easiest and damn near cost the same at the parking lot a block down.

As I handed my keys over I gave my normal warning ……

"Dude, she's my girl. Anyone handles my girl wrong or treats her in a disrespectful way, I beat their ass. You got it?" Poor kid just looked me up and down.

"Umm, y-yes sir I got it. Um…. We're talking about the truck right?" He asked as he looked over towards Ellie who was now trying to hide her laughter. I looked over at Ellie then back at my truck.

"It goes for both of them,"I said as I gave him a wink and then turned towards Ellie, grabbed her hand and walked towards Halcyon. As soon as we were far enough away she let out the laughter she was trying so hard to hold in.

"Ohhh holy shit! That was funnier than hell. I mean, you had that poor boy scared to death Gunner. Do you always say that when you valet park?" She asked as she was still giggling.

"YES! She is my girl. That truck means a lot to me. She served my Gramps well on the ranch and she has been nothing but faithful to me since the day I got her. I love that damn truck," I said with a wink as I opened the door to the coffee shop.

You would've thought Ellie had never set foot in a place like this. She worked in a coffee shop for christ's sake. I saw her looking all around. We walked up to the counter to order and that's when I saw Crysti. Fuck me…why the hell did she have to be working today. SHIT! As soon as she saw me walk up she walked over and told the girl who was taking orders to switch with her…or at least that's what it looked like. I handed Ellie a menu as we stood in line to order.

"Oh my gosh, I love it here! Thank you Gunner for bringing me here." She said with such excitement. She grabbed my arm with her good hand and quickly let it go. Boy this was going to be easy winning this girl over if just something this simple made her happy.

We moved to the counter and I took a deep breath….I could see the daggers Crysti was shooting at Ellie. Good lord, I went out with this girl once as a favor for Jeff who was going on a date with her friend Jemma. She was nothing but a pain in the ass the whole time. She called me for like two months before she got the hint and moved on.

69

"Hey there Gunner baby, how are you doing? Long time no see!" Crysti said as she leaned over the counter trying to expose her chest more than it already was. Fuck me…nope she has not moved on.

"Hey Crysti, how's it going?" I asked in the most uninterested voice I could muster.

"It's going good…even better now that I see your handsome face!"

I took a peek at Ellie who was trying very hard to keep looking down at the menu. This fucking sucked. Last thing I needed was for this bleach blonde bitch to cause problems.

"Ellie do you know what you want?" I asked as I turned to look at that beautiful face and those drop dead gorgeous blue eyes.

"Um, yep…I think I'll have a Turkey Pepper Jack Panini with the chips and a Salted Carmel Mocha Frapp please," Ellie said with a smile to Crysti who was still looking at Ellie like she wanted to jump over the counter and attack her.

"Ookaaaaay. What about you handsome?" Crysti said with such seduction I wanted to hurl right there in her face.

"I'll have the same Panini as Ellie and a Chocolate Espresso Martini. Can we also get the tableside S'mores…..for two?"

Crysti just looked at me like I was some kind of a freak. "Sure….yep…I'll get that in for you. Please make sure you stay inside since you are getting the S'mores."

Ellie was looking around after I paid for a place to sit. I took it upon myself to guide her to the back corner booth. Thank goodness it was open as most of the tables were taken except a few high tables right by the bar.

We slid into the booth and Ellie looked at me and smiled. Then she looked over to where Crysti was standing behind the bar. I took a quick glance up and noticed she was staring at us. I looked at Ellie who turned to look at me. She gave me a weak smile and then looked away.

God I hope Ellie didn't think I had something going on with Crysti. That's all I would need….

What the hell? As soon as we walked into Halcyon I could not miss the dirty looks the girl behind the bar was throwing my way. I was so happy before we walked in here. Even if Gunner's reference to me being 'his girl' was just to make a joke, it still felt good. Then we walked in and this Crysti bitch is all but taking her breasts out of her shirt and flirting with Gunner. I mean come on skank. I know we are not on a date but she doesn't know that….. good grief. Wait till I tell Ari about this fucking bitch.

I wonder if Gunner went out with her. What the hell did he see in someone like her? I looked up at her and sure enough she was staring. I looked over at Gunner and he was looking at me with that melt my panties crooked smile of his. If he went out with someone so beautiful as the blonde behind the bar….he would never want someone like me.

You will never be wanted by anyone……………

"Hey….I'm sorry about Crysti being so rude like that. She's just a bitch and that's her problem. Don't let her spoil our fun day okay?" Gunner said as he took his hand and lifted my chin up to look at him.

God his eyes…..I tore my eyes away from his and moved to look at his lips. I would give anything to kiss him. Just then I saw him leaning down towards me…oh shit….

"Is she an old girlfriend?" I just blurted out in my sheer panic. SHIT! Shit shit shit! Gunner instantly stopped and sat back. He moved his hand through his hair….god why did that turn me on so much. I looked away because I thought I already knew his answer.

"No, Ellie she's not an old girlfriend. She is just some girl I took on a date once," Gunner said as he looked back over at the bar. Why did he seem mad all of a sudden? I guess I had no right to even ask. I mean…maybe I'm just imagining all of this. Was he really leaning down to kiss me? No….he wasn't you fool. He's just being nice to me because of Jefferson. Or maybe he looks at me like a little sister. I don't know. I'm getting mixed signals here. Fuck…who am I kidding. I don't even know what signals to look for!

For some reason my mouth was talking before my brain thought it through. "So how come you went out only once. She seemed to act like she knew you pretty well."

OH.MY.GOD……did I just really say that?

Gunner let out a small laugh. "I only went out with her as a favor for Jeff." OH? This has me intrigued now. "Jeff asked Crysti's roommate Jemma out, and she said the only way she would go out with him is if I went out with Crysti. So we all went out on a double date. Longest four hours of my entire life. She is a self-absorbed bitch. Same went for Jemma. Jeff was not the least bit interested after about two hours into the date. It was more like five minutes into the date when I lost interest. I remember I kept checking the Rangers game on my phone pretty much the whole time."

I let out a laugh at the way Gunner described their double date. Come to think of it…..Jefferson has never really had a long term girlfriend. I wonder if Gunner has. According to Jefferson he hasn't.

"Have you ever been in a long term relationship with anyone?" I asked just as they called out Gunner's name for our drinks. Gunner jumped up and walked over to the bar. He said something to the guy at the bar who I could tell said 'sure thing.'

Gunner set our drinks down at the table and then slid back in. This time I noticed he sat a little closer to me. I could practically feel his body heat. Hells bells….there went that ache between my legs again. I squeezed my legs together to try and relieve it. Jesus…..why did I never feel this with Ryan? What was going on with me?

Friends Ellie….only friends.

Just when I thought I was going to explode Gunner started to talk. "To get back to your question Ellie, no I've never been in a long term relationship. Longest I ever dated one girl was maybe four or five dates? I don't remember. It was when I first came to UT," Gunner said as he took a sip of his drink.

Okay, so shouldn't I feel relieved that he has never been in a crazy love fest relationship? Or did this just confirm what I was also thinking….someone like Gunner would never settle down with a girl, especially a girl like me. Totally unworthy of him, that is all I was.

Once we finished eating our lunch, the guy who Gunner talked with at the bar earlier brought out our tableside S'mores. It was the coolest thing I'd ever seen. It was a big wooden bowl and in the center was a little burner. Around the burner in the bowl there were two sticks, some marshmallows, a Hershey candy bar and four packs of graham crackers. Gunner picked up one of the sticks and stuck a marshmallow on it. He handed it to me and I roasted it over the little flame. He opened the crackers and the candy bar and had it all ready to go since my right hand was still sore. Good god could this guy just not get any better? Just then my marshmallow caught on fire and I laughed! Gunner grabbed my hand and blew it out then took the marshmallow and sandwiched it in between the crackers and the chocolate. I was still trying to recover from him grabbing my hand and sending electricity through my overly sensitive body when he took the cracker and put it up to mouth for me to eat it.

Holy fuck…he was feeding me the S'mores. Yes…..yes he could get better!

Gunner started to laugh when the marshmallow trailed from my mouth to the cracker he was trying to pull away. I reached up and tried to break it. Shit it was getting everywhere.

We both laughed as he tried to make and feed me S'mores. I totally forgot all about the bitch working behind the bar. At one point I looked up and if looks could kill, I'd be dead on the spot right now.

Gunner finally ate his last S'mores and walked up to get two glasses of water. Bitch Crysti was trying to make a conversation with him but I could tell Gunner was not the least bit interested. For one brief moment I let myself believe we were here on our first date. It could not have been any more perfect.

Gunner set the waters on the table and then slid back in. "Thank you so much for lunch Gunner; this really was fantastic. I'll never eat a S'mores again without thinking about you!" I said as I used one of the wipes to clean my hands and mouth.

"Good because that was my plan all along," he said to me with that smile.

"What was your plan?" I asked as I looked at the piece of marshmallow that was on the side of his perfect mouth. I could not pull my eyes away from his mouth.

"What're you looking at Ellie? Is there something on my face?" Gunner asked with a smile.

I don't know what came over me but I reached up with my left index finger and tried to wipe the marshmallow off his mouth. Gunner grabbed my hand, and before I knew what he was doing he put my finger into his mouth and sucked on it.

Holy hell….I'm pretty sure I let out a moan…..the ache down between my legs grew ten times stronger. I just stared at him. I could not tear my eyes away from his mouth. It was the hottest damn thing I'd ever experienced in my life. I didn't want him to stop…ever. He slowly took my finger out of his mouth.

"Now that was the best thing I've tasted all day," Gunner said with a wink and a smile. I just sat there stunned. I don't even think I was breathing. How did he do that? How could he make me want him so damn much? Did he know what he was doing? Surely he knew that was going to turn me the fuck on.

Okay….I had to clear my head and get away from him because I was so ready to just jump on him. NO!!! I could not do this. Gunner was not looking for a relationship, and I certainly was in no way looking to let someone in just to get hurt again.

"Um....I guess we should leave don't you think?" I said as I looked up at his beautiful eyes. His smile faded for one quick second and then it was back.

"Sure, you probably need to get things ready for tomorrow," Gunner said as he slid out of the booth. He took my arm and helped me up and guided me out the door with his hand on the small of my back. God please help me right now because every time he touched me, I thought I was going to explode.

As we stood and waited for Gunner's truck to be brought back up, he made small talk about graduation. What time was it, how long did I think it was going to last? Once we got the truck and got in and started towards my house he started to talk about the graduation party. Talk about trying to keep the small talk going.

"So did you invite any other friends to come tomorrow night?" Gunner asked trying desperately to make small talk.

"Um, yeah, I think Ari was going to invite our friends Amanda and Heather. They've been to a few UT frat parties with us so yeah I think they will be up for it."

"So just three friends is all you're inviting Ells? I mean this is your party so you can invite whoever you want. You know that right?" Gunner said as he watched me very closely.

Huh? What was he expecting me to say I was inviting a guy? My heart sank for just a moment. Was Gunner going to have a date there? I started to get angry just thinking about it. Really honestly Ellie....it's not like he's your boyfriend.

"I know. I really only have a few close friends and to be honest I want to start moving away from the high school crowd. I've been dying to come to one of y'alls parties for so long. I'm pretty excited about it!"

Gunner let out a laugh. "I know how that feels....wanting to get away from everything high school. Um, so tell me....what Frat parties have you and your friends gone to?"

Oh shit.....busted. "Gunner...*please* don't tell Jefferson! He would be so pissed at me if he knew. I mean he is so overprotective, and I'm so shocked he is even having this party for me and.....and....well I mean we only went a few times and it sucked each time we went. My god those college guys had their paws all over us. It was disgusting! Although, Amanda lost her virginity at one of the parties......but......"

Just then I heard Gunner start choking. OH...Oh no! Oh holy shit....I swear I have zero filters....ZERO.

"Oh my god....... are you okay? I mean oh my god, oh my god! I can't believe I said that out loud.....I mean....oh holy shit......oh no! Please

Gunner don't repeat that…ever! Oh god…first I slip about Ari to Jefferson and now Amanda! Holy hells bells Amanda is going to kill me and if Jefferson ever found out that one of my friends….oh my god I almost said it again……" There it went….my mouth talking when my brain clearly had checked out again.

"Jesus H. Christ Ellie please…just *PLEASE* stop talking! You're making it worse!" Gunner said as he had tears running down his face. Thank goodness we were stopped at a traffic light. I looked over at Gunner and busted out laughing. I laughed so hard and it felt so good. I cannot remember the last time I laughed so hard or had so much fun. I loved spending time with him. I didn't want this day to ever end.

Everything about him made me happy. His eyes, his smile, his touch….his laugh. We must have laughed for a good five minutes. God it felt so good to just be carefree and relaxed.

I was surprised Gunner knew where I lived. I don't ever remember him coming over to the house. "How did you know where I lived?" I asked as we were driving down the street that lead to our simple three bedroom house.

"I've been here plenty of times Ellie. You were just never home. I think you might have been home one time but I usually just waited out in the truck for Jeff," Gunner said with a smile. He looked up and his smile faded and was replaced by a look that scared the shit out of me. I looked over towards my house as Gunner parked his truck.

Holy hell. Ryan was sitting on the steps to my house.

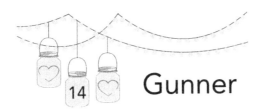

Gunner

As soon as I saw that bastard sitting on the steps I had to fight the need to pound his face into the ground.

"What the *fuck* is he doing here?"

Ellie was just as shocked as I was. "I don't know why he is here. SHIT! My mother is here also Gunner. She's going to ask questions about what happened! What am I going to tell her?" Ellie just about started to cry.

I didn't have time to worry about her damn mother. I just wanted to know what this little prick was doing here waiting for my Ellie…..I mean….waiting for Ellie.

"I'll get your stuff in the back, but let me help you out of the truck," I started to say but Ellie threw the door open and got out of the truck before I could stop her.

"Where the fuck have you been all night Ellie? I've been worried sick about you!" Ryan said as he jumped to his feet and started to walk over towards Ellie. I reached into the back seat and pulled out her two bags and her backpack. I so wanted to tell this douche bag not to talk to her that way but I needed to stay out of this or I might end up in jail for kicking his ass.

"What are you *doing here?* Why are you waiting on my porch for me?" Ellie kept looking back up at the house. What the hell was she looking at? Was she waiting for her mother to come out? I thought I saw someone standing in a window but I looked away when that little prick started yelling at Ellie.

"*Fuck* yeah; I've been waiting here for you. I was here last night waiting for you to come home but you never did. Where were you Ellie?" Ryan said as he moved closer to Ellie. I was standing behind her so I took one step closer to her and that stopped him in his tracks.

Pussy bastard.

"I don't know why you're here Ryan, and I have nothing to say to you. I'm sorry you waited for me but we are through. I thought I made that perfectly clear yesterday after I saw you with Jessica. As far as where I've been…well that's just none of your business," Ellie said with her shoulders straight and square. Good girl. Stay strong…I heard her voice crack while she was talking but I was so fucking proud of her.

Just then that little bastard laughed and looked at me. "What were you out fucking this guy because I wasn't good enough for you to fuck Ellie?" He did not just say that to her.

I immediately dropped Ellie's bags and backpack and went straight after that fucker. I had him pinned up against the house before he even knew what hit him. It took all of my strength not to beat the shit out of him for talking to her that way.

"You better apologize to her right now you fucking bastard," I said as I held him even tighter in my grip. I heard Ellie behind me let out a gasp.

"OH MY GOD Gunner, don't hurt him! Please just let him go he's not worth it." Ellie was trying with all her might to pull my arm off of Ryan's neck with her left hand.

"Ellie I need you to stand back. I'm not letting him go until he says he is sorry for what he said to you."

I could hear him trying to say something so I let up on my hold just a bit. "I want you to apologize to her, and then tell her you will never bother her again or I'm going to come after you with a few more of my friends and Ellie's brother," I said up against his ear.

"If you let go of me I'll tell her......just let go of me I can barely breathe dude." So I pushed off the fucker and stepped back a few steps. I stood next to Ellie and waited for the bastard to catch his breath.

"Um, Ellie I um, I didn't mean what I said, I'm sorry. I shouldn't have talked to you that way."

He acted like he was finished and wasn't going to go on with telling her he would leave her alone so I took a step back towards him.

"Yeah and I um, I won't ever bother you again. I understand we're over. I'm sorry I hurt you Ellie. I really am. I hope you believe me," Ryan said as he bent down to pick up his baseball cap that flew off when I pinned his ass against the house.

Ellie didn't say a word to him as she watched him walk away. As soon as he got in his car and drove away I saw her whole body just start dropping. Holy shit! I reached out and grabbed her to hold her up.

She looked up at me and smiled. "Thank you Gunner. You're starting to make it a habit of coming to my rescue," she said with a weak laugh. I pushed a piece of her hair behind her ear, bent down and kissed her forehead and smiled at her.

Just then I heard the front door to Ellie's house open. Ellie and I both looked over at the same time and Ellie pushed herself out of my arms and started to walk up the stairs. I walked over and picked up the bags and back pack I had dropped on the ground.

"Um, mom I'll be in the house in just one second." Ellie turned towards me and held out her hand. "I'll take those from you Gunner and thank you again for today. I had a wonderful time." Ellie let a small but weak smile come across her face. Just as I was handing them to Ellie I heard a raspy voice start to talk.

"I always knew you would turn out to be a whore. There's no other way you could get a man…nope, you will never be wanted by someone like that Ryan boy or by this handsome fella. You give it up for this one also you damn whore?"

Ellie's whole body started to shake and I saw the tears coming down her face as she slowly closed her eyes, almost as if she was trying to block out what this monster was saying to her. I could not believe this was her own mother who was talking to her this way. At that moment all I wanted to do was take her away from here, from this woman who was causing her all this pain.

I took a step back away from Ellie. I turned and walked over to my truck and put the bags back inside. I walked back up to her and almost threw up looking at her distraught face. Her mother was still calling her names and going on and on but I tried to block her out of my head and only look at my sweet Ellie.

I walked up to the step right below the one she was standing on. She opened her eyes and looked at me. I took my hands and wiped away her tears. She tried to smile but the tears would not stop. All the life was drained from those beautiful blue eyes.

Holy Fuck…my heart has never hurt so goddamn much in my life.

"Do you have a suitcase Sweetheart that we can pack your clothes in?" I asked as I heard her mother start to laugh. Ellie nodded her head yes.

"Let's go inside and pack up your stuff okay? Can you do that for me Sweetheart?"

My sweet innocent Ellie was just standing there broken. How could a parent say such hateful and hurtful things to their own child?

Ellie and I both turned to walk into the house. Just then her mother stepped in front of us.

"You can't take her away from here. She has to stay with me she can't leave me." Ellie's mom said in her drunken slurred voice. "She *has to* stay with me. She's not going anywhere with you so she can be your whore."

I took a deep breath and looked right at her. "You really think I'm going to let her stay here with you and take this abuse? I suggest you move out of the way Ms. Johnson. You wouldn't want me to call the police now would you?"

Ellie's mother looked at me with a stunned look on her face. She stepped out of the way and I led Ellie into the house.

"Show me where your room is Sweetheart."

Ellie walked towards her bedroom but stopped at a hall closet. She opened the door and I saw a suitcase sitting on the very top shelf. I reached up and took it down along with another bag and then walked with Ellie into her bedroom. I shut the door to her room only to hear her mother yelling.

"There will be none of that in my house you dirty whore! Pack your shit and get the fuck out of my house you no good for nothing bitch whore!"

I watched as Ellie slid down her door and hit the floor crying. My whole body started to shake. I balled my fists together trying to stop the anger that was growing inside. The emotions I was having were confusing as hell and scared the shit out of me. God I was being torn apart inside watching this beautiful girl fall apart. I just wanted to beat the shit out of somebody. I took a few deep breaths to calm down. I knew what I had to do. Now I just needed to do it.

I took out my cell phone and sent a text to Jeff. Did he know this was how his mother treated Ellie? Surely not….if he did he would've taken her away from this long ago. There's no way he would have let her stay here if he had known his mother was still verbally abusing Ellie.

"Ellie, where is your cell phone?"

Ellie reached in her back pocket and pulled it out and barely handed it to me before she just let her hand fall to the ground. Shit! It was her sprained hand too. Broken….my sweet girl was just giving up. Fuck I wish I could just take away her pain.

I slid down on the floor next to her and started to look for Ari's number. After I sent Ari a text I set the phone down on the floor and picked Ellie up and moved her onto my lap.

I'm not sure how long we sat there while she just cried in my arms. She finally stopped sobbing and looked up at me. Those beautiful blue eyes red and swollen and so sad. I made a vow to myself right then I would do whatever it took to always protect and take care of her. Always…..

"You have to stop doing this," Ellie whispered.

"Doing what Sweetheart?" I asked her as I looked into her eyes.

Ellie put her forehead up against mine and I thought I was going to die right then and there. "Stop coming to my rescue, I'm going to expect it from now on," she said with a slight laugh.

"Ellie sweetheart, I'll always come to your rescue. For the rest of our lives……I will *never* let anyone hurt you ever again," I said as I felt my heartbeat pick up even faster.

I stood up making sure I didn't let her go. I walked over and set her down on her bed. I opened the suitcase and started to take the clothes out of her closet and put them in the suitcase. I was starting to get a little freaked out because Ellie was not moving at all. She just stared at the floor. SHIT! Where the fuck was Jeff?

Then I heard him.

"What the fuck did you do to her?" Jeff was yelling at his mother.

"I don't know what you're talking about? That little whore was out all night sleeping around and then came back here to my house and caused a scene for the whole neighborhood to see. It was disgusting," Ellie's mother said as they walked down the hall towards Ellie's room.

"Shut up! Just shut the fuck up right now! What the fuck is wrong with you? That's your daughter you're talking about. She is NOTHING like you so don't you EVER call her a whore again. She is leaving, mom, and you will never see either one of us again. Do you understand me? That means no more money from me. No more help. My god......If I find out that you've been treating her like shit this whole time.....you will be out on the streets. When I paid this house off I made sure it was put in my name. You will have nothing! Do you understand me? NOTHING!"

Just then the door to Ellie's room flew open and Jeff looked at me and then down to his sister who was still sitting on her bed but, now she was crying again. I have never seen Jeff look so devastated before. I already knew he was blaming himself. Jeff would give up his own life for his sister. I could see it in his eyes.....he was hurting bad.

Jeff walked over to Ellie and fell to his knees and Ellie immediately wrapped her arms around his neck and just cried hysterically. God how I wish I could make her feel safe like that. Just then I heard Ari. I looked up and she was standing at the door. "Mother fucker......" she said as she looked at Ellie coming apart in her brother's arms.

She looked over to me and tried to give me a small smile. I just looked down at the suitcase and back up at her. She nodded her head yes to me. Next thing I knew she had taken over packing up Ellie's clothes and whatever little possessions she thought Ellie would want to take.

I just stood there. I had no idea what to do. What could I do to help her with this pain? Jeff got up and sat down next to Ellie who was still crying. He put his arm around her and just kept repeating... "Shhh it's going to be okay honey....it'll all be okay."

He looked over at me and gave me a look that clearly said thanks. I nodded back my acknowledgement to him. Once Ellie calmed down and somewhat stopped crying Jefferson started to talk to her.

"Ellie honey, you'll stay at Ari's house until we figure this all out. I need to run back and let them know I'm leaving so Ari is going to take you to her house okay? Are you okay with that Ells?" Jeff said as he looked over to Ari who was now standing there with Ellie's suitcase and another small bag. Ari gave Jeff a smile, and it looked like Jeff could not tear his eyes away from her. He seemed to be lost in Ari's smile. Something I knew a shit ton about after spending time with Ellie today.

He was fucked....just like I was.

Ellie started to talk and that snapped Jeff out of his day dream.

"Um….sure that's fine but can Gunner give me a ride to Ari's. I need to talk to him. I mean, if that's okay with you Gunner?" Ellie said as she looked up at me.

Holy fuck, the look on her face about dropped me to my knees. She wanted me…..not Ari or Jeff….she actually wanted to be with me.

"Of course it's all right sweetheart, anything for you."

I sat there on my bed devastated. How did this happen? What was Gunner going to think about me now after my mother called me a whore? Oh God I hope he didn't believe a word she said. My hands started to shake again, and I almost started to cry again. I could not lose him even though I knew we would never be more than friends but he truly did seem to care about me. I felt like I was in a box and everything was muffled. I could hear Ari and Jefferson talking. I looked over at them. What was Ari saying? Something about the cottage on her parents property. Gunner was standing next to me waiting. I was trying to find the strength to stand up.

Oh my God…we were going to have to walk by my mother again! What if she starts calling me names again?

"Ellie, come on sweetheart let's go. Jeff is going to walk out first and talk to your mom. Come on Ells, its okay. Let's go," Gunner said as he helped me to my feet. Ari came up and gave me a hug. "I'll see you back at my house okay Sweets?"

I just smiled and nodded my head yes. I just wanted to be alone with Gunner. I had to make him understand I was not the things my mother said I was.

As we walked out of my room and down the hall I saw Jefferson standing over our mother. She was passed out on the sofa. Perfect. Why couldn't her ass have been passed out 30 minutes ago? I'm not surprised……. this is just how my life goes. Another serving of shit served on a platter just for me. The Ellie special this week I guess.

Next thing I knew I was sitting in Gunner's truck. He was standing outside talking to Jefferson. They both looked so pissed off. I was the cause of all of this, or I should say my drunken mother was the cause. God I hated her more than anything right now. I never wanted to see her again. EVER!

Gunner opened the door and hopped in his truck. Once he had it started he turned on his iPod. I think he was trying to give me time to gather myself without there being an awkward silence. My god, could he be any more perfect?

I had no idea where we were going. I was finally able to open my mouth to speak. "Um, can we go somewhere quiet to talk Gunner? Somewhere we can be alone if that is okay?"

I noticed Gunner tightening his grip on the steering wheel. "Of course we can Ellie. Is there anywhere you have in mind Sweetheart? We can go anywhere."

Just then an idea popped into my head. "The canoes down at Zilker Park, I've always wanted to sit in one and just think….it seems so peaceful." I said as I stared out the passenger side window. I was so afraid he just wanted to get rid of me.

"Ellie please look at me sweetheart," Gunner asked as he used his hand to turn my face towards him.

"You've never been in a canoe?" Gunner asked with that drop dead smile of his. He made my heart hurt but for all the right reasons. Oh please take this pain away Gunner…..please…….

I let out a small laugh. "Nope….but I've always wanted to go. Pretty stupid huh?"

Gunner's smile got even bigger. God it was contagious because next thing I knew I was smiling back at him.

"What? What is it?" I asked him wanting to know why he was looking at me all goofy like that.

"It's just that I get to take you on another first today. I need to write down all the things you've never done before but want to do Ellie." Gunner said as he took my hand in his. I decided I wouldn't try to pull my hand away this time. I was going to just pretend we were together and this was a perfect first date. It was just Gunner and me…..together.

"Why do you need to know that?" I asked confused but very curious as to where he was going with this.

"Well, because I want to be the person who gives you all of your firsts. I want to experience them with you so I can see that beautiful smile of yours light up every time you do something new. I want to make all of your dreams come true."

"Oh…."

WOW….I was not expecting that at all. Maybe Gunner was different, and he might just be interested in more than what I was giving him credit for. Then again…….maybe he was just interested in a friendship like how Jefferson was with Ari. He would never want it to go past friendship.

The thought of Gunner and I never becoming closer than friends almost had me feeling sick again and ready to cry.

As Gunner pulled into the parking lot of Zilker Park my heart started to beat faster than ever. Was I more nervous about the canoe ride or about talking to him about my mother? It was clear he was not going to bring it up until I was ready to talk about it. I needed to do this. I HAD to do this.

"Gosh Gunner, I never even asked if you had plans today. I'm so sorry. I feel like shit now just assuming you would be able to spend the day with me," I said as I realized he might have actually had things to do today.

Gunner let out a laugh that moved through my body and sent chills up and down my back. "Sweetheart, I would much rather spend the day with you than run around and do errands. I just need to swing by James Avery to pick something up and that's it. I'm yours for the whole day!"

He looked at me and gave me a wink. Yep…my knees just felt weak as I tried to walk down to where they rented out the canoes. Oh shit….with how my stomach was feeling why the hell did I pick this? It just popped into my head….canoes. Jesus….watch me hurl right onto him. Good going Ellie…..picking a damn canoe ride. ARGH!

As Gunner was renting the canoe and getting our life jackets my mind kept thinking to what he said a few minutes ago. He needed to stop by James Avery? I wonder who he was buying jewelry for. He said he didn't have a girlfriend. Maybe it was his mother's birthday coming up or his grandmother's. It was driving me crazy! Why was it driving me crazy? It really was none of my business, but it was still driving me insane wondering who the hell he would be buying jewelry for.

Just then I felt his hands on my shoulder and he leaned down and whispered in my ear. "Are you ready to go on your first canoe ride Ells?"

Yep….I knew it the moment I leaned back and felt his strong chest against my back, I was so fucked. I didn't even care how this might look to him. The feel of his hot breath on my face and the touch of his hands on my body….I needed to lean against him before my knees gave out. He turned me around and lifted my face up towards his. He smiled, leaned down and kissed……….

My forehead. What the hell! SHIT! Why didn't he kiss me? I wanted him to kiss me so badly and earlier he tried to kiss me but I stopped him. What changed?

Maybe it was what my mother said. Now I really felt sick as he was walking me over and helping me climb into the canoe.

Holy fuck don't let me puke dear Lord…..just please don't let me puke.

Gunner

German Shepherds, Labs, Poodles, Rottweilers, German Short Haired Pointers........good god I was trying to name off every breed of dog I knew. The moment she leaned into me and I felt her body up against mine, my dick instantly rose to attention. I had to turn her around to face me before she felt me jabbing her in the back with my hard on.

I swear to God my dick was so hard and there was not much more room in my pants to accommodate my growing problem. As Ellie was getting settled I tried my best to adjust myself while thinking of other dogs. *Shit*, I wanted to kiss her so fucking bad. It was getting harder and harder to resist her.

After I got in and sat down the look on her face made my hard on go down in a matter of seconds.

"Ellie…what is it? Are you feeling sick? Do you not want to do this?" Her face was turning green right before my eyes. Maybe there was a reason she never went out on a canoe before.

"I'm okay…just give me a few minutes here to get used to this. Just….go slow, really really slow. AND don't rock the boat!" Ellie practically shouted at me. I had to laugh at her, she was so damn cute!

After about ten minutes of slowly rowing out we finally made it onto Town Lake. I could see Ellie start to relax as she sat back and lifted her face to the sun. Damn she looked so beautiful. I felt my phone vibrate in my pocket but decided to let it go to voicemail. I had sent Jeff a quick text to let him know where we were right before I rented the canoe.

Another few minutes passed before Ellie started to talk. She never moved her head and just continued to keep her eyes closed as she soaked in the warm June Texas sun.

"Please just let me get this all out before you try to interrupt me or anything okay?" Ellie said with a slight crack in her voice.

"Okay."

"First, I just wanted to say thank you again for everything you've done for me the last two days. I know we just met but I feel……well I feel like I can really count on you. Thank you so much for being such a good friend," Ellie said as she finally looked at me.

Ouch…there went that friends comment again. Could she really not see how much I wanted to be more than friends? Fuck…what more did I need to do?

KISS HER……..

She started to sit up straighter and I could see her starting to tense up again. She was looking everywhere but at me. I stopped rowing and just let the canoe drift in the current. I wanted to study her. I wanted to remember this moment for the rest of my life. The way her beautiful blue eyes stood out and the way her light brown hair was starting to fall down from her pony tail and blow in the wind. The way she smiled at me. Her smile…..I loved the way her smile made me feel. I wanted to wake up every fucking morning to that smile. I wanted to prove to her that her mother was wrong so damn wrong.

Ellie was nothing like her mother. She was smart, innocent, caring, and beautiful……. all the things her mother never could be. I was going to kiss her before this day was over. Yep, fuck the dogs. I was going to prove to Ellie I wanted to be more than just her goddamn friend.

"Gunner, about what my mother said. Well….um….I just wanted to let you know that everything she said was a lie. I mean….I'm not that way…I'm not a whore. I barely even ever kissed Ryan let alone slept with him. I know you probably already figured that out by the way Ryan left me and all. It was just really important for me to let you know what she was saying was not true. Honestly, I'm not a hundred percent sure why I needed you to know this….I just…..did. I just needed you to know." Ellie finished and now she was looking right at me.

How could she even think for one minute I would ever believe her mother? My heart was breaking all over again. I was so fucking confused. One minute she is calling me a good friend and the next she is telling me how important it is that I know she does not sleep around.

"Ellie sweetheart, believe me when I tell you this. I *NEVER* believed anything that came out of your mother's mouth. I'm so sorry she hurt you and that you had to endure all that verbal abuse from her over the years. Please don't ever let what she said to you ever stand in your way. You're a strong, beautiful, and very smart young woman. Don't ever forget that Ellie…..never forget that," I said as I reached over and took her left hand in mine. I lifted it up and placed her hand to my lips and pressed a soft kiss on the back of her hand. She gave me the sweetest smile in return. I let her hand go to start rowing again.

Ellie threw her head back and started soaking in the sun again. I would never get tired of watching her. I could watch her eat, sleep, laugh, smile….god you name it. I had this incredible urge to spend every spare minute with her. This was the perfect first…….day, not date, day. The perfect first day of many more to come.

As I rowed the canoe up to the shore, the guy who rented us the canoe held out his hand to help Ellie out. The way he looked at her just made my skin boil. Did he really think I couldn't see what the fuck he was doing?

Bastard!

Ellie laughed at something he said and I had to fight the urge to pound his face into the ground. I walked up and took her hand out from his hand. I thanked him and led Ellie away from this dickhead. I turned back around once to see him watching us walk away. Fuck wad douche bag go flirt with another guy's girl.

Shit....I needed to remember that Ellie was not mine....but I was going to change that and very soon.

We walked for a little bit along the trail as Ellie told me all about her plans for college. She was going to study business but was not one hundred percent sure that was going to be her major. After about fifteen minutes of talking about college, a young couple walked by with a baby and I watched Ellie smile at them as they walked by. I thought about earlier when I pictured her on the ranch with our little girl and a puppy. The idea made me smile and filled me with a warm sensation. I wanted a life with her. I wanted to wake up every day and look over at her sleeping by my side. I wanted her.

Ellie was staring out at the water, and I decided I had waited long enough. I walked around to where I was standing in front of her. She looked up at me and just gave me that beautiful smile I had come to love and need so quickly.

"Ellie sweetheart, I really need to do something I've wanted to do since I first laid eyes on you yesterday."

I took my hands and cupped her soft beautiful face. I leaned down and barely brushed my lips against her lips. Holy fuck…they were softer than I'd imagined them. I kept my lips just inches from her lips and waited just a few seconds to see if she would pull away. When she didn't, I took that as a sign it was okay to kiss her. I leaned back in and made the kiss deeper this time. I kissed her with all the passion and emotion that I had built up inside me from the moment I first saw her. She let out a small moan which vibrated through my whole body and instantly my dick started to get hard. God, what this girl could do to me was crazy insane.

I slowly slipped my tongue into her mouth and Ellie lifted further up on her toes and wrapped her arms around my neck. Holy fucking shit….I've died and gone to heaven. Pure heaven……… I slowly started to lift her off the ground as I wrapped my arms around her. I knew my erection was pressing into her body but I didn't give two shits. All I cared about was showing her how much I wanted her. She needed to know she was wanted.

If I died today I would die a happy man. I'd never in my life experienced such a kiss before. I was overwhelmed by the sensation, and my whole body was on fire from her touch.

I slowly started to slide her body back down along my body until her feet touched the ground. We both pulled away from each other only when we finally ran out of breath. I was completely breathless. Ellie's chest was moving up and down at a rapid pace. I stared into her eyes and she stared back into mine. I would remember this moment for the rest of my life.

I wasn't sure what she was going to say or do but the moment the smile spread across her face.....I wanted to jump up and down and do a few fist pumps. YES!

My sweet beautiful Ellie. I would never give up on her......ever.........

The moment Gunner's hand came up to my face I thought I was going to faint. His touch was so much better than any dream or fantasy could ever be. But his kiss......

Oh. My. God. His kiss was my undoing. I'd never felt so much emotion in just a single kiss. I wrapped my arms around his neck and prayed to God he would never let me go. When he picked me up I thought I was going to explode. I could not help the small moan that escaped from my mouth. I wanted to stay in this moment for the rest of my life.

Then I felt his erection. I could no longer doubt that this boy did indeed want me. Shit…I was going to owe Ari that purse. I had felt Ryan's erection plenty of times but it *never* had this kind of an effect on me. The throbbing ache in-between my legs was driving me crazy. I needed relief and was not sure how to get it.

Gunner slowly started to slide me down his body. Holy fuck….I just wanted to crawl inside his body and never leave. My god he was *huge* from what I could tell. I mean…I don't have much experience but from what I could feel…..he was definitely not on the small side. My stomach was doing flips. I was going to have to tell Ari about this and get her thoughts on the matter.

We pulled away from the kiss at the same time. I could hardly catch my breath. My chest must have been heaving up and down because he looked down at it and quickly looked into my eyes. We stood there and looked into each other's eyes for what seemed like forever. I never ever wanted to forget this moment. I needed to lock it away so that I could pull it out anytime I needed it.

I was scared to death to say anything. That had been one of the most amazing moments of my life. I have felt more alive with Gunner in the last 24 hours than I had my whole life. The way he made me feel with that kiss was beyond anything I'd ever felt before. He made me feel……..wanted.

The warm sensation that was still traveling through my body caused me to smile. I needed him to know how he had just made me feel. As soon as I smiled up at him, he smiled that damn crooked smile back at me. I never in my life felt the desire I was feeling right now. If we had been alone somewhere I might not have been able to stop, I would have wanted more of him. I KNOW I would not have been able to stop. I felt the blush creep up into my cheeks for the thoughts I was having. Gunner reached up and ran the back of his hand down the side of my face.

"I love to see you blush Ellie. You're the most beautiful thing I've ever laid eyes on," Gunner said with such a soft sweet voice.

Oh wow! Ohhh……I mean…..wow……….Okay…….Breathe Ellie….that was the most beautiful thing anyone has ever said to me.

I let out a small laugh and looked down. "Um, thank you Gunner. That is the nicest thing anyone has ever said to me."

He put his finger under my chin and lifted my face up towards him. "Well that is a damn shame because I've wanted to tell you that all day." He reached down and kissed me softly once more on my lips and then he said, "Shall we head over to Ari's house now? I'm sure Jeff is waiting for you."

Wait…Jefferson was at Ari's house?

"Jefferson is at Ari's house? Well that should be interesting, the two of them together….alone. They'll kill each other!" I said with a laugh as Gunner laughed along with me and grabbed my hand. We started to walk back to his truck, and I thought about what he had said earlier to the valet guy about me being his girl. My stomach was filled with butterflies and I couldn't help but smile. Could Gunner really be interested in me that way? Or was this attraction just because I was something that was always "Off limits" to him before?

Was I some kind of challenge for him?

No, I really didn't think so but….I was going to keep my guard up that was for sure. I wouldn't allow myself to be hurt again. I'd been hurt enough to last me a life time.

I literally felt like I was walking on cloud nine all the way back to the truck. I kept looking up at Gunner who was walking with the cutest damn smile on his face. I wonder if our kiss had affected him as much as it had me. Gunner held my door open and helped me up in to the truck.

He picked up my right hand. It was not nearly as swollen as it had been. He gently brought it up to his mouth and kissed it. I smiled at him and wondered what type of a family he came from. His mother sure did raise this boy right. I loved that he had kissed my body three different times in the last few minutes. I loved how his lips felt against my skin. I would forever long for his kisses now.

"How does your hand feel Sweetheart? Do you need to take a pain pill?" Gunner asked as he pushed a piece of hair behind my ear. Kisses and Gunner playing with my hair……..

Oh yes, a girl could get very used to this if she let he guard down, which I was *not* going to do.

"I'd forgotten all about it until just now!"

Gunner just smiled at me. "Good Ellie sweetheart. I want to take away all your pain. I'm sorry I reminded you about it. We'll stop at the store and pick up a few waters on our way." I smiled at him as he shut the door and walked around his truck.

God, with what just happened between Gunner and me, and Jefferson alone with Ari…..my mother was a million miles away and I was happy. I was so happy for the first time in a very long time.

Gunner started his truck and Ne-Yo's "Let Me Love You" started from his iPod. Gunner looked over at me and gave me that panty melting smile.

"What a perfect song," he said as he reached over and took my hand. Gunner gave my hand a squeeze as he pulled out of the parking lot.

Here I thought just thirty seconds ago was the happiest I'd ever been….now I was really floating on cloud nine! I couldn't tear my eyes away from him, he was singing along to the song and my heart just dropped into my stomach. This guy was too good to be true. If I was not careful I might start falling in love with him……or maybe it was too late…..

18 Gunner

I couldn't believe it when Ne-Yo's song started to play. Talk about perfect timing. This was turning out to be the best damn day of my life. I was still flying from the kiss Ellie and I shared. By the way Ellie had been smiling for the last hour; I would say what happened earlier this afternoon was far from her mind.

Jeff sent me a text letting me know he was going to meet us at Ari's once he was able to leave work but I needed to make one more stop now to pick up Ellie's graduation gift. We bought some waters at the store so she could take her pain meds. I looked over at her and she looked so tired, poor thing must be emotionally exhausted. It looked like she was fighting to keep her eyes open.

I pulled up and parked outside of James Avery. I saw Ellie tense up out of the corner of my eye. I knew what she was probably thinking. It had to be running through her head who I was buying jewelry for. Fuck I hated that she doubted herself so much.

"You want to run in with me or wait out here?" I asked hoping that by me inviting her in, it would ease her mind….or….it might make her think I was a total dick for buying another girl jewelry and asking her to come in while I bought it. Fuck me…..

"Um, no that's okay. I'm going to give Jefferson a call. I can't imagine what must be going on with him and Ari alone in her house!"

"Alright, give me two minutes then!" I said as I tried to give her a reassuring smile. She smiled back at me but the smile looked forced, not happy like it had just a little bit ago. SHIT!

"Ellie…….I'm not buying jewelry for another girl. I want you to know that okay?" I said as I placed my hand along the side of her precious face. How can one girl get into my heart this fast?

Ellie smiled a bit bigger and I saw her body relax just a little.

"Gunner, you certainly don't owe me any explanations of what you're buying. It's none of my business really."

I let out a small laugh. I wanted so badly to tell her after a kiss like that, it sure as fuck was her business. I had to remember slow…..slow and steady. Last thing I wanted to do was spook her.

I jumped out of the truck and went into the store.

"Hello, may I help you?" The short blonde working behind the counter quickly came out and was practically falling all over me. Maybe it was a good thing Ellie didn't come in.

"Hi, I um, I called in earlier this morning about a silver daisy charm that y'all were going to put on a chain for me. The last name is Mathews."

The blonde just about jumped for joy. "That was me you talked to this morning. What a wonderful choice. Daisies are my absolute favorite flower. We did indeed have the size of chain you requested and have it all ready for you. Let me show you."

I followed her over to the other counter. She went in the back and came out holding a small jewelry box. After she handed it to me, she leaned against the counter and waited for me to open it. I knew what she was doing but I was not about to look up. She already had on a low cut shirt and I'm sure she was doing her best to show her assets off.

No thanks.

"Would you like this gift wrapped? Is this for your mother or your sister?" Nice one but two can play at this game.

"Neither, it is for someone very special. She's having a big day tomorrow." I looked up to see the smile on her face fade. For about two seconds I felt kind of bad.

"Um, not to be rude but, I think I'll just take it without the gift wrap. I'm in a bit of a hurry," I said as I looked back out towards the parking lot. I could see Ellie sitting in the truck still and it looked like she was on her phone.

I paid, got the necklace and headed out. Ellie was still on the phone when I got back in the truck. I slid the box up under my seat and she didn't even notice she was so deep in conversation with Jeff.

"I'm sorry Jeff; I just didn't want to bother you with all of that. I know, I know all the things she said were just nothing but bullshit. Listen, Gunner just got back in the car and we're not far from Ari's house so I'll talk to you in a few minutes okay? Jefferson.....please be nice to Ari. Thanks."

I had to let out a laugh. "So how long has Ari liked Jeff?" I asked Ellie as she slipped her phone into her back pocket.

"*What?*" Ellie asked stunned. "What do you mean? What makes you think she likes Jefferson?"

I just looked at Ellie with a "REALLY?" look on my face.

"Well, for starters I see the way she looks at him. She can't take her eyes off of him. Then there is the fact that when she is around him she is a nervous Nelly and talks nonstop."

Ellie let out a sigh as her head fell back against the seat. "Ari has had a crush on Jefferson since I can remember. She acts like she can't stand him, but I know better. I think it's her way of dealing with how he treats her. The last few years have been hard for me. I feel like I'm in the middle. Ari keeps falling harder for Jefferson and Jefferson, well he keeps growing more and more annoyed with Ari. He literally acts like he cannot stomach to be in the same room as her. I'm not even sure why? He used to get along with her great then something happened. I thought maybe he might have had a thing for her but, when I asked him he blew me off about it," Ellie said with a shrug. "I just hope they have not killed each other by the time we get there."

"Ellie I think you are wrong about how Jeff feels. I really think he likes Ari.....*a lot*. He's just afraid to admit it to himself. I'm not sure why, but I think he feels like she is too young. The way he acts when he has been around her these last two days is just....well it's just weird to me. He also can't keep his eyes off of her."

Ellie looked deep in thought and shrugged her shoulders. I followed Siri's directions to Ari's house. She didn't live too far from Jeff and Ellie's house.

"You really think Jefferson thinks Ari is too young and that is why he is denying his feeling for her? Do you think I'm too young?" Ellie asked me. I looked over and she was batting those beautiful long eye lashes at me. I let out a laugh.

"No, I don't think you're too young. If I had I never would've kissed you!" I said as I took her hand in mine.

Ellie smiled a small smile at me. Then she said what I never ever wanted to come from her mouth.

"Gunner, I need to talk to you about that kiss."

FUCK! I knew I pushed her too soon.

"Do you regret kissing me Ellie, because I don't regret kissing you sweetheart, not one bit."

"NO! God NO! It was one of the most amazing moments of my life. I will never forget that kiss for as long as I live. Of course I don't regret it. I'm just.....you see.....well. I guess what I'm trying to say is, I'm not looking to get into a relationship right now. I mean....I really like you Gunner....a lot. But I think I need to just take it slow. I hope that you understand why I need time. With all the shit I just went through with Ryan, and now my mom. I just need some time for me to figure out who I am."

I looked over at her and she almost looked like she was going to cry. She had just gotten to where she was happy again, so I was not about to get her upset. Fuck it, if she needed time I would give her all the time she needed. I. Was. Not. Giving. Up. On. Her.

Ever.

"Ellie of course I understand. I'm sorry if I pushed you into moving too fast. I really am Sweetheart. Please know I would never want to rush you into something you weren't ready for." I gave her the best smile I could muster even though inside I was starting to die a slow painful death.

"So we can be…..friends?" Ellie asked as a blush started to creep up her face.

"Yes, Ellie we most certainly can be friends." Fuck, I really hope I don't throw up.

I hope I was not making a mistake by talking to Gunner about taking things slow. I saw the disappointment in his eyes when I said I wanted to just be friends. God that was the hardest thing I have ever had to say. I have no doubt that Gunner has feelings for me. I certainly have feelings for him. Strong feelings that were starting to scare the shit out of me.

This is for the best; I just need to keep reminding myself that I need time to think and this is moving too fast. These feelings….they're confusing me. I mean I'm going to be going to college now. I have to keep my options open right? I don't need to be jumping into another relationship the day after I just ended one.

Gunner reached down and turned up his iPod a little more. Taylor Swift's "Fearless" was playing. I had to smile. That song describes exactly how I felt today being with Gunner. I looked over at him and he seemed lost in thought.

Shit…I really hope I didn't just blow it with him. God if he only knew the way he made me feel. How all I wanted to do was jump into his arms and stay there forever.

How did he feel about me? I mean that kiss…..holy shit…..that kiss. It was amazing but, I still had this nagging feeling I was just a girl for him to conquer.

Gunner started to talk and pulled me out of my daze. I shook my head to clear my thoughts. I *was* doing the right thing.

"Holy shit…..this is where Ari lives?!" Gunner said as he pulled up to Ari's parent's 5,500 square foot house. He parked in the front of the house and jumped out of his truck.

"What the hell do her parents do?" Gunner asked as he opened my door to let me out. I quickly learned this is something he just did. If I got out first it seemed to upset him, so now I just waited for him.

"Her dad is a big time lawyer and her mom is a stay-at-home mom. You'll love them though. They are really cool. Ari's mom is a *huge* Katharine Hepburn fan. She's made us watch all of her movies. Her dad loves football and will *love* you just like he does Jefferson. Don't be surprised if he knows all your stats. He went to UT and is a big time UT football fan," I said as Gunner got the bags out of the back seat of his truck.

Gunner let out a laugh. "I already like him then! Anyone who likes football and knows his stats is an okay dude in my books!" We both laughed and turned when we heard Ari come running down the steps.

"Ells….thank God you're here! Where the hell have you two been? Jefferson has been here for forty five minutes driving me fucking crazy! Thankfully my dad came home and he's now talking to him about football." Ari stepped back and looked at me and then Gunner and then back at me again. A huge smile came across her face.

"I get the Coach purse don't I?" Ari said as she started to laugh and hooked her arm with my arm as we walked into the house. I just laughed and I turned back around to see Gunner with my favorite panty melting smile on his face. He gave me a wink like he knew what our exchange was all about. I smiled back at him as we made our way into the house.

Gunner and Jeff stayed for about an hour longer after we got there. Ari's dad Mark was in hog heaven having two starting UT football players in his house. Ari's mom Susan, begged the boys to stay for dinner but they said they needed to clean up the house for tomorrow night's graduation party for me.

Ari was acting so strange. She was much more talkative and seemed to be nervous. I couldn't tell if it was because Jefferson was in her house for so long or if it was something else. I noticed her staring at Jefferson a few times, and I actually caught him staring at her. What the hell was going on with those two? I was beginning to think Gunner was right about Jefferson liking Ari.

Ari almost seemed like she was trying to get rid of Jefferson and Gunner. God I hope she didn't want to talk. I was so happy right now I did not want to talk about my mother or what happened today with her or Ryan.

"Okay, well I think it's time for you two guys to take off. We need to unpack Ellie and get ready for graduation tomorrow so…..you can leave anytime you want," Ari said as she looked directly at Jefferson.

"Arianna Katherine Peterson! We do not treat our guests that way," Ari's mom said.

"Yes Arianna Katherine Peterson. You keep being so rude you won't be invited to Ellie's party tomorrow night," Jefferson said with a wink directed at Ari.

Ari got up and walked over to where Jefferson was sitting. She bent over and got right next to his ear.

"Fuck off, dick head!" She said loud enough for Gunner and I to hear but not her mother. Gunner and I both laughed as Ari stood up and walked back over to where she was sitting next to me. Jefferson's face was red. Was he blushing or was he just pissed?

"Come on dude...I have stuff I need to take care of anyway. We can stop and grab a beer on the way home," Gunner said has he slapped Jefferson on the back.

Jefferson got up and walked over to me. I stood up because I knew I was about to get one of my brother's bear hugs. After he gave me my hug he leaned down towards Ari.

"Watch your language Squirt; you wouldn't want to make mommy and daddy upset with you," Jefferson whispered into her ear.

"Stop calling me Squirt and while you're at it.....go to hell asshole."

Jefferson let out a laugh and walked over to Mark and Susan to say goodbye.

Ari grabbed my hand and started to lead me upstairs. I stopped to say goodnight to Gunner. I wished we were alone because all of a sudden I started to panic. What if I made a mistake by telling him I just wanted to be friends? What if he went out with someone tonight? Or brought a date tomorrow night!

"Um, thank you again for everything today Gunner. I really enjoyed myself," I said as I gave him a smile. He smiled back and for a second I wanted nothing more than for him to kiss me again.

"I really enjoyed today also Ellie. Good luck tomorrow at your graduation and you too Ari and congratulations on Valedictorian."

"Thank you Gunner, and thank you so much for taking care of Ellie today. I guess we'll see you tomorrow night," Ari said as she walked Gunner and Jefferson out.

I turned to find Mark and Susan smiling at me. They know.

"We are heading out to the club for awhile. Let Ari know we will be back later this evening Sweetheart," Susan said as she gave me a kiss on the forehead.

"Okay I'll be sure to let her know. Thank you Susan and Mark for um, everything."

"No thanks are needed my sweet girl," Mark said as he kissed my cheek.

Ari and Jefferson must have filled in her parents because they never said a word about me staying there except to tell me I was always welcome in their home. They had been like my second parents since I was ten. I use to stay over at their house for days at a time. I loved them more than I think I loved my own mother.

"Come on let me show you your room!" Ari said as she dragged me upstairs.

"My room, wait, I'm not staying in your room like always?" I asked Ari as I came to a stop at the top landing.

"Nope...I've been dying to talk to you ever since you got here with hotter than hot Gunner!" Ari said with a laugh.

"Shut the fuck up bitch!" I said as I punched her in the arm with my left hand.

"Okay so I want all the dirty deeds on what went down with you two today, and *don't* try to say nothing did. I saw the look on your face when you were walking up with him. You either lost your virginity today or that boy has magic fingers." Ari said with a wiggle of her eyebrows.

"OH. MY. GOD! You're impossible! *No*…I didn't lose my V card you bitch!" I said as I followed Ari down the hall. She stopped outside a door that was right next door to her room.

"Your room Sweets," Ari said as she opened the door to the guest bedroom. My bags were already in the room and sitting on the bedside table was a bouquet of fresh daisies. I walked over to the flowers, leaned down and gave them a good long smell.

"Oh my gosh, how sweet of your mom to put these in here!" I said as I sat down on the bed. For the first time since I'd left my mother's house today I actually felt like things were going to be okay.

"It wasn't my mom who wanted the flowers in here Ellie. It was Gunner," Ari said as she sat down on the bed next to me.

Gunner? What! How? Why?

"Wait…..It couldn't have been Gunner, he's been with me all day today Ari, how could he have bought flowers and put them in here?" I asked as my head started to spin.

Ari laughed. "Jesus, Mary and Joseph, how are you third in the class you shit head! Gunner sent me a text earlier today. He said he was taking you canoeing, something you requested I take, and he asked me to pick up some daisies to put in your room. He wanted them to be here when you got here."

"How the hell did he know daisies were my favorite flower? Did you tell him?" I asked confused as hell.

"Nope." Ari said as she made her P sound like a pop.

"Jefferson?" I asked.

"Nope." Ari said again with a shit eating grin on her face.

"I told you that boy wanted in your panties Ells!" Ari said as she fell back on the bed laughing her ass off.

"Arianna! I'm so confused. Did he just guess? Please just tell me. My god this guy has my head spinning and my heart pounding, and his kiss just about knocked me off my feet," I said as I fell back to lie next to her.

I heard a scream and saw Ari jump up.

"What the *fuck* Ellie, he kissed you? He *kissed you*? When? I mean, oh my God you bitch, you kept something this HUGE from me?! I can't believe you….. how could you?" Ari just kept going on and on.

"Holy shit Ari, if you would just shut up we've only been alone a whole five minutes I'll tell you," I said laughing at how Ari was still jumping up and down.

I told Ari all about our morning and how perfect it was. I even told her about that Crysti bitch. We talked about how sweet Gunner was after we left my mother's house, the awesome canoe ride. Then I told her every single detail about the kiss.

"Holy hells bells…..Jesus……did you orgasm from that kiss?" Ari asked while pretending to fan herself.

"OH MY GOD! Arianna! I can *not* believe you!" I said as I threw a pillow at her.

"Really Ells…..that sounds like it was fucking hotter than hell. I mean, just looking at that boy makes me have naughty thoughts. I can't even imagine kissing him!"

"Damn Ari….I can't believe how he makes me forget everything. It was the most amazing moment of my life. I've never been kissed like that before."

"Ryan didn't kiss good?"

I started to laugh. "Ryan barely ever kissed me, and when he did it seemed like he was forcing it. The first few months he tried to take it further but…..I just never felt like it was right. He never made me feel…..special." I looked up at Ari who was smiling at me with the most ridiculous smile I had ever seen.

"And, does Gunner make you feel….special?" Ari said as she bumped her shoulder into mine.

"He does but……I have to wonder. Am I just something that he wants to conquer since I'm the forbidden sister? Or does he really feel something for me? I'm just not sure. At any rate, I told him I just wanted to be friends."

"You told him *what?* Are you fucking nuts Ellie? What the hell is wrong with you?" Ari said as she turned to face me. Clearly she must have forgotten the whole Ryan just cheated on me thing?

"Ari come on, a guy like Gunner interested in me? Puh-lease! Besides, I just found out yesterday my boyfriend was cheating on me. I'm not ready to get into any kind of relationship. I need to take some time for myself. Figure out where I want to go and what I want to do."

Ari just stared at me for the longest time.

"What?"

"First off, you stupid bitch….YES…. a guy like Gunner could very well be interested in you! Second, do not ever refer to that asshole Ryan as your boyfriend again! Third, okay I get that you need time. What did Gunner say when you told him you only wanted to be friends?"

"He was very understanding. He told me he would always be my friend. He really is amazing and almost too good to be true. I mean he opens car doors for me….all the time! I actually think he gets disappointed when I open it and get out myself!"

"Well, I think you're crazy for pulling the friends card out. With the sound of that kiss can you imagine how he is in bed! I bet a girl can get at least three to four orgasms from that guy."

"OH.MY.GOD! ARI! How the hell are you still a virgin for fucks sake!"

Ari just shrugged her shoulders and winked at me.

She stood up and looked down at me. "It's getting late, and I still have to finish my speech. Are you okay Ellie? I mean with everything that happened with your mom today? You know you can talk to me anytime about anything sweets. You do know that right?"

I got up and walked towards my best friend. I would be lost without her and Jefferson. I hugged her as tight as I could. "I love you! Thank you, goodnight girl.

"Night Ells, try not to dream about your prince charming too much tonight!" Ari said as she threw her head back and laughed.

That night I slept the best I've slept in ages. My hand didn't even really hurt anymore. For the first time in a long time, I felt like things just might work out for me in a good way. Too bad I couldn't get rid of that nagging feeling in my stomach.

20 Gunner

Jeff had left for Ellie's graduation earlier this afternoon. Ari's parents where planning on taking them all out for dinner afterwards so I had plenty of time to get things ready for the party. Jack was already here setting up his equipment. He was probably one of the best DJ's in Austin. I only had to promise him two 50 yard line seats to get him to do this party.

"Alright dude…I got my shit all together and ready to go. I'm going to go and grab some food. What time do you want me back here?" Jack asked as he threw his backpack over his shoulder.

"Seven sound good?" I asked as I saw Jeff walk in the front door and slam it shut.

"Sure…see y'all then."

"Hey, how was the graduation?"

Jeff walked by me and into the kitchen. He reached in the refrigerator and pulled out a beer. He slammed the door shut. "Fucking great….just fucking great."

Well holy shit, what is going on with him? "Dude what's going on? Oh fuck, please tell me your mom didn't show up at the graduation."

"What? No…no man she didn't show up. The graduation was perfect. It was the fucking dinner afterwards that sucked. I swear to God, I want to just ring that Ari's fucking neck!" Jeff said as he slammed his empty beer bottle down and grabbed another beer. Wow…he downed that beer fast.

"Fuck Jeff, you're going to be trashed before Ellie even gets here. What the hell did Ari do?"

Jeff just started laughing. "What does that girl not do? She never fucking shuts the hell up for one thing. I mean I just wanted to reach across the goddamn table and shove a piece of bread in her damn mouth. Then that prick showed up and all he did was fucking flirt with her over dinner and she flirted right back with him. It made me sick."

Ahhh, so now we get to the big picture.

"Who was this….prick….. who showed up? Someone they graduated with?"

"I don't know who the fuck he was….some asshole she use to date in school. He was having dinner with his family at the same restaurant. Fucker sure didn't have any manners since he practically sat with us the whole time and left his family sitting there just waiting for him to come back."

"Okay, so what exactly did Ari do that has you so angry with her?" I asked Jeff as I watched him get another beer out.

Holy fuck....he had it bad for Ari. Why the hell couldn't he admit it?

Jeff laughed as he walked over and sat down on the sofa. "I pulled Ari aside and told her how inappropriate it was for her to be flirting with this guy so openly in front of her parents."

"Oh holy fuck....only knowing Ari for a few days, I'm pretty sure that probably pissed her off Jeff. What the fuck did you do that for? It's not like she's your girlfriend."

Jeff threw his head back and laughed. "Funny fucking thing.....she said the same damn thing to me as you just did. First, she just about called me every name in the book, told me to mind my own damn business and ended it with 'I'm not your goddamn girlfriend....I'm just Squirt...you little sister's best friend.' Then she smiled at me, leaned in and whispered against my ear and told me how it was such a shame I was a spineless dickless prick because she didn't go for guys like me! Bitch!"

OUCH! Talk about sexual tension.

"Jeff, why can't you admit you have feelings for Ari? It sure would make things easier on Ellie, you and Ari." I said as I sat down next to him.

Jeff just turned to look at me and then smiled. It was such a sad smile.

"I need to focus on Ellie right now; I don't have time to jack around with some baby drama queen who obviously needs way too much attention to keep her happy. Let her little high school prick friend do that. I need to go jump in the shower before Ellie and her friends get here. I told them to come any time after seven. I also called Rebecca and invited her and some of her friends. Told them it was Ellie's graduation party but most of the normal folks would be here. Do me a favor and keep your eye on Ellie and her friends tonight. I don't want any of these jack asses trying something with any of them. I already gave Ellie the lecture about taking any drinks from anyone." Jeff ran his hands through his hair and started to walk to his room.

"Hey dude, you didn't tell Rebecca to invite Crysti did you?" I asked as I reached down and picked up the two empty beer bottles Jeff had downed since he sat on the sofa.

"I told her I didn't care who she brought along. The more of them here the less likely the guys will hit on Ellie and her friends. Ellie was adamant about having college students here, something about leaving her high school years behind," Jeff said as he walked away from me.

Fucking great.....the last thing I needed was that bitch Crysti hanging around me all night with Ellie here. If Jeff thought having some UT bitches here were going to stop the guys from hitting on Ellie and her friends....he was seriously not thinking clearly.

An hour or so later people started showing up. Ellie and her friends had yet to arrive. Jeff had drank two more beers and was now arguing with Brad about which of them could bench press the most. Jack had the music spinning and there were already people dancing inside and out.

Just then I felt all the hair on my arms stand up. She was here. I could just feel it.

I looked over at Jeff who looked towards the front door and got the biggest smile on his face. I followed his eyes and saw Ellie walking up to him. *Fuck me* she looked beautiful. She was wearing a short white dress with cowboy boots on and her hair was pulled up into a pony. She had a bit more makeup on today than she did yesterday. As soon as she got to Jeff he picked her up and spun her around. She threw her head back and laughed. I looked behind Jeff and noticed Brad and Josh were standing there with their goddamn mouths hanging open.

Fuckers. I didn't like how they were looking at Ellie like she was a piece of fucking meat. As Jeff started to talk to Ellie I walked up to where about six or so of our friends were standing.

"Hey Gunner what's up dude? Check out the fresh meat! Holy fucking shit, Jeff's sister is HOT and her friends are just as fucking hot!" Josh said as he whistled.

"Listen you mother fuckers…I'm giving you this warning once. None of you get any ideas about Ellie's friends. This warning comes from me and Jeff."

Josh let out a laugh. "Alright well you didn't say anything about baby sister so if y'all will excuse me," Josh said as he started to walk towards Ellie. I stepped in front of him and put my hand on his chest to stop him.

"I don't think so. Ellie is off limits….*Period.* You so much as fucking look at her wrong, and I'll beat your ass, you got that?"

"What the fuck Gunner? You calling dibs on the baby sister?" Brad asked as they all started to laugh.

"As a matter of fact, I am asshole. I'm dead fucking serious….do not so much as talk to her wrong."

Josh and Brad exchanged looks and Brad held up his hands and took a few steps back. I could hear Josh saying something about how this was not fucking fair.

I turned to see Ellie walking up to me. I smiled at her as she walked closer. Her smile grew bigger. God how I had missed her and it had only been a day since I last saw her.

I could see Ari and two other girls start laughing and talking to each other. I wonder if Ellie told them we had kissed. I hope she told them because that meant she was thinking about it. I better make sure I gave her something tonight to keep her thinking about me.

Ellie walked up and stood on her toes and gave me a kiss on the cheek. My heart jumped up into my throat, and my dick started to get hard.

"Hey Gunner, how are you doing tonight?" Ellie asked with that beautiful smile of hers.

"I'm doing much better now that you're here. How was graduation?" I looked over Ellie's shoulder to see Ari giving me a shit-eating grin. Yep....I knew Ellie had told her about the kiss just by the way Ari was looking at me.

"Ari...... how are you? How'd your speech turn out?"

"Hey Gunner. Oh yeah...the whole speech thing. It went pretty good, I about pissed in my pants from being nervous. I looked out and saw Jeff so, I just pictured his ass naked and sucking his thumb and strangely enough...... I calmed right down." Ari said with a shrug and the most serious face I'd ever seen. I kind of believed she was telling me the truth. I shook my head and laughed. Damn I liked this girl.

"Well shit...I'm going to have to remember that one when I stand in front of a group pitching an idea for a new building." Ari just gave me a wink.

Ellie introduced me to their two other friends. "Gunner this is Amanda, Amanda this is Gunner." Ahhh, so this was Amanda who lost her virginity at a frat party. It was hard for me to keep a straight face but somehow I managed. She had short brownish-red hair right to her shoulders and she was probably dressed the most provocatively in tight jeans and a brown tank top that showed her assets really well.

"It's a pleasure to meet you Amanda," I said with a smile.

"We've heard so much about you Gunner....seems you made an impression on our Ellie here."

I laughed as I saw Ellie give Amanda a dirty look.

"Anyway, if you are done Manda, Gunner this is Heather." Heather was a little shorter than Ellie and Ari, and the only blonde in the group. She had shoulder length hair and blue eyes. She reminded me of Ellie in a way. Her innocence was pouring off of her.

"Heather it's very nice to meet you."

"The feeling is mutual, thank you for inviting us Gunner." Innocent and southern charm...these girls were in for a wakeup call tonight.

Both girls were more than pretty, and I could already see the vultures swarming. I gave all four of them my lecture about no leaving with anyone, not even a girl. No taking any drinks from anyone other than each other, Jeff or me. I also made sure Amanda and Heather had plans for a ride home. Heather had drawn the smallest straw so she was not drinking tonight.

Jeff had already told Ellie that she and Ari could stay over. Something he was regretting just thirty minutes ago when I mentioned Ari staying over all night. I thought he was going to come undone.

Once I got the girls a beer and Heather a Diet Coke, they all moved out to the back yard and were quickly dancing. I had to smile at Ari....man that girl knew how to get attention. There must have been at least four guys dancing around her. Amanda was holding her own and seemed to have Brad's full attention. Ellie and Heather were dancing with each other and both seemed oblivious to the guys who were desperately trying to get their attention. I looked over as Jeff walked out the sliding glass door with Rebecca in tow. He scanned the people dancing. He saw Ellie and smiled. Then his smile faded and was replaced by pure anger. I followed to where he was looking.

Ari.....she was dancing with another girl and two guys. Christina Aguilera's "Your Body" was playing and wow....Ari could sure dance. She saw Jeff and gave him a smile and a wink. I looked at Jeff and he had his hands balled up in fists. Shit that girl had him under her spell, whether he wanted to believe it or not.

Just then Ellie walked up to me and bumped my shoulder.

"You enjoying your first college party?" I asked as I gave her a wink. I looked into those beautiful blue eyes and my heart started to pound. The white lights we had hanging in all the trees were casting sparkles in her eyes and it took my breath away.

"YES! I think Ari is trying to make a statement though," Ellie said with a nod of her head towards Ari.

"I think you might be right. By the look on Jeff's face I would say it's working. Where the hell did she learn to dance like that?"

Ellie laughed. "She's been taking lessons since she was five years old. She loves to dance." Ellie said as she looked over to Jeff. I saw her smile fade from her face.

"Who is that with Jefferson, and is that the girl from the coffee shop behind her? What was her name, Crysti?"

Fuck.....

"The girl is Rebecca. She is the cheerleader who Jeff went out with Thursday night. Crysti is another cheerleader and is one of Rebecca's friends. Jeff invited Rebecca but I'm not sure why because he can't stand her."

"Probably to piss off Ari I'm guessing. They had some kind of fight at dinner and Ari won't tell me what they argued about."

Ellie stared at them for a good a minute before she turned back to me and smiled, but it didn't touch her eyes. I reached for her hand and brought it up to my mouth and kissed the back of her hand.

"Don't worry Ellie." I gave her a wink and slowly let her hand go.

"I'm not worried. I'm sure Jefferson knows what he's doing. I just hope he didn't invite this girl to make Ari jealous. They were both in piss poor moods when they came back in from outside. Ari just told me Jefferson was being a dickwad. That seems to be her favorite word to describe him the last few days!" Ellie said with a small laugh.

I looked back out to the dance floor to see Ari dancing pretty close to Josh. I took a peek at Jeff and he was trying to pay attention to what ever Rebecca was saying to him but he kept looking out on the dance floor at Ari. He looked worried and he should've been. Josh has probably slept with every girl at this party except for Ellie and her friends. The way he was looking at Ari though…I know what that fucker was thinking.

"Gunner, can I use the bathroom in your bedroom? Jefferson said y'all keep your rooms off limits. There was a pretty long line waiting for the bathroom when we walked in."

"Of course you can sweetheart. Just be sure to lock the bedroom door when you go inside."

"Will you wait right here until I get back?" Ellie asked as a blush crept up her cheeks.

"I'll be right here," I said as I leaned down and kissed her forehead.

Ellie stopped to talk to Jeff for a quick second. I saw Rebecca and Crysti staring her up and down.

Bitches.

Jeff walked over to me and slapped me on the back. "So you think my baby sister is having fun at her first college party?"

I looked at Jeff who was clearly getting himself drunk. "Jeff, man what's going on with you tonight….you never get wasted like this. You're leaving me totally responsible for watching your sister and her friends."

"It looks like Jeff's little sister's friends are taking pretty good care of themselves," Rebecca said with a laugh. Crysti and some other girl who I'd never seen before started to laugh as they looked out to where everyone was dancing.

Just then Ari started to walk over to where we were standing. She was out of breath from dancing. I reached into the cooler I was standing by and handed her another beer.

"Whew! I haven't danced that much in forever! Where is Ellie? She needs to get her ass out there and dance with us," Ari said as she took a sip of beer.

She looked over at Jeff and then noticed Rebecca hanging onto him. This was not going to turn out good. Ari's eyes traveled up and down Rebecca and landed at where she had her hand on Jeff's waist.

"Who is your friend dickwad?" Ari asked Jeff.

"Rebecca, this is Ellie's best friend….. Squirt. Squirt, this is Rebecca…..a *friend* of mine." Jeff stressed the word friend and I saw Ari's whole body just stiffen up. What the fuck was he doing?

"Hello Jeff's *friend* Rebecca. The name is Ari, nice to meet you," Ari said as she reached for Rebecca's hand to shake it. Rebecca, being the bitch she was, just looked at Ari's hand and laughed.

Jeff just stood there with a grin on his face. Why in the hell was he letting Rebecca be so rude to Ari, this was not like him at all.

He leaned closer in to Ari like he was going to say something only to her.

"Better be careful dancing like that out there Squirt. You're playing with the big boys now. You might just lose your V card if you keep dancing like that Honey."

HOLY FUCK! OH shit……..he did not just say that!

Jeff practically shouted it to Ari. Rebecca and Crysti started to laugh. I just stood there stunned. This was not Jeff. He would never purposely hurt anyone.

I turned and looked at Ari. She just stood there staring at Jeff, the tears were slowly starting to build in her eyes. She looked over at the two bitches who were laughing still.

"Rebecca, knock it the fuck off or you can take your friends and leave," I said as I walked in between Ari and Jeff. She looked like she was ready to knock the shit out of him. He just stood there smiling at her. After what felt like forever I saw Ari's shoulders square off and she stood up tall.

"Fuck you Jeff! It's not the first time I've played with the big boys and it certainly won't be the last." Ari turned and walked over to Jack. It looked like she was asking him to play a song.

I turned and just stared at Jeff. "Rebecca, will you and your friends give us a few minutes please?"

"Sure, I'll be inside baby." Rebecca reached up and kissed Jeff on the cheek. He briefly closed his eyes like he couldn't stand the contact.

"Jeff, what the fuck is your problem? Why the hell would you embarrass Ari like that?" I pushed my hands through my hair….what the hell was he thinking? "Holy fuck dude, that was a real douche bag move."

Jeff just took a swig of his beer and shrugged his shoulders.

Next thing I knew, "I'm a Slave for You" by Britney Spears started playing.

Oh fuck….. this can't be good. Just then Ellie walked back up and had a confused look on her face.

"What the hell?" Ellie said just as Jeff looked out to the dance floor. His jaw dropped. I didn't want to turn around but I did.

Dammit……I shouldn't have……

Ari was dancing with Josh. I mean she was *dancing* closely with Josh. There was some major grinding going on. I'd never seen a girl move like how she was moving. There must have been at least a group of ten people standing around whooping and hollering. I saw her look over towards Jeff and the look on her face was sending a clear message.

"Gunner, do you know why Ari is dancing like she's starring in the next Dirty Dancing movie?" Ellie asked over the music. Fuck....what was I supposed to say. She was going to be pissed at Jeff.

I looked at Jeff to see if he was going to say anything. Nope. He couldn't pull his eyes away from where Ari was dancing. We just stood there...watching Ari. Amanda and Heather joined in on the dancing. Josh looked like he had died and gone to heaven. Even I was getting turned on just watching Ari dance with Josh.

A slower song started to play, "Fall Into Me" by Brantly Gilbert. I shook my head at Jeff and looked down at Ellie.

"I love this song......will you dance with me Ellie?" I asked as I took my hand and ran it down the side of her face.

Ellie looked over at Jeff; clearly she knew something had happened, and then she looked over at me and smiled.

"Or course I'll dance with you."

I scanned the dance floor and saw Ari was dancing with Josh. I thought I saw her quickly wipe a tear away from her face but I wasn't sure. Shit....Jeff fucked up big time.

I took Ellie in my arms and held her close. I took a deep breath in and breathed in her smell. She would forever smell like daisies to me. She molded perfectly into my body. She was tense when we first started to dance but I could feel her relax more and more as the song went on.

I looked up to see Rebecca and Jeff dancing....and kissing. Jeff didn't even have his eyes closed. It was almost like he was on auto pilot.

Stupid drunk bastard.

I was going to fucking kill him tomorrow. I kept Ellie turned away. I didn't need her leaving me now to go bitch out her brother. I closed my eyes and pictured Ellie and I all alone just the two of us dancing.

The song ended and Ellie looked up at me with the most precious look on her face.

"Gunner.....you have a beautiful voice," she said as she stared into my eyes.

I could lose myself in those beautiful blue eyes. If I had not known any better, I would have thought my knees were about to give out from under me. Wait......what did she just say? I had a beautiful voice? Was I singing?

"I didn't realize I was singing out loud. I'm sorry!" I said with a laugh. "That must have been pure torture!"

Goddamn, there comes that smile I would die for. It slowly spread across her cheeks along with the blush that I have grown to love so damn much.

"No….it was……it was one of the most romantic things ever. It took my breath away," Ellie said as she looked down and away from me. She looked back up with a weak smile.

"You're going to make some girl very happy someday."

Fuck. I had my work cut out for me. It was pretty damn clear she was sticking to this whole friends bull shit. She was just going to keep pushing me away. Patience is all I needed. If it meant ending up with Ellie the rest of my life….then I was going to have to learn to give her the space and time she needed.

Ellie and I danced together most of the night. I was pretty sure I didn't see Ellie dance with any other guy. Not that they were not asking her to. I saw her turn down more guys tonight than I cared to count.

I stopped drinking after my fourth beer. I needed to have a clear head. Between keeping the vultures off of Ellie and her friends, watching dick head Jeff and trying to keep Crysti at bay, I needed to be as sober as I could.

The most interesting part of the night was when Ari stood right next to Jeff and Rebecca and danced to "Shut Up" by Christina Aguilera.

"Okay, what's going on with those two?" Ellie asked me while she watched Ari dance and never once did Ari look away from Jeff. He looked like he was going to blow any minute. I was just hoping that they didn't rip each other's eyes out.

I shrugged my shoulders and prayed that Jeff didn't kick Josh's ass since he was dancing pretty damn close to Ari and she had a shit eating grin on her face the whole time. Jesus those two were going to be the death of me tonight.

The party started to wind down around midnight. I was standing in the kitchen talking to Scott and Brad when I felt someone come up behind me and wrap their arms around my waist. I instantly knew it was *not* Ellie.

"Hey there handsome, what do you say to a dance with me?" I took the arms that were wrapped around me off my waist and turned around to see Crysti standing in front of me. She looked like she was wasted. Fuck, I wish her and her Barbie doll friends would just leave already. Rebecca had been clinging to Jeff damn near all night.

"Ah, no thanks Crysti…..you might want to start gathering up your friends. We're shutting things down soon," I said as I gave her a blank look. Last thing I needed to do was encourage her anymore.

"What the hell Gunner…..you have a few high school girls at your party and we all have to go to bed early tonight? I know who I want to go to bed with ……" Crysti said as she threw her arms around my neck.

Of course that would be the moment Ellie and her friends had walked into the living room. She was scanning the room. Probably looking for Jeff but he fucking disappeared about thirty minutes ago. She caught my eyes. She tried to keep her face natural but I was not stupid. Her whole body tensed.

I pulled Crysti's death grip arms off of my neck. I held her arms and pushed her back slightly.

"Crysti that's enough, I already told you no and asked for you and your friends to start heading out. Party is over. Jack is packing up his stuff so there's no more dancing."

Crysti looked like she was going to cry but then she started to laugh. What the hell?

"Oh. My. God......tell me you're not into that little girl? Come on Gunner....don't you remember how good we were together? I bet she can't make you feel the way I did."

Fuck....Ellie was now just standing there listening to the whole thing. Could this get any worse?

I should not have asked......just then I heard Rebecca with her obnoxiously loud laugh. She and Jeff were walking out of his bedroom and down the hall. Rebecca was throwing her hair in a pony and Jeff was slipping a tee shirt on over his head.

Oh, fuck no, Jeff you didn't......

Ellie and Ari both spun around and looked at them. Then Ellie turned back around and looked at me.

"It's time to go Crysti, and take your tramp friend Rebecca with you," I said as I grabbed her arm and led her into the living room.

"Hey.....take your hands off of me you dick," Crysti shouted.

"Get out now Crysti." I said as I looked around for Cooper. He was taking them all back to their sorority house.

Once I got them all out the door and gone I started to clear out the rest of the house. This party was over since Ellie was sitting on the sofa with a clearly upset Ari. Amanda and Heather were all surrounding Ari so I didn't notice Ari crying until Amanda stood up to say goodbye to Brad. Did he just hand her a piece of paper?

Amanda and Heather walked up to me. "Thank you so much Gunner. We had a really great time. We would say thanks to Jefferson but, we can't find him," Amanda said with a weak smile.

"You girls are more than welcome. I'm glad you had a good time and Heather you haven't had anything to drink right? You'll be okay driving home?" I asked as I looked over their shoulders at Ellie watching me talk to her friends. God this girl was my undoing....just a smile from across the room could bring me to my knees.

"Nope…I haven't had a drop! Thanks again Gunner. Hope to see you around soon," Heather said as they headed back over to Ellie and Ari.

"Um, yeah sure. See ya around," I said.

Ellie walked them to the front door. Everyone was now gone. I watched as Ellie walked back over to the sofa and sat down next to Ari.

I decided it was time for me to find out where the fuck Jeff went and what the hell he was thinking. I walked outside and he was sitting in a chair just staring off into space. He was the only one outside, just sitting there alone.

"You want to tell me what the fuck has gotten into you tonight dude?" I asked as I grabbed a beer out of the cooler and pulled up another chair to sit next to him.

Jeff looked up at me and I'd never seen him look so damn upset. "I don't want to talk about it."

"You've got to know what an asshole you were tonight, not only to Ari but to your sister as well. Dude, I can't believe you fucking slept with Rebecca. What a stupid-ass move man." I took a long swig of beer and looked over at Jeff. He had his face buried in his hands.

"I don't want to fuckin' talk about it Gunner. I know I fucked up okay? Just leave me the fuck alone."

"I have *never* in my life been so goddamn disappointed in you Jefferson. NEVER!" I heard Ellie shout.

I looked up to see her standing in front of Jeff with her hands on her hips. She looked so fucking cute standing there all mad.

"Ellie, why don't y'all head into my room and get some sleep okay honey?" Jeff said without looking up.

"*What?* You really think either one of us wants to go and sleep in a bed you just *fucked* a girl in! No thank you, Jefferson. I'm calling a cab and we are going back to Ari's house." Jeff flinched when Ellie shouted the word fucked.

"Ellie, no don't leave sweetheart. Ari has had way too much to drink. You both can sleep in my room tonight," I said as I stood up and walked Ellie away from Jeff.

"I can't believe he did this Gunner! I just can't believe it. Ari just told me what he said about her losing her virginity. Oh my god Gunner……this….. this *person* sitting here is not my brother." Ellie was now on the verge of tears. She looked over my shoulder at Jeff and screamed out, "You are *just* like mom! You drink and you spit out hateful hurtful things you prick!" Ellie pulled out of my arms and started to walk into the house.

I turned around to look at Jeff and saw something I never thought I'd see……..he was crying as he watched Ellie walk back into the house.

I was shaking from head to toe after I walked back in the house from yelling at Jefferson. I thought I was going to throw up the moment Ari told me what Jefferson had said to her earlier in the night. It all made sense now. I was wondering why Ari had been dancing so provocatively with a few guys. I noticed Jefferson a few times watching her but I had no idea he had said that to her.

Oh. My. God.....he was such a prick! I was mad at myself also. If I had not slipped and said Ari was still a virgin, Jefferson would've never have said anything to her.

Then......to see him walk out of his bedroom with that whore who had been hanging on him all night. I couldn't believe it. If he did this kind of shit at each party maybe it was for the best if we made this our first and our last party.

I had to stop and settle my anger. I was not only pissed at Jefferson but that fucking Crysti chick had been hanging all over Gunner when we walked into the living room. It looked as though he was trying to push her away but.....if my own brother could do it......I got a glass of water and drank it down quick. I was feeling sick to my stomach. Ari was now just sitting on the sofa lost in thought.

FUCK!

"Ari, honey let's go get changed and go lay down. I'm not feeling very well." I said as I walked in front of her.

"There is no fucking way I am sleeping in his bed Ellie.....*no*....I will walk home if I have to. No...not after what he did in there with that slut. Did you see her smile at me when she came out of his room? Did you see that? I mean....oh my god....she actually gloated right...right in my fucking face!"

Ari threw her hand up over her mouth...shit....I think she was about to get sick. Next thing I knew she was flying down the hall to Jefferson's bathroom. Right then Gunner walked in with Jefferson. They both saw her go running by and down the hall.

"What's wrong?" Gunner asked me as he walked in.

"Ari is about to throw up. Shit! Shit! Shit! Do you have a towel I can get wet to bring to her?" I asked Gunner as I turned and saw him walking into the kitchen. He was already making his way to the sink with a small towel and running it under warm water. My goodness, this guy was too much. Everything he did made my heart skip a beat. I walked over and stood next to him. I bumped his arm with my shoulder.

"You really are something else do you know that?" I said with a smile. Gunner smiled at me and handed me the towel. Just then I heard Ari yelling.

"DON'T TOUCH ME! DO. NOT. TOUCH. ME! Get the fuck away from me you fucking asshole!"

"SHIT!" Gunner and I both said it at the same time as we ran towards the bathroom. Jefferson was standing in the bathroom holding a towel out for Ari, trying to hold her hair back. He looked completely shell shocked.

Ari was throwing up bad and when she wasn't throwing up she was screaming for Jefferson to leave her alone.

I walked up and took Ari's hair out of Jefferson's hands. Jefferson just stepped back out of my way.

"Gunner....please get him out of here. He's only making it worse."

Gunner nodded his head and led Jefferson out of the bathroom and into his bedroom.

Ari just kept saying "Oh.My.God......Ohhhhh my god!!!" Over and over. I wasn't sure if it was the thought of seeing Jefferson coming out of his room with another girl, or if it was the alcohol that was making her so sick. It was probably both.

Once it seemed like she could not possibly throw up anymore she sat back and leaned against the wall. The tears were just pouring out of her eyes.

She started to laugh. "Oh my fuckin' holy shittin' son of a bicthin' hell......how could I be so fucking stupid? What would make me think he would *ever* be interested in me Ells? So fucking stupid!" Ari shouted out.

I bent down and pushed her hair back behind her ears. "Stop crying right now Ari. What would your mother say right now if she saw you? She'd be pissed and probably telling you some stupid Katharine Hepburn quote. Pull yourself together.....you're a beautiful, smart young woman. Come on.....let's get you to bed. You'll see, in the morning you will feel so much better sweets."

Ari stood up and I helped her across the hall into Gunner's room. It had been the third time I had been in his room. Well, really the second time being fully in his room. I still could not get over how neat he was!

I helped Ari get her shoes off and her shirt. She pulled her shirt up over her head and crawled under the covers. I swear as soon as her head hit the pillow she was out.

I picked up her clothes and laid them over a chair. I walked over to Gunner's dresser and looked at the few pictures he had. One picture was of an older couple. They looked so happy and so much in love. I bet these were his grandparents. Then there was a family picture. A handsome young man in a military uniform and a very beautiful girl, she must have been in her late 20's or early 30's along with a very handsome boy. This must be Gunner and his parents. I had to smile at the little crooked smile he had even then. There were a few other pictures of just the young woman. She really was beautiful. She had shoulder length brown hair and beautiful green eyes. Gunner had her smile.

I looked back at Ari who was sound asleep. I guess I should go clean up the bathroom. I walked into the hall and stopped when I heard Jefferson and Gunner talking. I shouldn't have, but I put my head up to the door so I could hear them.

"Jeff, you got to explain how the fuck you ended up sleeping with Rebecca. You can't even stand her." I heard Gunner trying to whisper.

"I don't know, okay?! I had too much to drink and she was fucking coming on to me all fucking night. Then watching Arianna out there practically dry humping every fucking guy she was dancing with….I. Don't. Know. I just snapped. I sure as shit couldn't have Ari. Rebecca kept hinting around about having sex and I guess I just gave in."

I could not believe my ears. My own brother….all I could think of was Ryan and how he said almost the same exact thing. Maybe my mother was right….all men are just out for one thing.

No…not Jefferson….I won't believe he did this on purpose. He needs to explain to me why he just broke my best friend's heart.

"You just gave in? That's fucking bullshit and you know it. You were pissed at Ari before she even got here Jeff. You did this on purpose dude. You might not realize you did it on purpose, but you did. You invited Rebecca here knowing that she was going to be hanging on you all night. You might not have planned to sleep with her but you did. You were trying to push Ari away, Jeff, and I think you were successful by what I just heard her yell out in the bathroom."

"You don't think I can see that? It fucking killed me when she was screaming at me not to touch her. Knowing I'm the one who caused this…..oh god…….it's tearing me up inside Gunner. I'm no better than that fucker who hurt Ellie…..and worse of all…..I not only hurt Ari, I hurt Ellie. Oh god….did you see how she was looking at me Gun? I fucked up with Ellie big time."

"Dude you fucked up with Ari big time also. You know the girl likes you….what's with this you don't like her bullshit," Gunner asked Jefferson.

"I don't understand my feelings for Ari. She has me so fucking messed up all the goddamn time. She has for at least the last 5 years. FUCK!" Jefferson shouted so loud it caused me to jump and my elbow hit the door.

"Come in," I heard Jefferson say.

Fuck a duck! Shit.....I slowly opened the door and saw Jefferson and Gunner both sitting on the end of Jefferson's bed. I looked at the bed and it was a mess. I instantly felt sick to my stomach knowing what had happened in here not too long ago. I put my hands up to my mouth in a reflex. Gunner jumped up and ran over to me.

"Ellie what's wrong sweetheart? Are you sick? Do you need to throw up?" Gunner asked as he bent down to look into my face. I shook my head no and slowly dropped my hand away from my mouth. Just the feel of Gunner's hands on my shoulders instantly calmed my nerves. I looked around Gunner and saw Jefferson sitting there staring at me.

OH. MY. GOD.....he had tears running down his face.

My first instinct was to run to him. I'd never in my life seen him cry. I looked up at Gunner who was still looking down at me with worry in his eyes. I took a step back to get out of Gunner's grip. Jefferson started to stand up and walk towards me.

"Don't! Just.... don't Jefferson. What you did tonight, it was...it was just....I don't even want to think about it anymore. I only wanted to let Gunner know that Ari is asleep in his room. Did you need anything out of your room? I could get it for you," I said as I looked away from Jefferson and back to Gunner.

"Um, no it's okay I'll just wear a pair of Jeff's shorts." Gunner turned to look at Jefferson and then back at me. He walked me out of the bedroom and leaned in close to me. "Is Ari doing okay Ells? What made her sick? Did she drink too much beer 'cause I will feel like shit if that's what made her sick?" Gunner said with the most concerned look on his face.

Gesh, every time I think he cannot be any better....he goes off and does or says something that just makes him that much better. The heat from his body and his breath on my face instantly caused an ache between my legs. I shook my head to clear my wayward thoughts.

"No Gunner, I don't think it was the beer at all. I think it was seeing Jefferson walk out of his bedroom putting his shirt back on while some whore was smiling at her with a triumphant *fucking* smile on her face. *That's* what made her sick to her stomach," I said loud enough for Jefferson to hear me. Gunner just closed his eyes.

"I'm going to go clean the bathroom and then go to sleep. Thank you, so much Gunner, for the party....I enjoyed myself, most of the time anyway."

"Ellie just leave the bathroom Sweetheart it's fine. Jeff and I always have a cleaning company come in and clean up the house the day after a party....it's fine just go to sleep. Please," Gunner said as he followed me into the bathroom.

"Whatever….fine……I'm exhausted anyway. Goodnight and thank you again for letting us use your room. I really do appreciate it." I leaned up and gave Gunner a kiss on the cheek. He smiled from ear to ear which made my heart skip a beat.

I didn't even bother saying goodnight to Jefferson. I walked back into Gunner's room. I just wanted to get out of these clothes and go to sleep. My head was killing me from all of the beer I drank. God I just wanted to get this night over with. I remembered seeing a tee shirt in the bathroom when I was in there earlier. I walked in and saw it lying over the tub. I took my skirt and shirt off and pulled the t-shirt over my head.

Oh holy hells bells….it smelled like Gunner. Hmmmm…..I took a big sniff and buried my face in the shirt. Yep…I should sleep well tonight!

I crawled into bed next to Ari. She was snoring away. Man oh man…she was going to feel it tomorrow when she woke up. Maybe she won't even remember Jefferson sleeping with that bitch Rebecca! Oh, I could only hope.

Good lord….everything around me smelled like Gunner…..his pillow, the blankets…..hmmmm…..I could sleep like this every damn day. Wrapped up in his smell……the last thing I remembered before I fell asleep was dancing with Gunner as he sang in my ear. He really had such a beautiful voice.

It seemed like I had just closed my eyes when I heard Ari talking on the phone. I opened my eyes and sat up yawning. From what I could tell, Ari was talking to her parents. She was fine, yes the party was super fun, yes it was just us two and Jefferson and Gunner……we slept in Gunner's room. After a few more seconds she finally said goodbye and hung up.

"Hey there and good morning sunshine. Did you sleep well?" Ari said as she jumped up out of bed. Oh *hell* no….she has to be feeling something for fucks sake. I was and I didn't even drink as much as she did!

Just then all the memories of last night came flooding back to me. Jefferson and what he said about her virginity, and him sleeping with that Rebecca chick.

"Good morning Ari….you sure are just a little too chipper this morning. How do you feel?" I asked as I watched her go into Gunner's bathroom. I heard the faucet start and heard her laugh. I got up to walk in and see what she found so funny.

"What's so funny?" I asked her as I looked around on the counter.

"This…this shit is funny," Ari pointed down to my skirt and shirt that was lying on the bathroom floor. "I never thought I'd see your clothes laying on the floor of a fucking hot guy's bathroom….OR you dressed in said hot guy's t-shirt. Hot Ells….very hot!" Ari said as she pushed my shoulder with her hand.

I let out a small laugh and reached down to pick up my clothes. "I thought I picked them up last night. Gosh, I was exhausted. Um, Ari honey, are you okay? I mean do you want to talk about anything?" I asked as I watched her put her hair up in a pony.

She stopped putting her hair up and looked at me. For one brief second I saw the hurt in her eyes, but it was gone so fast I wondered if it was even there in the first place. She flashed that signature smile at me and shrugged her shoulders.

"There's nothing to talk about Ells. What's done is done. I had a silly crush on a guy who happened to turn out to be a real dickhead; sorry I know he is your brother. If he wants to go around and fuck every girl on the UT campus....I could care less," Ari said as she turned and walked out of the bathroom.

Ooookay.....that was not what I was expecting from her but I'll go with it.

"So, you mean to tell me Arianna that you are totally fine with everything that happened last night. You're not the least bit bothered that Jefferson slept with another girl," I said as I started to take Gunner's tee shirt off and put my own clothes back on.

"Nope....I'm not the least bit bothered by it Ellie. Matter of fact, Josh gave me his number and asked me out last night. I turned him down but....... now that I think about it, I'm going to give him a call today."

She turned and gave me a wink and headed towards the bedroom door. I saw her square up her shoulders and take a deep breath as she opened the door and headed out towards the living room. I could hear Gunner and Jefferson talking as soon as she opened the door.

Bullshit....she was totally putting up a front.

22

Gunner

I ended up sleeping on the sofa last night after Jeff finally passed out around 2:30 am. Once I sat on the sofa I could smell Ellie on the pillows. I probably looked like a stupid fuck with the way I was cuddling a goddamn throw pillow last night.

Jeff was up at six am dressed and ready for a run. Not sure how the fuck he managed that but he did. I got up and went for a quick run before I came back to make up some of my Grams' blueberry muffins.

I never got a chance to give Ellie her graduation gift last night, so I was hoping to do it this morning. I was pretty sure I heard Ari on the phone and then heard Ellie and Ari talking. Jeff had been gone for almost two hours. I started to wonder if he was staying away to avoid the girls.

Stupid bastard.

Just then the front door opened and Jeff walked in. Looking like he just had the shit beat out of him.

"What the fuck happened to you dude?"

"I went a few rounds with Bubba up at the gym. I needed to work all the fucking alcohol out of my system." Jeff said as he grabbed a water out of the fridge.

"Are the girls up yet?"

Jeff sat down at one of the bar stools and started to down his water. Man he looked like shit.

"Dude, I think you worked out too hard, you look like shit." I said as I took the muffins out of the oven.

"Fuck you dude…..I'm not the one acting like Betty Fucking Crocker!"

"Seriously Jeff, you feeling okay today, you get enough sleep?" I asked as I took a good look at him. He looked tired and his eyes were like a dead green sea.

"Yeah, I feel alright. I can't believe I drank that much last night. I fuckin' never drink like that," Jeff said as he reached over and grabbed the bottle of Advil that was sitting on the kitchen counter.

"Do you um, you remember everything that happened last night?" Shit…I hated to do it but I had to ask.

Jeff looked up at me and I swear his eyes glossed over with tears. "Yeah dude, I remember everything that happened last night. Believe me…I woke up wishing I had been drunk enough not to have remembered it."

Just then the door to my bedroom opened up and Ari came walking out. Damn….she looked just as good this morning as she did when she walked in yesterday evening. I could see Jeff sit up straighter.

"Good morning!" Ari announced as she came buzzing into the kitchen. What the hell? I looked over at Jeff who was just watching her every move.

"Did you make blueberry muffins Gunner? My god! No wonder Ellie has the hots for you," Ari said with a laugh.

"ARIANNA!" The sound of Ellie's sweet voice caused my stomach to do a few flips. I looked up and my breath caught in my throat. She looked beautiful. I wonder if she woke up every morning looking this fucking good. She gave me a shy smile….there was that blush…..I just wanted to take her in my arms and kiss the shit out of her.

"Good morning Sweetheart. Did you sleep okay?" I asked as I poured her a glass of orange juice. She sat down in the bar stool next to Jefferson, who was still watching Ari's every move.

Ellie looked over at Jeff and her smile faded just a little. When she looked back over at me she gave me that smile that would make me promise her anything in the world.

"I slept okay, thank you so much for giving up your room last night for us."

Jefferson shut his eyes for a second. Was he even planning on saying he was sorry to Ari and Ellie?

"Look Ellie….Gunner made blueberry muffins. Isn't that so sweet? Some guys are just like that…..caring….they know how the little things just make a woman so happy," Ari said as she leaned against the counter and stared Jeff down. She had been sending someone a text message right before.

I did not like where this was going.

"Ari, can I speak with you in private please?" Jeff asked as he stood up.

"Um, no…." Ari said as she picked up a muffin and started to put butter on it.

Jeff was running his hands down his face clearly getting frustrated. He let out a loud sigh. "Please….I *really need* to talk to you………please."

Ari looked up at Jeff and I swear if looks could kill, Jeff would have been on the floor. "Whatever you have to say to me you can say it in front of my friends. You know what those are, don't you Jeff? Oh…wait…the type of *friends* that you have……you fuck them in your room during your sister's graduation party."

"Ari that's enough, he just wants to talk to you," Ellie said as she looked back and forth between Ari and Jeff.

Fuck me….this was not going to go well at all.

124

"No this is fine Ellie. If this is how Ari wants to have this go down, then that is fine by me. I was going to apologize for my comment last night that embarrassed you. It was very insensitive of me to bring up the fact that you're still a virgin, and that your fucking dry humping every guy at the party might give them the wrong impression you were ready to give it up," Jeff said as he slammed his water bottle down.

This was like a fucking train wreck that I couldn't stop watching.

"*Jefferson*! Oh my god! How could you say that to her right now, after what you did to her last night?" Ellie said as she stood up and walked up to Jeff.

"What…what did I do to her Ellie? I was trying to apologize and she is being a bitch about it," Jeff said as he turned to look at Ari.

She was just standing there with a blank expression on her face. "You *slept* with that girl Jefferson. You knew that was going to hurt Ari…you knew it would," Ellie said with a crack in her voice.

"Is that what it is Ari? Are you upset because I slept with another girl, because the last time I checked Sweetheart….I didn't have a fucking girlfriend," Jeff shouted at Ari.

"Do not call me sweetheart you son of a bitch," Ari said as a tear started to roll down her face.

"Jeff, let's just back off here for a minute. Dude I see where you're going with this and I get it but….."

"What?" Ellie said as she turned and gave me a shitty look.

Oh fuck…..

"So Gunner…..you think what Jefferson did to Ari was okay, because they're not dating? You and I both know they have feelings for each other," Ellie said as she put her hands on her hips.

Shit she was cute when she was mad.

"Now wait a minute Ellie; don't turn this around on me now. That's not what I was going to say. I was just saying that it is true….Ari and Jeff are not dating and really he could see or date anyone he wants. I'm not excusing what he did it's just….it's just…." Oh why the fuck did I think I just stuck my foot in my damn mouth. Stop talking Gunner….

"Can I just please say that I could care less what this dickwad does okay? So Jeff…have at it ….fuck whoever you damn well please 'cause you're right, we have nothing together. Never have and you made it very clear last night, we never will. I got your message loud and clear," Ari said as she wiped a tear from her face.

"Fuck, Ari please just let me explain….I wasn't trying to hurt you last night. I just got angry and you were flirting and….."

Ellie wasn't done with me though and she cut Jeff off….."

"So wait…Gunner. Does this mean if I had been dancing with one of the other guys all night, and made you all hot and bothered, you would have gone off and fucked Crysti to help satisfy your hard on? Because that's pretty much what you did right Jefferson?" Ellie said as she walked over to Ari who was now just as confused as I was. How the hell did this turn around onto me?

"No! Ellie, I wouldn't do that to you, but they're not dating."

"Neither are we Gunner……thank god for that!" Ellie turned and walked to my bedroom.

Oh holy fuck……..I started to follow her. How the hell did this just happen?

"Ellie wait a minute. How did this turn to me doing something wrong to you?" I asked her as I walked into the bedroom. Ellie turned and looked at me. She threw one of my tee shirts at me and shouted, "Because you're all fucking alike! Every goddamn one of you…..even my own brother. All you do is use your dicks to think with."

Ellie grabbed her bag and pushed past me and walked back out into the living room. Ari was standing there waiting at the front door. What? Where were they going?

"Ellie let me drive you both home Sweetheart," I said as Jeff walked up to try and ask Ari if he could take her home.

"We don't need a ride thank you Gunner and no Jeff, you cannot take me home so we can talk. We have nothing to talk about.

"How are you getting home Ari?" I asked while I was looking at Ellie who would not even look at me now.

"I sent a *friend* a text message asking him if he could take Ellie and me back to my house.

"What friend?" Jeff asked clearly annoyed.

"Josh, he gave me his number last night, and asked me out on a date. I told him no last night but I seemed to have woken up with a much clearer head this morning," Ari said as she smiled at Jeff.

"The *fuck* you will. There is no fucking way my sister, or you, are getting in a car with that asshole!" Jeff said as he took out his cell phone. I already knew what he was doing.

"Josh, this is Jeff……..yeah I know and I want you to listen to me, you come anywhere near my sister or Ari and I promise you I'll break you in fucking two pieces you got it? Good…….lose her number…." Jeff threw his cell phone onto the sofa and walked down the hall into his bedroom and slammed the door shut.

"Great….just great….I guess I'll call a cab Ells," Ari said as she took out her cell phone again.

"Wait……Ari please just give me five minutes." I turned to look back at Ellie. I practically begged her to let me have five minutes with her in private.

I took Ellie back into my bedroom and sat down on the bed while she stood up near the door.

"Ellie sweeeee......um, look I don't know what the fuck just happened out there, or what I said or did that pissed you off, but you have to believe me. I have no.....absolutely no interest in any other girl but you. I already told you....I won't give up on us Ellie. I'll wait forever if that's what it takes to prove to you how I feel about you. I know we just met and you think I'm moving too fast and I promise you I won't push you but please Sweetheart.....please just don't push me away," I said as I watched her whole body relax.

I looked over and saw the James Avery box. I got up and walked over to it. I picked it up and walked over to her.

"I wanted to give this to you last night but, I never could find the right time to do it," I said as I handed her the box. Her eyes lit up when she saw that it was the James Avery gift I picked up yesterday. I guess she was putting two and two together now.

"Wha.....what is this for?"

"It's your graduation present Sweetheart. I wanted to make sure you got it this morning before you left," I said as I pushed a piece of her hair behind her ear.

"Gunner.....you really didn't have to get me anything!" Ellie said as her blue eyes captured mine.

"Open it...please before you get mad at me again," I said with a laugh.

Ellie let out a giggle that just traveled through my whole body. I could listen to her laugh all day.

She started to open the box and when she saw the daisy necklace her head snapped up and looked at me. She looked so confused. Why?

"How.....I mean......how did you know....the flowers at Ari's house and now this?" She took the necklace out and handed it to me to put on her.

"How did I know what Sweetheart?" I clasped the necklace and turned her around to face me.

"Did Jefferson tell you daisies where my favorite flowers?" Ellie asked me with such a confused look in her eyes.

Well I'll be damned. I can't believe it, they're her favorite flower! If only I could pump my fist in the air right now.

I smiled down at her causing her to smile at me.

"Ellie, when you were in Jeff's truck right after the whole Ryan thing...I leaned in to whisper in your ear and I thought you smelled like daisies. Every time I see a daisy I think of my Grams who has a whole garden of them, and now I will also think of you sweetheart." I said as I traced the side of her jaw line with the back of my hand.

Ellie looked down at the necklace and then back up at me. She threw herself into my arms.....fuck I have died and gone to heaven again!

"Oh. My. God! Thank you so much Gunner! Thank you for being so sweet to me and just knowing how to make me feel so much better. I love this! I will *never* take it off....ever." Ellie said as she held onto me so tight. I didn't want to let her go. I wanted to take a few steps back and lay her down on my bed, and just make love to her slowly and sweetly. I felt my dick jumping......... DOGS! I needed to think of dogs!

Ellie started to let go of my neck. She stepped back and smiled up at me. I leaned down and kissed her softly on the side of her lips. "You are most welcome my Ellie. Now, can I please give you and Ari a ride home? Please?"

Ellie started to laugh. She nodded her head and we headed back out into the living room. Ari was now sitting on the sofa holding Jeff's cell phone. She had a huge ass grin on her face.

"What are you doing Ari?" Ellie asked as she walked up to Ari.

"Oh nothin', just deleting Rebecca's number from Jeff's phone." She set the phone down on the table as Ellie and I busted out laughing.

Yep....Jeff was in for a wild ride whether he wanted it or not!

23

Ellie

It had been four days since the party and I had not seen Gunner yet. I talked to him on the phone everyday at least twice a day. He called me first thing every morning because he wanted to be the first person I heard each day. Then every night he would call to tell me goodnight. By the third day I was so excited just waiting for his calls.

It was Wednesday and Ari and I were going to go looking at apartments. I was stressing out about it as I was going to have to work to help pay my share, and I was taking a pretty heavy load the first semester. Just then I heard my phone on the side of the table and I reached over to answer it.

"Good morning Gunner," I said with as much of a purr to my voice as I could.

"Good morning to you Sweetheart, how did you sleep?" Gunner asked with a laugh.

"I slept okay. I have a lot on my mind so I tossed and turned a lot. How about you? How did you sleep?"

"Like shit….your smell is gone from my bed so I can't sleep in it anymore. I'm going to need you to come to my house right away, get naked and roll around in my bed…..while I watch of course!"

I let out a laugh. He always knew how to make me laugh. I loved to hear his voice over the phone. It made my whole body just tingle. Shit if he only knew how much I would love to do just that but…….I can't go there. We have to stay friends.

"The only way I would do that is if you had those blueberry muffins ready and waiting for me," I said with a giggle. I shouldn't be flirting with him like this but damn….it was so much fun! Ryan never flirted with me like this.

"Fuck Ellie….don't tempt me or I'll be baking all damn day! What're you doing today? I want to see you," Gunner said so soft and sweet.

"Argh….Ari and I are going to look at apartments so she made me block out my whole day for that. I'm not sure how this is going to work out though. I'm a bit nervous about it."

"Don't worry Sweetheart, it'll all work out. Do you think we could go out for dinner tonight? Not on a date….just as friends?" Gunner asked as I heard a bunch of people yelling in the background.

"Um, yes I would love that! Where are you? It sounds like there is a party going on there." I asked as I heard a knock on my door. Ari opened it and I waved for her to come in and sit down on the bed.

"Yeah....I'm at the gym," Gunner said as he sounded a bit distracted.

"My goodness, what time do you get up to go to the gym Gunner? It is only 7:30 in the morning!" I said as Ari started to giggle next to me.

"Jeff and I try to get in a run and a workout first thing each day. That way if I have the time I can sneak in another one later on. Makes it easier for me to just get it done with in the morning and......."

Gunner's voice trailed off. Then I heard Gunner start cursing.

"Oh shit....I knew this was going to fucking happen," Gunner shouted.

"Gunner? Gunner! What's wrong?" I shouted back into the phone.

"Um, Ellie sweetheart.....I need to let you go for a second. Jeff has been sparring all week since the party and he just got knocked out. Let me call you right back okay Sweetheart?" Gunner said in what sounded like a bad attempt to keep me calm.

"*What!* Oh my god...is he okay? Gunner, please call me right back as soon as you can. I'm getting dressed now!" I shouted into the phone.

"Ellie...listen to me....calm down okay. Give me five minutes and I'll call you back."

I started to cry, oh my god what the hell was Jefferson doing fighting? I managed to let out an okay before Gunner hung up.

"Jesus, Ellie what the hell is wrong?" Ari asked as I flew up out of bed and started to throw on a pair of jean shorts and a UT t-shirt.

"It's Jefferson! He's hurt or knocked out or something! I don't know!" I started to say in between my sobs.

"Jeff is hurt? Oh my god how? Wait....let me go get dressed!" Ari flew out of my room while I went and brushed my teeth and threw my hair up in a pony. Please Gunner call me back.....*please*.........my heart was beating so fast I could hardly stand it.

I was putting my sneakers on when Ari busted through the door again. She was already dressed.

"What's going on Ells?" Ari said with tears in her eyes.

"I'm not sure.....I mean, I was talking to Gunner and he mentioned that he was at the gym. Jefferson must have been there with him....I heard all this yelling in the background, Gunner seemed to be distracted when he was talking to me, and then Gunner just started swearing and said something like he knew this was going to happen. Um...something about Jefferson had been sparring ever since the morning after the party and he just got knocked out! Oh my god Ari...if anything happens to him....." I broke down and cried hysterically.

Ari took me in her arms. I saw her wiping away tears from her face as she rocked me back and forth.

"It's okay sweets…..don't worry. Gunner would never let anything bad happen to Jeff, and besides Jeff is huge! Even if he was boxing with someone, he would for sure kick their ass! I'm sure it is going to be fine…..shhh…don't worry Ells….." I think Ari was trying to calm herself down more than she was me. I could tell she was just as worried as I was.

My cell phone rang.

"Gunner, please tell me he's okay!" I practically screamed into the phone.

"Ellie, he is awake now but he's really confused. He has a big gash in his forehead and he is going to need stitches. I'm taking him to the ER right now," Gunner said in such a calm voice.

"What do you mean he's confused? Which hospital are you taking him to?" I saw Ari's face drop when I mentioned hospital.

"Seton main, but please be careful driving here okay Sweetheart. Why don't you make sure Ari drives okay? I have to go so I can drive."

"Okay! Please get him there fast Gunner, and please be careful driving. I'll get there as soon as I can." I jumped up and grabbed my purse. Ari was still sitting on the bed.

"Ari! We need to get to the hospital now!" I shouted at her.

She jumped up and ran down the stairs. We both ran right into Ari's dad.

"Hey….whoa what is going on girls? Why are you in such a rush and why the hell are both of you crying?" Mark asked.

"Jefferson, he's been hurt and Gunner is taking him to Seton we need to get there!" I couldn't believe I managed to get it out my voice was shaking so bad. Ari just stood there…not saying a word.

Mark pulled out his cell phone. "Okay….well there is no way either one of you is going to drive this upset. Let me get Brian to pull the car up and he'll take you both."

Next thing I knew, we were heading to the hospital and Ari was just sitting in the back seat with me staring out the window. I managed to stop crying when I got a text message from Gunner saying that they were at the hospital and they had taken Jefferson back.

My heart was beating so fast. I had not talked to Jefferson since Sunday morning and I never even said goodbye to him when I left. The last thing we did was yell at each other. Oh my god…please….please dear God I'll do *anything*……Please just let him be okay.

We pulled up at the ER and I jumped out of the car. I turned around and Ari was just sitting in the back seat still. "Ari? Are you coming Honey? Did you change your mind about coming with me?" I asked as she turned to look at me. The tears were just pouring down her face…..she shook her head no and started to slide out of the car. I thanked Brian and told him we had a ride home.

I rushed into the ER and the first thing I saw was Gunner sitting in a chair. He stood up as soon as he saw us walk in. I flew into his arms so hard he lost his balance for a second. I lost it and started to cry again.

"Shhh…Sweetheart it's going to be okay. Don't cry Baby……please don't cry," Gunner said as he stroked my hair with his hand. I grabbed onto his shirt and almost let out a yell, my hand was still hurting.

"What's going on? How is he?" I said between sobs.

"Honey they won't tell me anything because I'm not family, so I don't know what's going on. Let's head over to the nurse and let her know you're here okay?" Gunner said has he wiped the tears off my face.

I looked at Ari and she was sitting down. She had stopped crying and had wiped her face clear of any evidence that she'd been crying. You could tell she'd been crying though because her eyes were red. I smiled at her and she smiled a weak smile back at me.

"I'll just sit here and wait if that's okay?" Ari said so quietly I almost had to strain to hear her.

I saw her take her iPod out of her purse and put her head phones in. I heard Colbie Caillat's "Realize" start up and my heart broke. Shit……Ari must be feeling even worse than me. I didn't even think about how this was affecting her?

Gunner took my left hand into his hand and guided me over to the nurses' station. I looked back at Ari one more time and she just looked so scared and lost.

The nurse told us that Jefferson had a mild concussion and that he was confused about what had happened. He didn't seem to have any memory loss that they could tell but, because he was a football player the doctor wanted to do a CT scan. He also had a pretty big cut above his eye that they were putting stitches in.

I asked if they needed me to fill out any paper work, but she told me Gunner had filled out most of the paper work and I just needed to sign a few papers. I looked up at Gunner who just gave me that crooked smile and my heart melted again….how will I ever survive without him in my life now?

"When can we go back and see him?" I asked the nurse.

"Once he comes back from getting the CT scan I'll take you back there. If the scan comes back normal we will start the process of discharging him," the nurse said with such a sweet smile. Of course I noticed how she kept eyeing-up Gunner. I guess that's to be expected with how damn good looking he is.

I thanked the nurse and walked over to where Ari was still sitting. She had her eyes closed and her music was blaring out from her iPod. She was going to end up with a massive headache if she kept listening to the music that loud. I sat down next to her and touched her arm. She jumped and opened her eyes. As soon as she saw me she pulled the ear buds out.

"Well? Is he okay…..will he be alright? Do we know what even happened to him? What did they say?" Ari and her nervous jabber.

"Um….well….he's okay. He has a mild concussion and he is a little confused but they don't think he suffered any memory loss. He has a really bad cut that they are putting stitches in. They did take him to do a CT scan just because he's a football player and the doctor just wants to make sure everything is okay before they discharge him." I saw Ari's whole body relax just a little and she let out a small sigh.

"So he can go home today?" she asked as she looked up at Gunner and then back down to me.

"Yes, if the scan comes back normal but I'm sure it will. I've seen him take a lot harder shots in the head then what he took today," Gunner said with a small smile.

"What happened? What is he doing fighting?" Ari asked Gunner as he took a seat on the other side of us.

"Yeah, what is this all about…has he been sparring every day? I didn't think Jefferson had boxing as part of his workout routine," I said as I reached for Ari's hand.

I pretty much already knew the answer before I asked it. I remembered Jefferson sparring in high school to let out steam. It was always after our mother had gone on one of her drunken escapades. Jefferson took a bad hit once and walked around school with a black eye the whole week. I asked him to stop doing it and he did. That is until Sunday morning.

"Um…..well…..I guess this is just his way of letting off a little steam. He was pretty upset with himself the day after the party. He stayed in his room almost the whole day until he told me he was going back to the gym to do a little sparring. He's been doing it at least twice a day. I tried to tell him he was going to get hurt but he told me he needed to do it." Gunner had been looking everywhere but at Ari and me. Ari squeezed my hand and looked at me.

"Just like when he was in high school," she said as a tear rolled down her face.

"What do you mean just like in high school?" Gunner asked.

"When my mother used to go on a week, or sometimes more, drunken binge Jefferson would head down to the Y and started sparring with a few of the guys that were training for fights. He got hit so hard once time that he got knocked out and it caused him to get a black eye. I made him promise me he wouldn't fight anymore to let off steam. That's when he took to running." Just then the nurse walked up to us.

"Miss Johnson? Your brother is back from his scan and he's asking for you. He can have two visitors at a time." The nurse smiled a small smile at me and turned to Gunner and gave him a wink before she walked off.

I just rolled my eyes. Gunner didn't even flinch or give her a smile back; he just kept looking over at me and Ari.

"Do you both want to head on back?" I'll wait here."

Ari shook her head no. "No, that's okay. I'm fine waiting out here for right now. I think the two of you should go on back first."

I leaned over and gave her a kiss on the head. "Be back in a few minutes sweets." Ari gave me a weak smile as Gunner and I turned and walked towards the nurse's desk.

When I walked behind the curtain and got a look at Jefferson my heart jumped in my throat. Oh. My. God. He looked terrible! I let out a gasp and threw my hands up to my mouth.

He opened his eyes and looked at me and then at Gunner. He looked behind us like he was looking for someone else……..he was looking for Ari….

"Hey there little sis, what brings you here today?" He said with a chuckle.

"Dammit Jefferson this is NOT funny! You scared the shit out of us! You promised me you would never do this ever again. Why? Why did you do this?" I asked him trying to bite back the anger I was feeling.

"What do you mean us?" Jefferson asked me.

"What?" Oh God….he is confused.

"You said us….you scared the shit out of us…..who is us?" Jefferson asked me as he kept looking over my shoulder.

"She's in the waiting room. They only let two come back at the same time, Ari had Gunner and I come back first," I said, knowing now what he was asking.

"Jeff, do you remember what happened? Do you know why you're here?" Gunner asked.

"Yeah….I remember why Gun. I remember everything…..I wish I didn't. I wish I could just forget it all," Jefferson said with such a lost look in his eyes.

"So all of this Jefferson, all this fighting the last few days was because of what happened Saturday night?" I asked as I took his hand in mine. He closed his eyes for a few seconds. When he opened them a tear rolled down his face and he squeezed my hand. His tear soaked eyes captured mine.

"I'm so sorry I disappointed you. I'll never forgive myself for hurting you. You're all I have Ells…..I promise I will never disappoint you again. Please tell me you forgive me for being such a prick. *Please Ellie*….."

My heart started to pound. Oh my God Jefferson.

"Of course I forgive you Jefferson. I love you more than anything, you know that. Jefferson you can't keep doing this…you have to stop. Having someone beat up on you like a punching bag is not going to make it go away, you have to talk to Ari. You have to tell *her* how sorry you are," I said as I looked up at Gunner who was watching me intensely.

"I've been trying to tell her I'm sorry. She won't fucking answer her phone when I call. I've been texting her to please call me and she just ignores me!" The heart monitors they had Jeff connected to started to beep faster and faster…..

"Jeff, dude just calm down…..let me go out and get Ari….she's right outside Jeff. Let me go get her," Gunner said as a nurse walked in.

"Mr. Johnson is everything okay in here?" the nurse asked as she looked between Gunner and me.

"Jefferson, please just take a few deep breaths okay? It's alright Gunner is going to get Ari right now. Everything is fine….he um, just started to get a little upset. When can we take him home?" I asked as the nurse starting taking all of Jefferson's vital signs.

"As soon as the doctor says he can leave we can start on the paper work. Until then…..please try to keep him calm," Nurse meanie said as she walked back out the door.

"She's pleasant, she been your nurse the whole time?"

Jefferson laughed. "Yeah, but she's been pretty cool. I'm sorry Ellie I scared you. I love you sis….more than life itself. I wanted to take you shopping last Monday for your graduation gift. Maybe we could do it tomorrow. What do you say?"

"Ohhhh….what type of store do we need to go to for this gift?" I said as I hopped up and down. Jefferson was the BEST gift giver! I couldn't wait to see what he was going to get me.

"A car dealership…….that type of store," he said with a smile.

"Wait…..what? A car dealership…..shut the hell up Jefferson! You're buying me a car? OH MY GOD! How can you afford to buy me a car?" I practically screamed out.

"Gesh Ells, try to keep it down. There are sick people here and my head is fucking killing me right now. Don't worry about how I can afford it. I work and I must say I'm a pretty damn good investor when it comes to money. Think about what kind of car you want honey and we will go shopping tomorrow."

I started to jump up and down I was so excited. The smile on Jefferson's face melted my heart. Just then my phone beeped alerting me to a text message. I grabbed it out of my back pocket. It was from Gunner.

Ari left…..she left a message with the nurse that she was heading back home.

Fuck a duck! Why did she leave? I looked up at Jefferson. His smiled faded when he saw my face.

"She left, didn't she Ellie?" he said with such a sad look in his eyes.

"Yes, I'm afraid she did. I'm so sorry Jefferson," I said as I took his hand again in mine.

"S'okay....I didn't even really expect her to be here after what I did to her so...it's no big deal. Um, can you go see about getting me out of here? I'm really ready to get home."

I nodded my head and headed out the door. When I walked out to the nurses' station Gunner was already talking about Jefferson being able to leave. They told him they were getting the paper work together and it shouldn't be much longer.

"Hey....everything okay with Jeff, does he know Ari left?" Gunner asked as he held open his arms for me.

I melted into his body. Only he could take away the hurt I was feeling. Hurt for Ari, for Jefferson.....shit....my own damn hurt. It all just melted away in his arms.

"Yes, he knows she left. And no....he doesn't seem okay. He's hurting so bad Gunner. What do I do?"

"I don't know Sweetheart.....I really don't know," Gunner said as he held me tighter in his arms.

Gunner

I woke up Thursday morning with a sick feeling in my stomach, like I was worried about something. What the hell was that all about? Yesterday turned out to be a fucked up day. With Jeff spending most of the day in the ER, then bringing him home and getting him settled, before I brought Ellie back to Ari's house. Ellie sent me a text saying that Ari had not been home when she got there and was still not home when Ellie went to bed and she was really worried about her. The fact that Ari left the hospital without seeing Jeff made Ellie upset.

What a fucked up mess. I sure as shit hoped Jeff and Ari could work out this cluster fuck 'cause it was taking a toll on Ellie.

My sweet Ellie….god every time I thought about her I smiled and had to adjust my damn dick. This whole friend thing was turning out to be harder than I thought it would be. She was worth the wait though. She would always be worth the wait.

After I got back from a run and a quick workout I walked in the front door and saw Jeff sitting on the sofa. He sure looked a lot better after a good night's sleep. He was on the phone with someone.

"Sounds great Brad, I'm in the mood for a night out. Yeah, Gunner just walked in so I'll let him know. See ya tonight dude." Jeff put his cell phone down on the table. He looked up at me and smiled.

"You want to go to Rebels tonight?" Jeff asked while wagging his eyebrows up and down.

I just laughed. "Shit dude, don't you think you should take it easy? Are you sure you're ready to go out on the town tonight?"

"Shit yeah! I guess our friend Brad hooked up with Ellie's friend Amanda. They're heading down there tonight. Want to call Ellie and see if she wants to go?"

"Brad and Amanda huh, Ellie should find that amusing," I said with a laugh while Jeff looked at me confused.

"Whatever dude, I'm going and thinking of calling up a few of the other guys so are you up for it?" Jeff asked as he got up and headed into the kitchen.

"Yeah, sure but um, if I call Ellie you know she is going to invite Ari. Are you okay with seeing her right now?"

Jeff turned and gave me a weak smile. "Sure yeah whatever.......I'm fine with her going along. She sure as shit likes to dance so she'll love it there. I've tried to call her, even this morning and she doesn't want to talk. She pretty much made it clear how she feels so I think I'm done with that whole thing. I'm fine dude, really."

"Dude, you sure you want to just walk away from this? I know you care for her Jeff. I've seen how you look at her and I saw how upset you were when she was dancing with Josh. Man, why don't you just ask her out to dinner....see where it goes. What's the big deal?" I said as I grabbed a bottled water out of the fridge.

Jeff took his hands and ran them through his hair and then down his face. Clear sign he was frustrated.

"Shit.....Gunner......man I have fought my feeling for this girl for as long as I can remember. We used to be really great friends....the three of us would do everything together. I used to love spending time with those two. Then it all changed. Ari started looking at me differently; she started changing right before my damn eyes. She kept getting more and more beautiful. Then she went away with her parents the summer before they started high school. She came back not looking at all like my little squirt...she came back fucking hotter than hell. That damn smile of hers.....fuck I swear my dick comes to attention when she is within fifty feet of me. If we started to date and it ended badly....she would be gone out of my life forever. I would rather have her in my life as a friend than not have her at all."

I just shook my head. "Jeff, you can't be afraid of losing her friendship. Fuck dude...your sister has turned my damn world upside down. She keeps pushing me away but I'm NOT giving up on her. I don't think you should give up on Ari. I really think you should think about taking this friendship a little further."

"I can't......I think we're better this way. I'm not even sure we're still friends to be honest. I just need to move on and I think she already has moved on. Anyway dude, enough of Ari....what's going on with my little sister and you. I haven't seen her so damn happy in a long ass time. I appreciate you not pushing her Gun. She needs time to figure shit out."

"I'm going to be honest with you Jeff. I know she is your sister, and I appreciate you giving me your blessing but, holy fuck. She has turned my world upside down, and I think I'm going crazy with this whole she just wants to be friends shit," I said as I pushed my hands through my hair only to have Jeff start laughing at me.

"What the fuck is so funny?"

Jeff got up shaking his head and punched me in the arm. "You! Damn Gunner....I've never in the three years that I've known you seen a girl get to you like this. The last thing I thought you were looking for was a relationship. Dude….you even said….you had three loves….Football, the ranch and football!"

"Yeah….tell me about it, just the thought of her going out with anyone else drives me insane. I think I would want to kill the fucker if I ever saw her out with another guy."

Jeff's smile faded a brief second but then it came back. "Well, just give her time. She went through a lot of shit with my mother and then the stunt Ryan pulled on her. She'll come around Gunner. I see the way she looks at you. Trust me dude….she wants to be more than friends just as much as you do. Holy fuck…I need to get off this conversation…..that's still my baby sister."

I looked at Jeff and laughed….."I sure hope you're right. Until then I just plan on waiting for her, I'm not giving up. Speaking of your baby sister……." I took out my cell phone to give her my normal morning wake up call.

Jeff just laughed and headed back to his room. "Hey, tell Ellie not to forget….car shopping today!" Jeff shouted from down the hall.

"Hello?"

"Good morning Sweetheart! How did you sleep?" I asked once the lump in my throat was gone from hearing her voice.

"Good morning Gunner…..I slept okay. I heard Ari come in pretty late though. I think she was out on a date but I'm not sure who with. It breaks my heart Gunner. Why can't they both stop being so damn stubborn."

I had to laugh at that….this was the pot calling the kettle black right here. "I'm not sure Ellie. I talked to Jeff this morning and he pretty much said he had no intention of ever dating Ari. Said he would rather have her has a friend than to not have her in his life at all." By now I had walked out to the back yard. I didn't need Jeff hearing me talking about him and Ari to Ellie.

"ARGH! They're both so frustrating. They act like they can't stand each other, how does he think that is a friendship? Oh shit…never mind. This is their problem not mine," Ellie said after a long sigh.

"You're right Ells……it's their problem. It will all work out honey, don't worry. Jeff can't ignore how he feels for Ari forever."

"Yeah….but for how long will Ari wait for him to make up his damn mind…….." Ellie went silent.

I took a deep breath knowing she was thinking about us. She was wondering the same thing about me. How long will I wait for her to decide this whole friendship thing was just plain stupid?

I would wait forever for her…..

"Hey, Jeff wanted me to remind you that y'all are going car shopping today. You excited?" I said as a smile came across my face. I could just picture her jumping up and down right now.

"Oh my gosh! I'm super excited! Are you going to come with us? OH please say you're coming! It will be so much fun." God I could hear the excitement in her voice.

I started to laugh. "Only if you let me be the first person you kiss in your new car."

"Oh….um….." She started to giggle. "OKAY! It is a deal. You will be the first person I kiss in my new car"

"On the lips……"

Ellie let out a louder laugh. "On the lips, you bet."

"With tongue….none of this chicken peck shit!"

"*Gunner*! You're terrible!" She was still laughing. "Okay….you'll be the first person that I kiss on the lips with a little bit of tongue…you're not getting anything else out of me."

"I'll take it and I'll hold you to it. I will not forget, I have an incredible memory," I said as I walked back into the house. Jeff was walking into the living room with a towel wrapped around his waist. He must have just gotten out of the shower. He picked up his cell phone and made a strange face when he looked at the screen.

He looked up at me and mouthed the word Ellie. I nodded my head yes. "Tell her I'll be there in forty-five minutes to get her," Jeff said as he started to listen to a voice mail.

"Hey Sweetheart, Jeff just said he will pick you up in forty five minutes. If I'm going with y'all, I need to hop in the shower and get ready. I'll talk to you soon okay?"

"Sounds good Gunner and I'll see ya soon," Ellie said with such sweetness in her voice.

"Bye Ells…."

"Bye Gunner." she practically whispered it and my heart rate took off through the roof. Damn….I was already getting excited just from knowing I was about to lay eyes on her beautiful face again.

Just then I heard Jeff shout "FUCK!" along with the sound of his cell phone hitting the wall.

I set my cell phone down next to me in bed. Holy hell….I just had to hear his voice and I got an ache between my legs. Why did he have this affect on me? It was insane! ARGH…this whole friends thing was starting to really suck. I knew Gunner wanted more but, I just was not ready to give up my heart again. I trusted him with my life but still, I barely knew him. This is what was scaring the shit out of me. I couldn't get dependent on him like I was Jefferson all those years. I needed to get my big girl panties on and figure my shit out.

I got to see him today though, and I had to smile with just the thought. I was already wondering what he would wear. He always looked so damn good when I saw him. Shit, he could have on a paper bag and still look good. Speaking of looking good….I needed to get up and get going!

EEEPPPPP! I can't believe Jefferson is buying me a car! I turned on the shower and threw my hair up in a pony tail. After a quick five minute shower, I hopped out and went to the closet. I pulled my hair out of the pony and started to look for something to wear. Shit, I really needed Ari's help picking something out. Just then I heard her open the door to my room.

"Well….look at you all ready to start your day!" Ari said as she came and sat down on my bed. She was already dressed herself in a pair of white shorts and a navy blue sleeveless shirt. Her hair was in two braided pigtails and she had on a pair of cowboy boots.

"Shit Ari….how do you put these outfits together like this? You look adorable! What the hell are you doing up and dressed so early anyway. I heard you come in last night. Why did you leave the hospital? Jefferson wanted to see you," I said as I sat down on the bed next to her. I saw her eyes light up when I mentioned Jefferson wanting to see her.

"Why did he want to see me?" Ari asked trying to sound disinterested.

"I think he just really wanted to talk to you, apologize for everything. He said he has been trying to call you but you won't return his calls," I said as Ari closed her eyes briefly before opening them again.

"I'm sorry I skipped out on you yesterday but, once I heard he was fine I figured it would be for the best if I just left. I ended up calling Brian back to the hospital for a ride home. Once I got home I went with my mom to the club to play a game of tennis and I ran into Jason Reed from high school. We talked for a bit, he asked me out to dinner so I figured why not. I came home and left to meet him at Hula Hut. We ended up going and shooting some pool and then I came home. I actually enjoyed myself for once. I forgot what a nice guy he was," Ari said as she stared down at the floor.

"Oh....um....wasn't Jason a few years older than us, he played football and hung around Jefferson and them right?" I asked as I got up and started looking for something to wear again.

"Yep...that's him. Anyway, he called me this morning and asked if I wanted to have lunch with him. I told him I would see what your plans were and call him back."

"Oh, well....Jefferson is taking me to get my graduation present today along with Gunner."

Ari sat up a little straighter. "Do you know what he's getting you?"

"Yep and you won't believe it! I hardly can!" I said as I jumped up and down.

Ari threw her head back and laughed. "Well.....what is it bitch? Don't just leave me hanging here!"

I cleared my throat and looked at her. "He's getting me a CAR!"

Ari jumped up and screamed "WHAT THE FUCK! A car? He's getting you a goddamn car? Oh my gosh. What kind of car or do you get to pick it out? Is there a price max? How the hell can he afford to buy you a new car?"

Gesh this girl..... "Ari if you would just take a breath I could fill you in!" I said with a laugh.

"Oh yeah....sorry...go...fill me in....I'm all ears!" Ari said as she sat back down on the bed clearly trying to keep quite.

"Okay well...he told me he had some money saved up from working and that this was my graduation present. Yes, I get to pick it out and no....he has not told me a max price...YET! I was really hoping you would come along with me to help me pick it out but if you made plans with Jason that's okay."

Ari's smile faded. She started fiddling with her shirt. Was that tears building in her eyes? When she looked back up at me a single tear started to slide down her face.

"Oh my god, Ari what's wrong?" I asked as I pulled her towards me and hugged her.

"Oh Ellie.....I want to go but I don't think I could see Jeff, not today anyway. He left a voice mail this morning asking me to please call him back and for me to stop acting like a baby. I don't know why I did it but, I called him back and I shouldn't have because I was so pissed off with him calling me a baby. It was his voice mail so I left him a message." She started to cry hysterically.

Oh no……."What did you say sweets?"

She was now just sobbing and shaking. What the hell?

"Ari….*what* did you say?" I asked her as I pushed her away from me to where I could look into her face.

"I….I just said…..I said that I accepted his apology and that he was right, I needed to grow up. I told him he didn't need to worry about my virginity anymore because……because….."

Oh. My. God……I knew where this was going.

"Ari just tell me what you said in the voice mail!" I yelled at her.

She started to settle down a bit. She took a deep breath and started talking again. "I told him he didn't need to worry about my virginity anymore, because I gave it up last night to Jason Reed."

No……oh please God no!

I felt like I was going to throw up. I had to stand up and go into the bathroom and splash water on my face. I was leaning up against the counter listening to Ari crying. Oh my god, how could she do this? Why would she do this? This was all so wrong! I took a deep breath and walked back into the room. I was so mad at her for doing this.

Ari looked up at me with tears streaming down her face.

"Of all the stupid ass, fucked up shit, you have ever done! How could you be so stupid Ari! I'm so disappointed in you right now, you have no fucking idea!" I was shaking from head to toe.

"WAIT! Ellie wait! Let me tell you….." Ari jumped up and started to walk over to me.

"I can't believe you would sleep with some guy you barely know just to get back at Jefferson. What the fuck is wrong with you two anyway? Does fucking other people help you two solve your problems? You probably just ruined everything Ari…..everything!" I shouted at her.

"No wait….ELLIE *please* just let me talk," Ari begged.

I just stood there and waited for her to start talking. Nothing she was going to say to me was going to make any this better. Jefferson was probably devastated thinking he drove Ari to have sex with someone.

Ari wiped the tears away frantically. "I didn't have sex with Jason! I was just so angry and hurt that all I wanted to do was hurt Jeff back. I know it was a childish thing to do…..believe me I know. I just…..shit, I don't know what I was thinking."

I stood there for a second taking every bit in that she just said. I felt like I wanted to slap the shit out of her. "You bitch! I don't know what's worse. You making me believe you lost your virginity or the fact that you just hurt Jefferson like this. How could you do this? I'm so mad at you right now, I don't even want to talk to you!" I shouted at Ari. I picked up my cell phone to call Jefferson. It went straight to voicemail.

"*Great*! It's going to his voicemail. You have to tell him the truth." I said as I looked at Ari with pure disgust on my face.

"No...."

"What do you mean no? You can't make Jefferson think that you slept with Jason just because you got your feelings hurt. You're behaving just like he did Saturday night," I said as I walked to my closet. I needed to get dressed and ready before Jefferson and Gunner got there.

"I think this is for the better. If Jeff thinks I've moved on then he will be able to move on as well. It's pretty fucking clear Ellie that Jeff never had any intention of taking things past friendship. This way maybe we can somehow be friends again later on down the road. He can date whoever he likes....I need to move on and I think Jason might be the guy I need to move on with," Ari said as she walked into my closet and pulled out a pair of white Capri pants and a black sleeveless shirt. "I have a pair of black flats and a belt that will look really cute with this."

And just like that....she was moving on.

"Do you really think that telling Jefferson you had sex with another guy last night is going to make him just...... move on? Ari, I *know* Jefferson has feelings for you. Why don't you...."

"I said NO! I'm done with all of this; I'm not talking about it anymore. I'm going to get you the shoes and belt then I'm heading out to meet my mom for breakfast, and then I'm going to call Jason. Tell Gunner I said hi."

She turned and walked out the door. I put on the pants and shirt and walked back into the bathroom. I tried messing with my hair but nothing looked good so I ended up pulling it back up into a ponytail. I put on a little bit of makeup and ran my fingers over the daisy necklace. I had to smile at the memory of our first kiss. Good God how I wanted to kiss him again so badly. To feel his warm breath against my face, his hands wrapping around my body to hold me close to him. I closed my eyes and dreamed of that kiss. Everything about it was perfect. He was perfect.......but did he truly want me? Was I good enough to keep someone like Gunner?

I shook my head to clear my thoughts. This is why I needed time. I needed to get my feelings and thoughts in order.

Here I was pushing Ari about Jefferson and I was too damn afraid to admit my own feelings for Gunner. I heard the bedroom door shut so I walked out to see if Ari had come back. She had left a pair of black flats and a black belt lying at the foot of the bed.

I looked at the clock. They would be here any minute. I tried to call Jefferson again....right to voicemail. I tried Gunner's cell next.

"Hey Sweetheart, we're almost there." My goodness my heart stopped beating for a second when I heard his voice. I would never get tired of hearing him call me sweetheart. Never.

"Okay great. Um, I've been trying to call Jefferson. Does he have his phone turned off do you know?" I asked.

"Yeah, um about that….we have to stop and pick Jeff up a new phone. He kind of, well he kind of broke his phone earlier so….that's why it's going straight to voicemail."

"I see…..I take it he got Ari's message then?"

"Oh yeah……" Gunner said in a hushed tone.

"Right….well I guess I'll just meet you out front. Ari might still be here and she was pretty clear she didn't want to see Jeff today."

Gunner laughed a nervous laugh. "Okay Ells, we'll see you in about three minutes."

I hung up and grabbed my purse and headed downstairs. Sure enough Ari was still home. I heard her on the phone as I walked to the front door.

"Lunch sounds great Jason. Do you want to just pick me up or should I meet you?"

I had a terrible feeling in my stomach. What was this about? I poked my head into the library where Ari was sitting and waved goodbye to her. She smiled up at me but the smile was so lost and insincere. She then looked out the window and her smile quickly faded. She looked back at me and I could see the tears building in her eyes as she tried to give me another smile and a wave.

Shit……

As soon as I walked outside Gunner jumped out of Jefferson's truck and helped me into the front seat. He kissed the back of my hand and his smile grew larger when he saw the blush creep up onto my cheeks. Shit! Why does he have this affect on me?

Snap out of this Ellie!

I turned to look at Jefferson who leaned over and gave me a kiss on the cheek. I saw him look past me like he was looking for Ari to be right behind me. There went that sick feeling again.

"Good mornin' Honey!" Jeff said as he looked over my shoulder. "Um, where's Ari? I thought for sure she would be coming with you to pick out your new car." He kept looking at me and then back at the house.

"She um, she really wanted to come, but she'd already made plans for today." I said as I tried to think of a way to change the subject before he asked me what her plans were.

Too late…..

"Oh really? What could be more important than her best friend getting a new car?" Jefferson said as he stared at Ari's house.

"I guess she had lunch plans," I said with a shrug and turned back to look at Gunner.

"Gunner, I'm so glad you're coming with us."

"Do you know what kind of car you want Ells?" Clearly he knew I was trying to change the subject but Jefferson was not letting this go.

"Who did she have lunch plans with?" He asked before I could answer Gunner.

Fuck a duck....why me? Damn Ari right now for putting me in this spot.

"Um...with um, an old friend from high school or something," I said as I looked up at Jefferson who was staring at the house still. I turned to look and I could see Ari standing in the window talking on the phone, probably to Jason still.

"Is it Jason Reed? Is he the *old friend* from high school?" Jefferson asked as he looked back at me.

God when I got back I was going to lay into Arianna! Her stupid childish behavior put me here in the middle of all of this........ FUCK!

I looked up at Jefferson and did the only thing I could do. "Yes Jefferson, she's having lunch with Jason Reed today. I guess they ran into each other at the country club yesterday."

"Did he take her out last night?"

"Umm.....she mentioned something like that." Oh dear God, please Gunner change the subject.

Just then Gunner cleared his throat and Jefferson seemed to snap out of it.

"Brad called earlier to see if we wanted to join him and Amanda at Rebels tonight. Do you think you would maybe like to go?" Gunner asked me as Jefferson started to pull out of Ari's driveway.

Oh God if I could jump across this seat right now I would so plant my lips onto his. I turned around and he winked at me. I smiled back.

"Heck yeah, I w'd love to go! Ari, Amanda, me and Heather have all been there once before. Are you going to ride the mechanical bull?" I asked with a smile and a wink.

Gunner threw his head back and laughed. "No! But Jeff here.....he can ride that thing like he grew up in the damn rodeo!"

"Wait.....did you just say Amanda *and* Brad were going? Like as in, they're going together...as like a couple?" I asked as it hit me what Gunner had just said.

Jefferson and Gunner both let out a laugh.

"Yep....looks like your little friend Amanda left an impression on Brad!" Jefferson said as he raised his eyebrows up and down.

"I guess so," I said as I laughed along with them.

"Why don't you go ahead and invite Ari to come along tonight also. Maybe her and her *friend* Jason would like to go," Jefferson said with sarcasm dripping from his mouth.

"Oh okay yeah, I'll send her a text. What time do you think we'll go?" I asked as I turned to look at Gunner.

"How about I pick you up early and we grab a bite to eat. Then we can just meet everyone there. Does that sound okay to you Jeff?" Gunner asked as he gave me a wink. I saw his eyes look down and land on my daisy necklace. I reached up and touched it with my fingers and his eyes instantly snapped back up and captured my eyes. His smile just about melted my heart. I tried not to, but I dropped my eyes to his lips. Those beautiful soft lips.....Shit.....I wanted those lips on mine so damn bad. I felt my tongue run over my now dry lips as I looked back up at Gunner.

Oh my....... The smile that was on his face was replaced by a look of pure lust. I felt a tremble go through my whole body and the heat instantly on my cheeks. He leaned forward and brushed his hand along the side of my face and gave me that crooked smile of his. He sat back once Jefferson started to talk.

Holy hell.........I could still feel the heat on my face from where his hand touched my skin.

"That sounds like a plan. We'll just plan on meeting there around 8:30. Now.....Ellie......what kind of car do you want?" Jefferson said as he looked over at me with a huge smile on his face.

"Well, do I have a price range I have to stick with?!"

Jefferson laughed...."Not really, just no BMW's okay?"

"Okay, then I'm thinking fuel efficient here."

Jefferson and Gunner both laughed. "I'm sure you are Honey." Jefferson said with a wink.

"A Honda Accord, if that's something we can afford," I said as I watched Jefferson's face.

"Somehow I knew that's what you were going to say. Let's go get you a car."

I never thought shopping for a car would be so much fun! I ended up with a silver 2013 Honda Accord. Between Jefferson and Gunner, the poor salesman had no hope. They got it for $300 below invoice and Jefferson wrote a check for the whole amount. When he saw my shocked expression, he told me he had put money aside from our grandmother's inheritance and had been adding to it the last three years plus what it earned in investments.

I ran into his arms and gave him a huge hug.

I would be so lost without him.

I was on my way to pick up Gunner in my new car with Taylor Swift's "Fearless" blasting from the speakers. This song reminds me of how I feel when I'm with Gunner. I had to smile as I was singing along to the words. I had invited Ari to come along but she said she'd made other plans with Jason and said maybe another time.

I pulled up to Gunner's house and he was sitting on the front porch on his cell phone. As soon as he saw me he smiled and must have said he had to go to whoever he was talking to. He jumped up and jogged over to the car. I turned Taylor down and put the car in park. He hopped up and leaned over and kissed my cheek.

SHIT.....there goes that all too familiar ach between the legs.....I tried with all my might not to let out a moan........ for Pete's sakes it was just a kiss on the cheek Ellie!

Gunner and I ate at a little Mexican restaurant in Hyde Park and then headed downtown to Rebels. We spent most of the night just sitting at a table talking. Amanda and Brad sure were getting along. They practically hung on each other all night. Jefferson seemed disappointed that Ari was not there but he quickly recovered and spent most of the night dancing. I swear every time he sat down 6 girls would walk up to him and ask him to dance. He tried being as polite as he could and danced with most of them, but by 11:30 he was exhausted. He started turning them down.

I was shocked at how many girls completely ignored me sitting with Gunner and asked him to dance. He turned them down even though I told him I didn't care. I mean, we were just friends....right?

Then *she* showed up.

I noticed her chatting it up with Jefferson first, but when she first walked up Gunner said hi to her. Her name was Lori. From what I could tell she must be majoring in Architectural Engineering as well. She soon turned her attention on Gunner. He introduced us and she did pretty much everything she could to keep me out of the conversation.

"So, your name is Ellen did you say? You're Jeff's little sister right," Lori said to me with a fake ass smile.

"It's Ellie....and yes, I am Jefferson's sister," I said back with a fuck you smile of my own.

"So Gunner, I didn't know you were dating someone, let alone Jeff's baby sister."

Gunner looked at me. I know he was waiting for me to respond. So...... me being the idiot I am....I answered the question for Gunner.

"Gunner and I are just friends Lori. We're not dating." A smile spread across her plastic looking face.

That was all the bitch needed to hear. She jumped up and grabbed Gunner's arm and pulled him half way up.

"Then let's dance!" Lori said as she was smiling at me.

Gunner went to sit back down, "Um, no really, I'm here with Ellie, Lori and..."

"It's fine....go dance Gunner, we're not together, you can dance with someone else." What the fuck? I said that before I could stop myself.

Gunner turned and looked at me. I saw the hurt in his eyes and he just shook his head. He looked mad.

OH MY GOD! I just wanted to slap myself for being so fucking stupid. I'm sure I just pissed him off with my whole 'we're just friends bit.'

"*See*....she wants you to dance Gun," Lori the bitch said as she winked at me and walked with her arm wrapped around Gunner's.

Just then Usher's "Hot Tottie" started. *Really?* Why that song of all songs?

Because life was serving me up another plate full of shit.

I just sat there and tried not to watch them dancing. I looked over at Jefferson who was watching Gunner. He looked over at me and gave me a small weak smile. Well fuck......that just made me want to look at them all the more.

Holy hell....this girl was fucking grinding all into Gunner, and that bastard was giving her just as much as she was giving him but he had his eyes closed for some reason. She turned and put her ass on his dick.....then she looked over towards me and put her finger in her mouth and sucked it as she pushed her ass into him further. She lifted her other hand and ran it down his face and side. He had his hands on her hips moving right along with her.

Oh. My. God. I was going to throw up.

I stood up and walked over to Jefferson. "Can you please walk me to my car?"

"You're leaving? Honey, what about Gunner?" I looked out to the dance floor.

"It looks like he found someone else to go home with."

"Ellie, he is just dancing and you told him to." Jefferson looked back out to the dance floor. I saw him frown. I looked back out.....they were still going at it. Now she was turned back around but Gunner still had his hands on her hips and they were really moving. Gunner's back was facing me now.

"I want to leave....*now*," I shouted at Jefferson.

"Okay Ellie Jesus....." Jefferson took my hand and we started to leave. I took one last look towards Gunner. He didn't even know I was leaving. My heart felt like someone was squeezing the life out of it. This is why I could not give my heart to anyone again. If he truly wanted me he would not be dancing with some girl like he was ready to fuck her right there on the dance floor. All I could hear was my mother's voice over and over in my head.

You will never be wanted by anyone.........

As soon as we got outside the club I stopped and took a deep breath in.

"Ellie, I don't understand why you're getting so upset. You have told Gunner y'all are only friends. You told him to dance with Lori and then you get upset because he does."

"What?" I shook my head to clear my thoughts. "Did you not see how they were dancing? Did you not see what I saw, because to me they were practically fucking on the dance floor!" I screamed back at Jefferson louder than I wanted to.

"Oh my god Ellie….they're just dancing. Everyone dances like that! Stop acting like this and decide what you want. Do you want Gunner as more than a friend or not? If you do then go back in there and tell Lori to take a fucking hike….if not….then…...."

"Then what Jefferson? What? Please tell me because you are *such* an expert in this field." Jefferson looked stunned.

"You're right. I need to just keep my mouth shut. Let's get you to your car."

Jefferson walked me the short distance to my car in silence. "I'm sorry Jefferson, it's just that I'm so scared of the feelings I have for Gunner. I don't see what he really sees in me when he can have someone like that Lori or Crysti." I said as a tear escaped from my eyes and rolled down my face. Jefferson wiped it away.

"Ellie, like I told you before honey, you are exactly what Gunner is looking for. You're beautiful, smart and you make him happy. You're not one of those girls who will fall into bed with the first good looking guy who gives them attention. You have to stop hearing mom's words play over in your head. You are not mom. You never will be. You have to stop pushing him away. He wants to be with you."

"He sure didn't look like it tonight while dancing."

"I know you think that Ellie, but honey you have to see it from his point of view. You practically pushed him to her tonight. Of course she is going to try and make you jealous 'cause she's a bitch who's been after Gunner for three years now. I'm sure he was hurt by you telling him to go dance. He made a mistake Ells." Jefferson said has he lifted my chin to look up at him.

"I know how it feels to make a stupid decision. Please just talk to him when he calls you okay?"

I took a deep breath and tried to smile. "I just want to get home. Thanks for walking me to my car Jefferson. You're a great big brother. I love you," I said as I stood on my tippy toes to kiss him.

He bent down and gave me hug. "I love you too Ells…more than you will ever know."

I got in the car and watched Jefferson walk back towards Rebels. My hands started to shake and all I could hear was my mother's voice telling me how I would end up alone like her. I would never be good enough to keep someone like Gunner Mathews happy for long.

I pulled out of the parking space and started driving back home to Ari's. That same sick feeling I kept getting off and on today was now back. I felt the tears rolling down my face as I touched the daisy necklace around my neck.

You will never be wanted by anyone..........

26 Gunner

I was so pissed at Ellie for pulling out the fucking friend's card again. Even after I tried to tell Lori I didn't want to dance, Ellie practically pushed me onto the dance floor. Soon as the music started Lori started grinding her ass into my dick. I had to close my eyes and act like it was Ellie I was dancing with just to get through it.

Lori did a pretty damn good job keeping me turned away from Ellie. When the song ended I turned around to see Ellie was no longer at the table….neither was Jeff. She was gone.

FUCK!

I made a beeline towards the table. Lori ran up and grabbed my arm. "HEY! Where are you going? Let's have some fun tonight. I made sure your little *friend* got the right impression," Lori said as she looked up at me with a smug look on her face.

"What the fuck are you talking about?"

"Well, you know….I made sure she knew she was a little too young to be trying to play with the big kids…if you know what I mean," she said as she stuck her finger in her mouth and sucked on it and then tried to put it on my mouth.

I jerked my head back away from her. "What the fuck did you do? I swear to God Lori, if she left, you will regret whatever it is you did." I pushed her out of my way.

I ran up to the table and asked Amanda where Ellie was.

"Well, since you were practically fucking that girl on the dance floor, Ellie told Jeff she wanted to leave and asked him to walk her to her car." Amanda said as she gave me a look that should have knocked me to my knees. That girl just gave new meaning to 'If Looks could kill'……

As soon as I got out of the club I started to run towards where I had parked Ellie's car earlier. I heard Jeff call out my name.

I stopped and turned around to see him walking across the street.

"She's gone," Jeff said has he walked up to me with his hands in his pockets.

"No! *Fucking hell!* What the hell did I just do?" I yelled out as I jammed my hands through my hair.

I looked at Jeff who just had a blank look on his face. "Why did she leave? Was it because I was dancing with Lori? She *told me to*. She made sure she let Lori know we were only friends and told me to go dance. I tried to tell Lori I didn't want to. Oh fucking hell......" I said as I started to pace back and forth.

"Dude, did you fucking know how you looked out there? You were grinding your dick all into Lori's ass while Ellie sat there and watched it. Then Lori's little stunt of sticking her finger in her mouth and sucking on it while you held onto her hips grinding away on her you prick. What did you think she was going to do? Sit there and watch."

I had to lean over. I had that sick feeling in my stomach again that I woke up with earlier this morning.

"No.... no...... shit no...I had to fucking keep my eyes closed the whole time. The whole fucking time all I was doing was picturing Ellie dancing with me. FUCK! I was so pissed at her for pulling out the fucking friend's card again, I guess I was just pissed and not thinking about how it would look to her."

I had to lean back over again....."Oh shit...I think I'm going to get sick."

Jeff slapped me on the back of the head. What the fuck?

"First off fucker...that's my sister you are day dreaming about.....and second....you better fucking make this right somehow."

Next thing I knew I was throwing up and Jeff was telling me he was going to get his truck. I had to talk to Ellie. I had to explain.....

It had been three weeks since I last saw Gunner. He called me every morning and I never answered. I thought after the first few days he would just give up. Same thing every night and each time he would leave me a message. I cried every time I listened to him beg for me to call him back. This morning he left the longest message and it tore me apart.

He said since I wouldn't call him he was just leaving it on my voicemail. He told me how upset he had been that I made him dance with Lori, he said he had to close his eyes and imagine that he was dancing with me. He just kept telling me how sorry he was and that he was so pissed he didn't even realize how it looked….It almost sounded like he was crying as he begged me to call him back. He was starting to sound just as bad as I felt.

Ari knocked and opened the bedroom door. "Hey, we're moving into the cottage today."

"Sounds good…..I just need to get a few more things packed up," I said with a weak smile. After looking at apartments near campus the last two weeks and deciding we would have to work a full time job to afford anything, we took Ari's parents up on their offer to let us live in their 2 bedroom cottage guest house.

Ari came and sat down next to me. "Did he call again Ells?"

I started to cry and handed her my cell phone. Ari listened to the voicemail.

"Holy fuck Ellie. Can you not hear it in his voice? He said he's sorry…he's begging you!"

"I can't get the image of him dancing with her out of my head Ari!"

"Ellie, he said he was thinking of you. Do you not think that maybe that is why he got a little bit too much into the dancing? You went out with Rich last week and you even said you had to pretend it was Gunner almost all night just to get through the date. Why is it so impossible for him to have to do the same thing? He made a mistake Ellie, and in a way I'm sure you confused the shit out of him with you offering him up to that bitch like that."

I looked up at Ari. She had a point. She had talked me into going on a double date with her and Jason and Jason's cousin Rich. I had a terrible time and thought about Gunner the whole time. I did push him into dancing with Lori….I knew that. Damn, it was just hard to admit it.

"Ari it's impossible for me to do this. I'm so scared of being hurt and I have such strong feelings for him....it scares me shitless!"

Ari let out a laugh. "I'm going to pull a Susan on you..... '*Nothing is impossible. The word itself says I'm possible*'....The great Audrey Hepburn, but we won't let mom know we didn't quote Katharine!"

I started to laugh. Ari always had a way of making me laugh when all I wanted to do was cry.

"I guess we could use some help moving?" I said with a small smile on my face.

"Yes we could! Jason is leaving for Europe today so maybe Gunner can help. Call him Ellie...you have been miserable sweets."

"What about Jefferson? I haven't seen him in two weeks. Would you be okay with him coming over?"

"Of course I would be. We need to get things back to normal between us. Besides, I'm happy with Jason so being around Jeff will be fine," Ari said as she attempted to give me a sincere smile.

Bullshit! She was not happy and I could tell. When she was around Jason she seemed lost. She actually seemed happy when he told her he was going to Europe with his dad and brother on a hiking trip and was not sure how long it would be until he got back.

"Call him Ellie."

I picked up the phone and dialed his number. The moment I heard his voice the tears started to roll down my face. Oh god how I missed him.

"*Ellie*......thank you for calling me sweetheart....." Gunner said my name with such a sadness I almost couldn't talk.

"G...Gunner......" It was all I could get out. I lost it and started crying.

"Oh baby no....please no don't cry Ellie."

"I'm so sorry.....I .....I just..."

"No...don't you apologize for anything Ellie. Please don't, it was entirely my fault....don't cry Baby please."

I sat there for another minute or two and cried. Gunner waited patiently for me to settle enough to where I could talk. This was it....I was going to put my heart out there and pray to God it would be safe with this man.

"Gunner, I'm just so scared......I'm so scared of the feelings I have for you. They are so strong and I'm so afraid if I give you my heart it will shatter in a million pieces if you break it, and I'll be left like my mother. I can't let that happen.....I *won't* let that happen. But.............I can't live my life without you in it either. I'm so confused."

I heard Gunner take a sharp intake of air. He slowly let out his air and I thought I heard him.....crying.....no now I was just hearing things. He started to talk but had to clear his voice.

"Ellie, I have never in my life.....*ever* sweetheart....experienced these feelings that I have for you. You walk into a room and I have to catch my breath at the sight of you. You flash your beautiful smile at me and there's not a damn thing in this world I wouldn't do for you. Your laugh moves through my body like a jolt of electricity. Your eyes captivate mine; your lips bring me to my knees. I want to know every part of you Ellie. I'm just as confused by these feelings as you are Sweetheart, but I want you to know something, I'll never push you or give up on us, I promise you that. Please Ellie, please just let me in. Let me prove to you how much I want to be with you. "

Oh my.......in my deepest hidden fantasies I never dreamed of hearing anyone say such beautiful things to me. *Never.* My heart felt like it was going to jump out of my throat. I know Ari heard every word Gunner said because she was sitting right next to me holding my hand, and she was crying just as much as I was. We both looked at each other and Ari smiled and mouthed to me 'I told you so.' I wanted to laugh but I didn't want Gunner to think I was laughing at what he just said to me.

"Ummm....Ellie you still there?" Ari hit me in the shoulder to snap me out of it.

I cleared my throat and tried to wipe away my tears. As soon as I wiped them away more tears just rolled down my face. "Yes Gunner, I'm still here. I.....I don't even know what to say but...but.... that was the most beautiful thing anyone has ever said to me. I'm afraid I might be dreaming and...." I couldn't say another word.

My eyes captivate his.....my lips bring him to his knees......

Next thing I knew, Ari took the phone from my hand.

"Um yeah Gunner, I think you've left her in a speechless state of happiness here. She is just staring off into space with a dopey smile on her face." I felt like I was listening to Ari speak from a bubble.

You walk into a room and I have to catch my breath at the sight of you.........

"We're moving into the guest house on my parents property today, since the last two weeks of apartment hunting got us nowhere but fucking depressed. We sure could use a little man power to help us move. I know Ells mentioned she wanted to see Jeff so, if he's available also? Great! Y'all come on over anytime. Let me see if she is able to talk now."

Ari handed me the phone and I just smiled before I even heard his sweet voice.

"Gunner...."

"Ellie, I'm on my way over right now." I had to let out a laugh. The butterflies in my stomach went into hyper speed mode. I had not seen him in three weeks and he was on his way over right now. I jumped up off the bed.

"Okay....I'll see you soon!"

"Bye sweetheart," Gunner said so soft and sweet.

I started to cry again......I was really doing this. I was going to give him my heart and pray to god he guarded it with his life.

"Bye......be careful driving." Was all I could get out and that I barely got out.

"Always." And then he hung up.

I turned to look at Ari who flew up and wrapped me in her arms.

"OH. MY. GOD! How..... How can I feel this way about him Ari? I just met him and I feel like I'm....I'm...." I could not say it.

Ari was about to say it.... "No! Don't say it. I'm not sure that is what this even is! Please don't say it."

Ari laughed and guided me into my closet that was pretty much packed up. "Let's find you a hot moving day outfit!" We both started laughing and for the first time in three weeks it didn't feel like I had someone sitting on my chest. I could breathe and I could smile.

Gunner was coming for me......

28 Gunner

I set my phone down on the coffee table and looked up to see Jeff standing there waiting for me. We were planning on going and picking up some stuff for Brad's birthday party tonight, right before I got the call from Ellie.

"Holy shit dude…you get a part time job with fucking Hallmark that you didn't tell me about! You almost had me in tears. I take it Ellie had a positive reaction since it sounds like you're heading over there now," Jeff said as he walked up and slapped me on the back. "Just make her happy and treat her right Gunner. That's all I care about."

"You got it dude," I said as I took his hand and slapped his arm. I was happy at this moment and I wouldn't have cared who heard me talking to Ellie.

Jeff knows the hell I have been through these last three weeks. The first week I wouldn't even get up to go work out. The second week I worked out so much I almost injured myself and this week all I was doing was getting drunk every night.

"You going over there right now?"

"*We're* going over there right now. Ellie wants to see you, and they're moving into the guest house on Ari's parents place and need help moving some shit," I said as I walked over to grab my keys and wallet.

"Well why can't Ari's boyfriend Jason help them move?" Jeff said as he sat down on the sofa.

"I don't know; I didn't ask Ari when she asked if we *both* could come over to help out."

Jeff sat up straight. "Ari asked for me to come over too?"

I nodded my head yes and Jeff jumped up and jogged back into his bedroom. Well I guess that solves that. I saw Jeff walking back down the hall….what the fuck?

"Dude….did you change what you were wearing?" I asked as I looked up and down at the khaki shorts and the tight ass red t-shirt he put on.

"What? I didn't want to wear jeans if we're going to be moving…fuck it's hot outside already."

I just nodded my head and headed out the door. The whole drive over to Ari's house Jeff was quiet. I knew he was excited to see Ellie since he hadn't seen her in about two weeks. The way his knee was bouncing up and down I would say he was excited to see Ari as well.

"Do you want to invite the girls over tonight for Brad's party?" I asked Jeff as he looked out the window in silence.

"Um, I don't care. I'm sure Ari will want to bring Jason. That guy was a fucking prick in high school who fucked every girl who let him. I can't believe she would give it up to that fucker."

Jeff had been kicking himself in the ass for the last month for pushing Ari into sleeping with another guy. I knew it was killing him inside. About a week ago we all went out and got trashed, when we got home Jeff and I sat in the back yard for a bit. He told me how fucked up he had been feeling since he found out Ari gave up her virginity to this Jason guy. He blames himself for pushing her into it. He just kept saying it should have been special for her....I knew what he was talking about. I think about Ellie all the time. I pray to God I'm the one she is with for the first time. I'll do everything in my goddamn power to make sure it is special for her. Of course I can't talk to Jeff about that, unless I want to get my ass kicked.

"Jeff, what's done is done. You can't take any of it back dude. You haven't seen this guy in how many years. He might be a nice guy who will treat her good," I said as I saw Jeff look over at me.

"Yeah well, I guess you're right. I just hope she's happy."

Jeff looked back out the window and I saw his body tense up as I pulled into Ari's long ass driveway. Damn these people had a shit load of money. As we got closer to the house I saw Ari and Ellie outside putting stuff in their cars. My dick instantly started jumping when I saw her.

Fuck....it had been too long since I laid my eyes on her beautiful face.

"Well, I guess I'm about to see if Ari still hates me," Jeff said with a chuckle. I pulled up behind Ari's jeep and my eyes caught Ellie's. My God....her smile just does me in every time.

Jeff hopped out of the truck first and then I got out, never taking my eyes away from hers. I thought for sure she would go up to Jeff first, but I was shocked when she started running over to me. I just stopped in my tracks. She ran and slammed into me so hard I almost lost my balance.

I just held her as tight as I could and breathed in her smell. God I've missed her so much.

" Ellie I've missed you," I whispered as I kissed the side of her head and held her even tighter and lifted her off the ground.

"Gunner! Thank you so much for coming over! I've missed you too." I gently set her back on the ground. When she looked up at me she had the sweetest smile on her face. I bent down and brushed her lips gently with mine. The fact that Jeff was standing here watching all of this left me a bit....uneasy. Ellie sucked in a breath as our lips touched. Holy hell, I wanted to just kiss the shit out of her right now. She must have been feeling the same way because she opened her eyes and looked up at me and started to laugh.

"What do you need help with Sweetheart....the calvary has arrived to help with whatever needs moving!" I said as I looked up at Jeff who was now just looking over at Ari.

"Hey Ari, how's it going?" Jeff said as Ellie walked up and gave him a hug.

"It's going good. I hear y'all are having a party for Brad tonight for his birthday," Ari said back to Jeff. I could tell she was trying very hard to act like everything was back to normal.

"Um, yeah did Amanda tell y'all?"

"Yep, she did. So are we invited to this little party? Ellie and I are going to need a break after moving today," Ari said as she winked at Ellie. Ellie looked back up to me and smiled.

I got to hand it to Ari....she was Oscar worthy.

"Yeah sure, I mean y'all are always invited to our parties. That's an open invitation. Feel free to bring anyone with you if you want," Jeff said as he walked over and started to pick up a box that was on the ground by Ari's Jeep.

"Cool....but it will just be Ellie and me tonight. There's more stuff in the house that is too heavy for me to carry if you don't mind getting it," Ari said as she moved towards the front door with Jeff following her on her heels.

I leaned down to Ellie and whispered, "Nice...is that her way of letting Jeff know Jason will not be joining us tonight?"

Ellie tried not to but she let out a laugh. "Yep. He's gone for at least a month....backpacking in Europe with his dad and brother. To be honest Gunner, I don't even think Ari likes him."

"Well she must like him some to have slept with him," I said as I looked back up towards the house.

"Ahhhh yeah about that....can you keep a secret?"

"Will I get to kiss you if I say yes?" I said as I wiggled my eyebrows up and down. Ellie instantly blushed. Shit...jumpage in my pants again. I had to move to try and adjust my growing problem.

"Yes...yes you will!"

"Well then, I'm all ears. Spill it."

Ellie looked back up at the house, the front door was open and it looked like Mark was talking to Jeff and Ari.

"Ari never slept with Jason, she just said that to make Jefferson jealous."

Whoa...wait....

"*What!*" I shouted a little too loud. Jeff poked his head out of the door.

"Is everything okay?" He looked between Ellie and me.

"Oh yeah dude. Ellie just told me…… um…..a joke that I didn't get." Jeff gave me a strange look and then turned back to Mark and Ari.

I pulled Ellie to the other side of my truck.

"First things first….."

I leaned down and brushed my lips against hers. She reached up and put her arms around my neck so I deepened the kiss. God the moment I felt her tongue against mine my knees almost buckled out from underneath me. I let out a small moan that made Ellie smile. I pulled back away from her and gave her a smile in return.

"Goddamn I've been dreaming of doing that again Sweetheart."

Ellie giggled and looked back around to see where Jeff and Ari where. Now back to this other bullshit.

"Okay, so you mean to tell me that Ari is still an um, you know, an um…."

"Virgin? Yes she is. She was upset the morning she called Jefferson. She was in hysterics when she told me what she did and was so upset for trying to hurt Jefferson. I tried to tell her she needed to tell him the truth but in her mind she thinks this will help them both to move on. I of course think she is making a huge mistake, but it's not my place to get involved. Please don't tell Jefferson, Gunner."

"Of course I won't say anything but shit….why can't they see how they both feel? I want to just knock their heads together!"

"What the hell are you two doing over there? This is a family home for Christ sakes!" I heard Ari shout. I looked down at Ellie and right on cue….there went the blush in her cheeks.

"Come on let's get you moved into your new digs!"

The whole time we helped them move the little amount of stuff they had I kept thinking about what Ellie had told me about Ari. Watching Jeff and Ari together they seemed to be loosening up again and becoming more relaxed around each other. Jeff even asked Ari to stop talking when she was rattling on about something and she replied with a fuck off dickwad. Yep, I would say things were getting back to normal.

Once we got everything into the guest house and Jeff set up their new flat screen TV for them, it was lunch time.

"Well shit…I know where we're coming to watch football. This fucker is huge!" Jeff said as he sat back on the sofa.

"So where do y'all want to go for lunch?" Ari asked as she sat on the sofa next to Jeff.

"How about burgers, Mighty Fine sound good?" Jeff asked as he looked around to each of us.

"That sounds MIGHTY FINE to me!" Ari said as she jumped up and grabbed her keys. I'm driving….the weather is too nice not to take the jeep.

As we started to walk out to Ari's jeep, Ellie held me back. Just by me holding her hand it made my stomach do all sorts of flips and dives. Jeff and Ari had walked out the door and were heading to the jeep.

"What's up Sweetheart, everything okay?"

"No…..no it's not okay." She said with a serious look on her face. Oh shit. I started to replay the whole morning in my head. Did I say something? What the fuck did I do?

"What is it Ells? What's wrong?" I asked her as my heart started to beat out of control. Things were just getting back to normal. No…better than normal. We were past the whole friends status.

"It's just that I really need you to kiss me, like right now," she said with a smile that melted my heart right there on the spot.

Well shit….just when I thought it couldn't get any better.

"Nothing would give me greater pleasure than to kiss you Ellie," I said as I reached down and hugged her around her waist. She giggled when I lifted her up and took her lips with mine. Fuck….if my dick was not getting hard again. I just wanted to walk over to the sofa with her and make out. Touch her body and make her feel things she had never felt before.

Just as the kiss was moving from sweet and innocent to passionate and needy….Ari honked the horn. Ellie started laughing and even though I just wanted to shout out FUCK, I started to put Ellie back down. She had a huge smile on her face that only made me smile right back at her.

"Was that what you were looking for?" I asked as I gave her a wink.

She smiled and punched me in the arm. "YES! But more than anything I love the way you pick me up and hold me close to you." Right on cue……the blush crept up her cheeks. I'll never get tired of seeing that color on her face.

"That is just one of the many things I would love to do to you."

Ari honked again but this time she laid on the horn for a good five seconds. Ellie and I both laughed and started to walk out the door.

"She is probably pissed she's sitting in the jeep alone with Jefferson," Ellie said with a laugh.

After lunch we drove and picked up a few items for Brad's birthday party before heading back to the girl's cottage. Ari had sent a text message to their friend Heather and asked if she wanted to come tonight since Amanda would also be there with Brad.

"You better warn your friend Heather that Josh had his eyes on her," Jeff said with a wink towards Ari and Ellie.

"SHIT! All the bastard talked about every time I danced with him was Heather. Fucker had a hard on all night and it was *not* from dancing with me." Ari said as she pulled the last bag for the party out of her jeep and walked it over to my truck.

Somehow nothing that came out of this girl's mouth shocked me. Ari was actually a perfect match for Jeff. If only they could both see it.

"Okay well um, I guess we will see y'all later tonight right?" Jeff said has he looked between Ellie and Ari. His eyes lingered a little bit longer on Ari though…did Ari just blush?

"Yep. We have to pick up Heather on the way there but we'll be there around what, seven?" Ellie said as she just stared at me and smiled. I couldn't even think with her looking at me like that.

"Yeah, seven is good honey," Jeff said as he walked up and gave Ellie a kiss on the check. He turned and starting to walk towards Ari who was leaning up against her jeep. I saw her whole body tense up.

"I'll see ya later then." Jeff said as he reached around her and into the jeep for his tea.

Shit….for a moment there I thought he was going to lean down and kiss her. By the way Ari's body language was, she was thinking the same thing. He grabbed his tea, took a drink and winked at her. Once he turned around I could see Ari let out the breath she was holding.

I walked over to Ellie and put my mouth up against her ear. "I can't wait to see you later Sweetheart. Thank you for such a wonderful day." I kissed the side of her face before I turned and walked over to my truck.

I jumped into the truck and looked up to see her smiling at me. I had to fight the urge to jump back out and kiss her again. I waved goodbye as I pulled out of their small driveway onto the main drive leading off the property. I looked over at Jeff who had a shit eating grin on his face.

"You want to tell me what that was all about?" I asked as Jeff turned to look at me.

"I think we should invite Ellie and Ari to go to the ranch with us. Your grandmother and grandfather would love to meet Ellie," Jeff said as he started to go through my iPod.

"Funny you should mention that 'cause I was thinking about it earlier this morning when we were helping them move. You think they would both want to come?"

"I know Ellie is dying to get out into the country air. She has talked about moving to the country since she was a little girl so I know she'll be excited to go."

"What about Ari?"

Jeff let out a laugh and then looked over at me. "Ari, yeah she'll go if Ellie asks her to go. I'm not sure how that princess will do out in the country but, I sure as shit would love to find out!"

"Well damn…that's going to make for an interesting trip out to the ranch that's for sure. Let's just get you two through the party tonight shall we? By the way, back to that move you put on her reaching in to get your tea. I hope you noticed her reaction," I said as I looked over at Jeff.

"You liked that huh? I sure as shit noticed it and believe me, I intend on using that to my advantage."

I just shook my head.

"I have no doubt about that dude."

Ari and I took some time after Jefferson and Gunner left to unpack a few things and straighten up. The morning had been blissful and I felt like I was on cloud nine. Gunner had kissed me twice today and each time I felt like I was going to just melt in his arms. I definitely liked our move from friends to more than friends.

I was still nervous about it all though. I never felt like this with Ryan, not even close. The more time I spent with Gunner, the more I felt like I was stepping into a danger zone. The last three weeks without him where pure hell, and it felt so good to have him back in my life again.

Ari was being very quiet. I'm not really sure what was going on with her this afternoon. Jefferson and she got along pretty good and even bickered a few times which was a relief. I wondered if she was worried about going to the party tonight. After all, the last party at Gunner and Jefferson's house turned out pretty shitty for Ari.

Just then Ari jumped when a text came through. She bolted up and grabbed her cell off of the breakfast bar. Her face immediately fell.

"What's wrong? Is it bad news or something?" I asked her as I walked into the kitchen to grab a bottle of water.

"Oh um no…..not at all, it's actually from Jason. Looks like they landed in France a little bit ago and he was just checking to see how my day's been. Sweet huh?" Ari said with a small smile.

"Yep, that is sweet. You telling him we are going to Brad's party tonight?"

"I wasn't going to. I mean he doesn't own me, I don't have to tell him my every damn move!" Ari snapped back at me and walked off.

What the hell was that about? Ari was sitting on the sofa typing out a text message back to Jason. Gesh….she was in a mood all of a sudden.

"What the fuck? Are you fucking kidding me?" Ari shouted as she looked up at me. I was walking back into the living room and stopped in my tracks.

"Holy hell, he just told me I should probably stay home. Who the fuck does he think he is?"

WOW, I don't think I've ever heard someone tell Ari what to do. Stupid move Jason…..

"What're you going to tell him?" I asked as I sat down next to her. She was texting so fast I could practically see the steam coming from her fingers!

"I just told him he has *no* right telling me what I can and can't do. I mean holy fuck. I just spent the last three weeks of my life devoted to him one hundred percent. Now he goes to Europe and he expects me to sit home and wait for him. I told him sorry, that's not how I roll. If he doesn't like it he can fuck off!"

I had to let out a giggle. A part of me was thinking Ari was hoping he would fuck off. Her phone beeped again and she read the message. Her whole body just sunk down in the sofa. Oh no… maybe he was telling her to fuck off?

"What did he say Ari?"

Ari let out a sigh and looked at me. "He told me I was right, he had no right telling me what I can and can't do and that I should go and have a good time."

"And this makes you unhappy? Isn't that what you wanted him to say?"

"Of course it is! I mean yeah, of course it is. I guess I should wish him a good time," Ari said as she gave me a weak smile.

Okay….I was confused.

"Yeah you probably should. He's probably already missing you."

"Gesh….he said they're leaving in the morning for their first hike so he won't be able to be in contact with me for a few days at a time until he can get a signal. Huh….what a shame. Anyway, I think I'm going to go get ready. Do you have any idea of what you're wearing tonight?" Ari said.

I had to laugh. There is no way she was into Jason at all. I would be devastated if that was Gunner.

"Nope, I have not even thought about it. Want to help me pick something out?"

"Hells yeah I do! Come on, my closet first!" Ari said as she grabbed me and dragged me to her bedroom.

Ari and I spent the next two hours or so picking out what we were going to wear, taking showers and primping. Ari called Heather and told her what time we were leaving to pick her up. I still couldn't believe Amanda was dating Brad. Ari filled Heather in on Josh and I could hear Heather laughing through the phone. I was pretty sure I heard the words man whore in there somewhere.

Gunner had sent me three text messages since he got back home. The first one said he was back home safe and sound and they were getting the house ready for tonight. The second said he was thinking about me, and the third said he couldn't wait to hold me in his arms again. I felt the heat in my cheeks as I read the last one.

Is he really for real? Sometimes I feel like I'm going to wake up from this dream to find out I'm still living at home with my mother and Gunner never existed.

"You ready to go Chica? Because I'm ready to party! I have not been to a party since….. well….fuck since the last Jefferson disaster party!" Ari said with a laugh.

I started to laugh at how much of a good mood Ari was in from compared to a few hours ago.

"I'm ready, let's go!"

Ari was wearing a blue jean mini skirt with a pink sleeveless shirt along with her pink cowboy boots. Her hair was pulled up in a low pony and she had on a pink cowboy hat. I had on a white short dress with my plain simple cowboy boots. Unlike Ari, who owned ten pair of boots in every color, I opted for just one pair of simple brown boots. I decided to put my hair up also since I'm sure we would be spending most of the night in the backyard dancing.

"Oh, Jeff sent me a text asking us to pick up plastic cups so we need to stop at HEB to grab some," Ari said as we made our way out to her jeep.

Was she skipping?

"So what got your mood turned around Ari?" I asked as I climbed into the jeep.

Ari threw her head back and laughed. "I'm going to a party instead of the damn country club for dinner! God love Jason but he needs to loosen up a little! But hey….while the cat's away….the mice will play!" Ari said with another laugh as she wiggled her eyebrows up and down.

By the time we stopped and picked up Heather, and then the cups for Jefferson, we ended up getting to Gunner's place around 7:45. Ari pulled in and parked behind Jefferson's truck. As soon as we walked in the front door Gunner had me in his arms and was lifting me up again for a kiss. I'm not sure why but every time he did that it made me giggle.

"God I love the sound of your laugh!" He reached down and gave me a quick peck on the lips. The moment he put me down I was disappointed. Good lord, I needed to get a grip. I couldn't be acting like this, needing more and more of him every time I saw him. I would have liked a better kiss though.

Gunner grabbed my hand and led me into the kitchen where Jefferson, Brad, Josh and some other guy I'd never seen before were talking. Gunner grabbed a beer out of the fridge and handed it to me after he opened it. Then he introduced me to their friend.

"Jon, this is Ellie, Ellie this is Jon." I reached out my hand to shake his and our eyes met mine. WOW…he had the most amazing green eyes. I tried to pull my hand away but he held onto it another few seconds. The way he was looking at me instantly made me feel uncomfortable. He looked me up and down and then finally let go of my hand.

"Ellie, Gunner has told me a lot about you. It's a real pleasure to meet you finally." He said as he smiled at me with a smile that would knock any girl off her feet.

I looked over at Gunner who was watching my every move. "All good things I hope."

Oh Christ, what a stupid answer that was!

Jon threw his head back a little and laughed as he ran his hand through his blond hair. He was built but not as built as Gunner or Jefferson.

"Do you play football for UT also?" I asked as Gunner came up next to me and put his arm around my waist. I instantly felt the butterflies take off in my stomach and the heat from his touch pool in-between my legs. I was praying to God I was not blushing. For once I'd like to not show it on my face what Gunner's touch does to me.

Jon smiled at me and tilted his head while looking at me. What the hell? He looked down at Gunner's hand resting on my waist then back up to me.

"No my dear, I don't play football for UT. I do, however, play baseball for UT. Do you like baseball Ellie?"

My dear? Okay......why was it the way he spoke to me made me feel all weird?

"Um I guess so, but I really only ever watch football, sorry," I said with a shrug of my shoulders.

Jon let out a laugh again and looked at Gunner. "Lucky son of a bitch you are." Then he looked at me again. "We might have to just get you to start liking baseball Ellie now won't we?"

I just smiled; I didn't really know what to say to that. Gunner leaned down and whispered against my ear if I wanted to step away and I nodded my head yes. All I wanted to do was get away from this guy. I wondered if Gunner noticed the way he was looking at me. This guy totally freaked me out!

Gunner took my hand again and led me to the one place I was not expecting to go....his bedroom. My heart started to pound and my head started spinning. When he opened the door and led me in I felt like I was going to stop breathing.

OH. MY. GOD. NO! He didn't think I was going to sleep with him did he. Before I could even open my mouth Gunner had me in his arms.

"Don't think that Ellie sweetheart. I only brought you in here to give you a proper kiss in private. His ran his hand through my hair and then brought it up to the side of my face. He took the back of his hand and moved it up and down my face. All I could feel was a tingling sensation every where his hand touched. He then took both hands and cupped my face. He tilted my face up and smiled that crooked smile at me. I swear I felt my knees wobble. He leaned down and lightly brushed his lips against mine four times and it was driving me mad.

"More…."

I felt Gunner smile against my lips.

"More huh?" He asked as he let out a small laugh.

"Yes Gunner please…..I need more."

The next thing I knew Gunner's lips were back on mine and his tongue was seeking entrance into my mouth. I opened and allowed him in. He moved his hand to the back of my head and deepened the kiss so much it felt like all the air was being sucked out of my body. He slowly backed me up against the wall. Thank God because I needed something to assist me with standing before my legs buckled out from underneath me.

God I never wanted him to stop. The way he made me feel was unbelievable. I felt….cherished. When he finally pulled his lips from mine, I slowly opened my eyes to look at him. His beautiful blue eyes were looking down into mine. He slowly let a smile creep across his beautiful face. I couldn't help but smile back at him.

"Was that better Ms. Johnson?"

I let out a giggle. "Yes…yes it was Mr. Mathews. You have successfully bewitched me."

Gunner took his index finger and traced my jaw line and then ran it over my lips. My whole body trembled and the ache between my legs grew stronger. All I wanted to do was squeeze my legs together to ease it..

"I'm glad to hear I have you bewitched Sweetheart. I thought for a moment someone else might be trying to do the same thing," he said as he tapped my nose with his finger.

He did notice and that was why he brought me in here! I wanted to throw myself into his arms again and beg him to kiss me once more. I wanted to forget all about some guy flirting with me right in front of him. All I wanted to see was Gunner's beautiful eyes looking into mine.

"You ready for a party?"

"Only if you promise to keep your dance card open for me all night," I said with a smile.

"Done!" Gunner grabbed my hand and led me to his bedroom door. He spun me around and slammed me back against the door and kissed me deeply again. He pulled his lips from mine and I gasped for air.

"That's so you don't forget who has you bewitched," he said with a wink. I stepped away from the door so he could open it. My head was spinning again, but this time in a good way. As we walked out from Gunner's room and through the living room I felt eyes watching us. I looked over to the kitchen and Jon was watching Gunner and I walk by. The way he was smiling felt like he was trying to look into my soul and it sent a shiver down my back. I quickly turned my head and looked up at

Gunner who was smiling from ear to ear and leading us outside to the music.

Once we stepped outside the fresh air felt amazing. I looked around and saw Amanda, Ari and Heather all dancing. They all looked happy and that made me smile. Jeff had walked out the back door and pointed at some chairs for Gunner and me to sit at. I still had yet to take a drink of the beer that was in my hand.

"Do you want to go dance with your friends Ellie?" Gunner asked.

"Nope, I just want to sit here with you." The next thing I did was probably the boldest thing I've ever done in my life. Especially since my brother was sitting right here. Gunner sat down and I sat down on his lap before I chickened out. I think Gunner was just as surprised as my brother. I went to take a swig of my beer and then felt something…oh wow…was I making that happen? I stopped my beer right at my lips as I felt Gunner adjust me in his lap. Jefferson was busy looking at everyone dance so he didn't notice Gunner lean in and whisper against my ear.

"I'm sorry Sweetheart. I was not expecting you to do that and he kind of has a mind of his own."

I snapped my head and looked at Gunner. Did he just say that to me? He just told me I gave him a hard on. I started to laugh and leaned down and kissed him right on the lips. Jefferson or not….I wanted Gunner to know how I felt about him every second of the day.

"Jesus Christ…can you stop Ellie….I can take you sitting on his lap, but not sucking his face at the same damn time!"

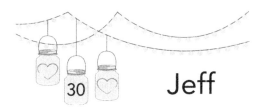

Holy mother fucking shit. I couldn't sit here and watch my baby sister suck face with my best friend while she sat on his goddamn lap. Christ a guy can only take so much. I looked back out to the dance floor and scanned for who I was looking for.

Ari…..

She was dancing with Amanda and Heather to Usher's "Yeah." Damn she could move. I wanted to know what she felt like in my arms dancing. They looked like they were heading over to get something to drink. I got up and walked over to Jack and asked him to play a certain song next. He nodded and I went and sat back down. Ari was drinking a beer and some of it ran down her lip onto her chin. Mother fucker……this girl has been getting my dick hard since I was 16 years old. She looked down at me as she wiped her chin.

"You been drinking long?" I asked as I smiled at her.

"Think you could teach me a better way to do it dickwad?" she said back to me with that damn sexy smile of hers. I didn't care how many times she called me names….as long as she was talking to me. I lucked out with douche bag Jason Reed out of town. Jack started up Rascal Flatts' "What Hurts the Most" right then. I jumped up and took the beer out of her hand and handed it to Gunner.

"Dance with me…..please."

She looked stunned but nodded her head yes. I took her hand and led her out to where a few other people were dancing. I pulled her into my arms and goddamn if she didn't fit perfect up against my body. I had not held Ari this close to me since she was 11 years old and fell trying to rollerblade.

I put my face into her hair and took a deep smell. I had to memorize every detail of how she felt, how she smelled and looked right at this moment. I felt her relax more and more in my arms. I prayed that she was listening to the song….she wouldn't ever let me apologize for my behavior and this was the best I could think of last minute. I pulled her closer to me as the words to the song played that I wished so badly I could say to her.

I felt her grip harder onto me and all I wanted to do was kiss her. God I wanted to kiss her so fucking bad…..she smelled like vanilla. Had she always smelled like that? I just held her tight against me while we danced.

The song was going to end soon so I leaned down and whispered in her ear.

"I'm so sorry I hurt you Baby. If I could take it all back I would do it in a heartbeat. I never want to hurt you again Arianna.....ever. It kills me you didn't get your special moment. I'll never forget that I took that away from you. I'm sorry."

I pulled away and looked down into her face.

Fuck...she was crying.......

"Jefferson I need to tell you something, and you're probably going to hate me after I tell you," she said in between sobs.

"Baby I could never hate you."

The song ended and we were just standing there. I reached up and tried to wipe away the tears that were falling down her face like rain.

"I....I never slept with Jason. I just told you that because I wanted to hurt you as much as you hurt me. I'm....I'm still a virgin Jeff. The moment I left that message I wanted to call you back but I was so angry still. I'm so sorry. I just wanted to hurt you as much as you hurt me." Ari spoke so fast I hardly was able to process what the hell she was saying.

Holy mother fucking shit.....I spent almost a damn month punishing myself for something that never happened.

I closed my eyes silently thanking God she didn't sleep with that asshole. Then I opened them and saw her staring up at me. I just smiled at her. If she had set out to hurt me, she did a good job of it.

"Well Squirt, it worked. I um, I need to go check on the food and everything. I'll talk to you later okay."

I turned and walked away from the one person I would always love.... but never be able to have.

The moment Jeff turned and walked away I wanted to go after him. Oh god...I just wanted to shout out MOTHER FUCKER as loud as I could! I didn't want to draw attention to myself so I just stood there, because you know....... standing in the middle of their backyard with tears running down my face wasn't going to draw any attention.

Fuck me!

Holy hells bells....the way he was holding me so close during that song....I knew the moment he asked me to dance what he was trying to do. It was his way of saying he was sorry.

I'm so sorry I hurt you Baby......... Baby I could never hate you......

I have waited eight fucking years for this.......eight years for him to call me something other than squirt, to hold me like he never wanted to let me go. Son of a fucking bitch!

Oh. My. God. I just messed up everything......I looked over at Ellie who was now getting off of Gunner's lap and walking over to me.

"Ari what did he say to you? I'll kill him for making you cry again that bastard!" Ellie shouted as she looked back towards the door Jeff just walked through.

I started to laugh. Why I have no idea....I found none of this shit funny. Ellie looked at me confused as hell.

"Ari what the hell is going on?"

"Oh nothing Ells....you know......Jeff just did the most fucking romantic thing anyone has ever done for me.....and I blew it. I fucking blew something I've been wanting for so long." I started to cry again. *Goddamn it*....the second time I've been to one of their parties and I'm crying! JESUS, MARY, AND JOSEPH!

"Come on, let's go sit on the front porch....." Ellie said as she turned to Gunner and pointed to the front of the house. Gunner looked concerned but just nodded his head like he understood.

"He's in the house...I can't let him see me crying Ells," I said as I panicked at the idea of seeing Jeff right that second.

"We'll walk through the gate okay?" Ellie linked her arm with mine and we walked to the front porch.

After I told her what Jeff said to me and how I told him the truth about Jason, she just sat back in the swing.

"Ari, clearly Jeff has feelings for you sweets. You have to see that right. Why didn't you go after him?"

"I don't know why I didn't Ellie. I mean, it's like he wants to be with me, but he doesn't. I don't know how else to explain it….I feel like he is attracted to me but he does nothing to act on it. Maybe he just can't see me as anything more than his little sister's best friend Squirt. He even called me Squirt before he turned and walked away. It killed me when he said that it worked……that me trying to hurt him worked."

"Well of course it worked. You had to know when you told him he would be upset. Give him time Ari. Maybe he just needs time to get used to the idea of you being something other than my best friend. What you need to do is show him that's not all you are. You're more than Arianna…Ellie's best friend….You're more than just Squirt………You need to make him want you Ari….want you bad! You need to show him how much he wants to be with you!"

Ellie said with a wicked smile on her face. We both started to laugh. Only Ellie could make me feel better when I felt like shit.

"Okay I have other news! So while you were dancing, Gunner asked if we both wanted to go to his grandparent's ranch next week for a few days. I SO want to go but I need you to go with me. Please say you will go!"

Ellie was so fucking cute when she begged! "Of course I'll go with you. Is um…..Jeff going?"

Ellie smiled that big ole smile of hers. "You bet he's going! Five full days of us in the country with two *really* good looking guys *and* the Llano River runs right through it…..I'm thinking Jeff might need to see you in your red bikini! "

"Well, when you put it that way…count me the fuck in!"

We both started laughing so hard we couldn't stop. So Ellie thought I should go after Jeff huh? I think I was up for that challenge! Just then the front door opened…….. speak of the devil……it was Jeff.

He opened the door all the way and stepped outside. "Is everything okay? Why are y'all sitting out here?"

"Well, we were just talking about how much *we* were looking forward to heading out to the country with you and Gunner," I said as I got up and walked towards Jeff.

Now it was his turn to be stunned. I walked up to him and leaned in so he had to bend down towards me to hear what I was about to say.

"I can't decide if I want to bring my red bikini or my white one? I might just have to bring both. What do you think Jeff?"

He looked like he was having a really hard time swallowing and if I didn't know any better I would say that Mr. Big football player was blushing. Oh yes…I thought to myself how much I liked Ellie's plan as I let a smile play across my face.

Game on Jeff………….

32 Gunner

Things must be okay with Ari because Ellie and Ari came through the front door giggling like school girls. Jeff was walking behind them and looked at me and just shrugged. I was standing in the kitchen talking to Brad and Amanda. I looked back up and saw Jon walking over to Ari and Ellie. What was that fucker up to? I watched as he put his hand on Ellie's arm. I immediately saw her tense up.

I couldn't tell what they were talking about but Ellie kept shaking her head no but held a polite smile on her face. He then leaned down closer to the side of her face and said something that made her laugh.

"Dude, are you even listening to me?" Brad said as he pushed my shoulder back. I tore my eyes away from Ellie and Jon and looked at Brad.

"Oh yeah sorry, I was distracted by something," I said as I looked back over to towards Ellie. Jon was clearly up to something that fucker.

"Listen Gunner, you better keep an eye on Jonathon Barker. That fucker is a man whore. Once he sees something he wants he won't stop at anything until he gets it in his bed," Brad said as he stared over at Jon and Ellie.

"I know all about Jon, but thanks for the warning Brad. Looks like he has his eyes on the one thing that he will not be taking to bed so if you will excuse me, Amanda, Brad….I have a girl to save," I said as I started to walk over towards Ellie.

I felt the heat moving up my body the more I watched him try to move closer and closer to her. I noticed Ellie take a step backwards away from Jon. I was already fisting my hands up so I needed to get a grip. When I walked up behind him I heard what he was saying.

"I really wish you would change your mind my dear and dance with me. I would really love to get to know you better."

Mother fucker…..in my own fucking house going after *my* girl, oh hell no. I looked over at Jeff and gave him a nod….if I lost it he better be fucking ready to pull me the hell off of this prick. Jeff was on his way over and walked up to Ari and whispered something in her ear. Jon didn't even notice Jeff walk up.

"Hey Sweetheart, are you ready for that dance?" I never took my eyes off of Ellie for one second the entire time I walked over to where they were standing. Ellie had seen me walking over and gave me the smile I would move heaven and earth to see every second of the damn day.

I slapped Jon on the back....hard.....causing his beer to spill a little onto the hard wood floor. He looked pissed but once he saw it was me he relaxed. Fucker better not think I'm harmless because I will break him in two.

Ellie tried to hide her giggle. "I'm more than ready for that dance!" Ellie said with a smile.

"Well, hold on a minute my dear...I just asked you to dance and you said no. Now you're just going to go running off and dance with Gunner? What's the deal?" Jon said with a laugh. Ari took Ellie by the arm and started to lead her away. Jeff must have told her to when he walked up. Ellie looked confused.

"It's okay Sweetheart, go on outside with Ari, I'll be right there," I said as I leaned down and kissed her cheek.

Once they started to walk away I turned and stood in front of Jon. He was giving me a shit eating grin, fucker.

"Hey bro, it was all harmless...I just wanted to dance with her that's all," Jon said as he took a sip of his beer.

"Listen Jon, I put up with your shit because you're friends with Josh and that's the only reason why. I don't really give two shits who you hit on, but if you ever lay a finger on Ellie again or call her anything other than Ellie, I will break both your arms and you'll never play baseball again? Do you understand.....*BRO?*"

Jon started to laugh. "Okay sure dude whatever, but in my defense, I always thought you were the fuck 'em and leave 'em kind of guy. You've never kept them around for more than a few dates."

Just then I hear a gasp and looked up. Ellie was still standing there and Ari was trying to get her to go outside. She had a look of horror on her face. FUCK! This fucking prick....I was going to kill him.

I was ready to punch the shit out of him and Jeff must have sensed it.

"Whoa...hey dude....You're one to talk. I think you need to either knock it the fuck off or leave our house. You don't talk like that to my best friend and you sure as shit don't talk like that with my sister right here you got it?" Jeff said as he stepped in between Jon and me. Jon gave me a fucking grin again.

"Sure you're right....sorry Gunner man, didn't mean to get you all upset. Put those Guns away dude. I'll stay clear of her for as long as she's your girl."

"You're goddamn right you will!" I practically shouted.

"Gun, man just cool off.....you need to go talk to Ellie. Ari got her to go outside."

I gave that prick one more look and started to walk off. I hit his shoulder as hard as I could as I walked by.

Fucking great...now what was Ellie going to think about me after this prick pretty much just painted me out to be no better than him.

When I walked outside Ellie, Ari and Heather were talking and laughing. Maybe everything was okay. She wouldn't believe that asshole would she? I mean, I'm not saying I haven't slept with my share of girls but fuck....it's not like I was a man whore. Fuck, I think Jeff has hooked up a hell of a lot more than I have.

Just then the music changed to an oldie but goodie. Christina Aguilera's "Dirrty" started playing and I smiled and made my way over to Ellie.

She smiled at me as soon as she saw me walking up to her. Fuck, it just about brought me to my knees. I leaned down and asked against her ear. "Please tell me you don't believe him. I'm not like that I promise you."

Next thing I knew Ellie's smiled turned to a very sexy grin. She started dancing....and I mean she was *dancing*. I did the only thing I could think of....I grabbed her and pulled her closer to me. She started to move her hips as she looked up at me with those beautiful blue eyes.

FUCK ME....I had no idea this girl could dance like this. She turned around in my arms and started grinding against me and I thought I was going to fucking explode. She reached up and put her hand behind my neck as she looked back at me with the most seductive look I had ever seen in my life. I moved my hands up and down her body and never in my life did I feel my dick this fucking hard. Holy shit this girl had the power to just blow me over. My whole body felt like it was on fire from her body being so close to mine.

She closed her eyes as she moved her ass as close to my dick as she could get. I didn't give a flying fuck that I was so hard. I'm not sure how long we danced like that before she finally turned around and faced me. I silently was hoping to God that Jeff was still in the house not seeing this right now. I'm pretty sure my face was giving away the fact that I wanted this girl more than my next breath. Next thing I knew, Ellie had her arms around me and was moving against me like nothing I'd ever experienced. Fuck I hope she never danced with Ryan this way. The way she was dancing...... it looked so fucking hot...her hands were moving up and down her body and then she put her hands on my chest and started to move.........

I had to stop. Holy shit....I had to stop before I did something I was going to regret. I began to push Ellie a little bit away from me. I needed to break this contact right now. Just then the music changed.

Oh thank the fuck.....I stood there as I ran my hands through my hair.

"Holy fuck Ellie, I think I need a beer and I know I need to sit down." Ellie let out a laugh and reached up to kiss me. Her lips where so soft and it was one of the most tender kisses I've ever received.

She smiled against my lips.

"*That* was to make sure you remembered that *only you* have bewitched me Mr. Mathews."

Right at that moment it hit me and it hit me harder than I would have ever expected it to.

I loved Ellie.

I loved her more than I loved anything in this world. She would forever be my whole life.

I stood there as Gunner looked at me....no....he was staring at me like he was trying to crawl into my soul. Then, slowly that damn crooked smile of his spread across his face. My heart started to pound. There was something so different about the way he was looking at me. I felt kind of bad because I know I just turned him on big time by dancing with him like that. Ari had requested that song and it was perfect timing for it to start because Gunner had just walked out. He looked angry when he first came out and I knew I had to set his mind at ease.

When I first heard Jon say that about Gunner sleeping around I started to panic, and felt a little sick to my stomach. Ari pulled me outside and she and Heather set me straight. I knew Gunner had been with girls before me. Jefferson had already told me Gunner never had a real serious relationship and dated maybe four or five girls off and on the whole time he knew him. I didn't for one moment think he slept around.

I looked over at Ari who gave me the thumbs up along with a smile. Okay...I wasn't the only one who noticed Gunner's moment of not being able to move.

"So, do you want to go get that beer and have a seat?" I asked trying to yell over the music that was now playing again.

Gunner just kept looking at me. "Gunner? Hello?"

Ari walked up and leaned into me and shouted in my ear. "I guess all the fucking blood left his brain and went to his dick!"

I couldn't even say anything to that. All I could do was laugh because I think she was right.

"GUNNER!" I shouted.

"Yep....okay....yeah....um....let's get a beer and sit down. I need to fucking sit down." Gunner said as he started to walk over to where Jefferson was sitting and talking to some girl who had her back faced towards me.

When we walked up Gunner reached into the cooler and grabbed two beers. He handed one to me as he sat down. He reached up and grabbed my waist and pulled me down onto his lap. I guess this will be his new favorite way to sit with me. I let out a giggle because it sure as shit was my new favorite way!

Just then I heard her voice. It almost made me want to throw up in my mouth.

"Jesus Gunner, you ought to think about getting a room next time you try to practically fuck Jeff's little sister on the dance floor."

Jefferson spun his head around and looked at Crysti, then at Gunner and me. Then I noticed Rebecca sitting next to Jeff. Oh shit....I immediately looked on the dance floor for Ari. She was dancing away with some guy and Amanda and Brad.

OH SHIT! OH SHIT! OH SHIT!

I gave Jefferson a "What the fuck are you doing" look. He just looked back at me and then out towards Ari and back at Crysti.

"Fuck off you bitch," Jefferson said to Crysti.

WOW! I wasn't expecting that.

"Yeah Crysti, I don't remember sending an invite to you and your little whore friend here," Gunner said as he downed his beer.

"GUNNER!" I said as I looked at him in shock.

"I'm sorry Ellie, that was rude of me wasn't it? Why don't y'all go on over and say hi to Jon and the rest of the baseball team. I'm sure they would love to ....party with y'all."

Crysti just glared at me. What was she giving me such a dirty look for?"

"Gunner's right Rebecca, it's time you moved along," Jefferson said as he reached for another beer and handed one to Gunner. Boy Gunner and Jefferson sure where drinking a lot tonight.

"Jeff! You haven't even called me since, well you know since when. Why? I thought we had something going?" Rebecca said with a whine in her voice.

Jefferson sat up straight and looked nervous as hell. I followed his eyes and saw Ari walking over with Heather. She had yet to notice Rebecca standing there.

"I think it would be best Bec if you just moved on and forgot about that night. That was a mistake and it's never going to happen again."

Jefferson never took his eyes off of Ari the whole time he told Rebecca to basically shove off.

"Wait one minute. Wait just one goddamn fucking minute. Do you like this bitch or something? Did you fucking use me to make her jealous? We had something Jeff, why can't you just admit that there was a connection?"

Ari now was standing directly in front of Jefferson looking at him. She slowly looked at Rebecca when she called Ari a bitch.

Gunner leaned over and whispered in my ear "And I thought I was the only one who wanted to beat someone's ass tonight. Ari looks ready to rip her hair out!"

I couldn't help it, I laughed.

"Rebecca come on, he's so not worth it. Let the little girl try and play with the big boys. Come on, I see Jon Barker is here….let's go have some fun," Crysti said as she tried to pull Rebecca away.

"No! I want to know right now you mother fucker….did you use me?" Rebecca shouted at Jefferson.

Jefferson ran his hands through his hair and sighed. Ari did something I was not expecting her to do.

She walked closer to Jefferson and started to laugh at Rebecca.

"It's a damn good thing this little girl knows how to play with the *big boys* isn't that right Baby?" Ari said as she walked over sat down and straddled Jefferson and then kissed the living shit out of him.

I'm sure I wasn't the only one who sat there stunned.

"HOLY FUCK!" Gunner said with a laugh.

Rebecca just stood there for a second and watched as Ari kept up the kiss. Jefferson sure was not stopping Ari as he reached up and cupped her face.

When I guess she had seen enough Rebecca looked at Crysti. "Come on let's leave."

Ari pulled away from Jefferson and looked up at Rebecca and smiled. Jefferson just sat there staring at Ari with a very confused look on his face.

"You can fuck off Jeff. Don't ever call me again you mother fucker. I hope you enjoy your little girl!" Rebecca said as she stomped off with Crysti right behind her. They went through the back gate so they must have been leaving the party for good.

Ari watched them leave and then turned to look at Jefferson. She smiled down at him.

"You're welcome!" She said as she hopped up and grabbed a beer.

"What….what the fuck was that all about?" Jefferson asked as he was desperately trying to get his breathing under control.

Ari shrugged. "You obviously wanted her to leave you alone so, I just gave her a reason to leave you alone. No big deal."

Jefferson sat there a minute with his hands just running through his hair and then down his face. He looked over at Ari and then back towards the house.

"Umm, I need to go check on something," Jefferson said as he jumped out of his seat and made a beeline for the house. Ari looked over at me and Gunner and we all laughed.

"Well played Ms. Peterson….well fucking played," Gunner said as he took his beer and hit it with Ari's.

Ari smiled at me and gave me a wink. I just shook my head. This girl actually knew what the hell she was doing.

Poor Jefferson, he didn't stand a chance.

34 Gunner

I sat there with Ellie sitting on my lap and I was in pure heaven. Listening to her and Ari talk and laugh, I was never more content. Every time she laughed or smiled I stopped breathing.

I love her……..

I had to smile every time I thought about how my world just turned upside. I knew Ellie still wanted to take things slow but, goddamn if I didn't want to just tell her, to just shout it out for the world to know.

Ari asked if Ellie wanted to dance and she looked down at me. "You mind?"

"No! Go and have fun. I'll just sit here and wait for Jeff to come back from whatever it was that he had to take care of," I said as I wiggled my eye brows up and down and smiled at Ari.

Ari laughed but Ellie didn't think that comment was too funny.

"Oh for the love of all things good….that's my brother Gunner! EEEWWWW gross!" Elli got off my lap and slapped my arm. I laughed and pulled her back down to me and whispered up against her ear, "Don't let Jon get anywhere near you okay?"

She looked at me with such a sweet and tender smile.

"Okay Babe!"

She got up and walked out into the yard and hugged Amanda and started dancing. Holy fuck….she just called me babe. I sat back in my chair and drank my beer while I watched her. I looked over towards where Jon was standing and noticed the fucker watching her also. I finished off my beer and grabbed another one.

"Jesus dude, you trying to get drunk. You got Ells back so what's the reason for getting wasted?" Jeff said as he grabbed another beer from the cooler.

"Fuck off...I'm celebrating douche bag." I looked over at Jeff and smiled. "So, what was it you needed to take care of so fast?" I said with a laugh.

"Very funny dick head but that's not what I was doing. Gunner, I swear that girl is going to be the death of me! I had to get away from her before I tore her fucking clothes off. I can't believe she did that to me. Shit! I saw Josh in the house and had to sit there and listen to him go on and on about Heather so I could try to lose my hard on."

I threw my head back and laughed. "That must have been entertaining."

"Fuck....to say the least. Dude has it bad for that girl. Jesus, I never in my life saw Josh this interested in a girl and this fucking nervous to actually talk to her."

"Yeah he has it pretty bad for her. Stupid fucker has not even talked to her all night. Speaking of stupid fuckers......what are you going to do about Ari?"

Jeff took a drink of his beer as he looked out towards Ari and Ellie dancing.

"Nothing."

"What the fuck do you mean nothing?"

"I mean nothing. I'm not going to do anything. She told me tonight that she never slept with Jason which was a relief because I would've hated myself the rest of my life knowing she just slept with him to get back at me. So, now that I know we're alright, I'm just going to move on," Jeff said as he took another drink of his beer. This time he damn near finished it.

"You've got to be fucking kidding me," I said as I shook my head and looked at him. "Jeff, can you not see that she has a thing for you. I mean holy hell, that kiss she gave you I'm pretty damn sure was more than just for show. Why do you insist on pushing her away?"

Jeff stared out at Ari. She looked over once and smiled and Jeff turned away. "I can't do it Gunner. I cannot risk losing her. If things didn't turn out she would be gone for good. I don't think I could live my life if she was not in it......even if that just means being friends."

I pushed my hand through my hair and let out a sigh. Looks like their mother not only fucked up Ellie's thinking of how love is, she fucked up Jeff's too.

"Jeff, I get that you don't want to lose her. I mean I *REALLY* get it," I said as I looked over at Ellie and smiled. "But what are you going to do when she gets tired of waiting for you. When she ends up with someone like Jason Reed? She'll get married; have kids, live a life that in the long run you will not be a part of. Do you think you can handle that? Are you going to be ready for that when it happens?"

Jeff tipped his head back and finished off his beer. "I don't know Gunner. I honestly don't fucking know dude."

"Well Jeff you better fucking figure it out, and do it soon. That girl is not going to just sit around and wait for you. If you want her....you better fight for her and let her know how you feel." I finished off my own beer and got up and walked towards Jack....I needed to dance with Ellie.

"Hey Jack, You got any Vince Gill?" I yelled into his ear over the music.

"You know I do! What are you looking for?"

"I want you to play 'Whenever You Come Around' next okay?"

Jack gave me that big ole smile of his and nodded. "You got it dude."

I walked back over to Jeff. Fuck I was starting to get a little drunk. I sat down and looked at him. I was going to bite the fucking bullet.

"I love her."

Jeff snapped his head and looked at me. "Ellie?"

"Of course Ellie, who the fuck else would I be talking about!"

Jeff just smiled at me. "When did this come about?"

"Earlier. It just fucking hit me like a brick wall. Scared the fuck out of me and it was a good three or four minutes before I could even talk or move." I looked over at Ellie who was now just standing in the middle of the dance crowd talking to Heather and Ari. God, there wasn't a damn thing I wouldn't do for her.

"Gunner, you know I trust you with my sister, I really do. I love you like a brother and there is nothing on earth I would rather see than my sister happy with you. Just take care of her dude, don't hurt her and please just be patient. She's been through a lot you know? Just....just don't push her into anything too fast okay?"

I looked over at Jeff. "I would die first before I let anything or anyone hurt her. I need you to know that Jeff. I really need you to know that I love her, and I will protect her with everything I have."

Jeff got up and slapped my back. "Well fuck dude....that's all I needed to hear. No wonder you're getting drunk!"

Just then Jack started to talk.

"Alright y'all, I'm going to slow it down again with a little Vince Gill."

I got up and walked towards Ellie who was now heading my way.

"Sweetheart dance with me?" I asked as I ran my hand down her face.

"Of course I will Gunner." She smiled at me and my knees just about went out from under me. Would these intense feelings every settle down?

The song started and I pulled her as close to me as I could. She buried her head in my chest and held me tighter. We danced slowly to the song as I started to sing the lyrics to her as I held onto her.

I loved this girl, and I'll spend the rest of my life proving to her how much I love and want her.

Ellie looked up at me with tears running down her face and my heart just stopped.

"Oh baby please don't cry, please, please don't cry." I said as I wiped away her tears.

"Gunner, I.....I've never felt like this before…you're so amazing and the things you say and do just leave me breathless. I'm so afraid I'm going to wake up and to find out this is all just a dream."

I smiled down at her and pulled her back into me as we finished dancing to the song while I sang along with Vince. "I promise Sweetheart, this is not a dream."

Everyone was slowly starting to leave Gunner and Jeff's place around 1 am. Jack had packed up long before and Jefferson just had the stereo playing for the last two hours.

I was a bit shocked at how much Gunner and Jefferson both drank. Ari was well on her way to being drunk. Because I'd had a few beers we decided to just spend the night here. Heather got a ride home with Amanda and Brad. Amanda was only drinking sodas all night since it was Brad's birthday party and she knew he would be drinking.

I started to clean up when I felt Gunner come up behind me and wrap his arms around me waist.

"Sweetheart we have someone come in and clean up. Come sit with me for a little bit," he said as he leaned in close to my face. The heat from his mouth set my whole body on fire. God the ache between my legs when he was this close to me was almost too much to take.

I turned around and smiled up at him. "Okay, inside or out?"

He returned my smile and took my hand. We walked past Jefferson and Ari who were at the moment complaining about who had to sleep on the sofa....Jefferson or Gunner or Me and Ari.

"Why the hell can't you just sleep with me in my bed? I promise to keep my hands to myself," Jefferson said to Ari with a wicked laugh.

"Yeah right dickwad...I may be drunk....but I ain't that drunk. You're on the sofa....I'm taking your bed," Ari said as she walked past Jefferson and walked to his bedroom.

Gunner and I went outside and sat down next to the coolers. He reached in for a beer.

"Umm, Gunner how much more are you going to drink?" I asked as he stopped the bottle before it even hit is lips.

"Why? You afraid I might get too drunk and take advantage of you tonight?" He said with a wink. I instantly felt my face blush. He let out a chuckle and took a drink of the beer.

"No, I'm not worried about that at all. I don't really think you're that drunk. Are you?" I asked as I looked down towards the ground.

"Ellie, I just wanted to celebrate tonight that's all. Come here and sit on my lap again......"

After all those years of watching my mother drink the last thing I wanted was to worry about Gunner drinking all the time.

"I know what you're thinking Ells and no, I don't drink like this all the time okay Sweetheart? I was just so happy that we're together and well....I just wanted to let my guard down a little tonight. I promise I do not make a habit of getting drunk."

Gunner downed his beer. I could tell he was getting wasted but he looked so damn cute.

"Are you excited about going to the ranch Ellie?" Gunner asked as he moved his hand up and down my back. My god his fingers tips had magic inside them. I could hardly breathe let alone think.

I took a deep breath and tried to clear my head. "*Yes*! I'm very excited. I've always wanted to go to a ranch and see lots of cows and ride a horse. Oh please say we can ride a horse," I said as I bounced in Gunner's lap.

"Fuck Ellie please don't move like that okay?" Gunner adjusted me on his lap and I of course felt the heat rise up in my cheeks.

"Oh...I'm sorry. How many girls have you brought out to meet your grandparents?" I asked as I looked at his eyes slowly starting to droop lower and lower.

"What?"

"You know, how many girls have you brought out to the ranch." Gunner's head looked like it was moving in slow motion as he looked at me.

"None....I've never brought anyone out to the ranch 'cept for Jeff and Brad and Josh.....never brought no girls there. I was waiting for you Ellie. Only you."

Oh wow, if that didn't make my heart start beating faster. I mean I knew he was drunk but I also knew he meant what he said.

"I want to kiss you Ellie.....but I don't think I can right now 'cause I might want to do more than kissing," Gunner said now with more of slur.

I had to giggle. "Like what kind of *more?*" I knew I shouldn't be going there but......I was.

Gunner gave me the most adorable grin. Just when I thought his panty melting crooked smile did it to me, there was nothing on his boyish drunk grin.

"Let's see...for starts. I would want to kiss you in more places than on your ips."

"My ips?"

"Your llllllipppsss. L.I.P.S...."

"Okay. Where would you move to after you kissed my L.I.P.S?"

"Hmmm, your neck and then down your throat to your chest and after I gave your chest enough attention I'd move to your stomach."

Holy mother fucking shit.......I never in my life wanted anyone like I wanted Gunner right at this moment. What the hell was going on with me?

"Umm...then what would you do?"

Oh shit I was treading in very deep water.

Gunner smiled up at me. "Ms. Johnson, are you flirting with me? Cause I have to tell you if we keep having this conversation any further, Jeff is going to beat my ass when I take you right here."

I can't breathe, deep breaths....through your nose...out your mouth Ellie......my god......my mouth is so dry. I leaned over and grabbed a bottle of water out of the cooler.

"Do you know how fucking beautiful you are Ellie? I can't wait to lie under the stars with you next week. I can't wait to show you everything about country living. I want to show you another first....lots of firsts while we are there Sweetheart."

"I can't wait either Gunner. I'm really excited especially knowing it will be you showing me everything." I leaned in closer to Gunner and whispered into his ear. "Spending five days with you all to myself is going to be yummy."

Gunner jumped up and almost knocked me to the ground.

"What's wrong?" I asked as I tried to help him stand up straight.

"I have to go take a cold shower Ellie.....I need to get these thoughts out of my head baby."

I had to laugh as he tried to walk away and was stumbling all over the place.

"Gunner, let me help you." I tried my best to help him into the house. Christ this guy was huge, and heavy! I saw Jefferson on the sofa passed out asleep. Ari must be in his bed asleep already. I guess I was the only one who was not drunk, good thing.

I guided Gunner to his bedroom the best I could. He must have hit everything possible on the way to his room. We made it to the door and I opened it. I led Gunner over the bed and tried to help him sit but he more or less flopped on it and took me with him. He was lying on his back and I was lying on top of him.

OH. MY. GOD. He had his eyes closed but slowly opened them and looked at me with his piercing blue eyes. Holy hell....he was beautiful. Could he really be all mine? Just then I remembered what Jon had said to Gunner. I wonder how many girls he has had sex with? I'm sure more than....three....five.....six? I started to get pissed off just thinking about another girl lying with him like this but naked. ARGH!

Just then he smiled at me. I smiled back at him. "Stay with me tonight Ellie....I promise to keep my hands to myself sweetheart. I just want to see what it would be like to wake up with you next to me."

"Have you ever had a girl spend the night in your bed before Gunner?" I asked as I searched his face for his reaction to my question.

He rolled over and took me with him so that we were both lying on our sides.

"What're you really trying to ask me Baby?" Gunner said with a slight slur.

I loved it when he called me sweetheart but when he called me baby.....fuck me I just wanted to crawl into his skin.

Should I ask? I mean he is drunk and would probably tell me the truth. Do I really want to know?

"Umm, how many women have you been with in the past?" I asked as I looked away from him.

"None that have ever really mattered or meant anything Ellie," he quickly said back.

Was that supposed to make me feel better? That could mean anything..... three, seven, fifteen. Oh my god, what if he has slept with so many he doesn't even know!

"I mean how many have you slept with?"

"Ellie, I don't think it matters sweetheart because the moment I laid eyes on you I forgot everyone else. You're the only person I want in my life and in my bed from now on."

Holy hell...I accept that answer!

"You never answered my other question though."

"What was it again, I forgets?" he said with a laugh. God he was a cute drunk!

"How many girls have you had spend the night with you in your bed."

"None......"

I let out the breath I didn't even realize I was holding in.

"Another first for both of us Baby," Gunner said as he closed his eyes. Next thing I knew he was out. I managed to get out from his grip as I started to take off his boots. Did I try to undress him?

Hmmmm...that could be a lot of fun....for me anyway.

I spent the next ten minutes trying to get his pants off and I could not get him to move. I decided it might be better if they stayed on since I was going to be sleeping right next to him. I walked into his bathroom and looked around. I smiled when I saw the new toothbrush in the box. He must have bought it for me. I opened it up and used it. After I washed my face I made my way back into his room.

I stood there for a few minutes and just watched him sleep. I slowly tried to pull the covers out from underneath him but I soon gave that up as well. I walked over to the chair and grabbed the blanket that was lying on the back of the chair. It smelled heavenly. I wonder if his mom or grandmother made it for him.

I crawled into bed and tried to put the cover over both of us. Gunner moved and started to mumble something. I shouldn't have done it but I leaned in to hear what he was saying.

"Ellie..........I love you Ellie........."

Holy hell and fuck a duck. Did he just say he loved me?

Gunner

I woke up with my head pounding. Mother fucker how much did I have to drink last night. I moved slightly and felt someone lying next to me. OH NO....oh fuuuuck....what the hell did I do? I started to panic before I realized I still had my clothes on. I slowly moved and looked over my left shoulder to see my sweet Ellie lying on her right side facing me and sleeping like a baby.

I didn't want to move another inch for fear of waking her up. Holy shit...she was beautiful and she looked so peaceful sleeping. I moved just a little more so that I could turn and watch her sleep. I wanted to see her eyes the moment she opened them.

If this wasn't a fucking dream come true, Ellie, in my bed all night.

Mother fucker! I just realized I was so fucking wasted last night I don't even remember coming to bed. Why did she stay? Did I ask her to stay with me? I kind of remember asking her to stay with me. Did I spoon her at all last night? Fuck I hope I didn't try to make any moves on her. I'd never had a girl in my bed all night.

Wait....did Ellie ask me how many girls I've slept with? Did I answer her? Oh shit I hope I didn't tell her. Fuck my head was killing me. I needed some Advil and a glass of OJ in a really bad way.

No, even drunk I wouldn't be that fucking stupid to tell her how many girls I've been with. It's not like it's a huge number. I'm sure Jeff has me fucking beat by at least ten. It doesn't matter though. None of those girls could hold a candle to Ellie.

Just then she started to move. I watched her as she stretched out and then opened her eyes. Four blue eyes just staring at each other. I could die right now and be a happy son of a bitch.

There was that smile.....I couldn't help but smile back at her. My heart starting beating faster the wider her smile got.

"Good morning Sweetheart."

"Good morning Gunner." She practically purred my name.

I reached over and pushed her hair behind her ear. So fucking beautiful.....

"Drew."

"What?" Ellie asked as she looked at me confused.

"My name, it's Drew. I just wanted to hear you say my real name," I said as I leaned over and gently brushed my lips against hers.

"Your name isn't Gunner? How did you get that name then?" Ellie asked as she looked at me with a smile.

"Say it first....say my name first. I want to hear you say good morning to me."

Ellie let out a laugh. "Good morning Drew. How did you sleep?"

The feeling that sped through my body when I heard her call me by my name was unreal. Why did that affect me so damn much?

"That's two firsts for me."

Ellie laughed. "Really? And what are they?"

"Well, first off I've never had a girl spend the night with me and tell me good morning. And second, I've never had a girl call me by my real name. I wanted you to be the only one to do it."

Ellie tried to hide her face but I saw the blush creep into her cheeks. Shit I would never ever get tired of that!

She peeked up at me and started to laugh as she pushed my shoulder back.

"Tell me how you got the name Gunner."

"Well, let's see. My sophomore year I was on the punt team. There are two guys that split out and they call them Gunners. Their job is to go directly to the ball and try to make the tackle while all the other guys fan out into zones to try and funnel the guy with the ball. I played that position, gunner. My coach used me as an example once because I made the most tackles. He'd tell the guys they needed to tackle "like ole Gunner here." It stuck and from that point on everyone called me Gunner for the rest of high school. I liked it so that's what I went by."

"Everyone called you that? Even your teachers?"

"Yep...everyone called me that."

"Did your parents call you that also?"

"No....they call me Drew, so do my grandparents." I said as I pushed the same piece of hair back behind her ear.

"I like Drew.....but I like Gunner better!" Ellie said with a laugh.

"I like Gunner better too Sweetheart. But I also like the way Drew sounds coming off your lips."

I leaned down and went to kiss her more deeply this time. She pulled back from me and jumped out of my bed.

"Um, I haven't brushed my teeth yet," she said as she walked into my bathroom.

Fuck I could get used to this. Ellie waking up with me every morning and me being the first person she spoke to.

After we brushed our teeth I watched as Ellie put her hair up in a pony tail.

"Let's go get breakfast shall we? I need something for my damn headache," I said as I took Ellie's hand in mine.

"Well maybe that will teach you not to drink so much Mr. Mathews. You were pretty wasted last night!" Ellie said with a laugh.

I immediately stopped and looked at her. "I didn't um, say anything to you that was out of line or anything, did I?"

Ellie smiled up at me, shook her head no and stood on her toes to give me a kiss. I reached down and cupped her face in my hands and deepened the kiss. Ellie let out a small moan that traveled from my mouth straight to my dick.

Then I heard a scream.

Ellie jumped back and looked down the hall towards Jeff's room. I looked over at the sofa and Jeff was already gone. He must have gone for a run...mother fucker had more to drink than me. How the hell does he do that?

Ellie took off towards Jeff's room and threw the door open. I was right behind her. We both came to a halt when I saw Ari standing in her pink sleeveless shirt and underwear. Jeff was wearing the same jeans he had on last night but no shirt on.

"You MOTHER FUCKER! What the *fuck* were you doing?" Ari screamed at Jeff.

Jeff looked like he had one hell of a hangover and Ari's screaming at him was not helping. He also looked confused as hell.

Ari quickly started to put on her mini shirt and kept screaming at Jeff.

"I cannot believe that you slept in here with me! I woke up to you SPOONING ME you dirty bastard! You said you were going to sleep on the sofa and Ellie were the fuck where you all night last night?"

Now Jeff really looked confused and then he looked pissed.....at me.

Jeff looked back and forth between me, Ellie and Ari. Then he narrowed in on me. He started to walk my way and I knew instantly what he was thinking. I threw my hands up in the air.....

"WAIT! Stop Jeff, nothing happened!" It must have dawned on Ellie what Jeff was thinking because she stepped in-between both of us.

"Get the fuck out of the way Ellie right now!" Jeff hissed between his teeth.

"Jefferson STOP! *Nothing* happened between us. Nothing! I slept in his bed and that's all we did was sleep. Gunner passed out as soon as his head hit the pillow," Ellie said as she was trying to push Jeff away from me.

"Jeff knock it off man…..you know me better than that!"

Jeff took a few steps back and ran both his hands through his hair and down his face. He turned to look at Ari and his face turned white.

"Oh my god….did we….we didn't…I mean, oh holy shit." He looked down and saw that he was still dressed in jeans and he sat down on the bed.

"*What? OH MY GOD!* No we did not have SEX you fucking idiot! What kind of girl do you think I am you mother fucking dickwad? I can't believe you thought….Oh that's just classic Jeff. And in the same bed you fucked Rebecca in too. Wouldn't that have made my first time so special? Drunk and in the man whore's bed to lose my virginity, yep just like always dreamed it would be."

"Arianna just shut the fuck up for two fucking minutes while I try to figure out how I woke up holding you in my bed!" Jeff shouted at Ari.

Ellie and I just stood there stunned. Jeff looked back at me and then over at Ellie and back at me again. I just shrugged my shoulders. Fuck if I knew how he ended up in here.

"When Gunner and I came in from outside you were passed out on the sofa Jefferson, so you must have woke up in the middle of the night and came to bed. Gesh, thank God I was in with Gunner!" Ellie said with a laugh.

Both Ari and Jeff looked at Ellie and gave her a dirty look.

"What? How weird would it have been to wake up with my brother spooning me?"

Ellie and I both started laughing. Jeff just dropped his head and I could tell he was laughing.

"Fuck off all of you!" Ari said as she grabbed her purse and walked out of the bedroom.

Ellie went after Ari calling her name.

Jeff looked up at me and I walked over and sat down on his bed. We both looked like hell and I'm sure he felt as bad as I did.

"You don't remember coming in here last night dude?" I asked as I looked at him.

He smiled at me with a big shit eating grin. "Nope, no memory of that at all but….. I'll *NEVER* forget waking up with a hard on pressed into the girl of my dreams' ass!"

"Oh fuck dude……that's just not right!" I said as we both laughed.

"Fuckin' a Gunner, this is the first time I've ever had a girl in my bed, all night and I never had sex with her! I actually enjoyed waking up and smelling her right there. At least I enjoyed it for about thirty seconds before she started screaming."

"Dude, tell me. I fucking woke up in heaven this morning. If I died today I would be a happy man!" I said as we both stood up.

"Holy shit what's happening to us?" Jeff asked as we made our way out to the living room.

"Hell if I know dude…hell if I know."

Today was the day! I jumped up out of bed and made a beeline to my bathroom. It was working out perfectly living in the guest house on Ari's parents' property. We both had our own bedroom and our own bathroom and best of all….we didn't have to pay rent to live here!

I had spent the night before last over at Gunner's again. That made three nights I'd spent over there now. I don't think Jefferson was too happy about it but I assured him nothing was going on. Ari finally got over the whole thing with waking up with Jefferson. She did tell me how for one brief moment she was thrilled to feel his hard on pressed into her and I had to stop her from speaking any further. Last thing I wanted to hear about was my brother's hard on. EEEWWW!

I heard Ari grinding coffee beans and hurried up getting dressed. I put on a pair of shorts and a UT football t-shirt. Flip flops were going to be my choice for the ride out to the ranch. I was so incredibly nervous about meeting Gunner's grandparents. I noticed he hardly ever talked about his parents. He would mention his mom every now and then but never talked about his father.

Just then my phone rang. I ran over and picked it up off the nightstand. Right on time!

"Good morning Drew! How did you sleep?" I had gotten into the habit of calling Gunner by his real name first thing every morning.

"Good morning Sweetheart! I slept like shit without you here. How did you sleep?"

I let out a laugh. "I slept okay but just sleeping with you for a few nights has spoiled me. I miss waking up to your smile."

"Jesus, same here Ells, you're all I think about when I go to sleep and all I think about when I wake up," Gunner said with such tenderness in his voice.

There was not a day that did not go by that he did not make me feel cherished. I really was waiting for the floor to fall out. Things like this just didn't happen to me.

"Are you getting excited?"

"YES! I'm packed and ready to go. I absolutely cannot wait to get going. How long will it take us to drive there?" I asked as I saw Ari walk by the bedroom with her cup of coffee in hand.

"Depends on how many stops y'all want to make, but it normally is about two hours and forty-five minutes."

"I'm really nervous about meeting your grandparents. What if they don't like me? Or disapprove of you bringing girls out there! Oh my gosh, that never even crossed my mind Gunner," I said as panic started to build up inside of me.

Gunner let out a laugh. I could picture him sitting on the sofa right now and that beautiful crooked smile and him throwing his head back as he laughed. Hmmmm.....I wish I was there r-ight now.

"Ellie, I asked them before I even asked you if it would be alright to invite you and Ari out. My grandparents have a huge ranch house with four bedrooms. Jeff and I will be in one and you and Ari will be in the other. Don't worry. My grandmother is dying to meet you Sweetheart, so please do not worry."

I let out the breath I'd been holding in. I wonder what his grandparents were like. I didn't even know if they were his dad's parents or his mother's. That was something I needed to know before I met them.

"So are these your dad's parents or your mom's?' I asked Gunner as I saw Ari walk back by my door. She was talking on the phone to someone and did not look happy at all.

"I never told you? I'm sorry Ellie. They're my father's parents. I spent pretty much every summer growing up at their ranch. I love that place. My father has a brother who has three daughters who used to join me every summer and boy did we all raise hell together. They were pretty much tomboys growing up with me every summer. Man how we all used to love swimming in the Llano River, watching my Grams make her famous apple pies and tend to her flower and vegetable garden. My Gramps taught me everything about cattle."

"Do they have help on the ranch? I mean they must need help, I can only imagine how much work that must be. Is your father or uncle going to take over the ranch someday?"

Gunner let out a laugh. "Yeah they have help. Drake is the foreman and has been since I can remember. His two sons, Aaron and Dewey, are the ranch hands. They're a good bunch of guys and would do anything for my grandparents. Drake doesn't get along with my father or my Uncle Jim. Jim's oldest daughter Shannon is actually getting married in the fall here in Austin."

"Why do Drake and your father and uncle not get along?"

"Not sure but I think it has to do with the fact that they both left right after high school and never looked back. They made it pretty clear that neither one of them wanted the ranch or anything to do with the ranch. Drake and my father used to be best friends. My dad joined the Army right after high school and left everything behind, including his best friend."

I just sat there. This was the most Gunner had talked about his father since I met him.

"So, Jeff and I are going to be heading out in a few minutes. Make sure you pack a few pairs of jeans, a sweatshirt and boots okay?" Gunner said as I heard Jeff talking to him in the background. He was saying something about Ari not bringing her whole bathroom.

"Should I pack the new bikini I bought from Victoria's Secret yesterday?" I said very timidly.

"Fuck yes you should pack that or not…we could always go skinny dippin'!" Gunner said with a wicked laugh.

"You wish! See you in a little bit. Be careful driving over here."

"Always Sweetheart, talk to you soon."

I walked out into the kitchen and Ari was still on the phone. I quickly figured out she was talking to Jason. The look on her face was priceless.

"I'm not sure I'm going to have a cell signal since we will be so far out in bum fuck Egypt. Jason really, I'm a big girl I think I'll be fine……it's just going to be Ellie and Gunner and me……..I'm not one hundred percent sure if Jeff is going……..his grandparents ranch……..yep just for like four or five days I think…….he is helping his grandfather fix a few things around their ranch……..okay well have fun hiking………Yep you too……bye……."

I looked over at Ellie as I poured a cup of coffee. I raised my eyebrows and turned my head down to give her a total mom look.

"Funny…sounded like you were having to explain a lot there."

"Fuck Jason….he thinks he can tell me where and what and *who* I can hang out with. No…sorry dude that position is reserved for my dad only and even he stepped down years ago. The fact that he is even upset about Jeff being there just pisses me off!"

I started to laugh, god I loved Ari. Her mother had us watching more Katharine Hepburn movies the other night and filling our heads with her girl power lectures. I see why Ari is so strong headed.

"Why would he be upset if he knew Jefferson was going to be there?" I asked because I was more curious than anything. How could Jason even know anything about Jefferson and Ari?

Ari stopped and looked at me confused. "You know, I'm not sure why he even asked about Jeff. That is kind of weird isn't it?" Ari said as she sat down and ate a banana.

"Maybe he knows Gunner and Jeff are roommates, have you ever talked about them?" I asked as Ari looked at a text message she just got.

Ari thought about it for a moment. "I must have....how else would he even know? I mean, I've brought up Gunner only because of you but, I honestly don't remember ever talking about Jeff. Oh well, it doesn't matter....I'm not one hundred percent sure Jeff is going until I see his handsome face sitting in the truck!" Ari said with a wink as she got up and walked towards her bedroom.

"I'm going to get dressed. Jeff just sent a text saying they were on their way." Right then my phone buzzed with a text message from Gunner.

My darling Ellie....we're on our way. I can't wait to see you ;-)

I let out a small EEEPPP and ran to the bedroom to grab my suitcase. I brought it back out to the living room and Ari was walking out with her suitcase. She was wearing short....SHORT blue jean shorts with a sleeveless black top. She had on flip flops and was putting her hair in a pony tail.

"There. Do I look country enough? I mean I know Jeff is expecting me to be all dolled up and probably wanting to bring four suitcases with me so I'm keeping it to a bare minimum."

I looked at her giant suitcase and then back at her. She had very little makeup on and had taken all of nail polish off as well.

"Well, I know how hard it was for you to take a smaller suitcase Ari....are you sure you got everything?" I said with sarcasm dripping from my mouth.

"Oh holy shit you don't know how hard it was for me to pack so light. I had to really think about my outfits and what situation I might come up in on a ranch. It was plain torture. Fuck...it better be fun!"

I let out a laugh. I couldn't believe she was fucking serious! Ari looked at me with a confused look on her face.

"What the hell is so funny?" She said has she put her hands on her hips and stared at me.

"YOU! That is a HUGE suitcase and what is with taking off all your nail polish? I'm pretty sure girls who live in the country wear nail polish. Did you pack jeans? Gunner told me to bring plenty of jeans."

"Of course I packed jeans what the hell Ellie....I've been to the country before!"

Just then I heard Gunner's truck driving and music blaring from it. Christ if he played "Truck Yeah" I would kill him. We walked over to the bay window and watched them park. They both got out of the truck at the same time and they were both laughing at something. My stomach took a dive and my heart starting beating like crazy.

"Holy fuck…." Ari and I both said at the same time. We looked at each other and started laughing.

"Jesus, Mary and Joseph no guy should look that fucking hot in a pair of Wranglers and cowboy boots. I think I'm going to have an orgasm just looking at his ass in those things!"

"Shit Ari come on! That's my brother….eewwwwAAAA!" I said as I hit her in the shoulder.

"Fuck me Ellie do you not *see* Gunner? Holy shit…..that fucker is hot!"

I smiled as I watched them walk up to the house. Gunner looked hotter than hot. I had to push my legs together to ease the ache that was present….again….from just looking at him. He had on a pair of Wrangler jeans and a white t-shirt. A tight white t-shirt just like the one he was wearing the first day I met him. I could see his tattoo through the white t-shirt and part of it was sticking out from his sleeve. I wanted to trace his tribal tattoo with my finger and then my tongue.

ARGH! Ellie stop thinking like that. Oh my god what was wrong with me. I had to shake my head to clear my thoughts.

"Hmmmm YUM….I see Gunner's tattoo…..sure as shit wish Jeff had on a white t-shirt stupid fucker! I hardly got to look at his tattoos the other morning," Ari said as she wiggled her eyebrows up and down.

"Shut up you bitch! Come on let's get going before they see us both drooling all over them."

Jeff knocked on the front door but then opened it and walked in. He stopped dead in his tracks when he saw Ari.

"You're wearing *that?*" Jeff asked Ari as he looked her up and down and ran his hand through his hair.

Ari shrugged her shoulders and looked at what she was wearing.

"Yeah, why, what's wrong with what I have on dickwad?"

Gunner walked up to me and leaned down and wrapped his arms around me as he lifted me up to give me a kiss.

"You look beautiful Ells. Did you pack enough pairs of jeans Sweetheart?" He said as he slowly lowered me to the ground. I loved nothing more than when he did that. To be so close to his body was amazing. I wonder what having sex would be like with him?

Wait….What? Holy fuck, where did that come from?

"Nothing is wrong if you're going to the beach or I guess the mall or something. For Christ sakes Ari, we are going out to a fucking cattle ranch. If you bend over a little I can probably see your ass those shorts are so short."

Ari looked at Jeff and gave him that signature smile of hers. "Well it's a damn good thing this ass doesn't belong to you now isn't it. You don't have to worry about it." Ari smacked her ass with her hand and gave Jefferson a wink.

"Whatever Squirt. If you want guys looking at you like you're some kind of whore that's up to you. Let me guess the giant suitcase right here is yours?"

Ari smiled and walked up to Jefferson as he picked up her suitcase. She stood on her tippy toes and purred up at him. "Are you jealous that the other cowboys will be looking at me and fantasizing about how good of a rider I might be?"

Jefferson dropped Ari's suitcase and it almost landed on her left foot. Ari was stilling leaning in close to Jefferson as she gave him a wink.

"Be careful there Jeff...I have very important items in that suitcase that I need to take care of...certain....*needs*..."

Jefferson looked over at Gunner and me and shook his head as if he was trying to erase an image. He quickly picked up her suitcase and walked out the front door. Gunner started laughing as soon as the front door shut. I mean really.....I think Ari just entertains the hell out of Gunner. I hit his shoulder and looked at Ari.

"Arianna! That was just plain mean! You and I both know you do *not* own any such items. And you......Gunner stop laughing. It's not funny. She's going to give poor Jefferson a heart attack by the end of the week," I said as I stared at both of them. They were both trying not to laugh but doing a piss poor job of it.

"What? I have my flat iron and hair dryer in that suitcase. Those are very important items to me. Gesh Ellie, get your mind out of the gutter you perv."

Gunner reached down and grabbed my suitcase and started to head out to the truck. "Come on ladies....let's blow this Popsicle stand!"

I was so excited I could hardly stand it! I grabbed my purse and stuck my iPod and my headphones into it as quickly as I could. I followed Ari out of the house and locked the door behind me. Ari leaned over and whispered in my ear.

"DO NOT make me sit in the back seat with Jeff or I will fucking kill you!"

I started to giggle when I saw Jefferson jump in the front seat of Gunner's truck. "I think you scared the shit out of Jefferson....he wouldn't sit next to you even if you paid him to!"

Ari looked over at the truck and then back at me and we busted out laughing. Gunner walked up and picked me up and spun me around. I let out a little yell as he gave me another kiss. He smiled at me and leaned in close to my ear.

"Do you want to sit in the front with me Sweetheart? I can kick Jeff into the back seat with the whore."

I started to laugh and hit his back. "Put me down and no! I'll sit with Ari in the backseat. I think if Jefferson and Ari had to sit near each other that long they would end up killing each other, and that would ruin my first trip out to the country!"

"Agreed! Let's go baby." Gunner walked over to open the truck door for me.

Ohhh.....I secretly wished he called me baby all the time. I wasn't sure why I liked it so much. I mean...the way it came out of his mouth it just sounded so.......

"Fuck it's hot when he calls you baby," Ari said to me with a wink.

"Yeah, it is hot isn't it?"

Ari jumped into the truck and slid all the way behind Gunner's seat. Gunner held my arm as I got in. Shit the electric jolt that traveled through my body when he touched me was unreal. Would I ever get used to it? He gave me one last peck on the cheek, smiled and shut the door. He jogged around the front of the truck and got in. He looked over at Jefferson and smiled!

"Alright! Let's get the hell out of the city and get us some fresh country air!" Gunner said with a smile.

Gunner looked back at me and gave me a wink and smiled.

"We have to listen to a little music to get us in the mood."

Gunner hit play and "Banjo" by Rascal Flatts started to play. Jeff and Gunner both gave each other a fist bump and said at the same time.....

"Hells yeah!"

I looked over at Ari and she looked at me.

She smiled and just shook her head.

"Men...." We both said at the same time.

Gunner

Christ almighty…….driving for three hours and listening to Ari go on and on was enough to drive me fucking nuts! She got a call from Jason and of course she took it. The minute she said Jason's name Jeff put on his headphones and didn't take them off for another hour. Stupid ass was just going to give up on the girl he wanted.

I looked back at Ellie one time and the smile on her face looking out the window told me all I needed to know. She already loved being away from the city. Would she love the ranch as much as I did? Could she see herself living there? Being a rancher's wife? Fuck I sure as shit hoped so.

I turned down the county road that led to the ranch and my palms started to sweat and my heart rate kicked up. What the fuck? I was never nervous coming to the ranch. Maybe it was having Ellie meet Gramps and Grams that was getting me all fucked up.

I looked back at Ellie and she looked like she was about to come out of her seat. Jeff took his head phones off and turned around to face Ellie.

"You excited Honey? This is your first time out to the country and to a working cattle ranch!"

I'm not sure what type of sound Ellie just made, but she was smiling from ear to ear.

"Holy shit I'm so excited I'm shaking!"

"Jesus Ellie….it's just a bunch of cows for Pete's sake. I'm more concerned with the fact that I've not had a cell signal for the last forty five minutes!" Ari said as she moved her cell phone all over the back of Gunner's truck looking for a signal.

Jeff let out a laugh. "Yep, you take the girl out of the city, but you can't take the city out of the girl. You won't die if you can't talk to your boyfriend for a few days Squirt."

"Fuck off dickwad."

"Can you two please just knock it off for at least two days? I really want to enjoy this time we all have together before Gunner and Jefferson have to report back to football practice okay. Will the two of you attempt to get along…….for me?"

Jeff just turned around and didn't say a word; Ari told Ellie of course they would behave. Right.....I didn't believe that load of shit any more than Ellie probably did.

We pulled up to the gate. It was a large black iron gate and above it read:

Mathews Cattle Co

I heard Ellie let out a gasp as I punched in the gate code and we made our way down the long country road that led to my dream. The driveway went on a good three miles before we got to the ranch house. One more turn and that big white house would be in front of us.

Fuck I loved that house. The house had four bedrooms with Gramps and Grams bedroom downstairs and the other three bedrooms all upstairs. Both the first and second stories of the house had wraparound porches all the way around the house. Each room had access to the porch and on cool nights Grams would open all the windows and doors to cool the house off.

The porch swing facing out towards the west was my favorite part of the house. I remember all the nights I sat on that swing with Gramps while he told me what it took to be a cattle rancher. I smiled at the memory. I turned to look back at Ellie. She was staring at me with a goofy little smile. My heart started to beat faster as I gave her a wink. I was fucking nervous as hell.

There it was....... the ranch house.......and there was Gramps and Grams standing out front waiting for us. I thought I heard Ellie tell Ari she was nervous about meeting my grandparents. We pulled up and I threw the truck into park as I jumped out and made a beeline straight to Grams. She was holding a bouquet of daisies in her hand. I reached down and gently lifted her up and gave her a small hug as I kissed her on the cheek.

"Oh, you big 'ole hulk, now you put me back down Drew!"

"Yes ma'am, I missed you Grams, I missed you so much." I slowly put Grams down as I turned to give Gramps a hand shake. He pulled my hand in and gave me a bear hug, just like always.

"How are you doing Drew? We missed you so much son. Son of bitch you keep getting bigger; good for ranch work," Gramps said as he gave me a once over.

Jeff walked up next and leaned down and gave Grams a kiss and a hug and then shook Gramps hand. Ellie and Ari were right behind him. Jeff turned around and took Ari's hand in his and brought her up to Grams and Gramps.

"Mr. and Mrs. Mathews this is Arianna Peterson, Ellie's best friend." Grams looked at Ari and smiled and then looked up at Jeff and raised her one eyebrow. She always knew when someone was hiding something.

"Humph, *just* Ellie's best friend huh sweetheart?" Grams said as she looked back at Ari. She walked up to Ari and gave her a hug and whispered something in Ari's ear that made Ari's face instantly blush. Ari then let out a laugh as she looked back at Jeff. Nothing got by my grandmother.

"Arianna dear, you are such a pretty thing…....please call me Emma."

"Thank you so much for having us; it's absolutely breathtaking out here! And please, call me Ari."

Gramps walked over and gave Ari a small hug and welcomed her. Ari thanked him and told him about her own grandfather's ranch where she spent almost every summer riding in the local rodeos barrel racing. Jeff looked shocked to say the least. Damn that girl never ceased to shock me one way or another.

Next thing I knew, Gramps was looking straight at me. "Now where the hell is this girl who has stolen our Drew's heart?" He had a huge smile on his face, the same smile he wore when ever Grams walked into a room.

It was time…..my hands started to sweat again and my knees felt like they were going to buckle any moment. I wiped my hand on my jeans and gently took Ellie's hand in mine. I walked up to Gramps first since he couldn't seem to tear his eyes from her.

"Gramps, I'd like to introduce you to Ellie Johnson, Jeff's sister and well…um….the girl who has captured my heart and soul." Ellie turned and looked at me. She slowly gave me that goddamn smile of hers that melts my heart every time. Her beautiful blue eyes looked even more beautiful out here under the vast Texas sky.

God I loved her.

Ellie walked up to Gramps as he bent down and wrapped her in his arms and lifted her up. Ellie started to laugh. "Well aren't you the prettiest thing I've ever laid eyes on next to Emma here."

Gramps set Ellie down and her cheeks were a beautiful rose color. She smiled up at him and I swear he swayed a little. I knew right then and there she had bewitched him just as much as she had me.

Ellie turned to face me and gave me a wink. "I see where you get it from now."

I placed my hand on her lower back and brought her over to Grams. I thought I felt a shiver go through Ellie's body. As we got closer to Grams I thought I saw tears in my grandmother's eyes. What was that all about?

"Ellie, this is the most important woman in my life, I adore her and I know you will also. Grams.......*this* is my Ellie." I could hear my heart pounding in my ears. I looked around to see if anyone else could hear it also.

Grams walked up to Ellie and handed her the daisies. Ellie's smile grew bigger and she told Grams that daisies were her favorite. Grams threw her head back and laughed and told her she had heard that from a little fairy. Grams placed both her hands on Ellie's shoulders and looked her over. Her smile was all I needed to see to know she already loved Ellie. She brought Ellie in for hug and whispered something into Ellie's ear as well. Ellie didn't laugh like Ari did. She pulled back and looked at Grams shocked and then turned to look over at me.

"Trust me Ellie darlin', trust me," Grams said with a wink. Ellie smiled as Grams linked both Ari and Ellie's arms into hers and walked them into the house. Both girls started laughing at something Grams said to them. Ellie turned back around and gave me a smile. I returned her smile along with a wink as she turned her attention back to what Grams was saying.

Watching her walk into the house for the first time with Grams almost made my heart burst into two. I couldn't tear my eyes away from her retreating body. Just as the door shut Gramps slapped Jeff and I both on the backs.

"Well I'll be goddamned! Holy fucking shit boys, how the hell did you two luck out with those beauties?" Gramps said with a loud laugh. "You lucky sons of bitches. Now, let's head down to the barn and find Drake, I think I need a beer or ten. I'll get Dewey to bring the girls suitcases up to their room."

Jeff and I both looked at each other and smiled. We walked with Gramps to the barn while he got us caught up on all the work he had in store for us while we were there. Jeff leaned over and whispered in my ear.

"I don't care how many goddamn fences need mending...I just want to see Ari in a bikini."

I let out a laugh and shook my head. No way was I going to admit I wanted to see his sister in one also.

Jeff gave me a wink and slapped my back.....Bastard already knew I was thinking it though.

"Let's go boys...we have some catching up to do."

After Gunner's grandmother gave us a tour of the house and her garden, she showed Ari and me the bedroom we would be using. I was falling more and more in love with Emma. She had a tiny frame but looked like if you pissed her off she could haul off and knock the shit out of you. She absolutely adored Gunner and he adored her. The way he introduced her made me swoon, and I couldn't help but fall for him even more.

When she whispered in my ear how happy she was Gunner was finally in love, I almost passed out from pure shock.

"Ari, what did Emma whisper in your ear when Jeff introduced y'all?" I asked as Ari was unpacking her suitcase.

Ari started to laugh again and looked at me.

"She just said 'Stupid bastard will admit how he feels about you, don't worry!'"

I lost it and started laughing. "Wow. Looks like Emma has some kind of super power. She told me she was happy Gunner was finally in love."

Ari dropped her flat iron on the floor and just stood there looking at me.

"W…What did she say? Did Gunner tell her he was in love with you? OH. MY. GOD! Has Gunner told you he LOVES YOU and you didn't tell me YOU BITCH!"

"Jesus, Ari calm down! No….I'm pretty sure Gunner has *not* told her that, and no he has not told me that. But….." I left Ari hanging as I got up and started to unpack my things.

"BUT? But what Ells… holy shit don't leave me hanging here!"

I looked at Ari and then jumped onto her bed. I'd been dying to tell her but was afraid I had just taken it wrong.

"Okay, well I've been dying to say something to you but I thought it was just the alcohol and all of that. The night of Brad's birthday party when Gunner and Jeff got so drunk, I helped Gunner to bed right?"

"YES, YES…I know all of this….fast forward please….."

I laughed at Ari and shook my head. "Well, as he was falling asleep he might have said something like I love you Ellie.....I don't really remember exactly what he said because I was in shock."

Ari sat there stunned. Her mouth slowly started to drop open as she just stared at me. I reached over and used my finger to shut her mouth but it fell back open. I let out a giggle as she just kept staring at me.

"You trying to catch flies with that mouth open like that?"

"Holy shit....Jesus, Mary and Joseph Ellie......how....why in the *fuck* have you not told me this before now?"

I just shrugged my shoulders. "I don't know. I guess because he was drunk and all. I mean, a lot of people say shit when they're drunk that they don't really mean. I guess I've just learned to ignore what drunks say because of my mother. He might have just been saying it because I was helping him to bed or something."

"Or something! He might have been saying it because he actually DOES love you! What the fuck is wrong with you and your brother? You both can't see what is in front of your faces. Drives me crazy Ells."

I let out a sigh. A part of me wanted to believe that Gunner was in love with me but the other part...the other part that knew better.

You will never be wanted by anyone.......

"Ari listen, we've not even been together long enough for Gunner to fall in love with me. And three weeks of that time we were not even speaking to each other. It's way too soon for him to be feeling anything like that for me. Way..... way too soon."

"Whatever Ells, you may not notice it but I see the way he has to catch his breath when you walk in a room. Or the way he can't keep his eyes off of you for a single minute. The way he smiles at you even makes my ass swoon. I don't care what you say Ellie Johnson. Drew Mathews loves you."

I tried to give Ari a smile. I really wished I could believe her, but something was holding me back.

The rest of the day was spent helping Emma cook dinner. We learned how to make Chicken and Dumplings as well as Emma's super secret apple pie. I was in awe of Emma. She was everything I would have ever wanted in a mother. I was falling in love with her as each minute passed.

Ari never ceased to amaze me. I sat there and watched her as she moved around this country kitchen like she grew up here! The way she interacted with Emma like she was Emma's granddaughter and had known her for her whole life. A part of me was envious that Ari got to have such a normal childhood growing up. A mom and dad,

216

grandparents....... the whole thing and all I got was a drunken mother who told me every chance she got how worthless I was.

You will never be wanted by anyone...............

I must have been lost in my thoughts because I never even saw Emma walk over. She cupped my face with her hands and looked deep into my eyes and for some reason, my eyes started to tear up. What the hell? She really did have magic powers!

"Ellie, let go of the past sweetheart. Just let it fall away from you and look at what you have surrounding you right now. Look at the people who love you and want you to be happy."

I felt the tears running down my face. WHAT THE FUCK? I never cry in front of people. I looked over at Ari who was watching. She had flour on her cheek right under her eye and I just started to laugh when I saw it. Emma took me in her arms and held me. I had never felt loved so much as I did in that moment. Could Ari be right, could someone love you this much and this fast? I completely lost it and started sobbing.

"Oh my gosh...I don't know what's wrong with me. I'm so sorry," I said as Emma held me close to her and stroked my hair.

"Shhhh, baby girl." Emma turned and had Ari walk over to us. Ari knelt down and looked at me.

"I told you Ells....I told you."

Just then the door opened to the kitchen and I lifted my head to see Gunner walk in. His smile quickly faded and he looked like someone had punched him in the gut. I instantly felt like a stupid idiot.

"Baby what's wrong?" Gunner said as he walked up and dropped to his knees at my side. Emma let me go and smiled down at Gunner. She took a step back and looked at me with a smile that made my heart melt.

"Nothing is wrong Drew. Ellie just needed a good cry that's all. I think tonight would be the perfect night for your surprise for Ellie," Emma said as Gunner looked up at her and she gave him a wink.

What did Gunner have planned? My heart started to beat faster. I looked over and just stared into his beautiful blue eyes. They looked.....bluer for some reason. They had a spark in them I'd never noticed before.

"Your eyes Gunner....they're so.....blue."

Gunner smiled at me and for a second time within the last two minutes my heart melted. He had Emma's crooked smile. He reached up and wiped the tears from my eyes.

"My beautiful Ellie, please don't cry."

Just then something inside my chest hurt, but in a good way. I threw my arms around his neck and he wrapped his arms around me and held me close. The warmth from his touch spread through my whole body all at once.

"My beautiful, beautiful girl....I hate to see you cry, it cuts me to the bone. I just want you to be happy baby."

Oh. My. God......I think I just gave up my heart and soul to Drew Mathews.

I think ....

I think I was in love with him.

I pulled away from him and he cupped my face with his hands and kissed me so passionately that my head started to spin. I forgot all about Emma and Ari being in the same room and I returned his kiss. I kissed him with everything I had been holding back. The feel of Gunner's mouth on mine, his tongue dancing perfectly with mine, I wanted to cry again. He slowly pulled away and leaned his forehead against mine. We both took a few seconds to catch our breath.

"I want to show you what the stars look like at night Ellie, just you and me, tonight if you're up for it Sweetheart? I want to give you another first," Gunner said as he looked into my eyes.

I smiled at him because he had remembered our conversation from before. "I'd like nothing more than to do that." Just then I remember Emma and Ari. I felt my face get hot as I looked up.

"They left before I kissed you Sweetheart," Gunner said with a wicked smile as I shook my head at him.

"Come on, I need to wash up before dinner."

Jefferson and Garrett walked in just then laughing their asses off. Gunner jumped up and took my hand.

Gunner's grandfather took one look at me and then snapped his head over to Gunner.

"What the hell did you do her Drew? She's been crying!" Garrett yelled.

Emma walked into the kitchen with Ari laughing about something.

"Oh hush now you old goat. Drew did nothing to her and everything is fine. The girls helped with dinner so go wash up and don't think I don't smell that beer on you!"

Everyone laughed and Garrett walked up and kissed Emma with such passion I had to look away. Gunner squeezed my hand and looked down at me as I looked up at him. I didn't dare tell him my hand still kind of hurt from when I hit Ryan over a month ago.

Just then I saw Jefferson walk up to Ari who was leaning against the counter smiling at the display of affection from Garrett and Emma. I watched him as he gently wiped the flour off of Ari's face.

"You um, you had some flour on your face there," Jeff said as he smiled at her and then turned and walked away. As soon as he walked out of the kitchen Ari reached to her side and grabbed the counter. Her face was as red as the dish towel that was slung over her shoulder. She looked up at me and I smiled. I was going to have to have a talk with that brother of mine.

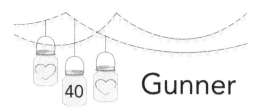

Gunner

Jeff, Gramps and I all cleared and cleaned the dishes while the girls went out and sat on the porch. I couldn't stop thinking about what it was that got Ellie upset. Did Grams say something to her? Maybe Ari said something? I'd have to talk to Grams about it when I was able to talk to her alone.

"Jesus Gunner….you're deep in thought," Jeff said as he was trying to hand me a plate to dry.

"Sorry dude, I didn't mean to space out on you."

"Women, they will do that to you. Best if you just get used to it now boys 'cause it will be like this the rest of your lives. When I met my Emma my whole world turned upside down. The boys used to tease me 'cause they said I walked around with a dopey look on my face all the time. It wasn't that, I was just thinking about her all the time. What was she doin' at that moment? Who was she with? Was she thinking about me? It totally scared the shit out of me too let me tell you. Now Drew, your grandmother was not the first girl I ever dated. But she was the first one that ever made me lose my breath when I saw her. The only one I ever thought about damn near 24/7." Gramps laughed and looked over at Jeff and me. We both were just standing there taking it all in.

"Shit, I still feel the same way about Emma after 49 years of marriage." He turned and leaned his back up against the sink. "I want you both to listen to me right now. I'm not stupid. You're both 21, almost 22 now. I know you've had sex with girls, probably a lot of them with your good looks. But let me tell you, when you find that one girl….. you'll know it in an instant. You won't want to just get in her panties and then leave her. Her eyes will hold your eyes captive, and she'll take the air out your lungs with just a smile. Her laugh, well shit……. her laugh will drive you mad and you will try to do everything under the sun to hear it as much as you can. Her tears will rip your heart out, especially if you caused 'em. Just the sound of her voice will drive you mad. When you find that girl boys, you found love. Not lust….but true love. You'll have found the girl who you'll spend the rest of your life loving, taking care of and just trying to make her so goddamn happy that you would gladly die doing it."

Jeff and I just stood there. I'd never heard my grandfather talk about women like this. I mean I knew he loved my Grams with his whole heart, that was never a doubt in my mind. But here he stood at 73 years old and it was like he had a window into my heart since the moment I met Ellie.

"When you find it, don't be stubborn and don't be scared. Fight for it boys....never let it go."

We just stood there in silence. Then Jeff let out a laugh.

"Fuck Gunner......I think your goddamn grandfather got a job at Hallmark also." Gramps slapped Jeff across the head.

"You shut the fuck up....I see how you look at Arianna boy. I might have to staple your damn tongue in your mouth because every time she walks in the room it just hangs out panting!" Gramps said as he finished up and started to head out to the porch.

"You know he's right," I said as I put the last of the dishes up. "She's not going to wait forever Jeff."

"Yeah, well....I don't know what the hell y'all are all talking about. There is nothing between Ari and me. Besides, she has a boyfriend or did you forget that?" Jeff said as he grabbed the dominos and headed for the door.

"Nah, I didn't forget but she sure seems like she has," I said with a laugh. Jeff just shrugged his shoulders and headed outside.

Stupid fucker.

We played dominos until the sun went down. I loved every minute of being with the ones I loved so much in my favorite place in the world. Watching Ellie with Grams warmed my heart more than I ever thought it would. Jeff was unusually quiet the rest of the night while Ari just went on and on from everything to how she loved dominos to how she was going to kick Jeff's ass at fishing tomorrow. I knew my Gramps liked Ari. She had a fire about her that he appreciated. You really would never know that this girl came from a shit ton of money.

I really knew he loved Ellie. How could he not? That smile, that laugh and those breathtakingly beautiful blue eyes. Grams had gotten up and went into the house. Gramps foreman Drake showed up with his two sons, Aaron and Dewey. I thought Dews was going to fall over when he saw Ari. Jeff noticed it also and I could practically see the steam coming from his ears.

We talked about going fishing tomorrow and to the river and Dewey made it a point to let Ari know he had tomorrow off and would love to join us if it was alright with us. I had no problem with it and when Ari said she would love for him to join us, Jeff got up and pushed his chair back so fast the damn thing fell over.

"I'm going to take a shower. Talk to y'all later, Drake, Aaron, Dew.....y'all have a good evening." Jeff gave Ari a look and headed into the house.

"What the hell was that all about, and why has he been so quiet tonight?" Ari asked as she looked straight at me like I knew what the fuck his problem was.

"I have no clue; he had been fine all day. Maybe he's just tired."

Drake and the boys excused themselves after they talked to Gramps about a few items that Jeff and I were going to take care of while we were there.

Ari stood up and leaned over and kissed Gramps on the cheek. "I think I'm going to go and grab a book and relax a bit if y'all don't mind. There's a sexy vampire named Kane who is waiting for me!"

"Baby girl you make yourself at home you hear," Gramps said as he stood up when Ari got up and walked into the house.

Just then Grams walked out with a blanket and a basket. Gramps looked over at Ellie and smiled as Grams sat it all down on the small white table that we had been playing dominos on.

"Now, Ellie darlin', Drew told us you've never seen the night sky away from the city lights. I think that is a crime right there that needs a fixing right away. Everyone needs to see the stars out in the country! It is a sight to behold." Grams said as she sat down next to Gramps. He took her hand and kissed the back of it.

Ellie let out a laugh. "No, I never have. That was one of the things I was most looking forward to coming out to the ranch for. I heard it's amazing!"

"Well, Drew why don't y'all take the blanket and goody basket your grandmother made up and head out to the west pasture. I think that one will give you plenty of space away from the lights up here."

I smiled at my grandparents. I knew exactly what they were both up to. My grandfather winked at me as my grandmother told Ellie what she had packed in the basket.

"There are is a mug of hot chocolate along with some fresh chocolate chip cookies I baked this morning. There is also some cut up cheese, crackers and fresh berries straight from the farmer's market."

"Oh wow Emma! Thank you so much for putting all this together! I'm so excited. It's a little chilly, I'm going to run and grab a sweatshirt and change into sneakers. Be right back!"

Ellie jumped up and kissed Grams on the cheek and headed into the house. I watched her as she practically skipped into the house. Her excitement was infectious.

"That's a pretty big ole smile you're wearing on your face Drew!" Grams said as I pulled my eyes away from the door Ellie just went through.

"Yeah well, that girl has turned my world upside down," I said as I gave Gramps a wink.

"Grams, what was Ellie upset about when I walked in earlier. The sight of her crying about had me fall to my knees."

Grams smiled and looked at Gramps. Something exchanged between the two of them and they never even said a word.

"Don't worry Drew, I think Ellie was thinking a little bit too much about the past and she got a little overwhelmed that's all. It's awfully clear to me how much that young lady adores you. Now you treat her right Drew Garrett Mathews or I will kick your ass up and down the west pasture do you hear me? I like that young lady….a lot."

"Yes ma'am, I won't let you down or Ellie for that matter. I um, I actually….well I think I um….I might be…"

"Holy shit son spit it the hell out, I ain't gettin' any damn younger!" Gramps said as Grams slapped him.

"Garrett!"

I took a deep breath and looked at the two most important people of my life.

"I love her."

I just blurted it out and I shook my head as if I couldn't even believe it still. "I love her so much I can't even breathe with the thought of her not being in my life forever. I dream about marrying her, having kids with her and sitting on this very porch and watching sunsets with her for the rest of our lives. I love her Grams and Gramps. I know you probably think it is too soon for me to even be thinking about Ellie like that but…"

"Drew listen to me and listen to me good. The first moment I laid eyes on your grandfather I knew. I knew I was going to be spending the rest of my life with him, and he felt the same way about me. You're preachin' to the choir son."

I took a deep breath in and let it out. "I'm not sure Ellie feels the same way about me Grams."

"Bullshit!" Gramps said. "I see how that girl looks at you. She can't take her eyes off of you, just the mention of your name and her eyes light up."

"Drew, remember what you told us about her mother. All of that negative crap that was pumped into her all those years. I'm sure that Ellie feels the same way about you. It's just going to take her a little longer to allow that to even be a possibility for her. Even if she has not admitted it to herself Drew, she loves you sweetheart. Just give her the time and space she needs sweet boy of mine. It will happen when it's meant to happen."

Just then Ellie came bursting out of the front door with the biggest smile on her face. She stopped dead in her tracks. "I'm sorry, did I interrupt something?" Ellie asked as she looked at my grandparents and then me.

"No sweetheart, not at all. Are you ready to get going and look at some stars?" I asked as I stood up and grabbed the blanket and basket Grams had packed.

Ellie did a little jump and let out a squeal. I couldn't help but laugh. She was so damn cute when she was so excited.

"I'm *more* than ready!"

"Let's go then. Will y'all be up when we get back?"

Grams started to laugh. "Take your time Drew and don't worry about waking us up when you get back. Your granddad and I tend to turn in rather early these days."

"Okay then, good night Grams, good night Gramps," I said as I leaned down and kissed Grams good night.

Ellie said goodnight to Grams and Gramps and skipped out to the jeep. I couldn't help but shake my head at her giddiness. It was funny how such simple things excited this girl.

"One rule Ellie....you cannot look up at all okay?" She nodded her head and took her finger and made a cross over her heart.

I hopped into the jeep and we set off for the west pasture. I knew the perfect spot I was going to take her to. There was a giant live oak that I used to lay under when I wanted to be alone and think. It was one my favorite places on the ranch to be.

Ellie sat next to me in the jeep and smiled the whole way. "It's amazing how I can see even though it's dark! I love it here already Gunner!" Ellie said with a smile.

"I'm glad to hear that Sweetheart."

I pulled up to the oak tree. After a quick check to make sure there was no manure around, I laid out the blanket and put the basket down. I turned the ignition over and tuned it to a country station. I had to laugh when "How Country Feels" by Randy Houser started to play.

"Well shit Ells, if this ain't the perfect song for you!"

Ellie laughed and sat down on the blanket.

I knelt down next to her and pushed a piece of hair that had fallen from her pony tail behind her ear.

"Close your eyes and don't open them until I tell you to."

"Okay...."

Ellie closed her eyes and slowly laid back. I saw her chest rising up and down so fast. God I could just lay here all night and watch her. I leaned in closer to her but was careful not to block her view.

"Open your eyes Ellie."

She waited a good thirty seconds before she finally opened her eyes. She sucked in her breath and her eyes grew wider. She didn't say a word. The smile that spread across her face was the sexiest thing I'd ever seen in my life. My fucking dick decided it liked it also. I moved and laid down next to her as I grabbed her hand and just looked up at the endless amount of stars. I never get tired of seeing this.

"It doesn't even look real. I never knew there were *so* many stars. There are millions of them!"

We laid there for I don't know how long just talking about everything. Favorite movies, songs, singers, bands, you name it, we talked about it.

"Gunner can I ask you something and please do not feel like you have to answer."

"Ellie honey you can ask me anything you want," I said as I kissed the back of her hand.

"Why don't you ever talk about your parents?"

I sat up and ran my hand through my hair.

"Um, well…I don't exactly have the best relationship with them. I haven't talked to my father or mother in almost three years."

Ellie sat up and looked shocked. "WHY?"

I let out a small laugh. "Well shit, where should I start."

"Gunner you don't have to talk about this if it's upsetting for you."

I looked over at her and my heart just swelled. I wanted to tell her about my parents.

"No, it's okay Ellie." I took a deep breath and started talking.

"My dad is a drill instructor in the Army, he and my mother live in Lawton, Oklahoma. My dad and I had different ideas about what I should do with my life. I wanted to play football back here in Texas. My dream was to go to UT, play football for them and then help out Gramps with the ranch. My father's dream was for me to go in the Army right after high school. Said it was the only way to make something of my life. He pretty much thought I was a loser for playing football and said I'd never get anywhere in my life. After I told him I got accepted into UT and got a football scholarship he told me if I went to school in Texas he was finished with me. My mother never did really have the nerve to stand up to my father so, on the day I graduated high school, he had my bags packed and he told me to leave."

"Oh my gosh Gunner, how could your own parents do that to you? Have you talked to them at all?"

"No, not since I started UT. My mother called a few times the summer after high school. I was staying here with Gramps and Grams. But once she realized I was not going to back down....well, I haven't talked to her since that summer. Not even at Christmas. Don't feel bad for me Sweetheart. It's really no different than your mother doing what she did to you all those years."

Ellie laid back down on the blanket and looked up at the stars. We sat there in silence for a few minutes.

"Do you want kids Gunner?"

My heart started beating a mile a minute. What if Ellie didn't want kids? I'd always dreamed of a little boy or girl I could teach to fish, ride a horse, learn about the cattle business. It was something I longed for. What if Ellie's mother had totally fucked up her thinking of kids? I panicked for a brief second.

"Yes, I want kids someday. What about you?"

Ellie stared up at the stars and then smiled. She turned her head over and looked at me and that smile of hers just blew me away.

"Yes, and I will love them unconditionally."

I let out the breath I was holding in.

Ellie wanted kids.

God how I hoped I was the one to make that another one of her firsts.

Gunner pretty much held his breath until I said that I also wanted kids someday. I wonder what he was thinking. I actually saw him let out the breath he was holding when I said yes. Was he thinking he wanted to have kids with me?

I could only dream. The thought of having Gunner's kids was too much to even think about. I could just see them now running around the ranch with Gunner chasing them. I bet he would make a great dad to our kids.

Oh wow....where the hell did that come from? *Our kids*..... I sat up quickly and shook my head. Fuck me why did I keep getting these thoughts?

Just then Lady Antebellum's "Just a Kiss" started to play. Oh God I loved this song! I jumped up and about scared the shit out of Gunner.

"Oh my God I *love* this song! Can I turn it up?"

Gunner laughed at me. "Of course you can Sweetheart."

I got up and started to walk over to the jeep. Just then I heard something. It was someone whistling and it was loud! Then I heard dogs howling. I let out a scream as I turned to run back to Gunner. I saw Gunner jump up and before I knew it I jumped into his arms and wrapped my legs around his body and buried my face.

"Holy fuck Ellie what's wrong? What happened?"

"OH MY GOD! OH MY GOD who is that whistling at us and do you not *hear* the coyotes! They're going to come after us!" I practically screamed into Gunner's chest.

Then I heard the whistle again. Holy shit it sounded like it belonged in the Amazon rain forest!

"There it is again!"

Gunner threw his head back and laughed. I kept my face buried into his neck.

"Holy hell Ells....those are Whipporwills. They're birds!" Gunner was laughing his ass off as he held me. I don't think I could have had my legs wrapped around him any tighter. I pulled back and looked at him confused as shit.

"Wait. What? They're birds? What kind of birds are out at night for Christ sakes, and how close are those coyotes?"

"They're not that close. Sound really travels in the country Ells. You could be a half a mile from me talking and I would be able to hear you. It's alright; there is nothing to be scared of."

Oh gesh....I felt like an idiot. He was smiling from ear to ear that beautiful crooked smile. Instantly I felt the ache between my legs. I didn't even realize it at first but I pushed my hips into Gunner. Gunner's smile faded and he leaned in to kiss me.

And kiss me he did. Holy fuck this might have been the most passionate kiss ever from him. I grabbed his hair and held him tighter and kissed him back with just as much passion. He started to walk while he held onto me and next thing I knew he had me pressed up against the jeep, he adjusted me to where I could feel his erection. We never broke the kiss. The ache between my legs was growing as he slowly started to move his hips against it. I instinctively moved my hips with his. Gunner slowly pulled his mouth away from mine. The look in his eyes was amazing. I'll never forget it as long as I live.

"Ellie, can I touch you?"

Oh. My. God.......

"Yes."

Gunner slowly placed his hand under my t-shirt. His hand started to move up my stomach and I thought I was going to explode from the inside out.

"Fuck Ellie....your skin is so soft."

I couldn't even think. His touch was driving me crazy. The ache between my legs was growing stronger and I was starting to feel weird. I shivered and Gunner stopped moving his hand.

"Touch me Gunner...please keep touching me." I begged. God I didn't want him to stop.

Gunner leaned in and started to kiss me again. I felt him move my bra and it released my breasts to him. His hand moved and started to caress each one. Then he started to play with my nipple. I let out a moan against his mouth and I felt him press his hips harder into me.

There was a strange intense feeling building in my body. What the hell was going on? I pressed my hips harder into Gunner and started to rock against him. He kept playing with my nipples, twisting them and pulling them. He pushed me harder into the jeep and took his other hand and grabbed the back of my head and deepened our kiss as he pressed harder into me.

Oh. My. Fucking. Hell.....

Something was happening to me....I pulled away from Gunner as it hit me full force. I started to scream out his name as the feeling got so intense I thought I was going to die. Gunner captured my screams with his mouth.

I thought for a brief moment I'd left my body. As I started to come down from the overwhelming pulsating sensations, Gunner slowed down his kissing and stopped playing with my nipple. He moved his hand around to my back. I felt so weak; I think if he were to put me down right now I would collapse onto the ground.

Gunner ever so slowly pulled away from my mouth as I opened my eyes. I was breathing like I just ran a fucking marathon and so was he. He leaned his forehead against mine and we didn't move until we both caught our breath.

"Baby, please tell me that was your first orgasm."

Fuck me....I just had an orgasm. I was going to fucking *kill* Ari for not telling me how amazing they were. Were all of them this wonderful? Maybe it's because it was with Gunner? I didn't even know you could have one without having sex.....Okay well, I did, but not just by kissing and a little hip grinding.

"Gunner....." It was all I could manage to get out of my mouth. I watched as a smile came across that beautiful face of his.

"Another first Baby?"

I started to laugh. "Yes, another first!"

Gunner grabbed me by the back of the head and kissed the shit out of me again. He pulled away and kissed the tip of my nose.

"My God Ellie, the things you do to me baby. I want to make you feel that good every day."

"I'd be okay with that!"

Gunner threw his head back and laughed.

"Ellie thank you for allowing me to do that for you. You've had a very busy day of firsts haven't you?"

I let out a giggle as he slowly started to lower me to the ground and I adjusted my bra.

"Yeah but I think that last one was my favorite out of all of them!" I said as I looked up at him. My god he was so handsome and his eyes were filled with.......love.

Gunner pushed me back up against the jeep and started to kiss me again. It was the most magical moment of my life and nothing would ever top it.

Gunner slowly moved his lips from mine but kept them just barley touching mine.

"Ellie.....I love you......."

Nope, I was so wrong.......that was the most magical moment of my life.

"I love you too Drew."

Gunner pulled back his head and stared at me in shock. I was pretty damn shocked myself that I just said that out loud. It was true though and it felt like the exact right moment to say it.

Then he smiled. I felt my body slowly start sliding down the jeep......my knees would not hold me up. Gunner reached around my hips and pulled me up and pressed me into the jeep again.

"You just made me the happiest man on earth Ellie Johnson. I will love you for the rest of my life baby."

Then he kissed me so slow and so sweet. My heart was squeezing in my chest. I did it; I gave my heart away to someone when I swore I'd never do it again. I prayed to God that Gunner was right....will he love me the rest of his life? Will he always want me?

You will never be wanted by anyone........

I felt a tear roll down my face. Gunner must have felt it too. He pulled back and wiped it away with his thumb.

"Please tell me that is a happy tear Sweetheart."

"Yes, yes it is. Promise me that you won't break my heart Drew. Promise me that will you?"

He looked at me and his eyes started to fill with tears. Oh my.....

"Ellie, I would rather die than ever break your heart. I have never in my life felt like this. I would lay down my life for you if I had to. I love you baby."

I reached up and wrapped my arms around his neck as he lifted me off the ground. I wanted to stay right here just like this forever.

In Gunner's arms laying under the stars at the ranch.

"You ready to head back to the house Sweetheart?"

Every time he called me sweetheart or baby my stomach did flip flops. I loved it so much. I loved him so much. Yes....I loved him, and if he was willing to take a leap of faith on us, so was I.

"Okay, except we hardly ate anything your grandmother packed. I feel so bad."

"Don't worry about it. We can take it with us down to the river tomorrow. Jeff and I have a few things to take care of in the morning around the ranch but we're free all afternoon. What do you say you and Ari meet us at the river around one?"Gunner said as he brought the basket back over to the jeep and I folded up the blanket and set it on the back seat.

"Sounds good, but how will we find our way to the river? This place is *huge!*"

Gunner let out a laugh as he went to start the jeep. It wouldn't turn over. Oh shit. After two more attempts it finally started.

"I need to tell Drake that the battery needs replacing in this thing. Make sure y'all take my truck tomorrow and I'll have Grams tell y'all how to get there in the morning."

Gunner reached over and gave me a kiss before he pulled out onto the gravel road and headed back to the ranch house. I had never in my life felt as happy as I did at this moment. I never wanted to leave. I thought I was so excited about starting school at UT in the fall but I found myself dreaming of starting a family with Gunner and living here on the ranch. What a silly dream….he was going to school to become an Architectural Engineer, not a rancher.

We drove in silence until we reached the ranch house. Before Gunner got out I reached over and held his arm to stop him.

He turned and looked at me with a smile. "What's wrong Sweetheart?"

I was not sure why I needed to ask him this, but it all of a sudden became very important to me.

"Nothing's wrong it's just….well I mean with us talking about wanting kids and everything I just…..well I just wanted to ask you…..shit….this is not coming out right!"

"Ellie, I've already told you sweetheart you can ask me anything you want. I'll never hide anything from you."

"I just was wondering where you saw yourself in the future? I mean, I know you only have one more year of college and your degree is in Architectural Engineering but you also love football so much. Jefferson mentioned that you already had NFL teams interested in you. Do you see yourself playing pro football?"

Gunner sat back in his seat and pushed his hand through his hair. Holy hell I loved it when he did that and I started to get that damn ache between my legs again. I had to fiddle around in my seat to ease it. Gesh how does he turn me on so easily?

Gunner looked over at me after sitting there for almost a minute in silence.

Oh shit….here it is….. I just knew he was going to say he sees himself playing pro ball….did I want to be with someone who would be traveling all the time….the women who would always be after his attention, I just couldn't imagine it….my heart just sank.

"Honestly Ellie, my dream ever since I was a little kid was to build and design buildings and to run this ranch. I figured I could do both so that's why I majored in Architectural Engineering. Jeff and I both are going to get hired on where we have been interning after we get out of school but I already worked it out to where I would do most of my work from out here. My number one dream is to take over this ranch. I would like to get married here, have my kids here and raise them right here on the ranch."

I was not expecting him to say that. It felt like at least one hundred butterflies went off in my stomach. Would he ever want that life with…..me?

"So, no pro football, even though you have teams trying to get you signed on?" I asked as I fiddled with my hands.

"No Ells, no pro football. I don't want to be away from the people I love. Especially with my grandparents getting older, I want to be here for them. Take the burden off of them with the ranch and I if I'm really blessed, I hope to give them great grandkids."

"Oh wow….um…that sounds wonderful Gunner." I turned to open the door to get out of the jeep but Gunner grabbed my hand and stopped me.

He started to laugh. "Well that's not really fair. You get to ask me about my future, what about yours?"

What was I going to say? Oh well okay…I have only known you for a little over a month now but I want to marry you, have your kids and live out here on your family's ranch. Yeah that would scare him the fuck off!

"Well, I guess I'm not really sure where I see my future. I'm starting college soon so I guess that's really about as far as I'm thinking right now, just going to college," I said with a shrug of my shoulders.

Gunner's face fell and it looked like he was devastated. What the hell? What did I say wrong?

He slowly gave me a small smile and let go of my hand. He got out of the jeep so fast I almost didn't see him grab the basket and head to the front door.

OH SHIT! I guess I pretty much just told him I didn't think I saw him in my future.

OH NO! FUCK!

"Gunner wait a minute. That's not the truth, that's not the truth at all."

"It's okay Ellie, we have different ideas about our future, it's not that big of a deal," he said as he turned to walk away. How could he say that? Why would he say that?

"Gunner please stop! Don't walk away from me after what just happened between us."

Gunner stopped and turned to look at me. "I would never walk away from you Ellie. Ever….."

I walked up to him and stood on the porch next to him. I was scared out of my mind to tell him what I really saw but I knew I had to. For some reason I had to let him know I saw the same future and I just prayed to God that it was me he saw in his future like it was him I saw in mine.

"Gunner, this is all moving so fast for me and...well..... it was huge for me to tell you how I feel about you. I'm so scared; you have no idea how scared I am. I love you. I love you with all of my heart, and the moment I got out of your truck earlier today all I could think about was being here, right here on this ranch, sitting on this porch with *you*. I want to watch sunsets and sunrises with *you*, seeing *our* kids running all over the place, and Emma teaching me how to make all your favorite foods. I've not been able to stop thinking about it all day and it scares the fuck out me!" I just spilled all that out and Gunner was just standing there staring at me with no emotion on his face. I had to sit down.

Oh shit...I think I'm going to throw up. Oh god I can't breathe!

I walked over and sat down on one of the chairs. I leaned my head down into my hands and cursed myself for being so stupid. How could I put my whole heart out there like that? OH MY GOD....

You will never be wanted by anyone................

I heard Gunner put the basket down and walk over to me. He got down on his knees and just stayed like that. What was he waiting for? What was he doing? I slowly lifted my head to look at him. What was I going to see? Probably pity in his eyes....just because he said he loves me doesn't mean he wants to spend the rest of his life with me.

When I looked up I let out a gasp. Gunner had tears streaming down his face! Holy hell......

"Gunner.....what's wrong? Why are you crying?"

The next thing I knew he put his head down in my lap and just.....cried. I was shocked. I picked up my hand and started running it through his hair. Why in the world was he so upset?

"Gunner I'm so sorry if I made you upset I...I don't know why I just told you all of that...I completely understand if you don't feel the same way about me......"

"Ellie stop talking."

I instantly stopped talking. He looked up at me and had the most breathtaking smile on his face. I didn't mean to but, I smiled back at him.

"When you told me earlier that you loved me....I just can't even begin to tell you happy you made me. For you to tell me that in your future you saw marrying me, having kids with me and living out here with me.......I feel like I could just explode I'm so fucking happy right now. I know we are so raw right now....it's way too soon to even be

235

talking about this but goddamn it Ellie. I want nothing more than to do exactly what you just said and do it with only you baby."

I was pretty sure I heard both of our hearts beating like crazy. I leaned down and grabbed his face and kissed him.

"I love you Ellie."

"I love you too. And can I just say since we're speaking out the truth here….It really turns me on when you call me baby."

Gunner threw his head back and laughed. He stood up and pulled me up along with him.

"*That* I'm going to have to remember! Come on, I need to get up early to help out Drake."

Gunner put his arm around my shoulder and led me into the house. When we walked in there was a small light on in the living room. Gunner and I walked in and Ari was sleeping in a chair with her book open. She looked so peaceful and so at home. If I had not known any better, I would say she was meant to be a rancher's wife. Not some country club ass hole's eye candy on his arm.

"Should we wake her up or leave her?" Gunner asked. After the night I just had, her ass was getting up so we could talk!

"I think we should wake her up. She would be more comfortable in bed." Just then Jefferson came downstairs.

"I thought I heard y'all. Did you have fun looking at the stars Ells?"

"Yes! It was *amazing*. The whole night has been *amazing*," I said with a little bit too much enthusiasm.

Jefferson just looked at me and then over at Gunner and raised his eyebrow. "Just how amaaaazing was it?"

I slapped him on the arm. "Jefferson Johnson! It was nothing like that and stop thinking that way! Gunner is too much of a gentleman to do anything like that!"

Gunner let out a laugh. "Jesus dude….give me a little bit more credit than that."

Jefferson looked over at Ari sleeping on the chair. "Has she been there the whole time? Her neck is going to kill her in the morning, and then I'm going to have to listen to her bitch about all day."

"I was just going to wake her up but sometimes she is hard to wake up when she's in a deep sleep."

We tried for ten minutes to wake her up. Finally Jefferson got tired of it.

"Fuck this; I'll just carry her up to your room." Jefferson bent down and scooped up Ari like she weighed nothing.

"Her bed is the one closest to the door," I said as he walked by and headed up the stairs with Gunner and me following behind.

Once we got in our bedroom I pulled the covers back as Jefferson started to lay Ari down. She opened her eyes and looked at him and smiled. He instantly stopped moving and just looked at her. Ari mumbled something about this being the best fucking dream ever and Jefferson smiled back at her and set her on the bed. Then he leaned down and kissed her on the cheek. Ari put her hand up to her cheek and smiled.

Then she let out a snore......I had to giggle.

"Figures," Jefferson said as he shook his head and turned to walk out.

"Night Ells...." Jefferson said as he leaned down to give me a kiss.

"Night Jefferson and sleep good."

Gunner took me in his arms and gave me a wonderful goodnight kiss. So wonderful I didn't want it to end. He pulled away and smiled at me.

"Think about me tonight okay?" I said as I gave him another quick kiss.

"Always!"

He turned and walked out the door shutting it behind him. I walked over to my bed and just fell back on it. I started to jump around like a school girl who just got her first kiss. Holy hells bells this has been the most wonderful day of my life!

I sat up quickly to look at Ari. I had to tell her or I was going to burst! Just then I heard her snore. Pesh, there would be no way of me waking her up. I'll have to just wait until tomorrow morning.

I tip toed into the bathroom, changed and brushed my teeth. As soon as I laid down on the pillow I drifted off into a dream.

Me...Gunner...and an open field filled with people looking at us...I never wanted to wake up.

42 Gunner

"Alright Gunner what the fuck happened between you and my sister last night asshole? You haven't stopped smiling all goddamn morning and my mind is going fucking crazy here!" Jeff said as we were mending the fence in the east pasture.

I stood up and took my cowboy hat off and wiped the sweat off my face with my shirt. I smiled over at Jeff and I thought for sure he was about to walk up and punch the shit out of me.

"Dude, nothing happened like what you're thinking happened. I already told you, I respect your sister and your friendship more than that."

"Well then shit Gunner, something must have happened because you're fucking walking around on cloud nine."

"I told Ellie last night that I loved her and she told me she loved me. We talked about where we saw our futures, she asked me if I was going to go play pro and I told her no. My dream was to be here and she pretty much told me she loved the ranch as much as I did."

Jeff ran his hands through his hair and looked at me. The smile that came across his face was all I needed to see. We walked up to each other and he grabbed my hand and smacked it and then shook it.

"Holy fucking shit…..Gunner Mathews is in love and it's with my baby sister. I never thought I would see the goddamn day! That's great Gunner….that's really great dude. I know you make my sister happy. I have not seen her this happy in…..well shit….I've never seen her this happy!"

I started to laugh as I slapped him on the back. "Well the feeling is mutual. She makes me happy Jeff and I can't stand to be away from her for a second. I just want to make her happy for the rest of her life."

"That's good to hear. Really good to hear 'cause if you ever hurt her Gunner, I'll fucking kill you and not think twice about it."

I stopped taking a drink of my water and looked at Jeff. He went back to fixing the fence like he didn't even just threaten me with my life.

"Well I don't ever intend on hurting her but, that's good to know dude….."

Jeff and I spent most of the morning fixing the back east pasture fence. Drake said they lost a few cattle last week so hopefully this will put a stop to that. I fucking loved it out here. Working with my hands in the Texas summer heat; shit there wasn't anything else like it.

"Shit, I'm ready to cool off. How hot do you think it is today?" Jeff said as he pulled his shirt off and wiped his face off with it.

"Fuck if I know.....Gramps said yesterday it got up to 101 but it sure as shit is different when you're sitting in a barn drinking cold beer!"

Just then we heard "Highway to Hell" blaring from up the gravel road.

"That has to be Dewey. Bastard always did like AC/DC," Jeff said as he grabbed his shirt and put it back on. "Why the fuck he is going to the river with us anyway? Did you see the way he was looking Ari up and down that asshole."

I had to laugh at Jeff. He won't admit his feelings for Ari but he didn't want anyone else to notice her either.....it was all too fucked up for me to try and understand.

Dewey pulled up next to Gramps' truck and parked. He jumped out and made his way over to us.

"What's up dudes? You heading down to the river? It's almost one and Ari said that's what time they were meeting you."

Holy fuck this bastard had already been drinking. That was not cool, not at all. I wonder if this is a normal thing for him.

"When did you talk to Ari Dew?" Jeff asked as he loaded the tools up in the truck.

"Oh I stopped by earlier this morning. Ari and Ellie were in the garden with Mrs. Mathews. Goddamn Ellie has a nice fucking ass."

I'm not even sure why I did it but I reached for Dewey and slammed him against the truck.

"Don't you *ever* fucking say something like that again about her or even look wrong at her Dewey or I swear to you, I will beat the shit out of you!"

Jeff came running over and tried to pull me off Dewey as Dewey threw his hands in the air.

"Dude! Holy shit I'm sorry I didn't think you were that serious about her....."

"Listen to me Dew; I'm going to marry that girl someday so you better keep your fucking distance from her you got me?" I said I as I gave him a good push and walked to the driver's side of the truck.

"Dewey we'll see you down at the river in a little bit...why don't you let Gunner cool off a bit before you come down there okay? And dude, don't talk about my sister like that ever again. Got it?"

"Um yeah sure sorry Jeff....see you in a bit."

Jeff loaded the last of the tools and jumped in the truck. "Jesus Gunner, I think you scared the shit out of Dewey," Jeff said with a laugh.

"Would you have let him talk about Ellie that way?"

"Fuck no...I was about to kick the living shit out of him but you beat me to him!"

"Let's just get to the river first before he shows up," I said as I put the truck in drive and took off. The thought of Dewey seeing Ellie in a bikini made me sick to my stomach. Goddamn fucker....

We pulled up and saw Ellie and Ari sitting on the tailgate of my truck and I had to smile. Just the thought of her driving around on the ranch in my truck brought a smile to my face. I looked over at Jeff who had a shit eating grin on his face. What was he up to?

"Do I even want to know what you're planning?"

"No. I don't think you do." Jeff said as he gave me a wink and jumped out of the truck. The girls jumped down from the truck and they were both dressed in short ass jean shorts and tank tops. I could see the white strap of Ellie's bikini top and just the thought of her taking off that tank top had my damn dick jumping. Ellie came running over and jumped in my arms as I spun her around.

"Good morning Drew!" She said in my ear. "I missed you this morning!"

The heat on my neck from her breath was about to drive me insane. Why is it that everything this girl does drives me crazy!

"Good morning Ellie. I missed you too sweetheart, more than you know. Did you sleep okay last night?" I asked as I put her down and pushed a piece of hair behind her ear.

"I did. I had a dream and I remember waking up so happy but I cannot for the life of me remember what the dream was about. It kind of pisses me off really."

I threw my head back and laughed at her. Damn she was so fucking cute! I swung down and picked her up while she let out a small scream and carried her back over to the truck. Jeff was already arguing with Ari. Jesus Christ those two......

"I seriously doubt I was calling out your name in my sleep you dickwad. You only wish I was."

"Tell her Ells, tell her how when I carried her up to bed she was saying how wonderful and strong and handsome I was."

"Um, that's not really how I remember it Jefferson," Ellie said with a shrug of her shoulders.

"Yeah you wish pretty boy! You could only dream of me wanting you."

"Whatever you say Squirt....you couldn't handle a man like me anyway." Jeff said as he lifted his t-shirt up over his head. We had already changed into swim trunks before we pulled up.

Ari stood there and just stared at Jeff and he looked at her and laughed.

"See what I mean Honey...you can't even think when you see my body!" Jeff threw his head back and laughed his ass off. Ari shrugged her shoulders and walked to the edge of the water. She dipped her toe in and then started to take her jean shorts off. Jeff instantly stopped laughing. She didn't just slip them down...she made a goddamn show out of it. Cue the strip tease music.

She tossed her shorts to the side and just stood there with her hands on her hips. I felt like I should be a better friend and go and pick Jeff's jaw off the ground but, he did bring it on himself.

I turned to look at Ellie who had a smile on her face, clearly amused by the whole scene that was taking place.

"How was your morning with Grams?"

"Oh my gosh, she is something else Gunner. She knows everything there is to know about gardens, and cooking and horses and cows, and what to do if you get bit by a snake or you roll around in poison ivy. She's amazing! I love her to pieces."

I smiled down at Ellie. I needed to bring her out here more often so that Grams can teach her everything she knows. I think they would both like that. Grams often mentioned how she wished she would have been able to teach her daughters-in-law more things about being house wives. I looked out at the river and was dying to get into it.

"Want to go swimming? I'm hotter than hell from working in the heat all morning."

Ellie's face lit up like a Christmas tree. Huh? Was she that excited about swimming in the river? I mean I know she had been out to Lake Travis plenty of times from what Jeff had told me. I wonder what was so exciting about the Llano River.

I started to pull off my t-shirt and heard Ellie suck in a breath of air. By the way she was eyeing my chest and my tattoo I now knew why she was so excited. Damn....she had been waiting for me to take my shirt off again. She has only seen me without it on twice. The times she spent the night with me I always kept my shirt on. She took a step closer to me and put her hand on my chest. I instantly felt the heat from her hand travel through my body and down to my dick. She started to trace my tattoo with her finger. She looked up at me, licked her lips and smiled.

"Like what you see?" I asked as I gave her a wink.

"Oh yes…..very *very* much! I've wanted to do that since the first day I met you and noticed your tattoo. How old were you when you got this?" She pointed to the Mathews brand tattoo.

"I had just turned 18 when I got it, birthday present to myself. I got the tribal tattoo when Jeff got his."

"Hmmmm….."

"I think that since you are drooling over my chest I should be able to do the same, don't you agree?" I said as I slowly started to lift her tank top over her head.

Holy mother fucking shit….she's more beautiful than I'd even dreamed. Her skin looked so soft and perfect. He breasts were amazing. She had to be at least a C cup. Ellie slowly started to peel her shorts down and when she had them off she took a step back and did a spin for me. I felt like my knees were going to give out on me at any moment. I had never in my life seen anyone with such a beautiful body. She didn't look like most of the girls I had dated…stick thin like they never ate. She had a figure. A beautiful figure, your typical hour glass shape and my God how I wanted to just take her right here in the bed of my truck. I had to step to my left to adjust my growing problem in my swim trunks.

"You like what you see?" Ellie said in a shy quiet voice.

"Um….yes…I more than like what I see, I want to lick every surface of your body with my tongue and explore every inch of you."

I looked down at her face and I saw that blush slowly creep up into her cheeks. I reached out and brought her to me and kissed her. She returned my kiss so passionately that I thought I was going to just die right there.

"Hey! That's my sister you bastard!" Jeff yelled over at us. Ellie started to smile against my lips. I did the only thing any other man would have done when he had the love of his life in his arms, with her brother yelling for him to stop kissing her.

I gave Jeff the finger.

"Can we leave and go find our tree?" Ellie asked as she pulled away from my kiss.

"Our tree?" I asked her confused.

"Yeah, last night watching the stars by the giant Live Oak. That had to be the biggest tree I've ever seen!" Ellie said with a laugh.

"So that's our tree huh? You know I used to go there when I was little just to get away, think or just enjoy the peace and quiet. I think I can share my oak tree with you." Ellie let out a laugh and jumped into my arms. I grabbed her and had to adjust her away from my rock hard dick that was starting to fucking hurt. It was time to get into the cold river water. I started to walk with her holding her close and tight.

"Where do you think you're going Drew Mathews? If you even attempt to put me in that water I swear I will…"

"You will what? What are you going to do Baby?" I said as I kissed her nose. I kicked off my shoes and started to run towards the water as she let out a scream. The moment we hit the water I had my breath practically knocked out and was gasping for air when I came up from under the water.

"HOLY FUCK….I don't remember this river being so cold!" I said as Ellie jumped up and tried to push me under the water. She kept pushing with all her might. Ahh…she was cute trying to act all strong. I just held her off while I yelled for Jeff to get his ass in the water. He and Ari were *still* going at each other on the shoreline about god knows what.

"I'm not getting in that water, it's cold as hell." Ari said.

"Come on Ari…it feels soooo good once you get in you big baby!"

"Fuck you Ellie."

Just then I saw Jeff come up behind Ari and throw her over his shoulder. I've never seen a girl kick and scream like Ari was. You would have thought Jeff was about to throw her off a cliff! He walked in waist deep water and slapped the shit out of her ass right before he gave her a toss. Ellie busted out laughing when Ari jumped up and was instantly bitching out Jeff.

"You mother fucking son of a bitch, dickwad asshole prick eating asswipe!"

"*Wow*! You kiss your mother with that mouth? We might need to give that filthy mouth of yours a good washing Squirt! I don't think I've ever heard anyone use all those words…….together like that!" Jeff said as he let out a laugh.

Next thing I knew I about jumped out of my skin when I felt Ellie's hand touch my dick. *Whoa*….I was not expecting that. I turned around and grabbed her hand.

"Ellie, what the fuck are you doing?" I whispered to her. She just gave me an innocent look and shrugged her shoulders.

"I just wanted to touch you," she said as she wrapped her arms around my neck and her legs around my waist. She pressed into me and I instantly pulled her off of me. She looked hurt but there was no way I could do this with Jeff 10 feet away from me. I really didn't feel like getting my ass kicked.

"Gunner what's wrong?" Ellie said as she moved closer to me. I moved back away from her as I looked over at Jeff who was now in a splashing war with Ari as they called each other every name in the book.

Just then Ellie let a sexy smile move across her face…..oh shit.

"What's wrong Gunner? What are you afraid of? I just wanted to hug you and give you a little attention...."

Who was this girl? Where did my sweet innocent Ellie go? She looked over at Jeff and smiled bigger which made me look at him. She made her move and I wasn't expecting it. She lunged at me and I tried to get away before she grabbed onto my neck and held on for dear life. The heat from her touch was more than I could stand. She took advantage of my moment of weakness and wrapped her legs around me as she moved her hand down my swim shorts and took my dick into her hand.

Oh holy fuck.....I was going to lose it. What the hell? Was I fourteen again? This girl was going to be the death of me.

Ellie started to kiss me as she moved her hand along my dick slowly driving me insane.

Jeff seemed too distracted with Ari to even notice what was going on.

"What's wrong Squirt? You too afraid to swing off the rope swing. You always were a bit of a scaredy cat weren't you?" Jeff said as he laughed at Ari.

"*Fuck* you Jeff....just watch what I can do on a rope swing!" I heard Ari shout back at Jeff.

"Move away from them Gunner........." Ellie said against my lips.

"Ellie you really have to stop baby....like right now......" I squeezed my eyes shut as she moved her hand faster. *Fuck me*! I was losing control fast. I pulled away from her as I looked over at Jeff standing in the water watching Ari about to swing from the rope swing. I started to walk away from them slowly.

"Kiss me Gunner now...."

I turned back and kissed her. Fuck it....it felt too fucking good to fight it anymore.

It only took her a few more pumps and I started to moan into her mouth as she deepened the kiss and I held her tighter. I slowly started to come back to earth but she was still moving her hand but slowed it down.

"Did you?"

Holy shit.....I was having a hard time catching my breath as I leaned my forehead against Ellie's. That was probably the most intense orgasm I'd ever had in my life. If her hand could make me feel this good what would it be like inside her? She slowly lifted her hand and wrapped her arms around my neck as she gave me that damn smile that made me weak in the knees.

"Yes baby I did." I leaned in to kiss her once I got my breathing under control.

"Thank you for letting me do that to you Gunner," she said against my lips.

I just started to laugh. "Well considering I could've had my ass kicked at any moment if you brother saw us, I would have to say that it was worth the risk of getting caught. Fuck Ellie you drive me crazy!"

She threw her head back and laughed as she looked over at Ari who had yet to swing off of the rope swing while Jeff just kept calling her a scaredy cat.

"Guess what?"

"What Baby?" I said as I traced her beautiful jaw line with my finger.

"That was another first for me," she said with a smile so sweet I just about had my heart explode in my chest. Fuck me.

"Jesus Ellie......" I cupped her face with my hand and kissed her. I couldn't believe what a lucky son of a bitch I was to have her experience all these things with me. What did I do to deserve her?

Ellie pulled away from my lips just a little and whispered against them.

"I love you Gunner."

"I love you too Ellie, more than anything."

Just then I heard Ari screaming at Jeff. "You fucking dick! You knew my top would come off if I did that! I *hate you*.....you dirty bastard!"

I'd never in my life seen Ari so mad. Jeff was standing in the water holding her bikini top in his hand laughing his ass off. Just then I heard music and saw someone pulling up. Jeff turned and then swam over to Ari as quickly as he could and started trying to put her top on.

"What the fuck are you doing? Get the hell away from me, and give me my goddamn top back!"

"Stop moving the fuck around Ari, stand still and let me put your top on before Dewey gets here!"

Jefferson sounded panicked. I swam over and took the top out of his hand and gave him a look. I helped Ari put her top on just as Dewey jumped out of his truck with two other guys and two girls.

"Who are they Gunner? Jeff asked as he looked over at Gunner.

"Hell if I know who they are; but I'm about to find out right now."

Gunner got out of the river and walked up to Dewey who grabbed his hand and gave it a slap. I couldn't really understand what they were talking about. I looked over and Ari was walking out of the river and Dewey was staring at her hard. Jeff started to get out and walked up next to Ari, blocking Dewey's view of her.

I saw Gunner running his hand through his hair. He only does that when something is wrong or he is worried. I started to get out and walked over to Gunner's truck. Next thing I knew Dewey and his group of friends got back in Dewey's truck and took off.

"What was that all about?" I asked as Gunner walked back up to us.

"Dewey had been drinking so I told him to take his friends and get them off of the ranch. I also told him if he ever did it again he would be gone. SHIT! I'm going to have to talk to Drake about this."

"Well, I think I'm about ready to head back to the house. I kind of lost the desire to go swimming and fishing thanks to dickwad here!"

Jeff let out a laugh and looked Ari up and down. I just shook my head. Gunner put his shirt back on over his head and walked over to me handing me my shirt and shorts.

"One More Night" by Maroon 5 came on the radio. "Jesus…..this is Jeff and Ari's song!" Gunner said with a laugh.

I started to laugh and Jeff and Ari both said "FUCK YOU GUNNER!" at the same time.

"You want to go riding Ells?" Gunner asked as he gave me that crooked smile.

"You mean horseback riding?"

He nodded his head yes and I jumped into his arms.

"*Yes*! Hell yes!" I shouted as Ari and Jeff started to laugh.

The rest of the afternoon was perfect. Well almost perfect, Ari and Jeff argued almost nonstop. When Ari challenged Jeff to a horse race I thought I was going to scream out with joy. While they took off Gunner and I made a beeline down to the south pasture and slowly walked along the river bank while the horses grazed in the field. It was probably the most perfect afternoon in my life. We stopped once and Gunner pushed me up against a tree and kissed the shit out of me. I so wanted to wrap my legs around him for a repeat of last night but the idea of Jefferson or Ari riding up on us had me thinking otherwise.

Speaking of, I could hear the two of them bitching at each other. I sighed loudly and Gunner gave me another kiss.

"Come on Sweetheart, let's get back to the stable and get the horses taken care of," Gunner said with a wink.

After we washed the horses and put them in their stalls, Gunner and Jefferson gave them all fresh hay. We made our way back up to the ranch house where Emma was making lasagna. Oh man it smelled heavenly!

Ari and I headed upstairs to clean up and get ready for dinner. Ari was not acting like herself and she was in a mood. She seemed to be happy when we first started to ride the horses but once we got back to the stables she was pissed about something.

"Everything okay?" I asked as she was lying on the bed staring up at the ceiling.

"No...."

"Want to tell me about it before we head to dinner?"

"I hate your brother......"

"This is not new news to me Ari. What did he do? You were so happy when we first started riding."

Ari sat up and sighed loudly. She ran her hands down her face and picked up the pillow and screamed in it. Shit, this was probably going to be bad.

"Why can he not admit he has feeling for me Ells? He is confusing me so much. One second he is dancing to a beautiful song and telling me how much he cares about me, and then next he is pushing me away as hard as he can. I just don't get it! Is he confused about how he feels? Scared? He treats me like a child one minute and the next second grabs my bikini top from me and he looks at my body like he wants to devour me.

I. Am. So. Fucking. Confused."

I wish I knew what to say to Ari. I got where Jefferson was coming from with his feelings. I wasn't sure why he was trying so hard to keep Ari in his life, but at the same time he was pushing her away. I really needed to sit down with him and talk to him.

"Ari, are you happy with Jason?"

Ari sat up and looked at me confused. She sat there too long....almost like she was really trying to think long and hard about this question.

"Of course I'm happy with him. I mean he is my.....well he's my boyfriend.....oh god....I'm so fucked up. I have a boyfriend and I'm pining over a guy who is not my boyfriend. Jesus, Mary and Joseph I'm headed straight to hell!"

I let out a giggle...she probably was. "Ari, if Jefferson said to you right now...be my girlfriend, leave Jason....what would you say."

"I would say Jason who?" Ari said as we both busted out laughing. It was clear that Ari had feelings for Jefferson, she always had.

"How long will you wait for Jefferson?" I asked as I raised my eyebrow up at her.

She let out a sigh and fell back on her bed. "I really want to say forever but...." Just then we heard a knock on the door. I hollered for whoever it was to come in.

Gunner poked his head in and said dinner was almost ready. I jumped up because I wanted to help Emma with the salad. Ari slowly sat up and reached her hand out to mine. I laughed as I pulled her up. As I walked by Gunner he slapped my ass and oh man..... OUCH!

"OWWW! That hurt!" I said with a giggle. Gunner let out laugh.

"We need to get you over that and back in the saddle tomorrow young lady."

Dinner was amazing. My goodness Gunner's grandmother sure knew how to cook. All Ari and I did was put together a salad to go along with the lasagna and Gunner gushed over it nonstop. Jefferson talked mostly to Garrett and I noticed he never once looked over at Ari. He was smiling at her when we first came downstairs until her phone beeped. Somehow Ari got a signal and a text message from Jason came through. Honestly, I think she was more excited about getting a signal than the fact that she got a message from Jason. Jefferson didn't see that though and his smile quickly changed to a frown. Maybe I could ask Gunner to beat some sense into my brother. The thought made me smile and Gunner looked up at me and winked. Cue the butterflies in my stomach.

Tonight the girls cleaned up the dishes while Garrett, Gunner, Jefferson and Drake sat on the porch and talked about the ranch. Gunner had already told his grandparents six months ago that he was planning on moving out to the ranch full time once he graduated from college, which was less than a year away. I heard Garrett talking to Emma about it earlier. The thought made my stomach hurt. That meant he would be leaving me. I tried to ask Gunner about it at the dinner table but his face turned white as a ghost and he just changed the subject. I'm not sure why but Emma and Garrett gave each other a serious look before the conversation got changed.

After the dishes were cleaned up we all went outside to sit on the porch. Even though it was damn near close to 100 degrees during the day the nights were wonderful out at the ranch. The breeze that blew was just enough to cool you off, that and a glass of Emma's sweet tea. Good god she made the best damn sweet tea I'd ever had. Jefferson and Garrett seemed to be in a deep conversation as I noticed Gunner standing up against the railing looking out into the dark pasture. I felt a warm sensation run through my body when I thought about what I did to him in the river this afternoon. I felt my face blush and I looked around like everyone might know what my thoughts were. Gunner turned right then and tilted his head and smiled at me.

"Penny for your thoughts?"

I laughed. "I don't think you really want me to talk about my thoughts out loud Mr. Mathews."

Gunner looked confused and then I swear I saw him blush. He grabbed me and pulled me to him as he whispered *I love you* in my ear.

"I love you too." I would never get tired of saying it to him or hearing it from him.

"Ellie, are we going too fast sweetheart? I'll slow things down if this is moving too fast for you. The last thing I want to do is spook you."

I hugged him closer to me and leaned up to kiss him. "I love that you worry about me but, trust me to let you know if I think we're moving too fast okay."

"Okay….but really all I want to do is sneak away and go up to your room for a little bit and make out with you," Gunner said as he wiggled his eyebrows up and down.

I let out a giggle and slapped his arm. "Behave Drew Mathews!"

He leaned down and the heat from his breath against my skin was pure torture. "Fuck it turns me on when you say my name…."

Oh….there went that ache between my legs. I desperately wanted to ease it now that I had a taste of what an orgasm felt like. I made sure to give Ari an earful first thing this morning when we woke up and I told her what happened with Gunner the night before. I thought her scream was going to wake everyone in the house up! She hopped onto my bed and told me to spill....so I did. Turns out miss smarty pants has only ever had one and it was self-induced while she was dreaming about Jefferson. EEWWWW that much I didn't have to know but it was already out of her mouth before she could take it back.

Gunner was yawning like crazy. I knew he was tired. Emma said he and Jefferson both got up at four am to work on the fence.

"Gunner babe, why don't you go to bed; you're exhausted," I said as I looked up into those beautiful blue eyes.

"Will you come with me?"

"Ahh no....."

"Can I come lay down with you then?" Gunner whispered.

"No!" *Yes*....

Then I noticed Jefferson stand up and shake Garrett's hand. He leaned down and kissed Emma goodnight and gave Ari a head nod with a faint goodnight. He walked up to me and kissed me good night as he slapped Gunner on the back.

Then it was like dominos. They all started dropping. Garrett and Emma excused themselves and said they were retiring to their room. Drake said he was going to kick his son Dewey's ass...Gunner must have told him about this afternoon down by the river. Ari headed up right after Dewey left and all that was left was Gunner and me. I could see he was fighting to stay awake just to be with me. I started to fake yawn and said I was really tired. That was all it took. Gunner jumped up, turned everything off down stairs and we walked up the stairs hand in hand.

In my mind I imagined we were married and there was a little girl with curly hair running up the steps in front of us with Gunner promising to read her a bed time story. The thought made me smile and I glanced over at Gunner. He looked so tired.

What would life be like for him if he worked here full time? Would he always be so tired? God he even looked handsome when he was dead tired. Oh how I loved him.

Gunner walked me to the bedroom door and leaned down to kiss me. He deepened the kiss and it nearly took the breath from my lungs. He pulled away and pushed a piece of hair behind my ear.

"Ellie......." That was all he said to me but it meant so much more. I could feel it in my heart. I smiled at him and I instantly got lost in his eyes. It was like he was trying to memorize every bit of me to take with him.

He leaned down and gave me a kiss that he pulled away from too damn quick. He turned and headed to his room.

I opened the door and stepped inside and as I closed it I leaned back against the door. My heart was beating so fast I could hear it in my ears.......This man has bewitched me.......I will forever be his. God I hope he doesn't get tired of me or fall for someone else. I would be devastated. This felt too perfect; too right....I was just waiting for the floor to fall out from underneath me. It was bound to happen...I just wish I knew when.

You will never be wanted by anyone......

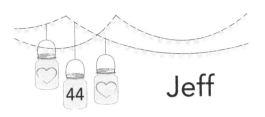

Jeff

Fuck! I could not sleep at all. All I could think about was Ari.....Ari in her bikini...Ari out of her bikini......Ari riding on that damn horse and racing with me....Ari smiling as she was just letting go while riding. It was clear to me she loved being on a horse and she was a damn good rider. We argued most of the damn day and I blamed myself for that. I just couldn't help it. She was so fucking cute when she was mad. Even though we fought most of the day....the normal conversation we had while we sat along the river letting our horses cool down was probably the best damn twenty minutes of my life. We didn't fight, didn't call each other names...we just talked. She told me she wanted to live in the country, on a place not as big as the ranch but with plenty of land for horses. My heart soared. I planned on buying the property that backed up the Mathews ranch. It wasn't anything like this ranch, only 250 acres but I'd been talking to Garrett tonight and the family that owned the small ranch was desperate to sell it. I guess their grandparents owned it and they just wanted it gone so they could keep up their city lives in Austin. There was a small ranch style home on the property, two wells and three tanks. Perfect for horses and a few cattle and Garrett already said I could let my cattle graze on the Mathews ranch as well as the horses. It was a dream come true. I hadn't even told Gunner about it yet.

On the trip back from the stables I decided I was going to talk to Ari. I needed to see if we could make a go at being something more than friends. Especially now that I knew she wanted the same life I did. I planned on talking to her after dinner. I was going to just tell her how I felt and pray she felt the same way. I dared to let myself get excited.

That was until I saw her bouncing downstairs right before dinner with Ellie and get so excited when a text message from the cheating bastard Jason came through. Her excitement sent a clear signal. She obviously loved him. Fucking prick didn't deserve Ari....she was way too good for him and he would end up cheating on her, just like he did with all the other ones.

I tried to clear my thoughts so I could get to sleep. After tossing and turning damn near all night, the clock read 4:30 am when my eyes finally closed.

The next morning I woke up to find Garrett and Ari sitting in the kitchen drinking coffee. Where the hell was everyone else?

"Where is everyone?" I asked as I poured a cup of coffee and sat down at the table.

"Emma ran into town to attend a church meeting, Gunner mentioned something about giving Ellie another first and they took off for town. Gramps here…he was just bitching to me about a fence that needs repairing."

I had to let out a chuckle at Ari's reference to Gunner's grandfather as Gramps…..only Gunner ever called him that.

"What fence needs fixin' Garrett? I can head out and fix it for you," I said as Ari quickly shot her head up and looked at me.

"Well it's on the north side of the ranch…butts up against the property you're interested in buying," Garrett said with a wicked smile on his face.

Fuck me….Ari sat up straighter and gave me a look of pure shock.

"*What*? You're buying property out here? Since when did you decide this? Does Ellie know? What about Gunner, does he know? What in the world are you going to do out here? I can't believe you didn't tell us…."

"For Christ sakes Ari, please shut the fuck up!" I said as I shook my head. Goddamn it, that girl could just rattle on.

Ari shot me a dirty look and I could tell she wanted to say something back to me but didn't because Garrett was sitting right there.

"Anyway, back to the fence….I can take the truck and head on over there right now." I said as I saw Ari still staring at me. I'm sure she had a million questions she wanted to ask me. Thank the fuck I was leaving to mend a fence.

"Oh Jeff that would be great since Gunner took off with Ellie, and Drake and the boys ran into town to get feed and run some errands. I don't want you going alone though….Ari you go with him. It will do you good to get some fresh air."

Ari and I both looked at Garrett and spoke at the same time.

"WHAT!"

"No really Garrett, I'm perfectly fine heading out there on my own, there's no need for her to come."

Ari nodded her head in agreement. "Yeah I mean, I was just planning on sitting in the porch swing and reading so…"

"Well then that's perfect. Take your book and read while Jeff fixes the fence. I have a strict rule…no one out in the pastures by themselves."

"Oh well um…." Ari said as she shrugged her shoulders and looked at me.

Fucking great…just what I needed. I was going to have to listen her go on and on for at least an hour while I fixed the fence.

"I want you to take the jeep though; I'll go and get it ready while you go change into some working clothes." If I didn't know any better I would have sworn he just gave me a wicked grin and then winked at me. What the hell?

I stood up to go change. I looked at what Ari was wearing…..short shorts, a tee shirt and some flip flops.

"Maybe you should at least put on some sneakers Ari."

She just looked at me, nodded and went up stairs.

Five minutes later I walked out to the jeep that Garrett had already pulled up to the house and had running. That was strange. I heard the front door screen shut and I turned to see Ari walk out in the same clothes but she changed into a pair of black cowboy boots.

Holy fuck….I'd never in my life seen anything so fucking sexy than this girl in a pair of shorts and cowboy boots. I had to take a few steps to ease my growing erection that was pressing into my fucking zipper.

She walked down towards the jeep and smiled at me as she hopped into the passenger seat. Damn, she even had on a cowboy hat….how the hell did I not see the hat. I let my eyes roam down her legs and then back up again. God how I wanted this girl so fucking badly but I needed to get a grip. She has a boyfriend…..she was not meant to be mine.

Garrett gave me a slap on the back and a wink. "I put plenty of water in there for y'all and even a few snacks…..just in case!" Then he laughed as he walked back towards the house. He waved and shouted back to us.

"Y'all have fun."

I got in the jeep and looked at Ari who just shrugged her shoulders and put her ear plugs to her iPod in. Yep…this was going to be fun.

I spent the next hour mending a fence that I swear looked like it had been cut in four different places on purpose. Nah….who the fuck would cut the fence on purpose. I was just about finished when I looked up at Ari sitting in the jeep kicked back and reading her book. She looked hot as hell with those legs propped up. They looked so smooth. I bet they were smooth. Just like her back was so smooth. I was able to get a feel of it when I was desperately trying to get her bikini top back on before Dewey saw her. I wiped the sweat off my face with my t-shirt and started to gather up the tools.

Fuck with it only being nine in the morning it sure as shit was hot out. I brought the tools back over and put them in the back of the jeep. I let the pliers fall hard against the metal floor and Ari jumped out of her seat. She ripped her head phones off and gave me a go to hell look.

"FUCKER! You scared the shit out of me!"

"Sorry...."

I grabbed a water from the cooler and took a long drink. I couldn't help but notice her watching me drink it. I wiped the sweat one more time off my face before I got in the jeep.

"Finally, it took you fucking long enough to fix a damn fence that should have been fixed thirty minutes ago."

"Well if you thought you could have fixed it sooner, why the fuck didn't you bring you sweet ass over and help me?"

"Pesh....yeah right. I kind of enjoyed the show," she said with a wink.

I turned the key over in the ignition and nothing happened. I let it off and tried it again. Nothing.....Strange....I turned it over again....Nothing.....I did this four more times and now Ari was sitting up looking at the ignition, willing it to start.

"Oh no...NO! NO! NO! NO! *NOOOOO*! Jeff, tell me that this piece of shit is going to start!" Ari practically shouted in my goddamn ear.

"Okay, this piece of shit is going to start."

Ari shot me a look and jumped out of the jeep.

"DO SOMETHING!"

"Jesus Ari, calm the fuck down, it's not like we are stuck in the middle of nowhere. Garrett knows we're here and when we don't come back in the next few minutes he'll know something is wrong. We need to just be patient and wait for someone to come looking for us."

I ran my hands through my hair as I watched her pace back and forth with that sweet ass swaying side to side. The thoughts that were running through my head were not good and I needed to stop. I had to reach down and adjust myself more than once.

I pulled my phone out to see how long we'd been gone, just a little over an hour and a half so if Garrett was the one who noticed the broken fence he would know that I should've been done by now and would be heading back.

After about thirty minutes of Ari pacing back and forth she pulled out her cell phone. She started walking all over the place holding her phone up. What the fuck was she doing?

"Ari, what the hell are you doing?"

"Well, while you're being a lazy ass just sitting underneath that tree, I'm going to try and get a signal to call someone to come save us."

"Save us?" I let out a laugh as she turned and shot me the finger.

"*Yes*! Save us. It's getting fucking hot out here and what if we run out of water? Did you ever think of that Jeff? HUH?" Ari jumped back up on the jeep and tried to get as high as she could.

"Jesus Christ Ari, it's not like we're going to be stuck out here for days. Stop climbing all over the fucking jeep. You're going to fall and get hurt."

"Fuck off dickwad! I got a signal last night maybe I will again."

"Oh yeah, when you got a text from your *boyfriend*….how's that working out for you Ari, dating a douche bag like Jason Reed," I said with a smile. I've never known that guy to remain faithful to any girl he has ever dated. I couldn't stand that mother fucker.

"Jealous much Jeff?"

"Hardly….." It fucking cut me to the bone knowing that that fucker got to hold Ari in his arms. Kiss her endlessly. The thought of him taking her virginity…..it just fucking pissed me off. He didn't deserve her.

"Oh. My. God! I can't believe this! We are going to have to be out here for hours. No one has come yet and it's been over two hours. What if they all left? What if they think we decided to go to the river and cool off, or you decided to check out your little piece of land you want. What if Garrett left and didn't leave a note where we were, and Gunner and Ellie come back and they think we're just riding or …or….or fuck I don't know……. What would two people who can't stand to be around each other be doing? *Fuck* why can't I get a signal!"

Ari jumped off the jeep and was now pacing and holding her phone up in the air again. I was going to fucking choke her if she didn't shut the fuck up soon!

"*Come on*! Fucking phone….why the fuck do I pay for all that extra shit if I can't even get a goddamn decent signal! Maybe we should start walking? Maybe we should just start yelling…yeah…then someone would hear us. Sound travels in the country pretty far right……"

OH. MY. GOD! I can't take it any longer. I need her to shut her up.

"Maybe if we just…."

I jumped up, grabbed her and pushed her up against the jeep…I looked down into those beautiful green eyes of hers and my heart fucking melted.

"Maybe Arianna, you need to just shut the fuck up."

I don't know why I did it, but I kissed her. My god her lips felt like heaven….just like the last kiss she gave me at Brad's party…the same kiss I had been fucking dreaming about every day since it happened.

I was afraid she would push me away but she opened her mouth more with a small moan and let my tongue start exploring. She deepened the kiss by grabbing my hair and pulling me in closer. Holy fuck….my head was spinning. Before I could stop myself I was pressing her up against the jeep harder. I wanted to crawl into her goddamn body and just stay there forever.

I started to put my hands under her shirt. Her skin was so goddamn soft I couldn't take it. She moved her hands under my t-shirt and started moving up and down along my back sending jolts through my entire body. I'd never in my life experienced such a powerful kiss.

Just when I didn't think it could get any better she reached in between us and started to move her hand along my erection. I moaned into her mouth and she pressed against me harder. I took my hand and started to unbutton her shorts and was about to slip my hand in her pants.

What the fuck was I doing? I needed to stop....right now before this went any further. I started to pull my hand away but she grabbed it.

She was practically panting when she barely pulled away from my lips.... "NO! Please don't stop Jeff....*please*....I need this so fucking bad!"

My brain stopped functioning and I put my hands down her shorts and into her panties. I ran one finger through her lips and slowly slid it inside her......*Fuck me.*

"Holy fuck you're so wet Ari." She moaned as she pushed her hips into my hand and started moving. I slid another and then another finger into her and started moving faster as I kissed her again.

Ari pulled away from my kiss and threw her head back. I couldn't take my eyes off of her. She grabbed my tee shirt and started moving her hips faster.

"OH MY GOD Jeff! *Ohhh god.....yes....* Oh Jeff yes!"

I reached up under her shirt again with my other hand and pushed her bra up. I pulled her shirt up and started to suck on her nipples. She smelled so fucking good....like vanilla....I teased her one nipple with my tongue and then pinched it with my teeth and that's when she started screaming out my name.

I thought I was going to die right there as I heard my name being called out from her beautiful lips. I pulled away from her breast and watched her as she came apart in my arms. I felt her clenching tighter onto my fingers and it was the hottest fucking thing I'd ever experienced. It seemed like her orgasm went on forever before she finally brought her head back straight and looked at me. I swear it was like she was taking a part of my soul right then and there. She slowly started to smile at me..... holy shit her smile....if she only knew how that smile could make me do anything she asked of me.

I couldn't breathe....my heart was beating faster than ever and pounding in my ears. Ari's breathing was getting back to normal as she just stared into my eyes. I couldn't stop looking at her. My eyes dropped to her lips as she licked them. Fuck my knees almost gave out on me. I pulled my hand out from her shorts.

What the fuck did I just do?

"Jeff…..I want you more than anything….I want to feel you inside me….*please I need you…...*"

WHAT? No! No, this was all wrong.

"No….no this was a mistake Ari…..this shouldn't have ever happened."

45   Ari

Oh…holy hells bells….I'd never experienced anything like that before in my entire life! I wanted more. I needed more. I needed Jeff so bad it physically hurt. I said it before I even knew the words were out of my mouth. I just came out and told Jeff I wanted to have sex with him…oh god why did I say that?

His face went white and he stiffened up.

"No…no this was a mistake Ari….this shouldn't have ever happened."

Wait…What? I had to shake my head to clear my thoughts. Did he just say what happened between us was a mistake? That it should never have happened?

"Wh….what?" I could barely get the word out of my mouth? How could he say that? That was the most magical moment of my life…..how could he say that? I saw the way he was looking at me. He felt it too. I know he did!

"I'm so sorry Baby…I should've never let that happen. I promise you, I won't ever do that to you again."

Oh my god, I'm so fucking confused right now I just want to scream. I threw my hands in my hair and shook my head to clear my thoughts.

"What the hell are you saying Jeff? How can you say that was a mistake? How….how can you do that to me…make me feel that way and then tell me it was a mistake. NO! That was not a mistake! I do not for one minute regret any of it."

Jeff pushed away from me and ran his hands through his hair. He looked me up and down and zeroed in on my shorts that were still unbuttoned.

"Jeff, I want you. I've wanted you for so long now, please don't say that this was wrong…" I started to move towards him but he put his hands up to stop me.

"No! I fucked up….I didn't mean to do that Ari. You….you have a boyfriend!" Jeff said as he looked at me shocked.

I shook my head back and forth….no….he was not going to use Jason as a way to get out of this.

"I don't want Jason….I want you Jefferson! I love *you*!"

He just stood there and looked at me stunned. At first he seemed relieved when I said I didn't want Jason....then it turned to confusion and now...I don't know how to read his face. The emotions running across his face were starting to freak me out. He looked........angry?

He laughed....Why the hell would he laugh?

"You love me? No you don't Ari, you just got caught up in a moment that I should've never let happen. It was all a mistake Ari....If I could take it back I would. It didn't mean anything."

I felt the water building in my eyes. No, I will not cry....he didn't mean what he was saying........how could he be saying this to me right now.

"I thought.....but I thought you wanted me Jeff? The way you were looking at me......"

He ran his hand through his hair again and turned away from me. I couldn't move.....I just stood there watching him. He took a deep breath and turned around to face me again. There was no emotion on his face whatsoever.

"I'm sorry Ari if I led you on. I.....I just got caught up in the moment and I wasn't thinking clearly. It didn't mean anything and I think we need to just forget this ever happened."

I can't breathe....oh my god I can't breathe....my whole world just turned the fuck upside down. The only man I have ever loved....ever wanted....just basically told me to fuck off. I felt a tear slide down my face. I couldn't even move my hand to wipe it away.

Jeff's face instantly looked like he was in pain.......he stepped forward and reached out to wipe the tear away.

I stepped back.

"Don't. You. Ever. Touch. Me. Again! You dirty rotten bastard. I can't believe you." I lost it and lunged at him and started to pound my fists in his chest.

"How could you? How could you *do* this to me?" He just grabbed onto me and held me while I pounded my fists on his chest.

Oh god.........my legs were giving out.....I started to slide down onto the ground as he came down with me and held me while I cried. I hated him.....I hated him with everything that I had.

NO! He was not allowed to comfort me after he just ripped my heart out. I pushed him away from me and stood up. I heard someone driving up.

Jeff stood up and reached out for me. He had tears in his eyes but I didn't give a fuck.

"I. Hate. You!" I said through gritted teeth.

"Ari...."

"No....no you don't get to stand there anymore and tell me how you fucked up you mother fucker! I will never......ever..... forgive you for this. Do you understand me Jeff....NEVER! I hate you! I fucking HATE you!"

I screamed it so loud at him he jumped back in shock. I buttoned up my shorts and walked around to the other side of the jeep. I was shaking from head to toe and I felt sick to my stomach.

It looked like it was Drake driving up. Thank god...I couldn't stand to be anywhere near Jeff right now. I felt like a cheap whore all of a sudden. How could I be so fucking stupid? To think that I stood there and asked him to have sex with me!

Drake pulled up in the ranch truck, jumped out and started to walk towards the back of the truck.

"Hey! Mr. Mathew's told me y'all took the jeep out. He must have forgotten that Gunner told him it needed a new battery. I picked one up in town this morning."

I turned to look at the asshole who was staring over at me still. He looked like he was going to throw up. I hope he did. Maybe I would put something in his dinner tonight so he got deathly sick and threw up all goddamn night. I turned away from him and walked over to Drake who was pulling the battery for the jeep out of the back of the truck.

"Drake, I um, I really need to get back to the house. Can you ride back up with Jeff please while I take the truck?"

"Ari...wait...we need to talk about......"

I spun around and glared at him, stopping him mid sentence. I never knew I could hate someone as much as I hated him right now.

"No...I believe you said all you needed to say, so now it's my turn."

I walked past a very confused Drake and got right up to Jeff.

"When I get back home to *Jason*, my BOYFRIEND, you can better believe he won't be telling me what a mistake it was after we get done fucking for the first time!"

Jeff briefly closed his eyes and then opened them again. His eyes looked like they were filled with pain but I fucking knew better.

I turned around and stopped in front of Drake.

"Are the keys in the truck?"

"Ahhhh....ummmm....yes." I kind of felt bad for the guy to have to stand there and hear all of that but, oh fucking well. I was done with all of this bullshit.

I barely made it back to the ranch house in one piece. I could hardly see through the tears running down my face. I saw Gunner and Ellie sitting on the porch with Emma. I tried to wipe the tears away but they just wouldn't stop. I pulled the truck down by the barn and started to make my way up to the house. I could see Ellie smiling at me but as soon as she got a better look her smile faded and she started to run up to me.

"Arianna....Oh my god what's wrong?"

"Your brother.....your brother is what's wrong Ellie. He is a dirty rotten good for nothing son of a bitch. I hate him. I fucking *hate* him."

"What....what did he do?" Just then she threw her hand up to her mouth and started to shake her head.....

"He didn't...."

I started to laugh, that was a joke. "No Ellie....I guess I'm a major turn off where that is concerned. If you will excuse me...I think I need to take a nice long bath and then lay down for awhile."

"Ari...tell me what he did," Ellie said as she grabbed my arm.

I turned and looked at her and the tears were back.

"He gave me hope for a few brief minutes Ellie, then he ripped my heart out and threw it on the ground and buried it deep into the dirt with his boots."

I turned and Gunner was standing there his hands balled up in fists. I tried to smile as I walked by and made my way up onto the porch. Emma stopped me and gave me a hug that caused me to go into another crying fit. She helped me into the house and upstairs. She led me into the bathroom and drew me a hot bath while I sat there staring off into space.

How could I have been so stupid?

"Arianna, men are stupid creatures. Sometimes they love something so much it scares them, and they try to push it as far away as they can." Emma said as she was pushing my hair back from my red tear swollen eyes.

I started to shake my head no. "Emma....no man who loved a woman would ever say the things that he said."

Emma let out a chuckle as she helped me get undressed. "You would be surprised my darling girl. You would be surprised."

I sat in the bath for I don't know how long. I got out only when I couldn't take the cold water any longer. I wrapped the towel around me that Emma had left and reached down to let the drain out. I slowly walked into the bedroom Ellie and I were sharing. Ellie must have come in and laid out some clothes for me to change into. They were my comfy blue PJ bottoms and sleeveless white shirt. I climbed into them somehow. My whole body felt numb. I never knew one person had the power to hurt another person so badly.

I sat down on the bed and that is when I heard Ellie yelling at Jeff.

"How could you? How could you destroy her like that?"

Then I heard Jeff and Gunner arguing. I got up and walked to the window. I could see them standing down by the barn closest to the house. I couldn't hear what Jeff said but the next thing I knew Gunner punched him. Ellie jumped in front of Gunner and told him to stop. My heart was beating a mile a minute.

SHIT! This was all happening because of me.

Garrett walked up and took Jeff by the arm and they walked off toward the stables. Ellie leaned back into Gunner as they watched them walk away. Jeff turned around and looked right up at the window I was standing in. It looked like he was crying.....

No....that cold hearted bastard didn't have an ounce of love running through his veins.

I hated him........

All of a sudden I got so tired.

Sleep....I just needed to sleep.

46   Gunner

I sat on the porch swing waiting for Ellie to come back from talking to Ari. I still can't believe I hit my best friend. I ran my hands down my face....FUCK! Why the hell did Jeff have to go and mess up so bad with Ari? Gramps wouldn't let me talk to him yet. They headed to the barn and that was the last I saw of either of them.

This had started out to be a great day and now it was just fucked.

I had brought Ellie into town to have breakfast at one of the local restaurants. I remembered her saying she wanted to go and eat in an old fashioned type restaurant. You just can't get any better than Miss Mayes restaurant in town. Best damn French toast I've had.

The plan was to eat breakfast, walk through a few of the little stores on Main Street, then come back to the ranch and ride. Ellie had really taken to horseback riding and practically begged me go again today.

When Gramps told us about his "plan" to get Ari and Jeff some alone time, I knew it was going to go down all wrong. Just how it went down wrong I didn't know yet. I heard the screen door open and saw the love of my life walking out with such a sad look on her face. I held out my hand and she came over and sat on my lap.

She laid her head on my chest and let out a sigh. God, what I wouldn't do to just stay like this forever and never let her go. I buried my face in her hair and took a deep breath. Fuck she smelled so good, daisies...she always smelled like them.

"So, did she tell you what happened?"

"Oh God Gunner.....I think Jefferson really messed up this time. I think he pushed her away for good."

Shit...I didn't like the way this was sounding. I'll fucking kill him he if forced her to do anything.

"He didn't...."

"NO! God no! Jefferson would never. But then again, I didn't think he would ever be so mean and hurtful as this either."

I felt Ellie shiver so I pulled her tighter into me.

"Can we take a walk? I don't want your grandmother to overhear us talking. I'm not sure how much Ari told her about what happened."

"Sure, let's head down to the stables." I reached down and took her hand in mine as we started to make our way to the stables. I needed to check on Big Roy anyway. He was a gift from Gramps when I was sixteen and somehow he cut his leg pretty bad; we needed to keep an eye on it for a few days for any signs of an infection.

Ellie walked for a few minutes in silence. Once we reached the stables I checked for Gramps and Jeff but they were nowhere to be found.

"No one is here Sweetheart."

Ellie started to cry. I walked over and held her in my arms. I was going to fucking kill Jeff for making his sister so upset. I don't care how fucked up he is.

"Oh God Gunner…."

"Just take a deep breath Baby," I said as I ran my hands up and down her back. Once she settled a little bit she sat down on a bale of hay and took in a deep breath.

"God I love the way it smells down here. I wish I could bottle it up and take it home with me."

I laughed and started to walk into Big Roy's stall. I checked his leg out and it seemed to be doing well. I gave him a bit of oats and shut his stall. I sat down next to Ellie and took her hand in mine.

"I guess when the battery went dead Ari freaked out a little bit…if you can imagine that. Jeff got pissed and pushed her up against the Jeep and well, one thing led to another. No sex but more than kissing."

I let myself go back to a few nights ago when Ellie had her first orgasm. The memory alone caused my dick to jump.

"What happened next?"

"I guess Ari made the mistake of telling Jeff she wanted to take it further and well…… he didn't. He basically told her he made a terrible mistake and that he wished he could take it back…….after she told him she loved him."

Shit Jeff……stupid fucker.

"She hates him Gunner but yet, I know she still loves him….I hate to see her hurting like this."

"I'm sorry Ellie, but I can tell you that I'm sure Jeff is hurting probably even more."

Ellie pushed back away from my chest and just stared at me. She looked confused and pissed at the same time.

"How in the hell do you think he is hurting more then she is Gunner?" Ellie hissed through her teeth.

"He's in love with her Ellie."

Ellie let out a laugh. "Yeah if that is how he shows love, than she is better off without him."

"Ellie, Jeff told me he loves Ari so much he's afraid that if they end up together something will happen, something bad and he'll lose her forever. He said he would rather have her in his life as a friend than to not have her in his life at all."

Ellie just looked at me for the longest time. I knew what she was thinking because I thought the same thing when Jeff spit out that bullshit to me.

"That doesn't make a lick of fucking sense Gunner. I hope you know that."

God I loved this girl.

"Ells I told him the same exact thing. I wish I could understand his stupid fucked up way of thinking, but I don't."

Ellie let out a sigh and we just sat there in silence. Fuck let this be a lesson for me *not* to fuck things up with Ellie.

Ellie and I spent the rest of the afternoon riding around the ranch. I showed her every square nook of it. Where me and my cousins used to play kings and queens, hide and seek and where in high school we would sneak off to with some of Gramps beer that he hid from Grams. Then I took her out behind the ranch house and showed her how to shoot a .22 gauge rifle. It was a perfect afternoon.

Dinner....not so much, Jeff didn't utter a word while Gramps mostly talked about the plans for fixing up the main barn. Drake and his sons lived there and their quarters needed some fixing up. I told Gramps I would come back the weekend of Thanksgiving and help out. We had a game that Thursday, Thanksgiving Day but, I could plan on getting here Friday after we reviewed the game, and stay until Sunday night. Jeff finally spoke and said he would plan on coming also. That led Grams to having Ellie come out also and we would cook up a Thanksgiving feast on Saturday. I thought Ellie was going to jump out of her chair she was so excited.

I looked up and saw Ari coming into the dining room. She was dressed in Jeans and a black Hulu Hut t-shirt. Her hair was pulled back in a low pony and she had the fakest smile I'd ever seen plastered on her face.

"Well crap...I see I'm late for dinner!"

I looked over at Jeff. He instantly sat up and looked at Ari. I could tell he wanted nothing more than to grab her and take her somewhere and talk to her. From what Gramps told me about his talk with Jeff, he pretty much told Jeff he just lost the best thing he would ever have, he then called him the stupidest mother fucker on the planet. He also let him know that if he ever wanted another chance with Ari he needed to back off, let her cool down, and once she did he better crawl on his hands and knees and beg her to forgive him.

"You're never late for dinners in this house my darling girl," Grams said as she gave Ari a wink.

Ari never once looked at Jeff. Grams handed her a plate and we all started to pass down the pork chops, mashed potatoes and green beans. I had never in my life seen a girl eat so much as Ari did tonight.

The rest of the night was spent outside on the porch talking, listening to Grams and Gramps tell stories, a couple rounds of dominoes and then we all headed off to bed. Before I went to sleep I let Gramps and Grams know we were leaving the next day. I killed me to leave knowing there was so much work to be done. But I thought it was for the best.

I had pulled Ellie off to the side and asked her if she wanted to go to our tree one more time and watch the stars. She jumped up and down and clapped her hands.

"Give me fifteen minutes and I'll meet you down at your truck!"

We ended up spending more time kissing and touching each other than we did looking at the stars. I was almost tempted to keep her out all night and make out but I knew we were heading back to Austin and we both needed to get some sleep. I kissed her long and passionately on the porch before I walked her to her room.

"Goodnight Ellie sweetheart."

"Goodnight Gunner. Thank you so much for such a magical week. I love you."

"You are more than welcome baby. Sweet dreams Ellie."

After Grams had packed up a picnic basket full of goodies we made our way back to Austin. Ari and Jeff both put their iPods in and never spoke a single word all the way home. It killed me I couldn't have Ellie in the front seat with me but Ari threw a fit at the idea of the "bastard from hell" sitting next to her.

When we finally pulled up to Ari and Ellie's house I thought Ari was going to bolt from the truck before I even had it stopped.

Jeff and I carried their suitcases in and then Jeff went back to the truck after saying goodbye to Ellie and Ari disappeared into her room.

"How many more weeks until football is starting back up?" Ellie asked me as she walked me back outside.

"Three….so once that happens and school starts I'm going to be pretty busy so you know I'm going to have to spend every minute with you from now until then."

Ellie laughed that beautiful laugh that warmed my whole body.

"Well….that sounds like a god awful punishment but I guess I can make it work!"

"You better! I'll call you when we get back to the house. Did you have fun Sweetheart?"

Right on cue there was that smile that could bring me to my knees. "Yes. I had a wonderful time Gunner, some moments stand out a little more than others, but wonderful all around."

I threw my head back and laughed. "Same goes here Baby!" I leaned down and kissed her goodbye and made my way to the truck.

As I pulled away I looked in my rearview mirror and already my chest ached from missing her.

The rest of the summer flew by. We went out to Lake Travis a few times and twice we took Brad's parents' boat out. It was huge! Amanda and Brad really seemed to be serious, I could tell Amanda had fallen hard for Brad and he felt the same way. Ari came once and brought Jason and somehow they managed to stay clear on the other side of the boat away from Jefferson. He had been there with some girl named Kassie…I think that was her name. Shit, I couldn't keep up with them anymore. Jefferson seemed to have a different girl on his arm ever since we came back from the ranch. I overheard Gunner talking to him in the kitchen one morning when Jefferson came back from a run about all the girls he had been bringing home.

"You can't fuck her out of your head Jeff….no matter how many girls you bring home, they'll never be Ari."

Gunner had been staying at my place more often than I stayed at his house. I could not bury my head in his pillows again while trying to drown out some whore screaming "YES OH GOD JEFF HARDER FASTER!" ARGH…….. It was just too much for my poor stomach to handle.

Ari seemed to spend every spare minute she had with Jason. For some reason I didn't like him, my gut was telling me he was not the right guy for her. I never liked him in school and I was pretty sure I remembered Jefferson talking about what a man whore he was when we were in high school.

This was the last night before Gunner had to report to football practice. We went to Chuy's for dinner, Gunner's favorite restaurant, and then back to my place to watch a movie. Ari was out with Jason and who knew what time she would be home. She was all dressed up and was going to the country club because it was Jason's parents' anniversary. So we were alone for most of the night.

Somehow Gunner and I were able to control ourselves and not tear each other's clothes off when we spent our nights together. I could tell it was getting harder for him to stop before things got too far. I had not had another orgasm since the ranch and I was practically ready to beg

Gunner. I think he was afraid of not being able to stop. To be honest so was I.

But there was something about tonight and the ache between my legs that was not going away. The way Gunner kept rubbing his thumb across the back of my neck was driving me fucking crazy. I was willing to take the risk of not being able to stop just to ease this damn ache.

I decided I needed to take matters into my own hands. I moved so fast I don't think Gunner knew what had happened. I swung my leg around and straddled him on the sofa. I started to bury my hands in that floppy messy hair of his that drove me mad. Then I did it…I rocked up against his already hard erection.

Oh god….it felt so good, but fuck I needed more. I let a moan escape from my mouth and Gunner grabbed my hips and held me closer to him. I pressed in harder against him and the next thing I knew Gunner had my shirt over and off of my head and was making quick time at taking my bra off. My heart started to pound. Oh wow….oh shit….this would be the first time he saw my naked breasts.

Once my bra broke free and Gunner slipped it down my arms he just stared at me. He licked his lips and I thought I was going to explode. He just sat there staring with a stupid ass smile on his face.

"Gunner….please touch me for fucks sake."

He looked up at me and gave me that damn crooked smile…oh my god…I could come just by that look alone.

"In a hurry Baby?"

I threw my head back and moaned….I needed more…..I pressed in harder wishing that his goddamn pants were off…..oh god it felt like I was so close.

"*Gunner*….." I could hear the desperation in my voice and I didn't care.

Just then he pulled my arms behind my back and grabbed my wrists and held them there with his hand. He leaned down into my chest and put his mouth on one of my nipples and sucked it. He used his other hand to twist and pull the other nipple.

Holy fucking hell…….I couldn't think straight. He was driving me insane.

"Ellie….ahhh fuck I love to watch you feel good."

I snapped my head back up and looked him in the face and yelled "Then fucking make me feel good damn it!"

That bastard laughed as he went back to sucking on my nipple. Just then he moved his hips and there it was…the relief I needed. I moaned again as he was hitting the spot I so desperately needed him to hit.

"Is that it Baby? Is that where you need it?"

Oh god.....my body was starting to get that tingling feeling....shit....I was so close. All it took was one more thrust of his hips into mine and I came apart right there.

"Oh my god! Gunner that's it!" I threw my head back and started to call out his name. I felt him stop sucking on my nipple but he never stopped twisting and pulling the other one. Oh. My. God. This feeling was fucking fantastic......

Oh holy hell I think I just left my body. I heard Gunner saying something to me but I was in a fog. He was moving me, why the fuck was he moving me.......he laid me down on the sofa....

What the fuck was he saying? I couldn't think......just when I thought the pulsing in my body had stopped it felt like it was going start all over again. Something was different though, something felt different. Oh my god....it felt so good.....

"Jesus Baby you're so wet. Open your eyes and look at me Ellie."

Wait.......... what?

I opened my eyes and looked into his beautiful blue eyes. He was lying next to me and I could feel.....Oh my god was that his hand??? Ohhhh holy shit......his hand was down my pants inside my panties.

"Ellie....you're so fucking wet for me baby."

All I could think of to say was "YES!"

He was touching my clitoris and it felt like so good I didn't want him to stop....EVER!

"Oh god Gunner...don't...don't stop."

He moved his lips gently across mine and nipped at my bottom lip. Then I felt him move a finger inside me. I bucked my hips up into his hand.

"Does that feel good Ellie? Tell me it feels good."

I tried to talk, really I tried but I couldn't...all I could do was moan. Then he placed another finger inside and then one more and started to move his hand faster as his thumb rubbed against my sensitive nub.

Oh shit....I felt it building again. I reached up and grabbed his arms as he leaned down and started to kiss me and nibble at my bottom lip again. One more thrust of my hips and I fell apart.

I was pretty sure I was about to black out from the intense feeling of this orgasm. It felt like it was going on and on and I actually needed it to stop before it killed me. I was screaming into Gunner's mouth and he never stopped kissing me.

Finally, the pulsing was slowing down and so were Gunner's kisses. I slowly removed my hands from the death grip I had on his arms. I opened my eyes and he was smiling at me. I couldn't help but smile back.

"Did that help ease that ache Baby?" Gunner said as he reached down and gently kissed me.

I was still trying to catch my breath. "I think so!"

Gunner started to laugh and sat up. I laid there for another minute or two until I got my breathing under control. I saw him adjust himself and then run his hand through his hair. I needed to be just as giving with him as he just was for me. I sat up and pulled my legs around to sit up on the sofa. I got down on the floor and turned to face him.

"Ellie what the fuck are you doing?" Gunner said as I started to push him back against the sofa and started unbuttoning his pants. He grabbed my hands and shook his head no.

"Why not Gunner?" I asked in a whiny voice.

He just looked at me and shook his head. "Ellie, I don't need to be taken care of sweetheart."

I ran my hand along his hard erection and raised my eyebrow at him.

"Um, it sure feels like you need to be taken care of."

I started back at unbuttoning his pants and unzipped his zipper. WOW....

"Commando huh?"

"Ellie...holy fuck...."

He threw his head back against the sofa and I had to smile when I saw the shiver run through his body as I touched him. Holy mother fucking shit...he was *huge*! Well, not that I really could compare him to any other penis because in all fairness, this was the first penis I've ever really seen...this up close and in person. I thought he felt big when I took him in my hand in the river at the ranch but seeing it....Holy hells bells how the fuck would that thing ever fit in me?

I started to move my hand up and down along his shaft. The way he was breathing made me horny all over again. The thought that I was making him feel this way was mind blowing.

"Am I doing it right Gunner?"

"Yes...my god yes.... Ellie don't stop....go faster baby!"

I let a smile play across my face and did just as he asked. Next thing I knew he was breathing even faster.

"Ellie, I'm about to come......*oh god Ellie....*"

My heart was beating like crazy.....what did I do? Do I keep going? Do I stop when he starts to come? Oh holy shit I should have asked Ari more questions about this. Just then Gunner let out a moan and called my name again but this time with so much more passion. I looked up and watched his face as I continued to move my hand up and down.

WOW! He was even beautiful when he was coming. I felt something run down on my hand so I pulled my eyes away from Gunner and looked down…..yep….it was cum….all over my hand. There it was. My second hand job and I was feeling pretty damn proud of myself. Thank god I never did this to Ryan when he begged me to.

Gunner lifted his head and looked at me and I smiled when he gave me such a sweet adoring smile.

Once he caught his breath he smiled at me. "You've never done that before the river Ellie?"

"NOPE!" I said as I popped my P!

"Jesus H. Christ that was amazing Sweetheart!"

Just then I heard Jason's car pull up the driveway. Gunner and I both looked out the bay window and then down at my cum covered hand still wrapped around his dick. I jumped up and grabbed my bra and shirt and we both dashed towards my bedroom and then into the bathroom where we both cleaned up and giggled like five-year-olds. Gunner turned me around and lifted me up and onto the bathroom counter.

"Someday Ellie sweetheart, when you're ready….we'll make love and I promise you it will be the most magical night of your life." He leaned in and kissed me passionately as we started to hear Ari arguing with Jason in the living room. It didn't faze either one of us because they argued all the time.

Holy mother of all creations, did this man know how to make the butterflies take off into flight in my stomach.

"I love you…..so much."

"I love you too Sweetheart. So, so very much."

Gunner

"Come on dude. We never fucking see you anymore Gunner except at Football practice and games. Let's just go get one beer, just one fucking beer," Josh said as he followed me out to my truck.

Football season started two months ago and between school, practice, games and everything in between, I had hardly spent any time with Ellie. I could tell it was starting to get to her. Especially on the away games and home games she always seemed nervous. Jeff said she was probably just worried about me getting hurt. I didn't think that was it.

When we did spend time together it was fucking magnificent. I loved being able to make her fall apart with my touch. Although, it was getting harder and harder for me to keep control, and I found myself dreaming about her and waking up jacking myself off in my sleep. I ran my hand through my hair and tried to tune Josh out.

I thought about last Sunday when I took Ellie out for her birthday. It was just the two of us. We went to Judges Hill Restaurant and Bar downtown and it was a perfect evening. I had to smile when I remembered how excited she got when I gave her the present I bought for her. It was a white gold bracelet with a single charm of two hearts on it. She felt her daisy necklace while I put the bracelet on her left wrist. God I loved her.

I threw my bags in the back seat and turned to get into the truck.

"Gunner, just one fucking beer dude that's all I'm asking. Spend some time with the team dude."

I let out a sigh. "Is Jeff going?"

"I'm sure he is. What the fuck happened to him this summer? He sure has been drinking a lot and going out to Rebels almost every night. Coach finds out and his ass is grass Gunner. Plus that fucker has banged more girls the last two months then I have this whole goddamn year. You need to sit down and have a come to Jesus moment with him Gun."

"Yeah, tell me about it. I've tried talking to him. He won't listen to me or Ellie."

"Is this over Ellie's friend Ari?"

"Yep, and tonight her douche bag boyfriend is throwing her a birthday party that I'm required to be at so I'll only be having one beer."

Josh slapped me on the back and smiled. "Hell to the yes my brother, make sure you tell Ellie I said hey!"

"Where we meeting?"

"Fado's dude...thirty minutes"

I jumped in my truck and called Jeff.

"What's up dude?"

"Hey you going to Fado's to meet some of the guys for a beer?" I asked as I heard some hoe in the background trying to get Jeff's attention.

"Fuck yeah I'm going. Pick me up?"

"Ah, yeah but right after I need to go straight over to Ellie's place, it's Ari's birthday and they're having a party for her."

Jeff didn't say anything for a few seconds.

"Fine by me. I haven't seen my baby sister in awhile."

"Where are you?"

"Sitting in the parking lot of the stadium still, where the fuck are you?"

"Same fucking place dick....where are you parked 'cause I only see a few of the guys cars and not your truck."

I heard the girl start laughing and I thought I heard that mother fucker moan.

"Yeah....around the back....give me two minutes."

Mother fucker this had to stop.

I called Ellie while I waited for the bastard to get his fucking blow job.

"Hey!"

"Hey back Sweetheart. How was your day?"

"Long and tiring and Jason is driving me fucking nuts with this party! He is freaking out about every detail. I want to punch him in the throat and give him a good kick in the balls and watch his face while he lies there in pain."

I had to laugh. God how I loved this girl.

"Listen Ells, Josh is giving me hell about not spending any time with the team. Do you mind if I go to Fado's for a quick beer and then I'll head over to your place? I'm picking up Jeff and he wants to come along to see you."

"Of course I don't mind Gunner. Just please make sure Jeff has not been drinking too much. It's Ari's birthday and I don't think he has seen her since September."

"I will make sure Baby and no...he sees her at every home game sitting next to you. I watch him look for her."

Ellie let out a sigh. "My heart aches for him Gunner. Will you please try to talk to him again?"

I didn't want to tell her I was waiting that very moment for the bastard to get done getting blown and that I thought he was a lost cause, so I agreed to talk to him again.

"Thank you Gunner. I love you and please be careful driving."

"I love you too and always Baby....."

I looked at the clock...I just gave him more than two minutes so the fucker better have the bitch gone. I pulled around the stadium and saw him leaning against his truck as some girl was pressed all up against him. I just shook my head. He was going to end up fucking up and getting someone pregnant if he didn't stop this bullshit.

I pulled up and honked the horn. He waved goodbye and jogged over to the truck and jumped in.

"Thanks for the extra few minutes," he said as he gave me a wink.

"Jeff...this is getting out of hand. I mean come on dude did you know her name?"

"What?"

"You heard me....did you even know that girl's name?"

"Of course I did. She's a bartender at Rebels and her name is Stacey........there are you happy fuckwad."

I shook my head as we made our way downtown to Fado's. I had my one drink and surprising enough Jeff only ordered a coke. We talked for a few more minutes with some of the guys and then Jeff and I took off for Ari's birthday party.

By the time we got to the party and pulled down their driveway there were already about fifteen cars parked all around.

"Mother fucker. What the fuck is Jon Baker doing here?"

Jeff looked around until he saw him leaning against a BMW talking to some bleached blonde.

"Hell if I know. Ari wouldn't have invited him so that means douche bag Jason must know him."

I parked my truck around the side of the cottage. By the time we got around to the front door Jon and the blonde must have already gone inside. I opened the door and was not surprised to see him standing there talking to Ellie. Fucking dick.

"Gun, just take it easy. He's only talking to her."

"Yeah and that's all he's ever going to do with her."

I started making my way over to Ellie. She smiled that big beautiful smile she saves only for me. She stepped away from Jon and started to walk towards me. I picked her up and kissed the fuck out of her.

"WOW! Was that because Jon was talking to me or are you just that happy to see me?"

Shit I loved this girl. I laughed as I kissed her quickly again. "Both!"

"I'll take both then, anytime!" I slid Ellie down against me and made sure she felt my already hard dick. Just looking at her turned me on. She gave me a wink and smiled. I needed to let her know how much I always wanted her.

"Hey sis…." Jeff said as he leaned down to give Ellie a kiss on the cheek and a quick hug.

"Thanks for coming Jeff. I'm sure Ari will be happy to see you."

Jeff just shrugged as he scanned the room. His head stopped and his eyes lit up for the first time in two months. I looked over to where he was looking and there was Ari. She was laughing at something Amanda and Heather were saying and she had not noticed Jeff yet. Just then she looked over and I could tell she sucked in her breath at the sight of Jeff standing in her living room. I looked down at Ellie and noticed she was holding her breath. When I looked back at Ari she smiled at Jeff. I swear it was the first time I'd seen that smile of hers since the day she was riding horses at the ranch. I turned to look at Jeff and he was smiling back at her. He then nodded and waved. She waved back and her face turned as red as a rose.

Huh….interesting. Ellie leaned up and asked if I wanted a beer and I shook my head no. I mouthed water to her, she smiled and turned to walk into the kitchen. I looked up just in time to see Jon watching Ellie walk into the kitchen. I think I was going to have to beat his ass, and soon.

Just then I heard Ari.

"Hey Gunner, Hi Jeff, um long time no see. How've you been?"

Jeff cleared his throat after his first attempt to talk to her failed.

"Um, I've been good. Busy with football and senior year and all. How about you? You look beautiful and um, Happy Birthday Squirt!"

Ari blushed again. I looked over her shoulder and saw douche bag Jason watching her every move. Fuck, I couldn't stand that guy. Something about him made me uneasy.

"Thank you for both the compliment and the birthday wishes. I've been okay……..busy. I miss hanging out with y'all. I'm thinking of going to the ranch with Ellie for Thanksgiving weekend since my parents are going on a cruise. Are you um, you planning on being there?"

Jeff must have felt the daggers being thrown his way by Jason because he looked up and smiled at the prick before looking back down to Ari.

"Yeah, I'm planning on heading there with Gunner."

Ari smiled a big satisfying smile. "Cool! Maybe we can have a rematch of that horse race you clearly cheated at," Ari said with a wink.

Jeff let out a laugh.

"You bet Ari, a rematch sounds great," Jeff said as they both just stood there and stared at each other.

Just then douche bag Jason hit a spoon on the side of a wine glass. What a fuck head. Ellie walked back up and Ari gave Ellie a questioning look. Ellie just shrugged her shoulders.

"Can I have everyone's attention please, quiet down please. Arianna baby, please come stand next to me."

Ellie leaned up and whispered to me…."What the hell is this all about? He *never* calls her baby!" Jeff must have heard Ellie because he snapped his head back over to where Ari was now standing next to Jason.

Jason turned Ari around so she was facing directly in front of us. Next thing I know, he stepped in front of her and got down on one knee.

"OH SHIT!" Ellie and I both said at the same time.

"Arianna, my sweet Arianna….these last few months have been nothing but magical for me."

Ari was looking down at this jackass with a shocked look on her face. I wonder if she was more shocked that he was about to ask her to marry him or that he just described their last few months together as being magical. Douche bag. All they ever did was fight!

"It would be my greatest honor if you were to take this ring and say you will marry me."

Ari looked up and looked directly at Jeff. She almost had a pleading look in her eyes. Jeff just stood there staring back at her.

"Jeff! Do *something*, say *something* for Christ sake!" Ellie whispered.

"Arianna, I know this might seem sudden but, baby will you be my wife?" Douche bag had to ask her again because she was still staring at Jeff. Oh this was going to be good.

Ari looked down at Jason and then back up at Jeff again.

"I need some fresh air….." Jeff said as he walked towards the front door.

"FUCK!" Ellie and I both said again at the same time. I started to go after him as Ellie pushed me from behind trying to get me to walk faster. I looked over at Ari who now had her eyes closed with a single tear rolling down her cheek. She opened her eyes and looked down at Jason but I never got to hear what she said because Ellie was pushing me out the goddamn front door.

Jeff was throwing up by the BMW that Jon had been leaning against earlier. Damn….I sure hope that was the asshole's car.

"OH MY GOD Jefferson! Are you okay?" Ellie said as she ran over to him.

"What the fuck is wrong with you mother fucking idiot! You just let the best fucking thing that will EVER happen to you go. You just walked away from her you goddamn stupid mother fucker," I said as Jeff kept throwing up.

"GUNNER! STOP!" Ellie shouted at me.

"Why Ellie? Because he just let the only girl he has ever loved end up with some fucking dick head who is going to end up cheating on her with some country club plastic Barbie? You fucked up again Jeff!"

Jeff was still throwing up and Ellie was just standing there rubbing her hand on his back.

"Shut the fuck up Gunner! You don't think I know what the fuck just happened. You don't think I lay in bed every fucking night and pray to God that Ari was mine and that I could turn back the clock and do it the right way? I'm getting what I fucking deserve. I don't deserve her, I never have!"

"Jefferson that's *not* true. Ari loves you..."

Jeff was still leaning with his hands on his knees looking at the ground. He let his head drop even more.

"You mean she used to love me Ellie. She's marrying another man." He threw up again. Then he stood up and looked up as he threw his head back and yelled out.

"FUCKING SON OF A FUCKING BITCH! I just fucking walked away from the only goddamn person I ever loved." Then he started to cry as Ellie took him in her arms. I heard a sharp intake of air and turned around to see Ari standing right behind me. How much of that did she hear?

She looked at me as she started to back up, then turned and went into the house. What a fucking mess.

"Gunner I think you should take Jefferson home," Ellie said as Jeff stood up and tried to calm down.

Fuck...I started to panic because if I left to take Jeff home that meant Ellie would be left here with Jon.

"Ells, please will you come with us?" Jeff asked as he started to walk towards the side of the house.

"Of course Jefferson, um..... let me go grab my purse." She walked by me and reached up to give me a kiss.

"We're around the side of the house by your bedroom window," I said as she gave me a sad smile.

I walked back to my truck and got in. Jeff was in the back seat already.

"You owe me, and don't ever call me all those mean names again you fucking bastard," Jeff said as he took a drink of water that was in the back seat.

"First off, that water has been back there forever and I have no clue who even drank from it last, and second, what the fuck do I owe you for."

"For asking Ellie to come along, you didn't really want her to stay here with Jonathon Barker hot on her tail did you?"

I stared at Jeff in shock. "You really are a smart mother fucker aren't you? I just hope that was the prick's car you were puking on."

We both laughed and when Ellie got in the truck she asked what we were laughing at.

"Nothing Sweetheart….just wondering who that BMW belongs to, they're going to be in for a rude awaking when they step in Jeff's puke."

"Jesus, Mary and Joseph it is fucking freezing outside!" Ari said as she bundled up under a blanket. I had to agree with her. It was chilly and my head was pounding and all these damn football fans were screaming even more than usual. Of course UT was winning and Gunner and Jefferson where playing great but, right now I was thanking the lord above that Gunner was not going pro. I could not do this every week. It already made me sick to my stomach to watch all these bitches throw themselves at the football players. Gunner always makes a beeline to the locker room but a few times I had to see a cheerleader or some stupid crazy bitch fan run up and start hanging all over him.

I hated it. I loved home games because of course Gunner was home that night but I hated watching all the girls. At least at away games I can't see that on TV.

I noticed there was a girl walking around on the sidelines, she looked familiar to me but I couldn't place her at all. Gunner had just come off the field and was standing there getting a drink when she walked up and he leaned down as she said something to him. He threw his head back and laughed. Ummm, hello...... that made me sit up straighter.

"Who the hell are you giving the evil eye to?" Ari said as she tried to look in the same direction I was looking.

"I'm trying to see who the bitch is that's talking to Gunner, he seems to be very captivated by her conversation."

"Ellie, trust me, you have nothing to worry about with Gunner. If you can't see how much that boy loves you then you need glasses bitch."

I shrugged my shoulders. Maybe she was right; I was acting like a jealous bitch. Then she turned around and I knew exactly who she was. Lori.

"That fucking bitch, how the hell did she get down on the field!"

"WHO? Who is a fucking bitch?" Ari sat up a little more interested after my outburst.

"Lori....the bitch that was dancing with Gunner at Rebels the night I left and we didn't talk for a few weeks. That's *her*! I knew she looked familiar. Why he is talking to her?"

Ari sat back and pulled her knees closer to her chest in an attempt to get warmer.

"Who cares Ells…..she's old news. It's not like he is hanging all over her, you have nothing to worry about. Gunner only wants you."

Just then Gunner leaned down and kissed her on the cheek.

"Or….maybe you do have something to worry about," Ari said as she saw the same thing I saw. That bitch leaned up and gave him a kiss back and then they hugged. WHAT THE HELL!

Gunner turned scanning for me in the crowd. Oh what's wrong dick head….checking to see if I just saw you kiss another girl. His eyes found mine and he smiled.

I was so pissed, no way was I smiling back at that asshole. His smiled faded and he waved. So I did what any other girlfriend would do in my shoes.

I gave him the finger and got up to leave.

"Wait…where're you going?" Ari said as she struggled to get out from under the blanket.

"I'm leaving. I think I've seen enough." I took one last look and Gunner was standing there staring up at me with a shocked look on his face.

I can't believe it….how could he…he knows I'm sitting right here and I can see everything! Why would he do that?

You will never be wanted by anyone…….

My mother's words just kept playing over and over in my head as we walked out to my car.

"SHUT UP!" I screamed out as I threw my hands over my ears.

"Jesus Ellie, I didn't say a damn word!"

I stopped and looked at Ari confused. "What?"

"What to your what? Why did you yell at me to shut up? I wasn't even talking!"

I shook my head to clear my thoughts. SHIT! I'm losing my mind.

"Fuckin' A…I think you're stressed out with school Ells. You took too many classes and you're stressed out from not seeing your man enough. I think you need a vacation. Like to a certain ranch under a certain live oak tree," Ari said as she used her elbow to hit my arm while she winked at me.

"Argh! The last thing I'm going to do is go anywhere with that prick. He can take Lori."

I started to walk faster. I needed to get out of there. I couldn't breathe.

"Ellie stop right now. ELLIE! STOP!" Ari shouted.

"WHAT?"

"Okay I get that you're pissed but holy shit. It was a kiss on the cheek in front of thousands of people including you....his GIRLFRIEND! Do you honestly think that Gunner is cheating on you with this girl? Don't you think it could be something totally innocent? Maybe you should at least let him explain before you fly off the handle."

I started to calm down a little. Ari was totally right. What the hell was wrong with me? I just couldn't shake this feeling that something bad was about to happen. The floor was going to fall out any day now I just knew it.

"You're right, let's go back." I turned and started to head back into the stadium when I saw the little bitch walking out. There was a guy standing there I hadn't even noticed when we walked by the first time. She walked right into his arms and they kissed. I stopped dead in my tracks. Wow...bitch sure does move from guy to guy.

Just then Lori the bitch looked up and noticed us.

"Ellie? Is that you? Gunner's girlfriend?" she asked as she walked towards me and Ari.

Well at least she got my name right this time and called me Gunner's girlfriend instead of Jefferson's little sister.

I smiled and introduced Ari to her.

"It's a pleasure. Um this is Michael, my fiancé."

WHOA...shut the front door! What did she just say? Of course I knew I could count on Ari right at that moment.

"Your fiancé huh? So what where you doing down on the field earlier?"

Subtle Ari...real subtle.

"My uncle is one of the trainers. I came to say good bye to him and a few of the guys I took classes with. I'm not coming back to UT after this semester. Michael's company is transferring him to New York so that's where I'm heading."

I finally found my voice. "Wow, that sounds exciting. So, did you happen to see Gunner to say goodbye?"

She smiled and shook her head. "Yes, you're very lucky Ellie. Gunner loves you very much. He couldn't stop talking about you the whole time. I'm really glad things worked out the way they did." She said as she looked up at her fiancé.

Okay..........I felt like a total idiot. Maybe Gunner will forget all about me giving him the finger. A girl can hope can't she?

"So are you going to keep ignoring me the rest of the night?" I asked Gunner as he sat there and watched TV. He looked exhausted and I knew he was. He played a good long hard game, and by the time he got to his house he was more than ready for bed. He didn't look very happy when he opened the door and I was sitting there waiting for him.

"Listen Ellie, I'm tired, I don't feel like watching TV anymore and I don't feel like talking…I'm not in the mood for your bullshit tonight."

My bullshit? What the hell! I haven't even said a word. Shit, was he still pissed I gave him the finger?

"Wait…….I've haven't even said anything to you. I got you a beer, made you a sandwich and just sat here while you came down from your game. Why are you pissed at me Gunner?"

Gunner slammed his hands through his hair and sighed. He stood up and looked down at me and shook his head. "Are you staying here tonight?"

"Do you want me to stay the night?" I asked as I looked up at him.

"I don't really give a fuck Ellie if you stay or not." He turned and walked to his bedroom.

I felt the tears starting to burn my eyes. I will not cry…I will NOT cry. I wish Jefferson was still up but as soon as he came home he went straight to bed. Some Thanksgiving this turned out to be. I slowly got up and grabbed the dish Gunner's sandwich was on and his empty beer bottle and set them in the kitchen. I grabbed my keys and purse and started to head for the front door. I had to hold it together just long enough to get in my car and leave, and then and only then would I start crying.

I quietly shut the front door and practically ran to my car. Just as I opened the door and was about to swing it open to get in I saw an arm come across and shut the door. I screamed and spun around ready to kick someone in the balls. Except I didn't see some strange mass murderer, I saw Gunner.

"What the fuck! You scared the shit out of me you asshole." I whispered realizing it was around one in the morning and my scream probably woke up one or two people.

"Ellie it's late, don't drive home this late. Come back inside," Gunner said in a tired voice.

"Well you shouldn't really give a fuck if I drive home now or not, now should you Gunner."

He took his hand and ran it through his hair….his signature I'm frustrated or angry move…..God why did that turn me on so much?

"Now if you don't mind, I'm going home, please tell Emma I'm so sorry but I won't be joining y'all for Thanksgiving dinner this weekend."

I turned and grabbed the door handle to open it and Gunner slammed the door shut again.

"Ellie, get your ass back in the house now."

I was so mad that I started shaking…how dare he tell me what to do!

I turned and looked at him. "FUCK OFF!" I tried to push him away but he wouldn't budge an inch that built mother fucker! I pushed again and again and even tried to put my foot on my car for extra leverage and nothing worked.

"Are you done yet?"

"No. How dare you tell me what to do. You're acting like a prick and I wouldn't stay here if you got on your hands and knees and begged me to."

Before I knew it he had lifted me up and was carrying me into the house. I instantly felt his erection which totally caught me off guard. I couldn't yell because it was so late and I didn't really want to end up in jail tonight.

Once we got in the house I started to struggle to get out of his arms. Jesus….he was strong and I was not making any headway. He grabbed my purse and threw it down on the sofa and forced my keys out of my hand all the while still holding onto me. I was trying to squeeze my legs tighter on him but I think I was only turning him on more!

He started towards his bedroom. SHIT! I couldn't yell because I would wake up Jefferson. Once he got in his room and shut the door with his foot, the next thing I knew he slammed me up against the wall and started to kiss me. At first I did nothing in return, but after I felt his erection pushing up against me and the sweet feel of his lips, I couldn't resist. I grabbed his hair in my hands and started kissing him back.

Oh god this felt so good and so right. I don't even remember why we were fighting. Oh yeah, he was acting like a prick. I started to pull away from the kiss.

"Baby I'm so sorry I said that to you. Please forgive me Ellie. It's just when you gave me the finger and got up and left I had no idea why and it fucked up my whole game after that. I dropped two fucking balls and got the shit knocked out of me three times."

Oh no! Oh shit, I had no idea that by me doing that it would mess him up. I put my head back up against the wall and closed my eyes.

"Oh Gunner I had no idea, I'm so sorry and it was a total misunderstanding that I don't even want to talk about. I came back into the stadium did you not see me? I was there the whole game!"

"No Ellie, once you and Ari left I assumed you were leaving for good. I never bothered to look back up there."

Oh I felt like a total piece of shit.

"You have to trust me Ellie," he said as he was kissing all over my neck. My body started to tingle all over again.

"I do trust you Gunner, I'm sorry I'm so insecure. I love you more than anything."

"As much as I want to keep this up, Ells I'm exhausted," He said has he carried me over to his bed. He was asleep as soon as his head hit the pillow. I'm not sure how long I watched him sleep. I really did love him but I just had the weirdest feeling. Something was about to happen, I could just feel it.

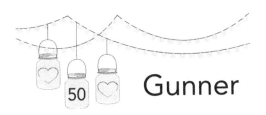

50

Gunner

Ellie was in heaven with Grams in the kitchen Saturday morning. My heart was racing just watching her learn everything Grams was teaching her about how to cook the perfect turkey, as well as how to make a homemade pumpkin pie.

I walked down to the stable to find Jeff saddling up Fire Star.

"You're going for a ride?"

"Yeah, I think I'm going to head out and clear my head. Maybe take a ride and check out that property again."

I nodded my head. I knew he was upset that Ari wasn't there. When I asked Ellie about Ari she just smiled and winked at me. I didn't even have the energy to ask what that wink meant.

"I still can't believe you plan on buying that property dude. Have you given any more thought about your plans for it? You still thinking of going the way you were thinking?"

Jeff looked over at me and smiled. "Yep, it just feels right. I talked to Jake at the office and the fact that they are going to let me work part time will help out. I always thought you were crazy to give up the position Jake offered you just so you could come out here but the more time I spend out here the more I know, this is the life I want also."

I nodded my head again. I had the strangest feeling in my stomach. I'd been having it for the last week, almost like I was expecting something to go wrong. Things with Ellie were going great…almost too good. While everyone around us had so much drama in their relationships, Ellie and I didn't, thank God. But still, something wasn't right. The fact that I saw Ellie talking to Jon at the football game didn't help matters either. That fucker clearly was not getting the message to stay away from her and for some reason, Ellie was too nice to him.

Fucker….

"I'm heading out for awhile. I'll be in the north pasture."

Jeff jumped up on Fire Star and gave me a smile. He had not had a beer for the last few days and I think he finally fucked all the girls in Austin he could. He had not gone out since the night of Ari's party. Maybe things were about to turn around for him. I sure as shit hoped so.

It was killing Ellie to see him being so upset over Ari. I saw him pull out his headphones and put them in.

"Have a good ride Jeff."

"Thanks dude, later."

I watched him ride off. I shook my head….I pray I never fuck up with Ellie. It would kill me if she was not in my life. I watched him ride until he turned around an oak tree and I couldn't see him anymore. I turned to leave and got the shit scared out of me.

"Holy fucking shit Ari! You scared the shit out of me. What're you doing here?"

Ari just smiled as she was leaning up against the stables. She was dressed in jeans, boots, a sweatshirt and a cowboy hat. I looked down at her hand looking for the ring but she had her left hand shoved into her pants pocket.

"Hi Gunner, nice to see you too asshole; and I told you I was planning on coming on out to the ranch this weekend."

Something was up….she had a shit eating grin on her face. I kept looking down at her hand. Why didn't she drive out with Ellie? Where was Jason? Jeff was going to flip out once he found out she was here.

"You're thinking too much Gunner. You mind helping me saddle up a horse?"

"No, I don't mind at all. You want to ride Chestnut again?"

"Who's Jeff on?"

I had to smile, damn this girl never ceased to amaze me. I shook my head as I walked over to the newest addition to the family. She was a beautiful paint horse who had a bit of spunk in her, fast as hell too and probably my favorite horse. Could be because Ellie named her Rose, said she loved the way she smelled. She smelled like a horse to me but who was I to argue.

"Jeff is on Fire Star. Rose here, she's the horse you want. She's a feisty five-year-old, has a mind of her own and sometimes she likes to just take over, push you to your limits. She tends to make you open your eyes and pay attention."

Ari looked over and smiled at me. "Sounds like my kind of horse. Now let's get her ready…I have a race to win."

I stood there and watched Ari as she rode off on Rose. Ellie came up behind me and wrapped her arms around me. God she felt so good. I was fighting the need to take her more and more. I was going to have to talk to her pretty soon to see where she was at with all of this. I needed her so fucking bad, but the last thing I wanted to do was push her into sex. I was pretty sure she was feeling the same way.

"So you knew she was coming all along?"

"Yep!" Ellie said as she popped her P.

"Why didn't you tell me?" I turned and hugged her close to me.

"I would have but she was not one hundred percent sure she was going to make it. She had a problem she was trying to deal with and he was not walking away as easy as she thought he would."

I pulled back and looked down at Ellie and tilted my head with a questioning look.

"She said no?"

Ellie laughed. "Of course she said no!"

"When did she say no? That night? Was it after she heard Jeff say he loved her when we were outside?"

"She pretty much told Jason she needed some fresh air and came outside after us. She heard what Jefferson said and went back in and pulled Jason aside to her bedroom and told him she couldn't marry him. He didn't take it very well and was pretty pissed. Turns out that Jason knew Jefferson liked Ari all along. I guess Jefferson used to talk about her in high school. One night when he was drunk, he told Jason and a few other football players he was going to marry her someday. She broke it completely off with him yesterday and told him she loved Jefferson and couldn't see herself with anyone else but him. Happiest damn day of my life, I could not stand him."

I let out a laugh and put my arm around her shoulder. "Let's go for a walk."

Ellie and I walked and talked for what seemed like forever. It was so nice to just have time to do nothing but talk to her. Usually one of us was running to class, the library, practice, the gym or some other bullshit. We sat underneath a red oak and just talked about everything.

"Gunner, what's going to happen when you graduate? You'll be moving out here and I'll still be in Austin. I thought the last two and half months were bad….that's going to be hell!"

I knew she had been worried about what would happen after graduation, but I had a plan to help ease her mind. I just couldn't tell her yet.

"Don't worry baby. I'm not moving out here full time right away. I have some other things I need to work out first and I'll be working at the firm pretty much full time this summer I think."

Ellie turned and looked at me with a strange look on her face.

"You didn't tell me you were working there full time this summer! That's awesome!"

She leaned back into me and we sat there not saying another word. I wish I could tell her my main reason for not moving out to the ranch full time right away but......I wasn't ready. The last thing I wanted to do was scare her away for good.

51

Jeff

I sat under the same Oak tree I was sitting under the day Ari and I got stuck out here. Fire Star was walking around eating as much grass as he could. Hopefully nothing spooked him and he ran off because I had my iPod on and wouldn't be able to hear it if he did.

Daughtry's "Life After You" was playing. I had it on repeat pretty much since the day I destroyed any kind of future with Ari. I closed my eyes and leaned my head back against the oak. I started to picture her up against the jeep. The sound of her calling out my name, the look on her face when she told me she loved me.

FUCK!

God….would I ever be able to get over her. My fucking heart was tired of hurting. I pretty much tried to fuck her out of my head but I even sucked at that. If only I could go back in time to that day under this tree. I would do so many things differently. I would tell her how much I loved her and wanted her. It was too late.

She was getting married…..

Just then I felt something hit my boot. I opened my eyes and had to close them again and rub them. Was I seeing things? Ari was standing in front of me with her hands on her hips. She was smiling down at me. My heart started to pound so hard I could hear it. What was she doing here? How did she even know where I was? What makes me even think she was looking for me.

"Are you just going to sit there and stare at me Jeff? Maybe you're trying to think of a way to get out of our rematch race?"

Wait…..what did she just say? I shook my head and pulled out my headphones. I couldn't move my body. I just sat there looking up at her.

"Wh…..what are you doing here?"

She threw her head back and started to laugh. Next thing I knew she was moving closer to me and started to walk with her legs straddling mine. She took off her hat and tossed it to the ground. Holy Fuck she was beautiful. She fell down onto the ground and was on her knees looking right at me.

OH HOLY FUCKING SHIT…..don't sit on me…please don't sit on me…….

"I came for our rematch race Jeff. Don't you remember the other day on my birthday, you *promised* me a rematch." She licked her lips as she looked down at my mouth. I had never in my life wanted to kiss her more than I did at this very moment. Why was she here though? She was getting married to someone else.

I looked down at her left hand and didn't see a ring. I snapped my head back up at her and she let the sexiest fucking smile I'd ever seen spread across her face.

"I...I um....I thought you wouldn't be here Ari because you're getting married so....I guess I just thought......I just thought....." Fuck I couldn't think enough to form any fucking words. She was inches away from my crotch and I was getting harder by the second with the heat coming from her body. Why was she doing this to me? Payback maybe?

She looked down at her left hand and shrugged as she held it up for me to see. Then she did it.....she fucking sat down on me. She raised her eyebrows up at me when she felt my erection. Fucking dick of mine.....sold me the fuck out. She rocked her hips just enough to drive me fucking crazy as she let out a small moan. She smiled as she looked at me.

"I don't see a ring on my finger Jeff. You see I'm not getting married, at least not right now, and certainly not to Jason."

Oh god, all I wanted to do was take her and make love to her right here right now.

"Why?"

She looked at me and shook her head while she kept that damn smile that drove me insane on her face. "I couldn't marry him when I'm in love with someone else." She wiggled again against my dick.

My heart was going to fucking explode it was beating so strong and fast.....please God....please let her say she loved me still.

I smiled back at her. She was the most beautiful thing I'd ever put my eyes on.

"Anyone I know?"

She reached up and cupped my face with her hands. She licked her fucking lips again as she looked down at my mouth again. She moved closer to me and lightly brushed her lips against mine. I felt a tremble move through my whole body. Then she did it again, but this time she kept her lips barely on mine.

"I always have been and always will be, in love with you Jefferson. Always."

I closed my eyes when I felt them burning with the threat of tears. I loved this girl so fucking much. I didn't deserve her love. I slowly opened them to see her staring at me.

"Ari baby, I've done some awful things the last two months. Things that I'm so ashamed of and, if I could take it all back....take back the day we stood here and I pushed you away.....you have to believe me when I say I would do it in a heartbeat baby. I......I....."

"Jeff, I'm going to ask you once and then I never want to talk about any of it ever again. I need you to be one hundred percent honest with me okay?"

"YES! You can ask me anything Ari; I'll never lie to you ever!"

She closed her eyes for a few seconds and when she opened them she had tears building up. FUCK! I can't believe how badly I've hurt this girl. I was going to have to get Gunner to punch me again, maybe a few times.

"When you were.....when you were with all of those girls...." She had to clear her throat and pause for a second. FUCK!

"What were you thinking about when you were with those girls Jeff? What were you trying to do?"

I sat there stunned. I can't believe she was asking me about my two months of man whoring. I didn't even care that I felt a tear rolling down my face. I needed to be honest with her. I needed to let her know what the fuck was going through my head.

"Ari..." My voice cracked and now it was my turn to clear my throat. "I was trying to erase you from my mind, from my heart baby. It was the only way I could think of to get over you but it didn't work. No matter what girl I was with, I just prayed to god she would be the one to get you out of my head, but it never worked. It never worked because I was so ashamed of what I was doing, I ended up closing my eyes and pretending it was you I was with. I completely tuned them out and just....I just fantasized I was making loving to you, not fucking some girl I had just met at a bar."

Ari had tears rolling down her face. *Fuck me.....* I was hurting her all over again. I hated myself....I fucking hated myself. If she found it in her heart to forgive me I would spend the rest of my life making it up to her I promised myself right then.

"Did you use protection Jeff?"

"ALWAYS!"

"Did you feel anything for any of them?"

"*Nothing*....."

"Do you promise me you're done fucking around?"

"I never want to touch another girl again my entire life!"

Ari raised an eyebrow up at me and tilted her head. I reached up and wiped the tears away from her face as she gave me a smile that if I'd been standing up I would have fallen to the ground.

"You sure about that last statement you must made Jeff?"

"YES! Of course I'm sure."

She started to giggle and was getting ready to stand up. I pulled her back down and held her there.

"Wait…where're you going?"

"Well, considering you just said you never wanted to touch another girl again in your life, I figured you wanted me to get off your lap!"

I smiled at her and pulled her lips to mine and kissed her. She let out a moan against my lips and I deepened the kiss. It was probably one of the most powerful kisses I've ever felt. Her love felt like it was rushing through my veins.

I pulled back away from her and waited for her to open her eyes.

"You're not just some girl Ari. You're the only woman I've ever loved and I'll spend the rest of my life proving that to you squirt."

Ari let out a laugh as she tossed her head back.

"Well holy fucking shit Johnson…..I think we're in for the ride of our lives then! But I have a deal breaker," She said as she looked over my whole body. I shivered from her intense stare.

"A deal breaker, anything…..just name it!"

"Okay………you're gonna to have to stop playing "Truck Yeah" every goddamn time we all get in your truck."

What?

"ELLIE! She put you up to this didn't she, that little traitor sister of mine!"

Ari laughed as she bent down to kiss me. Just then I heard "You Save Me" by Kenny Chesney coming from my ear phones. I had to smile. Perfect song. We sat there for another few minutes and just kissed each other senseless. In those few minutes of kissing the woman of my dreams, I'd never in my life felt so at peace and so loved by another person.

"I love you Arianna Katherine Peterson…….so fucking much."

"I love you Jefferson Michael Johnson. Now, let's get the hell back on our horses. I have a goddamn race to win!"

Emma, Ari and I spent most of the afternoon cleaning up and packing up food from our Thanksgiving Day feast. The guys all went out to the porch and I heard Garrett saying something about a Jess person bringing in a new horse. Ari's eyes lit up at that. Anything to do with horses and she was on board.

"Girls, why don't y'all head on down to the main stable and check out the new filly that just came in."

"How old is she Emma?" Ari asked as she took off the apron she had tied around her. She had been smiling from head to toe ever since she and Jefferson came back from their ride yesterday. I guess they worked things out because he couldn't keep his hands off her and she was the same way. Emma had to tell them to mind their manners at least five times during dinner.

"She's three and she's a beauty. Jefferson actually bought her for his new place." Ari and I both snapped our heads around and looked at Emma. She realized her mistake the moment it came out of her mouth.

"Wait, what new place Emma? Why is Jefferson buying a horse?" I asked Emma.

"You mean he hasn't told you yet?" Ari said in a stunned voice.

"No….I have no idea what either one of you is talking about!"

Emma shook her head and looked back to the sink where she was putting away the last of the dishes. "It ain't my place to tell you Jefferson's news Ellie."

Ari started to laugh. "Well it sure is shit is mine now! Jeff is buying two hundred and fifty acres of land that butts up to the north side of the Mathews ranch."

WHAT? Why would he not tell me this and more importantly HOW?

"How in the hell, oh sorry Emma, how in the heck can he afford to buy a two hundred fifty-acre-piece of land?"

Ari shook her head and shrugged her shoulders. I knew Jeff worked during the year after football season but that was only during the spring semester. Then I remembered my car. How did he afford to buy my car….with cash? Now he's buying horses? Something did not add up. No intern at an architectural firm could make that much money. I know he said he had money left over from our grandmother, and he was a good saver but come on. I was getting to the bottom of this right now.

I spun on my heels and made a beeline for the stables. Ari was right on my heels. I didn't talk the whole way there; I had too many things running through my mind. OMG...what if he was selling drugs!

"Stop thinking so much Ellie! Christ! I can hear your damn brain working in over time now. Just give Jeff a chance to tell you. Don't go running in and start accusing him of selling drugs or something."

Shit....how did she know that's what I'd been thinking? Did I say it out loud by mistake? We turned the corner and I saw Drake, Aaron, Jefferson, Gunner and......a girl?

She was probably my height and weight but she was dressed in super tight ass Wrangler jeans, cowboy boots and a tight Navy Blue t-shirt. What the fuck?

Gunner and Aaron were both talking to her and she was throwing her head back laughing at something Gunner had just said. I immediately didn't like her. I didn't know who she was, but I knew I didn't like her one bit.

"Jesus, Mary and Joseph, who the fuck is the tramp dressed as a cowgirl?" Ari said as she looked her up and down. Jefferson's eyes lit up like a Christmas tree when he saw Ari. He looked over at me and smiled as he walked up to me.

"Ells I wanted to wait until it was all final but it looks like this week it will be so....Um, yeah I bought some land out here. It butts up to the north pasture of the Mathews ranch. It's about two hundred and fifty acres." He then looked over to Ari and smiled even bigger. "I bought it hoping to turn it into a horse ranch, and I bought my first filly today. She's yours Baby. Whatever you want to name her Ari, she's all yours."

Ari looked stunned. I'd never in my life seen Ari stunned into silence.....EVER.....in all the years I had known here. She just stared at Jeff and I noticed his smile starting to falter. I looked back at Ari and she had a tear rolling down her face. Next thing I knew she was jumping into Jeff's arms and wrapping her legs around his waist.

"OH MY GOD! You bought me a horse! Jeff started laughing as he walked over to the filly while Ari was kissing him all over like mad.

"Jesus get a damn hotel room would you!" Gunner called out as he looked over at me and winked. He then turned his attention to miss bleached blonde tight ass jeans wearing fake ass tits cowgirl. She gave him a quick hug....HUH?......and then turned to hug Aaron. Old friend? Cousin? Who was this girl?

"Hey Sweetheart, want to see the filly, she's a beauty."

"I'm pretty sure I already got a look at her." Gunner gave me a confused look and looked back toward the horse. Stupid ass…..

"Sure, let's go meet Ari's new horse." I said as I just shook my head.

For the rest of the night no one brought up miss bleached blonde tight ass jeans wearing fake ass tits cowgirl, so neither did I. It was almost like she was never even there. I did corner Jeff about how in the hell he was able to buy all this shit. Turns out the money from our grandmother that he invested is doing pretty well. He had some set aside for a car and school for me and some left over if I ever wanted to use it for a wedding.

A wedding? Okay. I wasn't planning on that for a while. Gunner's whole body tensed up when I laughed about needing the money for a wedding. I thought it was weird but I was still pissed about miss tight pants to care right now what Gunner was thinking.

The next morning I got up to Ari already up and gone. Gesh, second day in a row she had hightailed it out first thing in the morning. I was beginning to think that she and Jeff were sneaking off to make out or something. EEEWWW….I didn't need that visual at all just now. Not first damn thing in the morning. I shook my head to erase the image from my mind.

I threw on a pair of sweatpants and a UT football sweatshirt. It felt like the cold front had moved through. I went down into the kitchen. 9:30? What the hell! Why did everyone let me sleep in so late? And where the hell was everyone?

I walked out onto the front porch to see Emma and Garrett in a deep conversation. They stopped the moment I walked out.

"Oh excuse me, I didn't mean to interrupt you," I said as I started to head back into the house.

"Nonsense Ellie darling, you could never interrupt us. Are you looking for Drew honey?"

I nodded my head and smiled.

"I believe he walked down to the barn a little bit ago. He was going to feed the horses."

"Oh….okay great….um thanks, I'll go him track him down." Why was I stammering over my words?

I headed down to the main stable and I heard voices. I turned the corner to see her…..leaning up against the barn and Gunner was leaning next to her with his arm resting up against a stall. She was smiling and laughing at something he said. I instantly had the same feelings I had when I came across Ryan. I just stood there. Finally Gunner looked up. He gave me that drop my panties crooked smile of his and dropped his arm and started to walk towards me. I was frozen. Why was he down here alone with this girl? I looked over at her and she was giving me a dirty look and then smiled a smirky smile at me.

I don't know why I did it but I turned and walked away. "Ellie?" Gunner called for me. As soon as I turned the corner out of their view I took off running. I had no idea where the hell I was going but I was running as fast as I could.

"ELLIE STOP!" Gunner shouted. I knew I'd never be able to out run him. Shit! He runs every damn day. I ran up to the tank and had to put my hands on my knees and lean over.

OH SHIT…I needed to start working out again. I was trying to suck in air but my lungs felt like they were closed up.

"What the fuck Ellie? What are you doing running away like that?"

Have. To. Catch. My. Breath…..

I stood up and tried to rub out the cramp I was now getting on my side. Holy fuck….I think I needed to start running……..okay maybe walking and then work my way up to running. Oh my god, I was rambling my own fucking thoughts now.

Gunner walked up and pulled me around to look at him.

"What was that about? Why did you run off?"

Once I got my breath back I just let go. I was tired, cranky, stressed out from school, never seeing Gunner enough, sitting and having to watch endless girls swoon all over his ass….and now this. He is down in the barn looking like he was about to kiss some bleached blonde tight…oh fuck it……BITCH cowgirl.

"Oh I'm sorry Gunner. It's just that it looked like you two needed a private moment to finish whatever it is you were about to start."

"What? Ellie what are you talking about."

"Go fuck yourself ok. You let me sleep in this morning so you could spend some time with tight jean wearing whoever the fuck she is bleached blonde. You sure looked cozy with each other. I would say her name but funny thing is, you never introduced her to me yesterday….especially after she gave you a nice long good bye hug…….Fuck this."

I started to walk away but fuck…I still had the cramp in my side. *Fuck me*!

"Ellie don't walk away from me. Stop for just one goddamn minute."

"I'm going home."

I watched as he threw his hands in his hair and then pulled them down over his face.

"Baby please stop…..I can't do this Ellie. All we do is argue anymore and you keep getting pissed at me and I have no fucking clue as to why. So you saw me talking to Jess, she's Drake's daughter. We all grew up together. Fuck she's like a little sister to me Ellie. I was not about to kiss her or do anything else with her for that matter. I love you dammit Ellie! Why can't you see that I love you....I only want you."

You will never be wanted by anyone.......

"SHIT! When will her voice get out of my fucking head!"

"Who's voice Ellie?"

I did it again. I turned around and saw the hurt in Gunner's eyes. Why was I having such a trust issue with him lately? I really didn't think they looked like they were about to kiss so why did I run off like that?

I felt sick to my stomach and just sat down and started to cry. Gunner was over and down on his knees in two seconds flat.

"Ellie! What's wrong? Do you feel sick?"

I just threw myself into him. He wrapped his arms around me and then sat down and brought me onto his lap. He was stoking my back and just kept saying it was alright. It wasn't all right though.

"Gunner, I don't know what's wrong with me. I keep waiting for the floor to fall out from beneath me. I'm so tired of school already, I'm stressed out, my mother won't stop calling me, you're hardly ever around and when I do get to see you, I have to watch girls throw themselves at you....I'm just waiting for you to get sick of me and leave." I started sobbing.

"Sweetheart I'm so so sorry. I didn't know your mom had been calling you. I wish you would have told me or Jeff. I know school is rough baby; you took way too many classes Ells. Football is almost over baby and we can be together more often. It's all going to work out. You need to talk to me Ellie, we can't keep fighting over little shit that means nothing okay?"

I nodded my head and looked up at him. His blue eyes caught mine and I sucked in a breath from the smoldering look he was giving me. He slowly started to pull me down and leaned me back on the grass and started to kiss me.

After I came back down to earth Gunner leaned in against my ear and whispered to me.

"Another first baby. Orgasm next to the tank."

I let out a laugh and looked at his beautiful smile. Maybe everything really was going to be ok.

December......

"I cannot believe you're getting married Amanda. What the fuck? Don't you think this is a bit too soon?" Ari said for the fifth time since we picked Amanda up at her apartment.

"Ari, I'm madly in love with Brad and he is madly in love with me. We want to get married as soon as possible so no, I don't think it is too soon.

"Y'all just got engaged just over two weeks ago for Christ sakes!" Ari said shaking her head.

Brad had asked Amanda to marry him on Thanksgiving right in front of his whole family. She of course said yes and they immediately started planning a Valentine's Day wedding. Classes were out for the semester and I finally felt like I could relax. When Amanda called and asked if we could go check out the Driskill Hotel we jumped at the chance to go and do something different.

Jeff was with Brad helping him fix something on his father's boat and Gunner was planning on meeting his cousin Shannon's fiancé James, who was flying in a day earlier than Shannon to catch up with Gunner. I guess Shannon and James were high school sweethearts and he went out to the ranch all the time when they were in high school. Gunner had not seen either of them in a few years. They were getting married that weekend.

"Okay ladies. So here is the drill. We're going to look at two different ball rooms. I'm trying to keep this small but I have a feeling Brad's mother is going to give me an invite list a mile long. So keep that in mind. I'm thinking no more than three hundred people."

"THREE HUNDRED PEOPLE!" Ari and I both said at the same time with equal amount of shock in our voices.

"I know.....I would like to keep it at one hundred fifty and that's my goal but not sure the future monster-in-law feels the same way. So just keep reminding me of that while we're looking. You're my bridesmaids.....this is your job."

I had to giggle because Amanda was the type of girl who would have just run off to Vegas to get married but Brad's mother.....she was something else. It shouldn't take her long to figure out that Amanda was not going to put up with her shit.

We toured a few different banquet halls and I knew Ari was just as bored as I was. I was in charge of taking notes and I swear to god if Amanda says "Did you write that down Ellie?" one more fucking time to me I am going to jam the notebook up her ass!

ARGH, the dude giving us the tour was a stick in the mud......he was an older gentleman and he just kept talking about servers, bartenders, chairs, linens, votive candles, china, silverware, flutes, dance floors....OH MY GOD! I couldn't take it anymore! Ari had walked ahead and was peaking in the doors to the kitchen.

We walked over and he was talking about catering .....

"Ellie, did you get that written down?" I just looked at her.

"Yes. Yes I did......" I said with a forced smile.

I saw Ari walking up to another door that led to the hotel rooms, that's what I wanted to see! I heard they were super romantic and Brad was planning on staying the night at the hotel before they flew out to Barbados. Just then I heard Ari suck in a deep breath of air.

"Holy fucking mother of all good, oh fucking shit."

Our tour guide instantly stopped talking and looked at Ari. Amanda gave her a dirty look and I tried to hide my giggle. Ari walked up to me and grabbed my arm and pulled me towards the door to the hallway.

"Thanks that was the most excitement I've had all damn day!"

"I thought you said Gunner was with his cousin's fiancé today," Ari said as she kept looking back at the door that lead down to the rooms.

"He is."

"Yeah, I don't think so....." She pulled me up and made me duck down and told me to look through the window.

Gunner? He was standing at one of the room doors. Just then the door opened and I heard a girl shriek. She instantly jumped into Gunner's arms and wrapped her legs around his waist.

Oh. My. God. This was not happening.....no.......

She looked so happy to see him and he looked so happy to see her. Then she kissed him. Not a deep kiss but a quick kiss on the lips. Then he walked her into the room and they shut the door.

I collapsed to the ground. That mother fucker was cheating on me. I was about to cry....I looked up at Ari who grabbed my arm and pulled me up to my feet.

"Oh no you don't....not here....let's go. AMANDA! Code blue......NOW!"

Amanda spun around and looked at me and then looked at Ari.

"*What? Now?* She turned and apologized to our tour guy. "I'll be back in touch with you but I loved everything! Thank you!" Amanda called out as she was running to catch up with us.

She finally caught up to Ari as we made it to the lobby and Ari sat me down in a chair. I looked up at them both.

"Go" they both said at the same time.

I lost it....I'd never cried so hard in my life. I was rocking back and forth and all I could hear was my mother...... *You will never be wanted by anyone*.......I threw my hands over my ears. She needed to get the fuck out of my head! I wanted to scream.....it was Bryce and Ryan all over again.....

"I knew it....I told you Ari...I told you that I had a feeling something was going on! I TOLD YOU! He has probably been trying to figure out a way to get rid of me. Even Emma and Garrett were acting strange over

Thanksgiving. He probably told them he was going to be breaking up with me."

Oh my god my chest was hurting. I couldn't breathe. Amanda dropped to her knees and pulled my face up to meet hers.

"Ellie, look at me....if it's true....."

"Mandy I saw him! I saw her....she jumped into his arms and kissed him and then they walked into a fucking hotel room together....."

"*IF* it is true Ellie, he doesn't deserve you. He is a stupid ass mother fucker who needs to have his ass kicked." Amanda looked up at Ari. "We need Heather....."

Ari took out her cell phone and next thing I heard was Ari saying code blue meet and us at my place in thirty.

I started to shake my head. I took a deep breath and then reached into my purse. I pulled out my cell phone. My hands were shaking. Ari looked at me and shook her head no. I put up my hand to her as I pressed Gunner's number.

"Hey Sweetheart! You having fun with the girls?"

Fucking bastard.....

"Yes....it's been a very informative trip to say the least."

"Ells, what's wrong. You sound upset."

"So are you with James Gunner?"

"Ahh, yeah we were just sitting here getting caught up on times and I got a little bit of a sur...."

"Don't. Ever. Call. Me. Again. I never want to talk to you again Gunner do you understand me?"

Ari reached down and pulled my arm to get me up and walking. She knew like I did, Gunner would be out of the that room in five minutes tops and last thing I wanted was to see him.

"Ellie, what're you talking about? What the fuck is going on now?"

"I saw you....I saw you with that girl. You fucking bastard you kissed her! I saw it this time Gunner with my own goddamn eyes!"

Silence......Busted....

"Ellie, I don't know who or what you saw, but it sure as fuck was not me kissing another girl. Where are you Ellie?"

"I know what I saw and what Ari saw.......we both saw you kissing on a girl and believe me you two were very cozy with each other and practically fucking out in public. I hate you.....I hate you Gunner!"

"Jesus Christ Ellie I don't know what the fuck you're talking about. Are you home? I'm coming there now!"

"Don't bother, I won't be there! Good bye Gunner...I hope she was worth it."

I hung up the phone and started to cry. Ari was back on the phone with Heather.

"Scratch our last meeting place…we're coming there."

I spent the rest of the night crying and then bitching; taking shots of something that burned like a bitch when it went down……I didn't even know what the fuck I was drinking. I ended up turning off my phone because Gunner wouldn't stop calling. Jefferson starting calling Ari's phone and when Ari told him what happened all I heard was Jeff screaming that he was going to beat the shit out of Gunner.

I finally passed out around 3:30. I woke up to banging on the door. I sat up and oh my god…my head was pounding. Heather ran over to the door and peaked through. She turned back and said it was Jefferson. She opened the door slowly to make sure he was alone. Jefferson walked in and as soon as he saw me he came over and sat down on the sofa. Once I was in his arms I started to cry again.

"Shhhh, Ellie honey it is okay. Don't cry honey…..shhh….I saw Gunner last night when he came home. He was crazy out of his mind worried because he couldn't find you. I don't think he even thought to look here at Heather's place."

"I don't care Jefferson, I don't care how worried he was because he sure as shit wasn't thinking about me when he was backing some bitch up into a hotel room!"

"Ellie are you sure it was Gunner. He swore to me he was with his cousins honey."

I pulled away from him and just looked at him. Then I looked over at Ari who shook her head.

"YES! Ari saw him first. We SAW him Jefferson….with my own two eyes I saw him!"

"Okay…okay I believe you, it's just that he was in hysterics and just really seemed believable."

"Yeah well, who knows how long he has been cheating. No wonder I never see him."

Jefferson looked over at Ari.

"Ellie it's been football season honey, even I was MIA for a good part of the time."

"I don't care….." I started to shake my head….I was done…. "I never want to see him again. Can you give me a ride home please?"

Jeff stopped at HEB so I could pick up a few items to cook for dinner. I was not planning on leaving the house anytime soon.

"Ellie…." I heard my name and turned around. It was Jonathon Baker. I let out a sigh. I was not in the mood for him.

"Hey Jon, what's up?" I turned back around and grabbed some strawberries.

"Ellie are you okay?" He looked at me with real concern in his eyes.

"No Jon I'm not....I just found out my boyfriend cheated on me so no...I'm not really okay."

"Fuck Ellie....I'm sorry to hear that."

I just kept on walking. I felt numb.

"Hey listen, a bunch of us are going to Rebels tonight, why don't you join us? I promise it is strictly a friend inviting another friend who might need to get her mind off of some shit.

At first I was going to say no but then something came over me. I needed a night out, and someone to get my mind off of Gunner Mathews.

"Okay....What time should I expect you to pick me up?"

Jon looked pleased....a little too pleased but right at that moment I didn't care.

"Dinner first?"

What the hell....

"Sure, why not."

"How about six?"

I nodded and tried to give him the best smile I could manage. "Sounds great...see you then."

Jefferson lectured me all the way home about how I shouldn't be going to Rebels tonight with anyone let alone Jon Baker. I told him a bunch of people were going. I was ready for him to just shut up. I still could get a few hours of sleep in before Jon came to pick me up. My head was pounding. I needed to have my head clear tonight so I could put my plan in place. Forget Drew Mathews ever walked into my life, starting tonight at 6 pm.

At five forty five the door bell rang. He was early that eager bastard. I had on a black dress that was barely half way down my thighs, and red cowboy boots. My hair was half up and half down and I put just enough makeup on to make my eyes stand out. I looked one last time in the mirror. Shit my eyes were red and swollen from crying.

I attempted to put on a smile as I swung the door open. My smile faded instantly.

Gunner......

I just stared at him as he looked me up and down.

"You going somewhere?" He sounded pissed. Pesh...if anyone was going to be pissed, it was me.

"Yes, as a matter of fact I am. I have a date so if you don't mind leaving; he'll be here soon to pick me up."

I started to shut the door put he stopped it with his hand.

"I have nothing to say to you so please leave."

"Ellie, I was not fucking some girl last night. I don't know why you keep doing this but honestly, I'm getting really tired of this game."

What?

"What game might that be Gunner?"

"You and this insecurity bullshit you have got going on Ellie. I have tried to be patient with you and bend over backwards not to push you too soon into anything, and all you do is accuse me of not wanting you, but always wanting someone else. It's bullshit and I'm fucking sick of it."

"Well good then, you don't have to worry about any of that BULLSHIT anymore because we…..are…..done. Please leave now."

"Who are you going out with Ellie? Tell me right now!" Gunner yelled so loud it caused me to jump."

Just then Jon came driving down the driveway in his BMW. I closed my eyes and prayed that Gunner did not beat the hell out of him. Gunner turned and looked at the car then slowly turned around and looked at me.

"Holy shit Ellie….that was fast. Maybe you've had Jon all along on the side huh?" I reached up and slapped him across the face. Jon got out of his car but stopped and just stood there.

"I hate you. Do you hear me? I fucking hate you and I NEVER want to see you again! NEVER!"

Gunner looked devastated and I almost wanted to tell him how sorry I was and that I didn't mean a word I just said…….until I remembered the bitch wrapped around his body.

"Fine, if this is what you want Ellie, don't worry. I'll never bother you again."

Gunner turned and walked away from me. That's it? He was just going to give up that easy?

I watched him get in his truck and peel out and race down the driveway. I had to put my hand on the door jam to hold myself up. Then I turned and ran to the bathroom and threw up.

53 Gunner

"Drew, are you sure you feel like going out? I mean you really don't have to entertain James and me."

My cousin Shannon had been talking about wanting to go to Rebels ever since we were sitting in her hotel room at the Driskill yesterday.....before my whole world turned upside down. I never told her why I had to run out on them. They were getting married this weekend and I didn't want to put a downer on things. James was supposed to fly in a day ahead of Shannon but she ended up surprising me by coming in early with him. I was so blown away when she opened the door to what I thought was James' hotel room. She screamed and jumped into my arms. Then I saw James sitting on the bed. It had been a great surprise, at least for a few minutes until I got Ellie's crazy ass call accusing me of sleeping with someone.

"Gunner are you going to ever tell us why Jeff punched you last night? Your eye looks terrible," Shannon said as she fussed over it again.

We walked into Rebels and I spotted Brad so I stopped and introduced him to James and Shannon. Brad I could tell was giving me the cold shoulder. I guess Amanda filled him in on my whole cheating thing. Whatever....I followed Shannon and James in and my eyes went right to the dance floor. It was like I instantly knew she was here. "I Cry" by Flo Rida was playing and Ellie was dancing with that fucker. What the fuck? She had a fucking beer in her hand and she dancing awfully close to Jon. Her ass was grinding all in his fucking crotch.

Just then Jeff and Ari walked up to me. Ari looked at me funny as I looked down at her. She tilted her head and looked at me and then looked out to Ellie. I looked back out and Ellie had her back to us but that fucker looked up and saw me. He smiled and then he reached down and kissed Ellie.

When they say you can't die from a broken heart they're right, but it sure as fuck hurts so much that you wish you were dead. My heart just shattered and I felt like I was going to be sick.

The song stopped and Ellie turned around and saw me. She stopped and stared at me. Then "Over You" by Miranda Lambert started playing. What fucking timing for that song to start playing. I felt a tear running down my cheek as Ellie shook her head and looked at me confused.

"I can't do this anymore. I can't love her enough for both of us....Jeff can you give Shannon and James a ride home?"

Jeff just looked at me and then out to Ellie who was just standing there while Jon was trying to get her to dance.

"Gunner why don't you try to talk to her.....she might..."

"I'm leaving and I need to know if you'll give my cousins a ride to their hotel please, they're talking to Brad and Amanda."

"Sure I will Gunner."

"Gunner, who was that you were with yesterday?" Ari asked me.

I just shook my head. "I don't know who you're talking about and I'm tired, I'm so tired of doing this. I'll see you around Ari."

I took one last look at Ellie who was still standing there and looking over at me. I turned and walked away from the only person I've ever loved in my entire life. I would love her for the rest of my life.

Now I needed to figure out how to forget about her.

Ellie

Was Gunner just crying? I was so confused why was he looking like I was the one who gutted him. I was pissed at Jon for kissing me. Asshole!

Gunner turned and was leaving.

Wait….where was he going? I started to walk over to where Ari was, she was looking at me like she was just as confused as I was. Jon started to pull me back onto the dance floor.

"JON! Let me go talk to my brother for fuck's sake!"

I started to walk towards Jeff and Ari and of course Jon was walking right behind me. Then I saw her…..my stomach instantly felt sick. I sucked in a breath and looked at Ari who looked over to where I was looking.

"Oh holy shit! That's her Jeff. That's the girl that Gunner was with yesterday." Ari said as she was pulling on Jefferson's shirt.

I couldn't believe it…he brought her here? I mean he didn't know I would be here. But oh my god….

Jeff looked at us confused. "Who?"

"The girl standing there with that guy talking to Brad and Amanda, that's the girl who was at the Driskill who jumped into Gunner's arms and kissed."

Jeff snapped his head at Ari and looked back and forth to both us like we were crazy.

"Fuck Ari you didn't tell me what hotel you saw Gunner at. Oh holy fuck!" Jeff said as he pushed his hands through his hair.

"What the hell does it matter what hotel it was at!"

"It matters a lot Ari. That girl over there…..…that's Gunner's cousin Shannon. She flew in a day early to surprise Gunner. That girl you saw jumping into his arms was his fucking cousin!"

No….. Oh my god no………this can't be happening again. I instantly felt the tears rolling down my face.

"Oh my god no…..OH MY GOD…..." Ari said as she looked at me.

"Where did he go Jefferson? Where did Gunner go?"

"Um, I don't know Ells, he was pretty torn up when he saw you on the dance floor kissing asshole here, who made damn sure Gunner saw him kiss you."

I turned to look at Jon and who was now pulling on my arm to go back out and dance with him.

"Let me go Jon…….Ari I need your car keys……..I need to go after him."

"No! Ellie my dear you need to come back out and dance with me. Just let him go."

"*Ari*….. I need your keys!" I was trying to push Jon away while trying to reach into Ari's front pocket for the keys.

"Ellie, I know for a fact you've been drinking…Jeff and I will take you anywhere you want to go."

Jon was still pulling at me. FUCK what was his deal.

"Hey, Jon…let my sister go right the fuck now!"

"Fuck you Jeff….your sister can make up her own mind." He took my arm again. This time I saw Jefferson coming after him. I ducked down when I saw the swing coming. Jefferson hit Jon right in the nose.

Ari screamed out when Jon lunged back at Jefferson. I grabbed Ari's arm and reached in her pocket and grabbed her keys. I knew she was going to be more worried about Jefferson than me reaching in and getting her keys out. I would be okay…I only had two beers.

I turned and ran over to Amanda and Brad who were still talking to Gunner's cousins until they saw Jeff and Jon fighting. Brad ran over to try and break them up.

"I need to find Gunner. Will you make sure Jeff and Ari get a ride home?" I yelled at Amanda.

There was so much commotion going on no one even saw me running for the exit. I had to get to Gunner. I had to beg him to forgive me. Once I told him what I saw he will understand how easy it was to misunderstand that. He had to understand….. OH. MY. GOD. Gunner! FUCK I had no idea where Ari parked! I started hitting her panic button as I ran to the parking lot she normally parked in. There! I saw her Jeep. I felt a little dizzy…….I only had two beers………

I jumped in her Jeep and took off…..the first place I needed to check was his house.

Gunner

Pounding...all I heard was pounding on the goddamn front door. Shit...my head was fucking killing me....I looked at the clock and it said 1:30 am. I left Rebels at 10:00 and came straight home and started drinking hard. I must have passed out around 12:30 am...at least that's the last time I looked at the clock.

Pounding again.... FUCK.....Make it fucking stop!

"I'm fucking coming, Jesus Christ."

I opened the door and saw Brad standing there. What the fuck was he doing here?

"Jesus Gunner, are you drunk?" he said as he pushed his way in.

I let out a laugh. "Not nearly drunk enough dude, not nearly enough."

"Where the fuck is your cell phone?" He looked around and saw it sitting on the coffee table. I turned it off around midnight when Ari kept fucking calling me over and over.

Brad turned it on while I walked over the kitchen to get a beer.

"You want a beer man or something harder...." I said with a laugh.

Just then I heard my phone beeping like crazy with notifications. What the hell?

"Gunner I need you to listen to me." He took the beer from my hand and looked at me. It was the first time I ever saw fear in his eyes.

"Oh my god, did something happen to my cousin?"

Brad shook his head at me....

"Your cousin is fine Gunner, she and James are back at their hotel. But there's been an accident."

My heart started to pound...oh god please no.

"Who?"

Brad swallowed hard. He ran his hand through his hair and when he looked at me again he had tears in his eyes.....holy fuck this was going to be bad.

"It's...... It's Ellie Gunner. She was in a car accident earlier and is at Brackenridge hospital. Jeff got a call around midnight and we've been trying to call you. I left the hospital to come find you."

Ellie.....in an accident......I felt like I was going to pass out.

"Whoa....Gunner sit down man...take it easy for a second."

I was instantly sober. I needed to get to her......

NOW!

"No, I need to get to her now Brad! Is she going to be okay? What happened? Who was driving?"

I was going to fucking kill Jon Baker if that asshole was driving.

Brad grabbed my wallet and we headed out to his truck. Once we got in his truck I started asking if she was okay again.

"I don't know how she's doing. They had her in surgery when I left."
Surgery?

"Surgery? What did she need surgery for?" Oh my god….my heart was pounding and my chest was killing me. I felt like I couldn't breathe. What if something happens to her? I didn't tell her I loved her, I told her we were done. She thinks I walked away from her. She thinks I left her and I promised I would never leave her or hurt her. I think I was going to throw up.

"Brad what happened?"

"Um, they think she might have swerved to miss a deer but she ended up hitting a tree….."

"Wait….Ellie was driving? Where the fuck was she going?"

"She was coming here Gunner to find you. After you left Rebels all fucking hell broke loose. It turns out that Ari and Ellie were at the Driskill with Amanda. They were there looking at ballrooms and shit for the wedding. Ari and Ellie saw you standing outside a room and then saw some girl jump into your arms and y'all kissed and then you walked into the room with her. That's when Ellie flipped out Gunner and thought you were cheating. She had no idea that was your cousin Shannon. She thought you were meeting James. Then when they saw Shannon at Rebels and Jeff told them she was your cousin Ellie just lost it. Ari said she was screaming for Ari to give her the car keys so she could go after you. I guess Jon was not having it and kept trying to pull Ellie back on the dance floor before Jeff got sick of it and punched the shit out of him. Then Jon went after Jeff, while that was all going down Ellie got the keys from Ari and she took off."

Holy fuck….It was all making sense. No wonder Ellie freaked out. Shannon had surprised the shit out of me and jumped into my arms and wrapped her legs around me like she always has when we saw each other. Did she kiss me?

*Fuck…*she did. It was quick but it was a kiss on the lips.

"Brad, please get there." I leaned my head back on the seat. My Ellie, I needed to be with her. She was coming after me. Oh god please don't take her away from me.

Please……

I walked into the ER waiting room and instantly saw Jeff and oh man, holy shit he looked bad. He jumped up and started walking over to me. Fuck…...he started crying……oh god no……please don't take her from me……..

He just slammed into me and hugged me and cried.

No…….Ellie…..

"Jeff, please tell me she's okay……please tell me she's okay, please."

He was just crying and Ari came up and stood to the side of us.

"We haven't heard anything in about an hour or so. The last thing they told us was they were taking her to surgery to repair her broken arm. Her ribs are bruised but not broken and they said she has a concussion. She's been unconscious since they brought her in but they did a CT scan and there were no signs of head trauma, thank God."

Jeff pulled away and walked back over to the chair he was sitting in. I practically had to hold him up, he felt like he was going to collapse any minute.

"If her head injury isn't that bad why hasn't she woken up?"

"I'm not sure. The doctor said something about her body trying to help her heal or something. I really wasn't paying attention I was in a fog when they were talking to us."

I walked over and sat next to Jeff. Shit he looked bad.…

"I must have missed some fight. I hope Jon looks worse than you do."

Jeff looked over at me and smiled. "Yeah, he looks worse. He's lucky Brad pulled me off of him. I'm pretty sure I'm not going to be allowed back in Rebels though."

I tried to smile. I couldn't stop thinking about my Ellie, all alone. Was she awake after the accident? Was she scared?

Just then the doors opened a tall guy dressed in scrubs came walking out and Jeff jumped up.

He told us that Ellie had a pretty bad broken arm. It was broken in two different places so they had to put pins in to help the bones stay stable. She didn't have any internal bleeding, but she had a concussion. He said something about memory loss a possibility but he thought she would make a full recovery. They would be moving her up to a room in about an hour and half.

Thank you God......thank you for not taking her away from me......

I was sitting on the sofa with my eyes closed when I heard the nurse come in again. Another four hours must have passed already if they were checking her vitals again. This time I just acted like I was asleep. I was shocked that the stupid bitch was flirting with me when my girlfriend was laying in a hospital bed unconscious. Once she left I got up and pulled the chair Jeff had been sitting in closer to the side of the bed.

I had finally talked Jeff into going back home and taking a shower and getting some real food. We both had been sitting in Ellie's room for the last 24 hours straight. When was she going to wake up? I was starting to get scared. Ari had been reading out loud to Ellie most of the day.

I just really needed her to wake up.

I had a terrible fear she was going to wake up and remember everyone but me. I took her hand in mine and tried to kiss it. Her left hand had all the tubes and shit coming out of it, since her right hand was in a cast.

I put my head down on the bed and just started talking to her again.

"Ellie sweetheart.....please wake up baby. I need you to wake up baby. I need to tell you how much I love you. You mean the world to me and I cannot live this life without you in it. You have to wake up so we can start planning our life together, you and me out at the ranch baby. I've been talking to Gramps and Grams a lot about us Ellie. I want to marry you sweetheart and spend the rest of my life loving you."

I thought I felt her hand move in mine. Then I heard her sweet voice.

"Okay."

Okay?

I looked up and she was looking right at me. Her beautiful blue eyes looked directly into mine and we just held each other's gaze. She smiled that smile of hers that just about brought me to my knees each time.

"Ellie.....oh baby you're awake! Wait, what were you trying to say sweetheart?"

I reached up and pushed the nurse's call button.

"I said okay."

Her voice was so soft, almost like she was having a hard time talking. She must have been confused..... why was she saying okay?

"Okay to what Ellie?"

"To marrying you, and you spending the rest of your life loving me, that's what I heard you say right?"

Holy hell........ I wanted to grab her and just kiss her. I loved her so goddamn much and she must remember me because she wouldn't be saying yes to marrying a stranger........would she?

I smiled at her and got up and leaned over and gently kissed her lips.

"Yes, Sweetheart, that's exactly what I said."

The nurse walked in and saw that Ellie was awake. She started to ask her if she was hurting anywhere. Ellie said her head and her right arm was hurting and her sides. Another nurse walked in and they started messing around with Ellie and taking some of the wires off of her.

I sent a text message to Grams, Jeff and Ari to let them know Ellie was awake.

"Are you hungry Ms. Johnson?" The nurse asked.

"Um, I think I'm thirsty more than anything right now."

I jumped up and told them I would go get some ice water but the nurse told me ice chips would be best for now. When I was walking out I heard Ellie ask the nurse how long I'd been there because I looked like shit.

I had to laugh to myself....she was going to be okay. We were going to be okay.

Christmas Day at the Ranch

"Emma please let me help out with something. I do have one good arm you know. I feel so helpless just sitting here."

Emma had been babying me ever since we got to the ranch two days ago. I thought Gunner was bad…..Gesh….he ain't got nothing on Emma.

After I got out of the hospital Gunner moved me into his place so he could take care of me. I thought it was going to be a huge fight between him and Ari about where I was going to stay, but then Jefferson reminded Ari that she could stay there also. So for almost two weeks now I've had Jefferson, Gunner and Ari waiting on me hand and foot. I was getting so sick of it. My only favorite thing was Gunner helping me with showers and that about caused Jefferson to beat the shit out of Gunner the first day he was going to give me a shower. That is until Ari whispered something into Jefferson's ear and he just smiled and then headed off into his room.

EEWW! EEWWW! EEEEWWWW! Just the memory alone made me want to throw up a little in my mouth. I knew they hadn't had sex yet because Ari told me. I guess Jeff was pulling a Gunner and "waiting for the right time." ARGH I was going to explode if I didn't lose my virginity and know what that man felt like inside of me.

Heather bent down and whispered in my ear.

"You better stop thinking about whatever it is you're thinking about….your blushed face is screaming your mind's dirty thoughts!"

I had to giggle. Ari was like my sister and by far my bestest of best friends but Heather, she was one of those friends who was your best friend but also someone who you could always count on to be there for you whenever you needed her. She was probably the least selfish person I knew. When Gunner invited her to the ranch for Christmas I could have kissed him. Both of Heather's parents had passed away this summer in a car accident and she had no one else to spend Christmas with. What Gunner failed to tell her was that he was inviting Josh Hayes, his UT football teammate, also.

Josh was probably the biggest playboy I'd ever met, well except for Jefferson's man whoring days this past fall. I see him with a different girl almost every day but Gunner seems to think Josh has a thing for Heather. I know when Heather first met him at my graduation party last summer she was instantly attracted to him. He was 6'2" and had light brown hair and beautiful green eyes and had a rocking body. Then she talked to him......and all interest was quickly lost. Or at least I thought it was. The two of them couldn't keep their eyes off of each other. Interesting......

I felt a warm body move up behind me and it sent shivers down my body. Gunner. I could always tell when he walked into a room....I could feel him. He leaned down and his warm breath instantly made me hungry for his touch. He had given me more orgasms in the last week than I thought possible. The first week home from the hospital he treated me like a china doll because of my bruised ribs. They still hurt but there was no way I was telling him. If I did he would stop touching me and I craved his touch so damn much.

"I have a surprise for you later this evening if you're up to it and are feeling okay."

Oh my god....the seduction in his voice gave me goose bumps. *Fuck yeah* I was up for it. I was feeling stiff from just sitting all day. I really needed to take a walk.

I turned and reached up on my tippy toes and gave him a kiss. God I loved him so much, and to think I almost blew it with my stupid insecurities. The thought made me feel sick.

"Will you walk with me for a little bit outside? I'm going crazy sitting here just watching everyone work."

Gunner gave me that crooked smile and my heart melted. I don't think I'll ever get used to how his smile makes me feel.

"Of course I'll walk with you Sweetheart."

Gunner told Emma we were heading out for some fresh air as he leaned down and scooped me up. I had to start laughing.

"Gunner I can walk you know...I only have a broken arm."

He threw his head back and laughed and then kissed me so passionately I almost wanted to cry.

"I know you can, but any excuse to have your body closer to mine and I'm going to take it!"

"Can we go see the new calf that was born yesterday?"

Gunner smiled and led me to the barn. I ohhhed and ahhhed over him because my god he was the cutest damn thing ever. Aaron pulled up in the jeep and I noticed Gunner's body stiffen. Aaron looked at Gunner and then at me and then back to Gunner. He gave him a wink and nodded his head.

"Did you get it all taken care of?" Gunner asked him.

"Yep, I did. Jenny is amazing. I think it will work out perfectly." Aaron said with a huge grin on his face.

"How is Jenny doing Aaron? I haven't seen her since Thanksgiving." Jenny was Aaron's fiancée. She was the sweetest girl and they made a wonderful couple.

"She's doing great Ellie, she had to leave to get to her parents place for Christmas dinner but she'll be around tomorrow so you'll be able to say hi to her."

"Great!"

Aaron walked towards us and gave me a quick hug before turning his attention onto Gunner who now seemed nervous as hell. What the hell was wrong with him?

"Dude, we took care of it. Don't worry…..trust me okay? Around what time in the morning do you want it?" Aaron asked Gunner.

"How about 8 am, is that too early?"

"Fuck no…I'll be glad to get rid of the damn little menace!" Aaron slapped Gunner on the back and headed off.

"Merry Christmas Aaron." I called out to him and waved.

"Merry Christmas Ellie." He gave me a smile that stretched from ear to ear and then let out a laugh.

Gunner looked down at me and smiled. I wonder what that was all about.

"I asked Aaron to take care of some things I needed done right away. I just feel bad asking him to do it on Christmas day," Gunner said as he looked at me and smiled bigger.

"Oh Gunner, don't worry about that. I know how much Aaron cares about you and your family. I'm sure he didn't mind one bit doing what you needed done."

Gunner smiled at me and stood in front of me.

"Do you know how much I love you?"

"Umm, I think you should probably show me."

He carefully put his arms around me and lifted me up. I swung my broken arm up and over his shoulder while I wrapped my legs around his waist. My ribs where throbbing with pain but I did my best to hide it. Gunner captured my lips with his and all the pain melted away. The only thing I could feel was his love rushing through my body. He slowly backed us up against the barn.

Oh god I could feel his growing erection and pushed my hips into him. He let out a moan that had me about to go crazy.

"Gunner, I want you so bad I can't stand it! Please….please…. I'm so ready to make love."

I could hear the pleading desperation in my voice and I didn't care. Almost two weeks of sleeping next to this man in his bed every night and not being able to have sex with him was killing me.

He just smiled at me. "I know baby, I feel the same exact way. The last couple of weeks have been killing me also Ellie….you have no fucking idea how hard it is to keep from ripping your clothes off and taking you right here."

I pushed up against his crotch again and let out a moan. I just needed this ache to be gone!

"Then do it Gunner…..no one will see us…."

"Jesus Ellie……please baby, I don't want your first time to be up against a barn."

"I do! Up against a barn, in the grass, in the bed of your truck….I don't care Gunner anymore. I just know that I need you so much."

Gunner took his hand and pushed a piece of hair behind my ear. He loved to do that and I loved it just as much.

"Ellie, I promise you soon baby. Very soon….please just let me make it special for you. I *need* to make this special for both of us."

I threw my head back and let out a scream. I didn't care who heard me. I looked back to see him giving me that damn crooked smile and I couldn't help but smile back.

"FINE! But I'm telling you right now…you have thirty days to make it happen and then I'm going to take matters into my own hands."

Gunner chuckled and kissed my nose.

"Deal. Now let's go get some food. I'm starving." He gently slid me down his body and then adjusted himself as we walked back to the ranch house hand in hand.

Thirty days…..the bastard only had thirty days.

Emma finally let me help out by putting away the dishes as Ari washed and Heather dried. The guys were of course all outside on the porch.

I looked at Ari who had a smile so big on her face I couldn't help but be happy for her. Jefferson had given her a beautiful bracelet from James Avery with a horse charm on it first thing this morning. Then he took her riding and when they got to the property line of his land and the Mathews ranch there was a huge black Iron gate that had the letters A and F together with a circle around it. It stood for Ari Forever.

Gunner told me I was getting my gift later this evening and I couldn't wait. Just then I saw Emma turn and look at me. She had tears in her eyes. She grabbed my hand and pulled me into the living room. She wrapped my body in the most loving hug ever.

"Emma what's wrong?"

"Ellie darling….nothing is wrong. Everything is just perfect. You're okay and here and Drew is so in love with you….I see it every time he looks at you. Do you know that every time you walk into a room he has to catch his breath? Thank you Ellie for making Drew so happy."

I didn't know what to say. I felt tears running down my face. To think I almost lost this just a short two weeks ago. I loved this woman more than I ever thought possible.

"Emma, I love Drew also….more than I love anything. He has the same effect on me but much more…so much more. His smile melts my heart and makes me long to do everything in my power to keep it on his face. His touch, well….I'm sure you can imagine how that makes me feel!" I felt my face blushing.

"I really should be the one thanking you for helping to raise such an amazing man. He not only has made me the happiest woman on earth but he……he literally saved me Emma, if that makes any sense."

She nodded her head and we both started crying and laughing at the same time.

Garrett and Gunner walked into the living room and they both looked so damn confused.

"Women. I'll never figure y'all out no matter how old I get!"

Emma walked over and kissed Garrett and I just happened to catch the quick slap on her behind he gave her. Gunner was just staring at me with those beautiful blue eyes.

"Are you ready for your surprise Sweetheart?"

My heart started pounding. He looked so handsome standing there but he also looked scared as hell. He was probably worrying himself sick if I was going to like what he picked out for me. I reached up and felt my daisy necklace he gave me for my graduation. Then I looked down at my bracelet. I never took either of them off and threw a fit in the hospital when I found out they took them off of me.

I walked over and took his hand and nodded yes.

I was so confused when Gunner started to lead me out to the Jeep. He helped me in and then gave me a quick kiss on the cheek. He jogged around to the other side and hopped in.

"Where're we going?"

"We're going to the hunter's cabin."

"The hunter's cabin? The one you showed me on my first tour of the ranch?"

"Yep! That's the one."

When we rode by it I remembered making a comment to Gunner about how romantic it was having a cabin out here in the middle of the ranch. It was a small cabin and was so rustic looking. It looked like at one time someone might have had a garden out front. It just screamed romance to me. Gunner laughed and said it was a dump and no one had been in it for years. Why the hell was he taking me there?

Gunner must have sensed my confusion. He reached over and placed his hand on my leg. The tingles instantly started in my leg and went right to my stomach. How did he do this to me still? I mean we had been dating for six months now. I thought it would wear off, but sometimes it felt like it was getting more intense.

The sun was starting to go down now as we drove on the gravel roads of the ranch. It was breathtaking. We came around a giant live oak and I saw the cabin. I'm sure my gasp was loud because Gunner snapped his head and looked at me.

It was the most beautiful thing I'd ever seen. The whole outside of the cabin was covered in white Christmas lights. As Gunner got closer I started to shake. OH MY GOD......I could see the inside lights were on in the cabin but I couldn't see in the cabin.

Gunner pulled up and parked. I just sat there stunned. He walked around and helped me out of the jeep. I looked up at him and was at a loss for words.

"When did you do all of this? How did you do all of this? My god Gunner it's beautiful!"

Gunner let out a small laugh.

"I didn't do it. Aaron and Jenny did it for me. Do you like it so far?"

"So far? There's more? I mean YES! It's so beautiful but, I thought you said this place was a dump."

"When you mentioned how romantic you thought it was I got an idea so I talked to Gramps about getting it fixed up and he agreed."

He took my hand and started to lead me to the front porch and when we stepped up on the porch I was stopped in my tracks. Daisies.....they were everywhere. In flower vases, buckets, laying on a bench and even in a bouquet of daisies in a cowboy boot.......holy hell.......I thought I loved this man before but now my heart felt like it was going to burst open from the love I was feeling.

I turned to look at Gunner who was watching my every reaction. "Gunner I....I don't even know what to say this is all so beautiful!"

"There's more inside Ellie....."

OH.....there was more?

Gunner told me to close my eyes so I did as he led me into the cabin and I heard him shut the door. He turned my body just a little and then I felt his warm breath up against my ear as he told me to open my eyes. I held them closed another few seconds before I slowly opened them.

HOLY HELL.....oh my god....

I started to cry as soon as I saw the small one room cabin. I looked around the room and was not sure what I loved the most. I quickly noticed a giant King size bed to the left side corner of the room. It had beautiful white linens on it and the whole bed was covered with daisy and rose petals. Next to the bed was a side table that had a few white candles on it that where already lit and a vase full of purple daisies.

I moved my eyes and they landed on a small writing table that had more lit candles on it and an iPod player. Just then Gunner reached up with a remote and "Magic" by Colbie Caillat starting playing. I threw my hand up to my mouth......how did he remember me saying I loved that song. I started to cry even more.

Gunner leaned down and asked against my face as he wiped a tear away if they were happy tears. All I could do was shake my head yes. I kept moving my eyes to the right. There was a small kitchen and every surface was covered in more white candles and vases of daisies in every color you could think of. There was a small dining room table on the right side of the room and it was covered in chocolate covered strawberries, fruit, more white candles and red and white roses.

I started to shake. Did Gunner plan all of this? I looked on the floor and it was covered in daisy and rose petals.

I closed my eyes to control the tears that were falling like rain. I spun around and looked into those beautiful blue eyes. Gunner leaned down and kissed me. I was lost in his kiss and I'm not sure how long we kissed for but now Colbie Caillat's "Stay With Me" was playing.

"Drew.....oh my god.....did you plan all of this?" I knew Gunner loved it when I said his real name. I said it every morning to him because he told me he loved to hear it from my lips first thing each morning.

"Yes Sweetheart. I told Aaron exactly how I wanted everything to look and he and Jenny started early this morning and did it all. Do you like it?"

I just stared at him. He reached over and pushed my mouth shut with his finger and laughed.

"Gunner...I don't even have the words to describe to you how wonderful this is. It's....." I turned around and looked at the entire room again. "It is magical."

"Good...that's what I was going for. Now, for your Christmas present my sweet Ellie."

"This isn't it?"

Gunner threw his head back and laughed.

"No baby this is just the beginning."

Oh my....my heart was pounding. I stopped dead in my tracks.

OH MY GOD! Oh holy hells bells. Gunner turned and looked at me.

"What's wrong Sweetheart?"

"Gunner....when you said you had a plan.....you....we're going to.....oh my god..." I put my hand up to my mouth again.

Gunner grabbed me and held me close to him. His heart was beating just as fast and hard as mine. No wonder he has been nervous all day.

"Yes baby......I plan on making love to you over and over again tonight."

Oh. My. God. My knees felt weak. Finally......I jumped into his arms and he held me so softly.

"OH....oh my god...you couldn't have made it any more special Gunner. I love you so much!"

"Oh but you're wrong Ellie. I still have your Christmas present to give to you." He pulled away and took my hand again. He brought me over to the table.

I could only imagine what he was going to give me. Ohh...... maybe something sexy to wear since he told me this morning he couldn't give me my present in front of everyone. I wanted to jump up and down I was so excited.

Gunner had me sit down in the chair. I noticed there was a bottle of champagne on ice sitting on the table. Oh hell yes! I'm going to celebrate me finally losing my virginity, and to the most wonderful man in the world. I smiled as I looked at the champagne and all of the fruit on the table. The roses smelled so good.

I never even noticed Gunner getting down on the floor. I looked back at him and sucked in a breath of air when I saw that he was kneeling down on one knee and he had a jewelry box in his hand. I couldn't breathe....oh my......I looked down at the box and then up at his eyes that were filled with so much love.

"Ellie, I had this whole thing planned out to say all of the reasons why I wanted you to be my wife. I've been practicing it for a week now. But...all those words....they cannot even begin to describe to you how much I love you. How much I want to spend the rest of my life with you. To be able to wake up every morning and look at your smile that turns my world upside down. To live on the ranch with you, have children with you.....to rock on the front porch with you when we're in our 90's. I love you Ellie so much, and I want to spend the rest of my life loving you sweetheart. Would you please do me the honor of becoming my wife?"

Gunner opened the box and revealed a beautiful vintage style oval blue sapphire engagement ring. The sapphire was framed with an intricate scalloped border and was circled by white diamond begets that continued down part of the white gold band. It was the most beautiful ring I'd ever seen.

I looked up at Gunner and just started to cry. How does this man remember every single thing I tell him? I told him once that I loved blue sapphires.

"*Yes!* Yes of course! Nothing would make me happier than to become your wife Drew." I'd never seen him smile so big in my life. I slid down onto the floor with him and we slammed our lips together. I had to kiss him with as much passion and love that I possibly could. I needed to show him with this kiss how much he meant to me, how much I loved him.

I'd never in my life felt so loved.

56 Gunner

Ellie pulled away from me after what I swear was the most powerful kiss of my goddamn life. She was panting hard as she looked at me. I had one more thing to do.

I took the ring out of the box and slipped it onto her left hand. Not that I was happy about it, but I was glad she broke her right arm instead of her left. She stared down at the ring for a few minutes before those beautiful blue eyes looked into mine again. I was about to ask if she wanted a glass of champagne when I noticed her eyes look up and over at the massive king size bed and then back down to me again.

Well well…..my sweet little Ellie was anxious to move to the more entertaining part of the evening.

She looked down at my lips while she started to lick her lips. Then she bit down on her bottom lip.

Holy fucking hell…..I never wanted her more than I did at this very moment.

"I still have thirty days……"

She let out a laugh and looked back over to the bed. This was it. I was really about to make love to her. My heart was pounding. I felt like it was my first time I was so fucking nervous. I stood up and reached down for her hand. She placed her left hand into mine and I helped her up and started to walk backwards towards the bed. I stopped right at the end of the bed. God she looked so beautiful in the candle light. Colbie Caillat, her favorite singer, was singing in the background. It could not have been more perfect.

"Are you scared Ellie?"

"No."

"Are you nervous Baby?"

"Yes."

"Don't be nervous Ellie."

"What if….what if I don't do something right?"

Oh my god could she be any fucking cuter?

I smiled at her and pushed a piece of her hair back behind her ear.

"Ellie you have nothing to worry about sweetheart. It's going to be perfect."

As much as I wanted to just toss her on the bed and get to it I also wanted to take my time and savor every single moment. I loved giving Ellie all of her firsts. This was the most important one. One she would remember the rest of her life.

She was dressed in blue jeans and UT football T-shirt. Ari told me how upset Ellie was because the red sweater she bought wouldn't fit over her cast. I reached up and cupped her face as I gently rubbed my lips across her lips a few times.

"More…"

I let out a laugh….."Greedy little thing aren't you?"

I felt her smile against my lips. She lifted her left hand and started to run it through my hair. HOLY FUCK! I sure hope I lasted at least two minutes inside of her…..she was already starting to drive me insane. I reached down with my hands and lifted her t-shirt up and pulled it over her head only breaking our kiss to get the shirt over her face. My hands started to shake as I reached down and started to unbutton her jeans. Once they were unbuttoned I slowly took my lips from hers and started to kiss down her neck….in between her breasts and then down her stomach until I was slipping her pants down her legs. She lifted one foot and then the other out of her pants. I leaned in and kissed her upper thigh as she let out a soft moan.

Fuck…….her body was perfect. As I started to stand up, I noticed she had on red thong panties….I just stared at them for a few seconds before I started to get up all the way and my eyes landed on the matching red lace push up bra. Mother fucker……she had the most amazing breasts. It felt like I was seeing them for the first time. I looked into her eyes and she was staring at me hard….watching every move I made. I leaned down to kiss her again softly on the lips. I took my hand and reached behind her to unhook her bra. I felt it pop open and I slowly used both of my hands to move it down her shoulders, out her left arm and carefully over her right arm and cast.

Even with that damn pink cast she had on she was still the sexiest thing I'd ever laid eyes on.

I stood there just looking at her breasts. I took my hands and cupped both of them as Ellie threw her head back and moaned. I leaned down and took one in my mouth as I slid my other hand down her stomach and ran my finger along her panty line. I felt her whole body shiver and it felt like my dick was going to explode.

"Oh god Drew."

"I know Baby….."

I went back to kissing and sucking on her breasts as I slipped my hand into her panties. She bucked her hips into me and let out a moan.

Holy fuck….I loved to feel her fall apart because of my touch.

I moved my mouth up to her neck and started to kiss along her neck and collar bone. I slowly slid one finger into her. She sucked in a breath of air.

"Ohmygod….."

Holy shit she was so fucking wet……

"Jesus Ellie….you're so wet and ready baby."

"Gunner….oh god that feels so good."

I took another finger and slid it in. God how much longer could I hold off…….

"More….please Gunner more."

I had to smile against her neck….she really was a greedy little thing.

I slid in another finger. She was so fucking tight…... so damn wet……..She leaned her head back and moaned again.

I took my thumb and started to move it against her sensitive nub. She started to buck her hips and grind harder into my hand. I started to slide my fingers in and out faster. I could tell she was getting close. She grabbed me with her left hand and started to scream out my name as she buried her head into my chest.

Mother fucker I could feel her squeezing my fingers. My head was spinning as Ellie just kept screaming out my name. Shit…this has got to be the longest orgasm she's ever had.

Finally she stopped calling out my name and I felt her body starting to go limp in my arms. I just stood there and held her as her breathing came back under control. She pulled her head back and looked up at me.

"WOW!"

"WOW is fucking right. I think that was the hottest thing I've ever seen Ellie."

Ellie started to laugh. Her smile faded as I felt her hand trying to undo the buttons to my jeans. Poor baby was having a hard time with only being able to use her left hand. I pulled my hand out from her panties and grabbed her hand and moved it away from my jeans. I slowly took off her panties and turned her to lay her on the bed. I felt her body starting to shake. I knew she was nervous, shit so was I. I just hoped like hell I didn't lose control and hurt her.

"Ellie baby lay down…."

Her eyes grew bigger and she grabbed onto my shirt. She started to sit down onto the bed. Fuck my heart was beating a mile a minute. I could actually hear it in my ears. She started to scoot back until she was laying back with her head on the pillows. I was kneeling along the side of her body since she never let go of the death grip she had on my shirt. I had to smile at how sweet and innocent she was. To think I was going to be the only man to ever be inside her made me almost start to fucking cry. Last thing I needed was to cry right now.

I leaned down and brushed my lips against hers. She captured my bottom lip with her teeth and started to smile. I pulled back to look at her. I just wanted to look at her perfect beautiful body laying there waiting for me......only me.

"Gunner?"

"Hmmm?"

"What's wrong......why are you just staring at me?" she said as her voice cracked.

"Nothing's wrong Baby......nothing at all. I'm just looking at your beautiful body. It's so fucking beautiful."

She started to cover up her breasts and I looked at her face that was flushed red.

"No Ellie, don't ever cover yourself up, I love to look at your body. This is the first time I've ever seen you totally nude sweetheart and I just want to take it all in."

"Ohhh.....okay."

SO. FUCKING. CUTE.

I stood back up and started to take off my jeans. Ellie's eyes grew bigger when I slid my jeans down my legs and stepped out of them. I saw her eyes moving up and down my body with a hungry look as she stopped twice to look harder, once on my chest and my tattoo and then again on my dick. Her mouth made a small o shape and she started to lick her lips. Shit I would love to have that mouth wrapped around my cock but not tonight.....tonight was for Ellie.

I reached down and pulled out a condom. She sat up and was sitting on her elbows.

"We don't need that."

"What? Of course we do Ellie."

"No Gunner we don't. I'm on the pill."

What? Why the fuck was she on the pill?

"After we came back from the ranch the first time I decided I better start protection just in case, you know well, in case we couldn't stop the next time." She shrugged her shoulders as she explained her reason for being on the pill. Fuck I loved her.

No condom. I'd never had sex with no condom on before. This was going to make it even harder not to come the second I entered her body.

"Have you always used a condom Gunner?"

"YES!" I can't believe she even just asked that.

"Is that why your face is white....the thought of not using one, does it have you scared because if you feel more comfortable wearing it..."

Holy fuck, she was worried about that?

"Ellie baby that's not what it is." I crawled onto the bed and moved over her and held myself up above her body. She let her head fall back onto her pillow.

"I'm worried that it's going to feel so fucking good I won't last thirty seconds."

"Ohhh….oh well….um…." she crinkled up her nose and smiled. I could not have loved her more in that moment.

"I love you Ellie……" I said as I leaned down and started to gently brush my lips against hers.

"Oh Drew….I love you too."

I could tell she was frustrated with her broken arm. She kept trying to lift it up and I finally took it and put it up over her head. She took her left hand and ran it though my hair. Then down the side of my face, neck and she finally ended up on my chest. I did not take my shirt off very often so I knew this was a treat for her. She had gotten a little tipsy the night of her birthday and begged me to let her lick my tattoo. I wanted so badly to let her but knew I would lose control. Tonight was a whole different ball game.

She took her fingertip and started to trace the tattoo. First on my chest then over my shoulder and down my arm….my body was starting to shake. She leaned up and kissed my chest and I let out a moan.

"If I lay on you Ellie is it going to hurt your ribs sweetheart?

She looked up at me shocked. She didn't think I noticed every time I hugged her or picked her up that she winced in pain each time.

"You noticed huh?"

"Yes Baby, I don't want to hurt you."

"Trust me……you're not going to hurt me Gunner…...you're killing me though by making me wait…."

I laughed and nipped at her nose.

"Where did this greedy little Ellie come from?"

"Umm, she's been here the whole time, she just can't wait for her future husband to make love to her any longer."

Future husband……..

I leaned down to kiss her and she grabbed me by the back of the neck. She sucked at my tongue causing me to let out a moan. She was pulling me further down as she spread her legs open wider.

*Holy shit….*My dick was pressed up against her. I reached down and slid a finger inside her. *Fuck me…*

"Jesus Ellie…...you're so wet baby."

"Yes, Gunner I want you so bad…...please…..." She begged as she pushed her hips up against me.

I slid two more fingers inside her and started to work my fingers in and out. Ellie let out a moan and started to move her hips. She was about to come again. I took my fingers out and moved over her again. She looked up at me briefly confused as to why I moved my fingers.

"I want you to come again but with me inside you Ellie."

She was panting hard…..her eyes captured mine and held me still for a moment. I was about to make love to the only girl I've ever loved. My heart was filled with so much love for her. Dear God please let me be slow and gentle with her.

I slowly pushed the head of my dick up against her opening. Her eyes grew larger and she had a moment of panic cross over her face.

"I'll go slow baby but you have to relax okay…can you relax for me Ellie?"

"What if….what if it doesn't fit?"

I didn't want to laugh at how innocent her question was. I leaned down and started to kiss her as I slowly started to make my way into her.

"It will fit baby trust me….relax Ells."

I felt her whole body relax. Even her grip on my arm that she was holding onto for dear life was relaxing. I pushed a little more and felt it sliding in easier with how fucking wet she was.

I saw her make a pained face and I stopped…I was hurting her. FUCK! I'd never been with a virgin so I was not sure if I should go slow or just thrust it in….like taking a band aid off…quick and fast….

Fucking hell I'm thinking about fucking band aids?

"Don't stop." Ellie was now pushing her hips into mine.

Oh sweet Jesus….I'd never felt such pure heaven in my life.

"Ohhh, Ellie, you're so tight baby and so fucking warm," I whispered against her ear.

"Gunner…...please…..."

Just a little more and I would be in all the way. Ellie let out a small whimper and it just about killed me. I slowly started to move in and out of her. Fucking heaven……

I captured her mouth with mine and she kissed me with such passion.

"OHMYGOD……Gunner…...oh god……it feels *so* good….."

"Ellie….you feel like heaven baby."

"Can you go faster?"

Did she really just ask me that?

"Yes Baby…..faster I can do!"

I picked up the pace and noticed she was moving right along with me. I wasn't going to last much longer doing it this fast.

Then I saw her whole body start to tense up. I literally felt her tightening around my dick. HOLY SHIT…come on Ellie baby please hurry.

"OH GUNNER! Oh god yes!" She arched her back and that was it….I lost it.

"Oh *Ellie!*"

We both came together. How perfect was that......to come together the first time we made love.

I was leaning on my elbows which were placed on both sides of Ellie's head. We were both panting like we just got done running a marathon.

I opened my eyes to see her watching me. Those blue eyes seemed to look brighter and her smile.....oh god her smile was to die for. We just stayed there like that for a few minutes. I slowly pulled out of her and rolled to her left side to avoid her broken arm.

"Gunner I never dreamed it was going to feel so good. I always heard the first time it hurt like hell. It hurt at first but then it quickly turned into nothing but pure pleasure."

I let out a laugh and ran my hand through my hair. I just made love to Ellie and I wanted to jump up and down on the bed and do a few fist pumps.

"I'm so glad baby that it felt good for you. It felt like pure heaven for me. I've never experienced anything like that before Ellie."

She smiled as she laid her cast across my chest. It was totally true. I had sex before but never have I made love.

"Um, Gunner, when can we do it again?"

"Jesus Ellie! Are you ready already?"

She looked at me with such an innocent look on her face and nodded.

She laid her head on my chest and before I knew it I heard her softly breathing as she slipped into a slumber. I closed my eyes and dreamed of the many more times I planned on doing that again. I just needed at least thirty minutes and then I could wake her up again.

I woke up feeling like I was on cloud nice. OH. MY. GOD....that was the *most* amazing experience of my life. I had my heavy ass cast resting across Gunner's stomach and my head on his chest. Hmmmm......he smelled so yummy. I took a peek at my engagement ring and then around the room. I cannot believe he did all of this for me. I could not have picked out a more perfect ring. I still can't believe we finally made love! EEEPPP! I wanted to jump up and down I was so happy. And it was so wonderful. The first few minutes it hurt like a son of a bitch and I almost wanted to tell him to stop but then it started to feel oh so good. I lifted my head to look at him. My goodness he was so handsome. I loved to watch him sleep. He looked so peaceful and happy. I loved him so goddamn much it almost hurt.

I wanted to marry him right away. I had already been thinking about this. I was not planning on going back to school next fall. Not if it meant Gunner would be here and I had to be in Austin. Now with us getting married I had even more of a reason not to go back. I would just take online classes and get my business degree. If I wanted to help Gunner out at the ranch, I would need a business degree for sure.

Gunner started to move and opened his eyes. He looked directly into my eyes and smiled. To think that this man is mine......that he......he actually *wants me*.

"Hey…"

"Hey back. Did I wake you up by moving around?" I asked as I looked down at my cast.

Gunner let out a laugh.

"Nope, I sensed that someone was getting ready for round two."

I felt the heat move into my cheeks. Would I always get embarrassed like this even after we were man and wife?

"Yes....can we umm....can we try a different um…." I had to look away. I can't believe I was about to even ask this.

"A different position?" Gunner asked with a wicked grin on his face.

I let out a giggle. "Yes....a different position."

"We can do anything you want Baby. Anything."

"Can I be on top?"

The widest smile ever appeared on Gunner's face.

"Ahhh, sure you can!"

Gunner sat up some and was leaning back against the head board as I crawled on top of him. ARGH this fucking broken arm of mine was driving me insane.

When I sat on him he already had an erection. Oh my god it felt heavenly pushing up against me. I bet if I just started moving against him I could come this way.

I moved my hips up a little as he reached down and helped to guide his erection in. I looked down and still could not believe that thing fit in me. As I felt the tip slowly start to enter I wanted to let out a moan. OH my god.....

I closed my eyes and sat a little further down burying him in deeper as I went. OH WOW! My eyes flew open and Gunner was smiling at me.

"It feels so different...like there is so much more of you." Gunner leaned up and kissed me. I sat all the way down and had to take a minute to get used to how full it felt. I could stay like this forever.....

"Are you going to move Ellie or just sit there sweetheart?" Gunner whispered against my lips.

"Feels so good...." I threw my head back and moved slowly.

"Does it hurt Ellie? Do you hurt too much sweetheart?"

"S'okay.....feeeelllsss soooo gooood...... stop talking to me for a second!"

Gunner started to laugh. Oh god...I was being stretched out to the max but it felt so fucking good. I slowly moved around in circles. Oh wow....oh yes I liked this position!

"Move baby...you've got to move soon or I'm going to take over."

I snapped my head back up and looked at Gunner. How did I move? Oh fuck......

"Up and down baby....just move however it feels good for you, it all feels good for me no matter what you're doing."

Okay......I can do this. I started to move up and down and oh.my.god......if I thought it felt good just sitting there this was......amazing. I needed more though. I started to move faster and I heard Gunner moan.....oh holy hell the sound of him moaning was even more of a turn on. I went faster even though my ribs where killing me.

"Oh God Ellie, I'm not going to be able to last much longer sweetheart."

I looked down into his eyes. I wanted to watch him come apart because of me. I didn't even care anymore if I came or not. I wanted to make him feel good. I moved faster and harder. Ohhhh that feels so good.

"FUCK ELLIE!"

YES! I was doing it, he was so close and I started to feel that familiar build up. Oh god yes......oh shit.....this was going to be big.

I swear I felt him getting harder inside and oh my god he was rubbing on a certain spot that felt......OH HOLY SHIT......Gunner started moaning more.

"Don't close your eyes Gunner...."

"Ellie baby I'm about to...."

It felt like a bomb exploded in my body and I started to cry out Gunner's name and a few other things..... I really have no idea what I was even saying. The look on his face was so amazing. He was saying my name and I was calling out his as our gaze never left each other's eyes. It was one of the most amazing moments of my life. I thought the first time could never be topped but this...…this I had no words for.

I slowly felt my body coming down from the overwhelming pulses as I closed my eyes for a second. When I opened them again our blue eyes captured each other. I felt like he was looking into my soul and I into his. I loved him so much.

"I love you Ellie.....I love you so much sweetheart."

I collapsed onto his chest and was trying desperately to catch my breath. I couldn't get the energy to even tell him I loved him.

"Gun......ner.....I lov…...love you…...too!"

He started to laugh and slowly rolled me over being careful of my ribs and my arm.

I laid there on my back with my eyes closed. I felt like I was about to fall asleep again. After another minute or two and my breathing was back under control.

I opened my eyes to see him smiling down at me. "Marry me...."

He started laughing. "I thought I already asked that and you agreed."

I laughed back at him. I never wanted to leave this cabin…...ever.

"I mean marry me today or tomorrow, I just want to marry you right now."

Gunner started to push my hair back with his fingers. Hmmmm it felt so good. I loved it when he touched me.

"Ellie, I would run off and marry you right now if I thought that was what you really wanted. But sweetheart I want to have a real wedding. I want to see you in a beautiful wedding dress, with Gramps and Grams there watching us, Jeff as my best man and Ari as your bridesbitch."

I busted out laughing.

"GUNNER! Ari is not a bitch! She's just....outspoken. And she would be the maid of honor."

Gunner leaned down and rubbed his nose against mine. Then he kissed me, so softly at first but it quickly turned to something more powerful.

He pulled away after a few minutes and left me breathless.

"Ellie, I would really love to get married here at the ranch if that's okay with you."

I smiled because I wanted the same thing. Ever since our first night looking up at the stars I'd been having the same dream over and over again. We were in that same pasture, Gunner and I were under the big oak and I kept turning around and seeing all these people looking at us. Every time I woke up from that dream I could never figure out what it meant. Now I knew.

"Nothing would make me happier Gunner. Except, I want to get married under our Oak tree. I've been having a dream, the same one over and over, with you and me standing under that tree. I never understood why I had that dream so much but now I know why. We were meant to be married there!"

"When Sweetheart?" Gunner said up against my ear. Oh god....was it possible for me to want him again, so soon? He started to move his hand down my body until he found his way to the ache that already needed relief from him.

"Umm, oh god......Drew......"

He rolled on top of me and made love to me again but this time it was so slow and sweet. Was it going to keep getting better each time?

"I love you Drew......"

"I love you more......"

58 Gunner

I woke Ellie up with a tray full of her favorite breakfast. Pancakes, eggs, bacon and orange juice. I thought for sure she would have woken up with all the noise I was making trying to cook it all in that tiny kitchen. Watching her sitting there eating I couldn't pull my eyes from her. I kept seeing that ring on her finger and I had to fight back the tears every time. She was going to be mine soon.

Ellie insisted on cleaning up all the flower petals even though I told her I paid Aaron and Jenny generously to take care of all of it. We made love two more times that morning and I wasn't even sure how I was able to get my dick to work so much the last twelve hours but I wasn't going to complain about it.

After we had things cleaned up to Ellie's satisfaction, we made our way out to the Jeep. Ellie was practically skipping the whole way. The sight of her so happy made my chest swell. I wanted her to feel loved and wanted every damn minute of every day. Just then Aaron and Jenny drove up, right on time. Ellie started to jump up and down when Jenny walked up to her. Jenny grabbed Ellie's hand and looked at the ring as they both let out a small scream. Then she leaned in and asked Ellie something. Ellie turned bright red and looked over at me. She turned back and said something to Jenny that caused a huge smile to spread across Jenny's face.

Aaron walked up and handed me a huge ass box. I sat down on the porch steps and called Ellie over.

"I have one more Christmas present for you Sweetheart." Ellie turned and looked at the box I was holding. She came and sat down next to me and smiled.

"What is it?" She asked filled with excitement.

"Well, the only way you're going to find out Baby is if you take the lid off!"

Ellie reached over and took the lid off and a 7 week old chocolate lab popped his head up. Little guy looked liked he had been sleeping.

"Ohhh! Oh my god! Is he MINE?"

I started to laugh. Damn she was so fucking cute.

"Yes, Baby he's yours."

Ellie reached in and lifted him out of the box and started to hug him. Aaron and Jenny looked on as Ellie smelled every inch of him and said how wonderful he smelled. Her smell senses and mine were clearly different.

She looked at the ribbon that was tied around his neck. The note I wrote was tied onto it. She took the note off and put the puppy down. Little guy went right over and peed in the grass.

"Oh sure, now the little fucker goes to the bathroom in the grass," Aaron said.

Ellie started to read the note out loud.

"Dear mommy, I'm here to help daddy watch over you and protect you and love you like there is no tomorrow. Love, Gus."

Ellie turned her head to look at me. Those blue eyes were filling with tears as she leaned over and kissed me. She pulled away from my lips just a little and smiled.

"Thank you…..I love him and I love that you remember every single thing I say to you Drew Mathews. I love you so much!"

"I love you too Ellie, more than you'll ever know."

It was 11:00 in the morning by the time we got back up to the ranch house. Ellie looked nervous as she was holding Gus in her arms while the little bastard slept in total peace. Lucky ass dog.

"What's wrong Sweetheart? You look like you just saw a ghost."

"Holy shit Gunner, your grandparents are going to know that we had…..that we had…..SEX!"

I started to laugh my ass off. Damn, she really was so cute.

"Ellie, we're adults, they knew what I was planning all along. Believe me; I got the lecture from them about protection yesterday before I took you to the cabin."

"But I would never want them to think badly of me for having sex with you before we got married."

I had to smile at how thoughtful her heart was. I pushed a piece of hair that had fallen out from her pony behind her ear.

"Ellie, don't let those two fool you. They were sneaking around in Grams' barn at seventeen having sex. Gramps talks a lot when he gets drunk."

Ellie threw her hand up to her mouth and started to giggle and woke up the little monster.

Just then I heard Ari and Jeff. I looked up and they were walking hand in hand down to the barn. I was so happy Jeff finally came to his goddamn senses. They both looked so happy. I wasn't going to tell Ellie but Jeff was planning on asking Ari to marry him graduation night.

Ari took one look at Ellie and she screamed. Ellie screamed back as she jumped out of the jeep, put poor little sleepy and lost looking Gus on the ground and ran over to Ari. Jeff just smiled and stepped out the way of two very excited females. Ari grabbed Ellie's left hand and screamed again.

Little Gus looked up at me like I knew what the feeling of not being in her arms anymore felt like. Little bastard thought like me already......I was going to love this dog. I reached down and picked him up.

"I know buddy......she has bewitched me also," I said as I held Gus in my arms.

"HOLY MOTHER FUCKING SHIT! You did good Gunner!! Fuck me that's beautiful!" Ellie turned around to face me with that sweet smile of hers. She gave me a wink and they both started to walk into the barn but not before she took the dog from my arms and gave him to Ari who went crazy over him.

Jeff started to make his way over to me. I had already asked Jeff for permission to marry Ellie last week. I knew how much he loved her and she didn't have a father so I felt like it was the right thing to do.

He reached his hand out to me and shook it along with a slap on the back. A hard fucking slap.

"Jesus...what the fuck did you hit me so hard for."

"I sure as shit hope you made it special for her or I'll kick your fucking ass. And goddamn if the puppy wasn't a nice touch. Well played dude."

I had to laugh.

"I sure hope I did Jeff. From how happy she's been all morning I would say I did a decent job."

Jeff smiled at me and then shook his head.

"You know Gunner, if she had to end up with anyone, I'm thankful it was you. I see how much you love my sister and I see how much she loves you. By the look on her face when y'all pulled up I would say you did more than a decent job dude. I've never in my life seen my sister with such a glow on her face. Thank you. Thank you for making it special for her. Now......I don't want to ever talk about the fact that you had sex for the first time with my baby sister on the night you asked her to marry you. You ever get drunk and tell me about it, I'll kick your fucking ass. You got it?"

I just stood there and stared at him. God I loved Jeff like a brother. I nodded my head yes and he laughed and pulled me into a head lock and we started to wrestle around before I heard Gramps yell out.

"Knock it the fuck off.....we got some male bonding to do, to the loft boys."

We had to leave in a few days as Jeff and I had a bowl game the next week. Our last game as college football players......I couldn't believe it.

The day after I asked Ellie to marry me I got up the nerve that night to finally talk to her about the wedding. I was so afraid she was going to be upset when I told her I couldn't stand the thought of her staying in Austin after we got married. I was so worried about it, I was sure she was going to tell me she didn't want to get married or that we were going to have to wait until she finished school but she just smiled.

"Gunner, I already made up my mind weeks ago I was not going back to school in the fall. I was coming out here with you to the ranch no matter if you had asked me to marry you or not."

"Ellie what about school, I thought you would be upset if I asked you to give up school to come with me out here. Are you sure baby this is what you want?"

She threw her arms around my neck. "YES! I already figured it out. I'm going to take classes online and finish up my degree in business. That way I can help you run the ranch when you take it over from Garrett someday." I was speechless. This girl never ceased to amaze me. I loved her so much. I leaned in and asked her if she was feeling daring and she smiled and wiggled her eyebrows up and down. We snuck off to the barn and made love. Another first…although I spent more time pushing Gus away, that little bastard was barking at me the whole time. He and I were going to have to have a man to man talk and soon.

Ellie was crying as she was saying goodbye to Grams. They had become so close and had been sneaking off all day yesterday with Ari and the puppy….I'm sure they were already talking about the wedding. Grams whispered something into Ellie's ear that caused Ellie to blush. She quickly looked over at me and smiled. I don't think I could ever be so fucking happy. Nothing would ever top this feeling.

June

"Gunner....dude you need to settle down. It's all going to be okay, trust me....come on." Brad handed me a beer and led me out to the deck that over looked Lake Travis. I didn't want a bachelor party so a few of the guys decided some male bonding up at Brad's parent's lake house would do the trick. Gus took his normal position at my feet. I was surprised Ellie let him come with me and not her. She fucking loved this dog and he loved her just as much, if not more. Damn dog followed her everywhere she went.

Ellie and the girls were at Ari's parent's lake house which was actually two miles up the road. All I wanted to do was talk to Ellie. We were getting married in three days and I was a nervous wreck. We were leaving tomorrow for the ranch. Ellie seemed so calm. Ari, Amanda and Heather were amazing friends to Ellie. They were handling so much of the planning for Ellie and were in constant contact with Jenny who we were using as the wedding planner. It helped Ellie not to stress too much so she could finish up school.

The only real break she took from school was for Brad and Amanda's wedding on Valentine's Day, and spring break when we all headed to the ranch. Jeff and I spent most of spring break getting his property ready for the horse stables he was having built this summer. He was going to tear the small ranch house down and start from scratch by building something bigger. He thought Ari wanted something big but turns out she's just a simple country girl at heart and wanted a simple ranch style home. They would stay in the existing house until they built their house. Jeff and I had both been putting in a shit ton of hours at the firm where we had been interning for the last two years. I'm still surprised they asked us to stay on as consultants.

Fuck just sitting here and relaxing felt great. Graduation was over and now the wedding. Jeff came walking out and slapped me on the back as he ran his hand through his hair. He sat down and let out a sigh.

"She still pissed?" I asked as Jeff took a drink from his beer.

"Yep......god she has me all tied up in fucking knots."

Brad and I just laughed. Ari was not speaking to Jeff ever since graduation night when he failed to pop the big question. Little did she know he was asking her the night of our wedding. He had Jenny working on the side taking care of it. I thought it was pretty cool he was going to ask Ari to marry him in the same cabin as I asked Ellie. Grams said it was a good sign. Ellie and I were going to be living in the cabin until we could get a house of our own built.

"Did you even acknowledge to her that you knew why she was upset?" Brad asked with a laugh.

"No....she's so pissed and just started calling me a mother fucking dickwad for no reason when we got back to her place so I just left and came home."

"*Damn* dude.....no wonder she's pissed at you. You better make it up when you do ask her this weekend," Brad said as he tipped his beer back and finished it.

"Shit......I think I'll text her."

Jeff sat there and typed out a text message to Ari as Brad and I talked about some last minute shit that needed to be done before the wedding.

"There. I just sent her a text telling her I knew why she was upset and that I wanted to wait until after Ellie's wedding. She just doesn't know it will be the night of the wedding."

Jeff's cell phone started ringing and he must have thought at first it was going to be Ari. He pulled it out and frowned when he saw who was calling.

"What do you want Rebecca?" Jeff said with no emotion at all in his voice.

"Well honestly I don't see what in the hell we would need to meet for lunch for. I have nothing to discuss with you. Fuck I haven't even seen you since what....last November."

Just then Jeff dropped the beer that was in his hand and it crashed onto the patio. Beer went everywhere and Brad jumped up.

"What the fuck Jeff!"

Jeff's face was pale. What the fuck was going on?

"Are you fucking kidding me right now Rebecca? That's impossible, I saw it and it was not broke. No you listen to me, you're wrong; I can't talk to you now I'll call you next week. No...I'll call YOU next week."

Jeff sat there for a second stunned.

"Jeff, what the fuck was that all about?"

"Jesus Christ Jeff you look like you're about to throw up! Man don't do it out here or my parents will kill me!"

Jeff turned and looked at me and he had tears in his eyes. Oh holy mother fucking shit...........

"She's pregnant isn't she?"

"Holy hells bells…..Jesus, Mary and Joseph! I asked you to keep an eye on her Amanda!"

"Don't yell at me Ari. She slipped out when I wasn't looking!"

"FUCK! That little shit is trying to make her way to Gunner! EVERYONE.….spread out and look for her."

"Um, Ari…who the hell are you telling to spread out to…it is just you, Amanda and me." Heather said with a laugh.

I started to laugh as I opened the bathroom door. "Um, ladies I just went to the bathroom."

"Jesus Ellie, stop doing that. I know you are just trying to throw us off you and your fucking horny little self trying to get to Gunner. Once Amanda here slipped and said he was two miles down the road it has been your mission to leave. Do. Not. Lie. To. Me!"

"I have no idea what you're talking about Ari."

"For Christ sakes, if she wants to go see Gunner I say we just take her. We can make a quick trip up there and say hi to the guys and then come back here," Heather said as she downed another beer.

All three of us turned and stared at Heather. What was going on with her?

"Ahhh, are you drunk?" Ari asked as she walked over and took the empty beer out of Heather's hand.

"No, I'm not drunk! I was just saying if Ellie wanted to see her fiancé that bad, who are we to stop her, that's all. Gesh…."

"Oh holy hell….."

Why was Ari smiling at Heather that way?

"Why are you looking at me like that Ari?"

"Mother fucker…you want to see Josh DON'T YOU!" Ari practically yelled out.

Amanda jumped up and down and was clapping her hands. "I *knew* you liked him! I knew it when I saw y'all dancing at the wedding."

"Wait…what? You like Josh Heather? Since when? I thought you couldn't stand him. Oh my god….where I have I been that I didn't know this." I couldn't believe Heather was falling for…...Josh…...playboy Josh!

Heather just blushed and shrugged her shoulders. "He has a certain something that I might find attractive. I don't know."

"Well you know, Brad told me that ever since the wedding, Josh has pretty much given up his playboy ways. The guys keep teasing him about losing his touch with the ladies."

We all looked at each other. Ari raised her eyebrow at me and I looked over at Amanda and then Heather.

"Hey, that lake house has six fucking bedrooms.....that is more than enough for all four us to get laid......" Ari said as she walked over and grabbed her purse. "Come on bitches.....let's go get some.....Jeff sent me a text and I've decided to forgive him and let him make it up to me with sex."

"OH MY GOD! I am not sleeping with Josh. Heather yelled out.

"Don't then.....all I know is my ass is wanting me some Jefferson......"

"EEEWWW! OHMYGOD! That's my brother for fuck's sake! GROSS."

"Come on girls, since I'm the only one who has not been drinking my ass off I'll drive," Amanda said as she grabbed her keys and we made our way over to crash the boys' party.

Josh opened the door and looked shocked to see the four of us standing there. Once he saw Heather he smiled.

"What the hell are y'all doing here? This is a private party."

"Get the fuck out of the way dickwad...." Ari said as she pushed past Josh.

"Hey Heather, how've you been?" Josh asked Heather in the sweetest way I'd ever heard him talk.

"I um, I've been good....feeling a little tipsy but good."

I thought I heard Josh mutter fuck. The way he was looking at Heather made me smile. If I had to guess I would say he was very interested in our little Heather!

"Where is Jeff?"

"He is sitting out on the deck with Brad and Gunner."

Ari started making a run for the deck......Jesus......if didn't know any better I would think she was the one getting married. As we walked up I could see Jefferson running his hands through his hair and Gunner and Brad looked like they both wanted to throw up. What was going on? Gunner looked up at Ari and at first frowned....HUH? But then he saw me and smiled that beautiful melt my panties smile of his.

Ari slid the door open and walked up to the back of Jeff. I noticed Gunner kick Jeff in the leg......almost like he was trying to get him to stop talking. Ari put her hands around Jefferson's eyes and whispered......

"Guess who was feeling a little lonely?" Jefferson flew up out of his chair and looked stunned. What was going on here? Amanda walked over and sat on Brad's lap as they started to kiss. I looked at each guy, first Brad, then Gunner and then Jefferson. Something was wrong. Really wrong. I could see it in Jefferson's face. He shook his head at me as if to tell me to leave it alone. Gunner reached up and grabbed my hand.

"Hey Sweetheart what are y'all doing here?" I sat down on his lap and I could instantly feel his erection growing. Hmmmm....this is why I'm here. I wiggled a little and smiled. I reached down and gave my second favorite guy a scratch behind the ears. Gus just wagged his tail and went back to sleep.

"She was horny you ass wipe, and kept trying to escape the wonderful spa party we had going on for her. So instead of trying to keep her away we hand delivered her ass to you," Ari said as she was rubbing her ass into my brother's crotch......BLAH......I was going to throw up. Jefferson spun her around and whispered something into her ear. I saw her nod her head yes. Jefferson leaned down and asked Brad something to which he replied "Third one on the left." Jefferson took Ari's hand and led her back into the house.

Holy shit......they were going to go have sex! Amanda asked Brad something and he laughed. They both stood up and started to go into the house. He leaned down and whispered to Gunner. "Take the master dude."

Gunner just nodded and then looked at me.

"Jesus......are they all really leaving to go have sex?" I asked as I watched Brad and Amanda walk in and say something to Heather and Josh who were standing at the kitchen bar talking.

"Looks like it Sweetheart. Now what's this about you being horny?"

I started to laugh. I leaned down and whispered into Gunner's ear.

"I really want you Mr. Mathews. Now."

Gunner had me off his lap and walking into the house faster than I even knew what hit me. As we walked by, Josh and Heather were so deep in conversation they didn't even notice us walking by.

Gunner and I made our way down to the master bedroom. Would I always feel so nervous with him? Just the thought of making love to him had my stomach doing flips.

"Oh my god....does it just keep getting better Gunner?" I said as I lay across his chest trying to catch my breath.

He let out a laugh as he stroked my back with his hand......up and down. God it felt so good.

"I have a feeling it is going to be even better when we're married."

I pushed myself up and looked down at him. He smiled at me but I could tell something was wrong.

"Gunner, what's going on with Jefferson?"

He let out a sigh. "Fuck Ellie, I can't be the one to tell you. I don't want to be the one to tell you."

Oh no....it was bad. Did something happen with the property? One of his horses, or oh god Ari's horse?

"Gunner…I saw the look on his face. It's big….tell me what's going on."

Gunner moved me off of him and sat up.

"Ellie you cannot tell Ari a word of what I'm about to tell you. Promise me baby you won't say anything."

Oh holy shit. Maybe I didn't want to know.

"Um, okay. I promise you Gunner. I won't say a word."

"Jeff needs to find out some shit before he talks to Ari about this."

"Okay…."

"I mean it all could turn out to not even be true."

"GUNNER! Just tell me!"

He ran his hands through his hair…....oh god how I wanted to do that…...oh gosh focus Ellie…..focus……

"Jeff got a call about forty five minutes ago from Rebecca. The girl he slept with that night at your graduation party."

"Okay…what did she want?"

"I guess Jeff hooked up with her the weekend before Thanksgiving. Ran into her at Rebels and ended up fucking her in his truck that night."

Nice……not the image I wanted in my head right now.

I just nodded and he kept talking.

"Well, anyway, she just called him and told him she was seven months pregnant and the baby was his."

Mother fucking son of a bitch. *No*…....

"Oh no! No Gunner no. This is going to destroy Ari! Why didn't he use protection?"

"He swears he did, he told her it was impossible but she said something about finding a piece of condom in her underwear later that night. But Jeff said he wasn't drunk and when he took the condom off it was not broke."

"Then she's lying Gunner. She has to be lying!"

"Jeff thinks she is but the only way to find out for sure is to wait until the baby is born and take a paternity test."

"Why did she wait until she was seven months pregnant before she said anything?"

"She said something about hearing from a friend he was about to get married. She must think he's getting married this weekend and she wanted to drop the bomb on him before he got married."

"Oh my god what a bitch! Ari is going to kill her Gunner."

"Yeah, I know. But hey, don't let this ruin our day okay? Jeff will take care of it. You have to trust him Ells to take care of it all okay baby?"

I nodded my head. Oh god. He was going to ask Ari to marry him Saturday night after the wedding. Is he going to tell her?

"Is he going to tell Ari?"

"Yeah, he just needs to talk to Rebecca first and then he's going to tell Ari."

"Is he still planning on asking her to marry him this weekend?"

"YES! Of course he is Sweetheart. He loves her more than anything."

"He needs to tell her right away Gunner. I don't think he should wait."

Gunner nodded but I know he was just as lost as I was.

I started thinking about the conversation I had with Ari just yesterday. We were wrapping up party favors that Jenny had sent up for us to do and Ari was talking about wanting to start a family right away. How she couldn't wait to see Jefferson's face when she told him for the first time she was pregnant. Oh god…my chest was hurting.

Poor Ari.

Saturday

The Wedding

"Do you want to go and check everything out before everyone gets here Ellie? If so, now would be our time to go."

Jenny was amazing! The way she was handling everything and doing such a great job at it! I had no doubt everything was going to look beautiful. She really needed to start a business doing this stuff with the way she made the cabin look when Gunner asked me to marry him; my heart was beating a mile a minute. She took us down to the wedding site first. It was a good thing my makeup was not done yet. It was exactly how I wanted it. The first thing I noticed was our tree. Hanging from the tree were about fifty small flower vases that we spent days making out of old bottles and mason jars. My fingers were almost raw from wrapping thin wire around and around the jars so that we could hang them in the trees. Daisies and other wild flowers were in each one. They looked beautiful. Then I saw all the hay bales. They were set in rows and had old quilts and blankets over each one. The way Gunner and Jefferson set them up there was a small back also so that people would be able to lean back while sitting down. Emma and her quilting club made pillows to put on the hay bales as well. The little fans on each row were perfect! They each had the letter M on them. I almost cried just thinking about how my name was going to be Ellie Mathews in just a few short hours.

The aisle that was made for the wedding party to walk down already had a few dozen red and pink flower petals spread around. Ari's little Cousin Lauren was the flower girl and her little brother Matthew was the ring barrier. They would both look so cute walking down the aisle.

I wanted the wedding site to be very simple, nothing more than the vases hanging in the tree. I did not want to take away from the beautiful location where we were getting married. I walked around and smiled. The memory of that night flooded back to me. The endless talking about our favorite movies, singers, songs, the beautiful stars......my first orgasm. I felt the heat rush into my face and I had to look around to see if anyone was watching me. I'm sure I was as red as those rose petals. This place was so special to me. Someday we would bring our kids here and show them the night time stars just like Gunner did for me.

"Is everything how you want Ellie?" Jenny asked as she walked around with a clip board and her cell phone ever present in her hand. I just smiled at her.

"I can never ever repay you for how wonderful you have made this day for me Jenny. It's perfect. Thank you so much for listening to me when I said I wanted to keep it as simple as possible. I just....I just love it."

Jenny smiled her shy little smile and shrugged her shoulders.

"I'm so happy you like it Ellie. Do you want to go up and see the reception area?"

"Is it safe? Where will Gunner be?"

Jenny laughed. I'll make sure that Aaron knows to keep him in the house and not to let him peek out the window."

We headed up to the ranch house and to the main barn. Drake, Aaron and Dewey spent days cleaning out the barn so that the slab floor would be ready for the reception. I was going to have to do something special for them.

We turned the corner and I saw three large white tents set up right outside the house and the barn. I sucked in a breath of air.

"Oh. My. God! It looks beautiful.....it all looks so beautiful."

We got out of Jenny's truck and started walking around. Ari grabbed my arm and we set off to explore. Each of the white tent legs were wrapped in white silk mesh tulle with soft pink ribbon wrapped around each leg. The white tables had white linen draped over the whole table with a smaller soft pink linen on top of that. I was so glad Jenny kept the white chairs plain though. She wanted to tie large pink bows on each but I wanted to keep it simple. I liked it simple and plain, it was more me I thought. Each table had a center piece of wild flowers in mason jars with a few small white votive candles.

I looked over to one table and they were setting mason jars all over it. That table would contain lemonade, sweet tea and ice water. Next to that was a giant trough that would have ice in it and filled to the max with beer. Last night Gunner was drilling holes and putting some tubing in it for the water that melted to drain out and away from the area. I smiled thinking about how handsome he looked last night. I looked back towards the house. I couldn't wait to see him.

The other table had the wedding cakes on it. The groom's cake was a 4 tiered chocolate cake that had an orange longhorn on the front of each layer. There were chocolate covered strawberries on the edge of each layer and on the top of the cake. All along the bottom of the cake were small chocolate footballs and helmets. The bride's cake was a three tier white butter cream cake with silver beaded accents on it. It was sitting on a piece of oak that Gunner had cut from a tree that had fallen in a spring storm. It was perfect! I wonder if Gunner had seen it yet.

Then I saw the fire pit that Gunner, Jefferson and Josh built yesterday. I smiled as I saw the table that had all the small pails with S'mores fixings in it. I laughed when I thought about how me, Ari, Amanda and Heather got so drunk while painting the pails with chalk board paint and then tried to write S'mores on them all. Gunner and Jefferson ended up having to finish them all. That was a fun night. The kids would have so much fun making S'mores and it reminded me of our first unofficial date at the coffee house.

The trees were all filled with white lights that would turn on right at dusk. I could not wait to see what it looked like! I looked around at all of the games that were set up everywhere. Horse shoes, croquet, washers…it was perfect. I had to giggle at the quilt on the ground with the chess set on it. That must have been Garrett's idea.

"Ellie honey, it all looks so beautiful." Ari said as we started to walk towards the barn. Oh my god….this did not look like the same barn. I don't know how Drake and the boys did it but, the slab floor was cleaned and white lights where everywhere. The band was already setting up in the corner along with the DJ. I was feeling overwhelmed yet so happy. I couldn't hold it back anymore. I started to cry. I was going to be Gunner's wife in just a few hours.

"Ellie! What's wrong?"Ari said as she took me in her arms.

"Nothing it's all just so beautiful. More beautiful than I could have ever imagined….." I was crying like a baby. Oh god…I was starting to hyperventilate. What the fuck was wrong with me?

"Ellie, breathe! Sweets you have to breathe! Hum, Jenny…..can you come here?"

I didn't even notice Ari and Jenny taking me back outside. I couldn't catch my breath. What the fuck was wrong with me? They walked me up to the ranch house and set me down on a chair. Emma walked out right then.

I can't get enough air…....OH MY GOD…… I'm going to die before I even get married!

"Ellie darling look at me. Look right at me," Emma said as she grabbed my face to look at her.

"Ellie take a deep breath in and blow it out."

I tried, I really did……all I could take was small gasps of air and that was starting to not be enough. Emma turned to Ari.

"Arianna, I want you to calmly go in the house and get Drew."

Ari turned and ran into the house screaming out Gunner's name.

Not thirty seconds later there he was. He came out of the screen door and our eyes met. He came running over to me and landed on his knees in front of me.

"Ellie baby what's wrong?" Gunner said with nothing but panic in his beautiful blue eyes.

He grabbed my hands and I felt that familiar jolt of electricity. I instantly felt the tightness in my chest let up and I was able to take a deep breath. I threw myself at him and hugged him as hard as I could. He got up and lifted me up with him. I wrapped my legs around him and he started to walk off to the other side of the porch away from everyone. God I loved to be in his arms like this. It was my favorite way for him to hold me.

He was running his hand down my hair. "Shhh Baby, it's okay. I'm here Sweetheart. Can you tell me what's wrong baby? Are you having second thoughts?"

What? NEVER!

I kept my face buried into him. My god he smelled so damn good. I was starting to get that ache in between my legs.

"NEVER! I want nothing more than to marry you Drew Mathews. I'm not sure what happened to be honest. All I know is I needed to see you and the thought of not being able to see you at that moment, I guess it made me panic. I love you. I love you so much.

"Jesus baby you scared me. I love you too Ellie. I love you so damn much it hurts."

I pulled back and looked into his eyes. "I feel the same way."

He just laughed.

"You know we're not supposed to see each other before the wedding. They say it's bad luck."

"I know for a fact that's not true. Emma told me that she and Garrett saw each other the morning of their wedding. Look how happy they are!"

Gunner just smiled at me as he pushed me into the side of the house and started to kiss me with so much passion I thought I was going to explode. Oh shit, I couldn't wait to spend the night with him tonight.

"Can we sneak off somewhere real quick?" I asked as I pushed myself into him.

"My greedy greedy little girl. What am I going to do with you?" Gunner asked as he bit my lower lip. I let out a low slow moan.

"Um, Ellie…we really need to get you back and start getting ready."

I looked at Gunner and made a sad face.

"Soon, Baby……soon." He slid me down his body in that oh so slow way he had.

"See ya soon?" I said as I looked up at him.

"See ya soon baby."

After we got back from checking everything out, I felt so much better. I think just being in Gunner's arms is what calmed me down. The cabin was so full of hair spray I thought I was going to die. Jenny must have sensed it was bugging me because she told her friends Ron and Jet, who were stylists from Austin, to spray outside from now on.

"I just can't figure out what the hell is wrong with him," Ari was saying to Amanda. I was pretty sure she was talking about Jefferson. I needed to push that from my mind today. I looked their way and they both looked beautiful. Ari, Amanda and Heather were all wearing their hair down but curled. Heather was getting hers curled right now and then she would be next for the spray down.

Jet was doing my hair and I loved it. She curled it all in big curls and then piled it all on my head. She pulled pieces of my hair down to frame my face and the back of neck. I smiled as I watched her put baby's breath all throughout my hair. I gave Gunner five minutes before he was pushing a piece of hair back behind my ear.

Jet was going on and on about something. I had tuned her out after the first five minutes and just thought about Gunner. I closed my eyes and pictured his blue eyes looking into mine as we said our vows.

"Ellie did you hear me honey?"

I opened my eyes to see Jet staring at me.

"Oh, I'm so sorry; what was that?"

"How do you like it Honey, your hair. Do you like it?"

I looked into the mirror. I looked perfect. I had just a small amount of makeup on but the way Ari did my eye makeup really made my blue eyes stand out. The tint of pink on my lips was perfect and my hair…...my hair looked beautiful. Was that even me in the mirror?

"Jet……it's just so amazing. I love it so much! It looks elegant yet simple."

Jet smiled from ear to ear then picked up a can of hair spray and sprayed the shit out of my hair. God I needed oxygen by the time she was done. Clearly she didn't hear the NO spraying hair spray inside rule.

I didn't even notice Ari, Amanda and Heather each going behind the giant sheet that was placed so everyone could change. I looked over and saw Ari walking out in the pale pink sleeveless sundress. Oh my…...she took my breath away. The gray silver cowboy boots she had on were perfect……just like she said they would be. She smiled at me as she put on her white cowboy hat. I wanted to jump up and down it looked so fucking good. Just then I saw Amanda and then Heather. They looked like super models……all three of them. I just stared at them. They started to laugh and Ari said something to Heather about getting the same reaction from Josh. Heather hit Ari in the arm and told her to go to hell.

Then Jenny walked up to me.

"Ellie, it's time to put your dress on."

Oh wow……this was it. I was putting on the dress that the four of us spent days searching for. We ended up finding it at the last bridal store we went to in Austin. I was so sick of trying on dresses I was ready to give up. I told Ari I was trying on one more dress and that was it.

When I looked at myself in the mirror before stepping out to show the girls I almost cried. MaryBeth, the bridal consultant who had been helping me try on dress after dress, leaned over and said, "That's the one. When you look in the mirror and want to cry.....then that's the dress meant for you."

I looked over at her as I felt the tears roll down my face. I didn't even bother wiping them away. I had to show the girls that very second.

I stepped out and heard three gasps at the same time.

"Holy hell!" Amanda said.

"Oh my Ellie, it's perfect honey!" Heather said.

"Jesus, Mary and Joseph, holy fucking shit......that dress is beautiful!" Ari screamed out as she jumped up. MaryBeth helped me up onto the platform and spread the train all out. Oh my god it was beautiful.

MaryBeth started to tell us about the dress as I stared at myself in the mirror.

"Ladies, this is a Jim Hjelm wedding dress. It's a Silk Satin faced Organza A-line dress with a strapless embroidered bodice with crystals and hand-cut Silk Organza, Chiffon and Charmeuse. The natural waist is accented with a Platinum moire ribbon and has a bias cut asymmetrical ruffle skirt with a chapel train."

All three of them just stared at poor MaryBeth. "Yeah....... whatever the hell all that means......Ellie it's beautiful! Just perfect. Get it.......Gunner is going to be jizzing in his pants when he sees you in this," Ari said as she jumped up and down.

I let out a laugh as I thought about that day. I stood up and walked over to the curtain. Jenny and Ari stepped behind with me and helped me get dressed. I started with a white lace bustier along with a pair of blue panties that Ari bought for my something blue. I slipped the garter belt on that had been used by Emma in her wedding, my something old, and started to roll on my satin thigh high sheers on. I was wearing cowboy boots under my dress but Ari insisted I wear thigh highs with a garter belt because it would driver Gunner mad when he saw me. I slipped the garter around my leg and up my thigh. It was pale pink and a gift from Heather, my something new. Now for the dress......I was shaking from head to toe.

Jenny and Ari carefully helped me into the dress and helped to adjust everything just right. I loved the platinum ribbon belt so much! Ari helped me slip on my cowboy boots and I walked out from around the sheet.

Amanda and Heather both let out a gasp and Heather started to cry.

"Don't make her cry! Damn you Heather, you're such a fucking sap!" I looked over at Ari and she was the one starting to cry.

Jenny's cell phone rang as Jet was handing the girls all their bouquets of daisies.

"Okay, they are here."

Gunner would not tell me how I was getting to the wedding sight; he just kept saying it was a secret. Jenny had a huge smile on her face as she handed me my bouquet of pink roses that had a small hanky that Emma carried with her bouquet, my something borrowed. I smiled down at Lauren, the flower girl. She was so sweet in her pale pink dress and pink cowboy boots. Matthew was beyond handsome! Gunner picked out what Matthew was wearing. He had on blue jean overalls, cowboy boots and a cowboy hat.

Amanda and Heather put their cowboy hats on and walked out first. The photographer had been there ever since we started to get ready and she had been snapping pictures nonstop. Then Ari, Lauren and Matt walked out. Jenny stepped aside so I could move out the door while she and Jet carried my train. I stopped dead in my tracks.

A carriage?

Fuck me…...I looked over and was shocked to see another one. Ari was helping Lauren and Matthew climb up into a pink carriage….a carriage for Christ sakes! My future crazy romantic husband had carriages picking us up. I had to laugh.

Oh…..….I was so going to give him a blow job tonight for this!

Jenny gave me a little nudge to move me along. I was helped into a beautiful white Cinderella looking carriage and I was shocked to see Garrett sitting there.

"Hello my sweet darling girl! Oh my holy hell…...if you ain't the most beautiful bride I have ever laid eyes on! And don't you be going and telling Emma I told you that!"

"OH MY GOSH Garrett! What're you doing here?" I reached over and hugged him.

"Well sweet girl, your brother really wanted to be able to walk you down the aisle but seeing as he is the best man, he asked me to do the honor for him."

Okay…...now I might cry.

"Don't you dare…...Ellie…...don't you cry," Garrett said.

I started to laugh.

"Okay, I won't."

Once they got my train all in Jenny ran over to her truck and took off like a bat out of hell. I was really going to have to do something special for her. I already had to force her to let us pay her for helping to plan the whole wedding.

We pulled up a little ways away from our tree. The first thing I saw was all of the people sitting on the hay bales. I still had not met Gunner's parents. I wasn't even sure if they would be showing up which broke my heart. Of course I hadn't spoken to my own mother in months. She was not invited to the wedding. When I called to tell her I was getting married she laughed and asked what I had to do to get Gunner to marry me, and then she asked if I was pregnant. I decided that was going to be the last time I ever talked to that woman again.

Amanda, Heather and Ari had pulled ahead of us on the way over so they were the first to get out. Amanda and Heather helped Lauren and Matthew get ready to walk down the aisle. I was watching them and my heart just melted. I was too afraid to look up and see Gunner. I knew the moment I saw him I would start crying so I just didn't look. Garrett got out and walked around to help me down. Jenny held my train up and off the ground. The music started playing so the kids must have started to walk. Ari was now by my side.

"Ells, breathe sweets. Deep breaths in and out."

I smiled at her. I really was feeling rather calm......which was strange.

"How does he look?"

Ari smiled. "He looks so handsome Ellie, and he has the biggest goddamn smile on his face I've ever seen!"

"Ari, Ellie, Garrett......are you ready?"

We started to walk and stopped right behind a horse. Jenny sure knew what the hell she was doing because once I got down out of the carriage I was blocked by horses and another carriage.

Ari leaned over and gave me a kiss.

"Here we go sweets…..." She winked at me and took off.

Garrett looked over at me and smiled.

"Are you ready Sweetheart?"

I had to smile at his choice of words. The fact that he called me sweetheart made my heart just start beating a mile a minute. I smiled and nodded. He took my arm in his and we started to walk.

We came around and stopped at the very beginning of the petal covered pathway. I looked around at all the people. The guests were mostly friends and family on Gunner's side. The rest were our friends, and Gunner's teammates. Everyone was smiling at me. Then the wedding march started. Garrett squeezed my arm and we took off.

I looked up and looked right at Gunner. His eyes captured mine and I instantly smiled. I let my eyes drift down his body. OHMYGOD......my knees felt weak and it must have been noticeable because Garrett lifted his arm up to what I'm guessing was to help me stay standing up. Gunner was dressed in black Wrangler jeans, black cowboy boots, a white button down shirt with a grey matching blazer and vest. He was wearing the bronze tie that we picked out together last week and his black cowboy hat.

I looked back up and my eyes caught his and it just took my breath away. He was giving me that damn crooked smile of his and I started to giggle. He raised his eyebrow up at me which made me giggle even more. It felt like it was taking forever to get up there and I found myself starting to try to walk faster. Now Garrett was the one laughing.

"Slow down there darling......this isn't a race you know!"

Finally we made up to the altar. I looked at Jefferson who looked so handsome and was dressed almost identical to Gunner but with a grey tie. He was next, him and Ari. He gave me a wink as Garrett announced he was the one giving me away. Garrett placed my hand in Gunner's hand and I stepped up on the last step. Gunner leaned down, pushed a curl behind me ear, and whispered so low I barely heard him.

"You look so beautiful Ellie; you take my breath away sweetheart. I love you."

Dear lord…...this man was amazing. I'm not sure what I ever did to deserve him but I will spend the rest of my life making him happy. That was a promise.

Gunner

I watched as Jenny walked Ellie back over to her truck and they took off for the hunter's cabin. Ellie turned back once and smiled at me and my knees about gave out. Will her smile always affect me this much?

"Yes."

What? I heard Gramps and wondered if I had just said my last thought out loud.

"Excuse me sir?"

"Yes, she is always going to do whatever it is you're feeling right now Drew, whether you can't catch your breath at the sight of her, your knees go weak from a smile or a kiss. She will always have you bewitched.

"Are you able to read minds now old man?" I asked as I watched the love of my life drive off.

Gramps let out a loud and gruff laugh. Then he slapped me on the back.

"Walk with me son."

We headed in the direction away from where everything was being set up. I looked over my shoulder and saw Grams standing on the porch watching us.

"Were you nervous the day you married Grams?" I asked after about three minutes of silence.

"Hell yes I was nervous. I threw up three times and my father kept telling me to man up. I was scared shitless I wasn't going to be able to make her as happy as she made me. I decided after the last time I threw up that I would rather die than not spend my life with her so I would just have to figure out a way to make her happy."

I smiled at the thought of my Gramps being scared. He was the strongest man I knew and didn't take shit from anyone, well anyone except Grams.

"I love her so much Gramps that sometimes I can't even think straight when I'm around her. I never in my life thought this was what love was going to be like. The moment I saw her I knew...... I just knew I had to make her mine."

Gramps let out a chuckle. "Drew listen to me son. Love like that, the love that you feel for Ellie and she feels for you. It's very rare. Only a lucky few will ever experience it and when you do, you fight for that love every single goddamn day of your life. You will both fight; make each other mad as hell. You might even think it won't work out but it will son, trust me it will. When you share a love so strong you can weather any storm."

"Like you and Grams? Did you think it wouldn't work out ever?"

"Yes, not long after we got married. I can't even remember what the fight was about but I remember packing up a bag to leave. The moment I reached for the door to open it, I was hit by this realization that if I left, if I walked out that door, I might not ever be able to get her back. It was not worth risking it so I put my bag down turned to see her crying and walked up to her."

Good lord what the fuck was wrong with me? My heart was beating a mile a minute as I hung onto every word.

"What happened?"

Gramps laughed. "I kissed her, picked her up and made love to her in the kitchen. It was one of the best fucking moments of my life."

Oh god……I think I'm going to be sick…...I didn't need that fucking image in my head.

"Ahhh shit Gramps……I don't want to hear about that…...man."

Gramps laughed. "I'm just saying Drew; don't ever give up without a fight. She loves you son. She needs you more than I think you know. The fact that only your touch calmed her down earlier was a testimony of how much she loves and needs you."

When Ari came screaming in the house for me I thought something horrible had happened. The moment I saw Ellie sitting there…...my only thought was to get to her. When I touched her and saw her almost immediately relax, I thought I was going to burst with happiness. Knowing I was the one she needed, not Jeff or Ari or Grams, it was me who she needed.

"Drew when you see her walking down that aisle, watch her every move. Don't look around to anyone else but her. Memorize how she looks, how she's smiling, how her hair looks, the dress she is wearing……every single thing. Tuck it away in your heart and never forget it. It will probably be one of the most amazing sights you'll ever see. And when she walks up to you, tell her immediately how she just made you feel."

I nodded my head and turned to look at the most important man in my life.

"Gramps, I want to thank you for everything you've done for me. Teaching me about the ranch, giving me the opportunities to be able to go to UT, play football and get my degree in something I loved. Thank you for teaching me to respect and be grateful for the love that I have found with Ellie. Thank you for loving me and believing in me. I love you more like my father than my grandfather."

Gramps stopped and turned to face me. He had a smile on his face and he just shook his head.

"I love you Drew, you make me so fucking proud son I want you to know that. You will always make me proud. Now let's go get you married!"

Jeff leaned over and looked at Ellie sitting in the carriage. Then he looked at me.

"You fucking bastard......a carriage, you got her a carriage? Jesus you're killing me here!"

I just smiled. He was still pissed about having to pay Jenny and Aaron so much to help out with his first night with Ari.

"Do you want me to make your sister happy or not Jeff?" I asked as I struggled to see my beautiful girl.

"Fucker......I knew you'd pull that card out. What the fuck are you going to do when she tells you she's pregnant for the first time? Fly her to Paris."

Just then the preacher coughed and looked at us. Hmm Paris? I'll have to remember that.

Jeff turned and looked at me and then went white. I just smiled at him.

"THAT was MY idea! I claim that one......you cannot have it dickwad! Paris is *my idea* Gunner."

"Boys!" Preacher Roberts said as Jeff instantly took a step back and looked down the aisle. Little Lauren and Matthew were walking down the aisle. So fucking cute. Lauren was skipping as Matthew was looking around at every one holding the pillow and snapping his overalls. Yep......I taught him that. Then I saw Heather walking. I took a quick peek at Josh and I thought he was going to break his face he was smiling so goddamn big. Then came Amanda and I heard Brad let out a cuss word that I'm pretty sure Preacher Roberts would be talking to him about later. Then I saw Ari. Jeff took in a breath of air and just stared at her.

"Holy fuck......she's beautiful," Jeff said at the same time he released all the air he sucked in. I had to agree, Ari looked breathtaking.

Then I saw her. Gramps had his arm around her and they started to walk. Our eyes met and I couldn't breathe. Oh. My. God. She looked......beautiful. Like a princess. She was looking me up and down checking me out, and man did I like it. It looked like she was about to stumble and Gramps had to hold her up. She looked back up at me and I smiled even more at the thought that I just made her weak in the knees.

Then she giggled. I raised my eyebrow at her wondering what she thought was so funny and she giggled more. If I didn't know any better it looked like for a moment she started to walk faster. Then Gramps laughed and whispered something to her.

It took forever for her to walk up to me. Once she got there and Gramps placed her hand in mine that familiar shot of electricity took off in my body. We stepped up to the altar and I leaned over to do just what Gramps told me to do.

"You look so beautiful Ellie; you take my breath away sweetheart. I love you."

She looked at me and her eyes filled with tears as she smiled at me.

"Drew, I love you too." Her voice was cracking and I knew she was having a hard time talking. I squeezed her hand and we both turned to Preacher Roberts. I smiled as the thought occurred to me for the first time that day.

Another first.........

"The ceremony was beautiful darling. Just beautiful! And you......you are the most precious thing I have ever seen!" Aunt Lacy said to me as she kept pulling me in for a hug and then pushing me out again to do a once over. I was starting to feel sick from the constant pushing and pulling.

I was finally able to break free from her and tried to sneak over to grab some sweet tea.

"ELLIE!"

SHIT! Dammit! I was just five feet from my sweet tea. I turned around to see Shannon and James standing there. Oh I still felt so bad about everything that happened. Gunner actually missed their wedding because of the car accident. I felt my face burning up.

Shannon leaned in and whispered in my ear. "Don't you even think about it Ellie. I know what you're doing and you will not feel guilty do you hear me?"

I smiled as she pulled away and gave me a kiss on the cheek.

"Have you met my sisters yet?" Shannon said as she put her arm in mine and led me away from my sweet tea. I looked around for Gunner. Where the hell was he?

Then I spotted him. He was playing horse shoes with a few of the younger kids. He looked up at me and we smiled at each other. I just wanted to leave......start our lives together, that and I really wanted some fucking sweet tea! If I had to talk to another person and thank them for coming I think I was going to hurl.

Shannon introduced me to her two sisters, Lynda and Clare. We talked for a bit and then I slowly started to make my way back to the sweet tea. I saw it......oh thank god my mouth was so dry!

Just as I was about to reach for a mason jar and fill it up with nice cold sweet ice tea, that only Emma can make......I was stopped again by someone saying my name. Mother fucker......now I was going to go off on someone.

"Ellie?"

"Mom?"

Wait....what?

I turned around to see a woman standing in front of me. I instantly recognized her from the pictures in Gunner's bedroom. Gunner was standing behind her and she slowly turned around to look at him. She ran into his arms as he picked her up and spun her around.

"DREW! Oh Drew! I've missed you so much. I'm so sorry baby boy, so sorry!"

OH. MY. GOD…...I looked around for Gunner's father but didn't see him. Bastard! I wonder if she had just gotten there. That made me feel sad if she had, she missed a beautiful ceremony.

"Mom……why didn't you let me know you were coming? Did you just get here?"

"No Drew, I was here for the ceremony. It was beautiful. You look so handsome Drew and look at you such a man now; you're not my little boy……. Oh my…...." She started to cry as Gunner drew her back into his arms.

My heart was hurting. To think of all the time she missed out because of Gunner's stubborn father.

"Mom please don't cry. You don't know how happy you made me by coming. Thank you so much."

"Drew, your father wouldn't come I'm sorry. He did tell me to congratulate you though," She said with such sadness in her voice.

Gunner laughed. "Sure he did mom! I don't want to talk about him. I want to introduce you to my wife."

I sucked in a breath of air. Oh god I loved hearing him say that!

"Mom, may I introduce to you my wife, Mrs. Ellie Mathews. Ellie sweetheart, this is my mother Grace Mathews."

I reached my hand out to shake hers but she came up to me and hugged me. More like squeezed the shit out of me. She pulled back and looked me up and down.

"So beautiful! You're such a beautiful girl."

"Thank you Mrs. Mathews."

"No, please Ellie sweetheart, call me Grace. Thank you so much Ellie for making my Drew so happy. I can see by the way he looks at you how happy and in love he is with you," She said to me with a smile.

I smiled back at her. She really was a beautiful woman and I could see so much of her in Gunner now that I saw her in person.

"Thank you Grace. I feel the same way about him. He's the most amazing man I've ever met."

Gunner walked around his mom and took me into his arms and leaned down and kissed me. Before he pulled all the way away from my lips he smiled.

"Do you want some sweet tea Baby?"

I had to let out a giggle. I wonder if he had seen my many failed attempts to get that tea.

"God yes!"

Gunner let me go and I watched as he poured me a glass of tea. I turned back to look at Grace and she was smiling at us with a big ole smile on her face. I really was so happy she made it, and I know it meant so much to Gunner. I just wished his dad would have come.

"Mom, you remember how good Gram's tea is, you want some?"

Grace laughed and shook her head no. "Drew I just spent nearly an hour in Emma's kitchen with her. She filled me up with three glasses of tea! I'm good honey thank you."

Grace and I took a seat at one of the tables and talked forever. She told me stories about Gunner when he was little, how he got into trouble in high school with fighting for a bit. It was like she was trying to make up for the lost time we had to get to know each other before I became her daughter-in-law. She raved on and on about Emma, told me to learn as much from her as I could if I was going to be a rancher's wife.

Jenny walked up to us and said Gunner and I really needed to have our first dance. We had both been so busy walking around and talking to everyone that the DJ and band just started up without us. I nodded and got up and followed Jenny into the barn. Gunner was talking to Jack, the DJ. I'm guessing he was telling him what song to play. I saw Jack nod yes to Gunner and smile. Gunner pretty much left all the wedding decisions up to me except for the song he wanted for our first dance. I had no problem with that since he had a pretty damn good track record with songs.

Gunner walked up to me and held out his hand. Jack announced that we were *finally* having our first dance. Everyone whooped and hollered.

"Will you please do me the honor Mrs. Mathews?" Gunner said as he kissed the back of my left hand and started to walk me to the middle of the barn.

As he pulled me into his arms he leaned down and whispered against my ear. His warm breath sent the butterflies into flight in my stomach and I felt a shiver run through my entire body.

"Don't ever forget how I feel about you; never, ever forget Sweetheart. I will *always* want you and only you. I would be lost without you Ellie; I love you more than life itself….."

Then he leaned down and kissed me so passionately I felt the love pouring from his body straight into mine.

Then the song started. Oh my god…….

"Wanted" by Hunter Hayes.

Gunner never let up on his kiss even when the song started. I felt the tears rolling down my face and Gunner grabbed onto me and held me tighter as I was slowly starting to sink down. I'm not sure how long he kissed me for but I started to sob. He pulled his lips away from mine and smiled down at me. He reached up and wiped away at the endless tears running down my face.

"Happy tears Baby?"

I couldn't find my voice. I loved him so much and he just made the most wonderful day so much more special. I didn't think it could get any better but again he showed me different.

I could barely talk but somehow I managed to speak.

"Yes Gunner, they are very happy tears. I love you so much. Th…thank…um……." I started to cry again. He pulled me into him and held me close as he started to sing the song to me so softly and sweetly.

I never wanted this moment to end. I never in my life felt so loved and wanted as I did at this very moment. I would love this man with everything I had in me for the rest of my life. I would do everything in my power to make him just as happy as he has made me.

I looked up at him and smiled as he smiled down to me.

"Drew……it's another first."

He looked at me confused. "What is Baby?"

"This……this feeling……it's a first for me."

"Tell me Ellie."

"I have never in my life…..*ever* felt so completely loved and……..wanted."

Gunner leaned down and captured my mouth again with his. It was perfect.

No, It was……..heaven……

Evening had already come and the lights in the trees were turned on by someone. Probably Jenny by the way that poor girl was running all over the place.

Gunner and I were both exhausted. I had never danced so much in my entire life, ate so much and laughed so much. It was all coming to an end.

"So are you going to change or stay in that dress?" Ari asked with a wiggle of her eyes.

Gunner walked over and whispered in my ear for me to keep the dress on. He wanted to slowly peel it off of at the hotel in Austin.

"I guess I'm keeping the dress on!"

Ari let out a laugh and hit Gunner in the shoulder.

"If you think she looks beautiful in the dress, wait until you see what she has on underneath the dress. Or all the little outfits I packed in her suitcase."

Gunner pulled me against him and pushed his hips into my backside. OH MY! I think it is time to go……

"Ari, I always knew there was a reason I liked you so damn much."

"Damn straight ass wipe, and you better spoil her rotten on the honeymoon or I'll punch you in the nuts and not think twice about it."

With that Ari turned and walked away. I had to laugh. I loved her so much. I thought about the whole situation with Jefferson. Ari didn't know it but Jenny was working double time tonight. With our wedding and also transforming the hunter's cabin into a romantic paradise so Jefferson could ask Ari to marry him tonight. I noticed her getting in and out of her truck for the last two hours running back and forth.

"We need to do something special for Jenny and Aaron for everything they have done Gunner."

"Baby I'm already one step ahead of you. I booked them a room at the Marriott in Austin for the next two nights. I had Jeff go and leave them some gift cards for a few restaurants also, and Gramps hired a whole crew to come and clean everything up and take it all down. Jenny doesn't have to worry about a thing."

I turned around and looked at him.

"You really are too damn good to be true do you know that?"

Gunner threw his head back and laughed.

Just then Jefferson pulled up in Gunner's truck. It was completely decked out in cans and ribbons and every window had something written on it.

Gunner grabbed my hand and pulled me to him.

"You ready to go and start our honeymoon Mrs. Mathews?" Gunner said as he wiggled his eyebrows up and down. Then he took his hand and ran it down my face.

I could feel the heat rising in my cheeks just at the thought of what it was going to be like tonight. The thought of making love to Gunner......as his wife for the first time had me blushing like mad.

"I'll take that as a yes."

Jenny came over and walked us around to the ranch house. She said Emma and Garrett wanted to speak with us in private before we left. We walked into the house and Emma was holding a bouquet of Daisies and smiling so big. Garrett was holding an envelope and his smile was even bigger than Emma's. Of course he looked at Gunner and winked which caused me to blush all over again. Emma handed me the flowers and hugged me.

"Welcome my sweet darling Ellie to our family. I loved you the moment you jumped out of Drew's truck and smiled at me. I absolutely cannot wait for you to move out to the ranch. You truly are the daughter I never had sweetheart. I love you."

I was at a loss for words......again......I hugged her back as tightly as I could and whispered in her ear how much I loved her and what a wonderful job she did helping to raise such an amazing man.

She pulled back and smiled. "He is, isn't he?"

I nodded my head yes. I looked over at Gunner and he had a tear running down his face. I reached up and wiped it away.

"A happy tear I hope."

"Yes Baby, happier than you can ever imagine."

Garrett cleared his throat and moved over to us. He looked like he was about to cry which made me start to cry.

"Drew, you continue to make us so damn proud. I can't begin to tell you how happy I am for you son. You did well, especially with this fine young lady here."

Gunner pulled me closer to him. I put my arm around him and felt his body shudder.

"I know you had your whole honeymoon planned out and wouldn't let your Grams and I help you with anything so, this is our gift to both of you. I want you to open it now before you leave."

Emma was standing there ringing her hands like she was nervous as hell.

Gunner took the envelope and opened it. It looked like a bunch of legal papers, a check and was that a deed to something? Gunner's face dropped as he handed me the check and looked at his grandfather.

I looked at the check and almost fell over. Was I reading that right? $550,000.....

"Gramps what are you doing? You can't afford to give us this kind of money. I won't take this."

I looked up at Emma and Garrett and they both looked pissed. I took a step back.

"Drew, don't you ever again tell me what I can and cannot afford to do young man. That house you lived in for four years in Austin, well I had a gentleman call me four months ago asking if I wanted to sell. I told him he could have the house the moment you and Jeff graduated and moved out here to the ranch. I sold it to him six days ago with the agreement that he give you until July 15 to move out. The money is from that house. Emma and I want you and Ellie to start right away when you get back from your honeymoon on building your home on the ranch. Anywhere on the ranch you like. That deed son, that deed is for the entire ranch. It is now yours and Ellie's."

Oh.MY.GOD...I had to sit down before I passed out. I looked up at Gunner who now had tears just rolling down his face. He walked over to his grandfather and hugged him. They exchanged a few more words to each other and then he hugged Emma. I couldn't think straight. The ranch was ours? I had to sit down.

"Gramps, Grams I don't even know what to say. Are you sure you're ready to turn it over to me to run? What if I fuck it all up?"

Garrett laughed. "Drew, I'll be here every step of the way to help you."

Gunner turned and took my hand to help me up. We kissed Emma and Garrett goodbye again; thanked them again for the *incredibly* generous wedding gift and made our way to the truck.

As we pulled away I started to get excited. Gunner looked over at me and took my hand and kissed my rings.

"You ready Sweetheart?"

I smiled at him and felt so nervous. I felt like it was my first time all over again.

"I'm so ready you have no idea! Can you possibly speed just a little? I'm not sure I can wait another three hours to be with you."

Gunner threw his head back and laughed as he drove just a little faster.

62 Gunner

"Ellie baby wake up, we're here sweetheart." I bent into the truck and started to lift her out. She opened her eyes and looked over at the valet who was waiting to get in and park the truck.

"Ummm, where are we?" Ellie asked all sleepy sounding. So fucking cute.

"We're at the hotel Baby. You fell asleep." I carried her into the lobby of the Driskill hotel. She looked around and smiled.

Ellie giggled as she whispered big spender in my ear. Her hot breath against my face almost brought me to my knees.

"Only the best for my wife, only the very best for you Sweetheart," I said as I kissed her nose.

I walked up to the counter and set Ellie down and told the receptionist I had a reservation for Mathews.

"Congratulations Mr. and Mrs. Mathews. Mrs. Mathews your wedding dress is absolutely breathtaking and I LOVE the cowboy boots with it!"

I smiled as I picked up my dress some and showed off my silver gray jeweled cowboy boots. Ari bought them and I almost killed her when I found out they were $350. She claimed they were a wedding gift from her parents. I did love them though!

"Thank you so much," I said as I willed her to hurry the fuck up. I just wanted to get out of this damn dress and....

"What are you thinking about Baby? You're blushing...." Gunner said against my ear.

I threw my hands up to my cheeks and smiled. Busted......so totally busted.

"Nothing....."

"Mr. Mathews we have you booked in a bridal suite with a king bed. Jason will bring your bags up to your room."

I looked over at Jason who was staring at me. I mean really staring. Gunner turned to look at him, frowned, and then snapped his fingers in front of Jason's face.

"Dude, that's not cool to be staring at a man's wife like that!" Gunner said. I started to laugh because Jason's face was redder than all get out.

We were standing outside the door waiting for Jason to put our bags in the room. He stepped out and Gunner handed him a tip but not before he gave him another look.

"Um, Mr. and Mrs. Mathews, enjoy your stay."

Gunner watched as Jason walked down the hall and then called him a fucker. I tried to hide my giggle but it slipped out. He looked down at me and gave me that crooked smile of his. He reached down and picked me up so fast I almost didn't realize what was happening. He walked through the door and shut it with his foot as he kissed me.

"Mrs. Mathews, welcome to your honeymoon suite." He oh so slowly slid me down and set me on the ground while he kissed me. Oh god......I was so nervous. Why was I so nervous?

"Mr. Mathews......it's perfect." Gunner smiled and stepped back and that's when I really got to take a look at the room. Oh. My. God. It was stunning!

Hard wood floors were throughout the room. The first thing I noticed was the four poster bed. It was huge, with a beautiful creamy yellow duvet and the most amazing throw pillows I had ever seen. There was a beautiful white lace fabric that draped down each post and was topped by a creamy yellow fabric that matched the duvet along with tassels hanging down from the fabric. It looked so old!

There was a giant piece of iron art work on the wall above the bed with satin fabric curtains draped across and hanging down on either side of the bed. It was beautiful! The walls were all painted with warm earth toned colors and the room was just so cozy.

I scanned the room; there was a private balcony and a living room. The furniture had such a European flare to it. WOW! Gunner took my hand and led me into the bathroom. I was stunned when I saw it. There was so much marble everywhere, the sink, the walls, the stand up shower, and the tub....oh my god the tub! It was a huge Jacuzzi tub and there were small white LED candles lit all around the tub. In the back corner were three red candles softly flickering, also LED's. There was a bottle of chilled sparkling wine with two flutes and a plate of chocolates sitting on the side of the tub.

"We will get to this in a little bit," Gunner said as he walked me back into the other room. He slowly walked backwards as he led me over to the bed. Sitting on the bed was a single yellow rose. And......what the hell was that?

I reached down and picked it up and started to read out loud. "Kama Sutra Getaway Kit.....contains a *Vanilla Crème Oil of Love*, OHHHH that sounds promising!" I said as I looked up at Gunner. "*A Sweet Honeysuckle Honey Dust with feather applicator*......that could be fun don't you think?" Gunner started to laugh. "Hmmm and a *French Vanilla Crème Body Soufflé*, I don't think I really need to say anymore with that one!" Gunner pulled me in closer to him. "OH there's more! There is also *a Love Liquid Classic Lubricant and scented romance candle.* I think I'm going to have to write a thank you note to someone!"

Gunner took the romance kit out of my hand and set it on the marble side table. He cupped my face in his hands and started to kiss me so passionately I about melted. He rubbed his lips all over my face and went right to my ear where he tugged on my ear lobe and whispered into my ear.

"Right now Ellie, the only thing I want to do is slowly peel you out of your gorgeous wedding dress."

"Okay."

"Turn around baby…."

I slowly turned around as Gunner ran his hand down my neck and onto my back.

"My god Ellie you are so beautiful. This dress looks stunning on you."

I had shivers going up and down my body and my heart was beating a mile a minute. I felt Gunner undoing the Platinum ribbon that was tied around my waist. Then I felt his fingers start on the buttons. If didn't know any better I would swear his hands were shaking. After he unbuttoned each button he kissed me on the back.

"Jesus Ellie, the way your body reacts to my touch turns me on so fucking much."

Oh god if you only knew!

"Gunner….." Was all I could manage to say.

After each painstakingly slow button he undid, he kissed me. I was going mad and the ache between my legs was growing. It was not going to take me long to have an orgasm.

After they were all unbuttoned he used his hands to turn me around.

I stood there looking into his beautiful blue eyes. He smiled and I swear to god I almost had a mini orgasm right there. I actually pushed my legs together to ease the throbbing.

He took both hands and pushed the dress off my shoulders and let it fall to a pool of Silk and Chiffon and whatever the hell else this dress was made out of.

Gunner sucked in a breath and just stared at me. He reached out and took my hand to help me step out of the wedding dress. I stood there……dressed only in my white lace bustier and blue panties, white garter belt and sheer satin thigh high stockings. Oh, and my cowboy boots! SHIT! Why the fuck didn't I remember to change into the white satin high heels.

"Holy shit Ellie……you look……you look….."

I felt the blush creeping into my cheeks. Damn, why did I blush so easy around him?

"Do you like it? Minus the cowboy boots I mean, I forgot to change out of them. I'm sorry."

He looked me up and down and started to lick his lips. I'm going to take that as a sign he likes it!

"Ellie my god sweetheart, I have…...I've never……*never* seen anything so fucking sexy in my entire life as my wife standing here in a white bustier and silver cowboy boots. I would have been so upset if you took them off."

I smiled up at him as his eyes traveled up and down my body in a greedy hungry look.

"Sit down on the bed Ellie."

I sat down on the bed and Gunner knelt down. He started to take my boots off. After each boot he massaged my foot for a minute or two. Oh my……it felt heavenly! Then he placed both hands on my legs and slowly moved them up and started to unhook my stockings from the garter belt. He slowly…...oh so slowly slid them down my legs and off my feet. Then he placed a kiss on the inside of each of my thighs. Yep……I was going to have an orgasm the moment he touched me.

"Slide back onto the bed Ellie," Gunner said in the deepest sexiest voice I'd ever heard him use. Holy shit! I slid back on the bed and had to close my eyes and squeeze my legs together or I was going to come just from hearing his voice!

I felt the bed dip as Gunner climbed on and was kissing me from the bottom of my feet all the way up my legs, then onto my chest, my neck and then my lips. He was lying to the side of me and I felt his……bare skin? My eyes flew open and I pulled away from his kiss to look at him.

OHMYGOD……he was naked. Beautifully naked. When the hell did he get undressed and how did he do it so fast?

"I want you so bad Ellie, so so bad baby," He said as he kissed my neck and chest.

"Oh God Gunner……I can't take much more please……I need you so bad."

"Anything for you my greedy, greedy wife." He started to take off the garter belt; slowly he removed it and set it on the floor. Then he removed the white garter that Ari put on right before we left. He left the bustier on though and crawled on top of me but sat back some.

"Sit up Ellie."

I sat up as he reached his arms around my back. The touch of his fingers was driving me insane. I swear he had magic in his finger tips the way his touch affected me. He took the bustier off and set it on the floor next to my other clothes. I laid back down and watched him just look at my body.

"As hot as you looked in that bustier, it had to come off…...I'll never get tired of looking at your body Mrs. Mathews."

He leaned down and kissed me so passionately I was lost in a world of pure passion.

We stayed up all night as Gunner made sweet passionate love to me once on the bed, once in the bath tub and once on the floor in the bathroom. We finally fell on the bed and collapsed in pure exhaustion at 5:45 in the morning.

"Sleep my sweet Ellie. We have a plane to catch at 2 pm." Gunner said has he brought me closer to him. I snuggled up next to him and sighed with contentment.

I yawned and asked when he was going to tell me where we were going. He just laughed and held me tighter against him.

"Baby you will find out soon enough. I love you Ellie, so very much."

"I love you more......." Gunner laughed and within minutes we both drifted off to sleep.

I dreamt about weddings, honeymoons, moving into a brand new home and sitting in a rocking chair on a porch watching the sun set while Gunner rocked a baby in his arms.

63 Jeff

I watched as Gunner and Ellie pulled away for their honeymoon. I was so happy for them I could hardly stand it. Ellie had looked so beautiful and so fucking happy. I shook my head at the idea of my baby sister getting married. I guess it was my turn next. The thought of Rebecca and the baby popped into my head. I fucking knew there was no way that kid was mine. I was not drunk that night and the condom was not broke. At least I swear it was not broke.

Jenny walked up to me with a huge smile on her face. I felt in my left pocket to make sure I still had the engagement ring. Ari felt it once in my pocket while we were dancing but I told her it was the box for Ellie's ring.

"Hey Jeff, the cabin is completely ready for you and Ari. I kept it simple just like you asked."

"Thanks Jenny. I'm not exactly like that over-the-top fucker best friend of mine."

Jenny laughed and gave me a hug. "Thanks Jenny, for everything you did for me and for Gunner and Ellie. The wedding was beautiful."

Jenny smiled and patted my arm. I watched her walk away as I saw Ari walking up to me with a wicked smile on her face.

"Hey you…....feeling a little lucky tonight?" she said as she reached up and bit my lower lip. I let a small moan escape and she smiled.

"I am indeed. I have a little surprise waiting for us back at the cabin." I said as I pulled her closer to me. God she smelled so fucking good.

"Well then, I think now that the bride and groom have left, the best man and maid of honor can leave as well."

"Best fucking thing I've heard all damn day Baby."

We turned to leave and was stopped dead in our tracks by Ari's dad Mark. FUCK ME!

"I think we need to talk."

Ari looked at her dad and gave him a confused look. He looked over at me and I swear if looks could kill I would have dropped right then.

"Um, dad is it something that can wait? I mean we're both exhausted."

"No Ari, I have been waiting to talk to you since yesterday. I didn't want to ruin Ellie's wedding but now that she and Gunner have left, we have a serious problem."

Holy fuck, what the hell was going on?

"Daddy you're starting to scare me. What has happened?"

"My office received a restraining order against you yesterday from a Rebecca Moore."

Holy fuck......I felt all the air leave my body in one second flat.

"Who the fuck is Rebecca Moore? I don't know anyone by that name daddy I swear."

Just then it must have hit her. She turned to look at me and I'm sure my face was pale as a ghost.

"Tell me that that's NOT the same Rebecca that you fucked!"

Holy shit! I cannot believe she just said that in front of her dad!

"Jesus Ari! Really?" I said as I looked over at her dad.

"Listen, Jeff, I don't know what the hell is going on. Two weeks ago you were standing there asking for my daughter's hand in marriage and telling me you planned on asking her to marry you the night of Ellie's wedding. Then there is some nut case girl claiming that she fears her life from Arianna. What the hell is going on?"

I threw my hands in my hair and dragged them down over my face. What the fuck? He totally just told her I was planning on asking her to marry me tonight. This was NOT fucking happening.

"Wait! What? You were going to ask me to marry you tonight? OH MY GOD!" Ari screamed as she jumped into my arms. Then she turned to her father.

"Why the hell would you just ruin that for me dad?"

"Do you want me to tell her Jeff?"

I shook my head no. I think I was going to throw up.

"Then start talking."

Ari looked back and forth between both of us. She looked confused and I wanted nothing more than to just take her away from all of this.

"Jeff? What the hell is going on?"

I looked up at her dad and then back at Ari. Here goes nothing. I was not sure how she was going to react when I told her. FUCK, I just wanted to find out if this was true or not before I even said anything to her. Spare her the hurt.......I had no choice now.

"I got a call the other night when we were at Brad's parent's lake house. It was from Rebecca; she just busted out and told me that she was pregnant and that the baby was mine."

Ari stepped back away from me and threw her hand up to her mouth.

"Oh my god......you cheated on me......with *her*!"

What?

"God no Ari! I swear to you I have not been with anyone but you since Thanksgiving. I swear to God!"

"Then how the fuck is she pregnant with your baby Jeff?"

I ran my hands through my hair again.

"She told me she was seven months pregnant. I ran into her at Rebels, the weekend before Thanksgiving and we.…...we um.…..." I looked up at Mark and he was glaring at me. Fuck....

"You fucked her Jeff? How many other girls are going to start showing up saying you got them knocked up! You promised me that you used protection! You PROMISED!" Ari screamed so loud it caused me to jump.

"I did Ari! I did use a condom baby. She's claiming it broke but I was not drunk when it happened and I would swear on my life the condom did not break. Ari I swear on my life!"

Ari stepped back away from me, no.…...no God please no.

"Why didn't you tell me you got a call from her? You must have gotten the call right before we came over. Why didn't you say anything?" Ari shouted at me.

"Ari I was going to tell you I swear to God, but I wanted to talk to Rebecca in person. To see if she was even telling me the truth because I didn't want to hurt you unless.…...unless.…..."

"What Jeff. Unless it was true.…...well now I know. I think we need to step back and take a break."

Fuck no.…...no way I was going to let her walk away from me again! Goddamn it I was going to fight for her with everything I had.

"NO! Ari this does not change the way I feel about you baby. I love you Ari. I want to marry you; I want to have kids with you I want...."

Ari started crying and shaking her head. She put up her hand to get me to stop talking.

"Do you know I was just talking to Ellie about this just the other day. I was telling her how excited I was to know that one day.…...one day.….." Her voice was breaking. Mother fucker.…...I fucking hated Rebecca Moore with everything I had right now.

"One day, I would be able to tell you we were expecting a baby. I wanted to see your face; I wanted to be the one to see your fucking face when you were told you were going to have a baby! Would you want a boy or a girl? Would you even care? I just wanted to be the one to tell you that."

"Baby I do want to have kids with you.…...more than you will ever know!" I walked to her and reached out for her.

"DON'T TOUCH ME! I will NEVER be the person who had your first child because you got some fucking whore knocked up. SHE gets to be the one who has your first child Jeff.…...NOT me!"

I looked over at Ari's father who was standing there looking torn. He looked at me with almost pleading eyes. What the fuck was I supposed to do!

"Ari I swear to you, I'm going to find out if this baby is mine. I really don't think it's my baby, I will get it taken care of I promise you."

"Well it looks like you're going to have to wait a few months to find that out now aren't you. Until then I don't want to see or talk to you."

"What!"

"Now Arianna don't do something based on your emotions right now sweetheart. Let Jeff talk to this girl before you do anything rash."

I could not believe Mark was on my side. If that was my daughter I would tell the fucker to leave and never come back.

Ari turned to her father and glared at him. He took a few steps back and turned to walk away a little.

She turned back to look at me. I could not lose her again. I won't lose her again!

I dropped to my knees in front of her. "Ari *please*, don't do this to me. *Please don't leave me again*......I beg of you!" I felt the tears running down my face and I didn't give two shits. I was pretty damn sure we now had an audience.

Ari was crying as she looked down at me.

"I love you Jeff, more than anything, but I can't handle this right now. I need time......I need to be alone and away from you while you work this out. I'm not leaving you......I just…...I just need to be away from you."

"Ari…...please tonight was supposed to change everything. Please."

"I'm going back to the cabin. Please do not come there. I'm going to ride home with Amanda and Brad tomorrow. Please just…...just......just leave me alone for awhile Jeff. If you love me you'll just leave me alone."

She turned and walked away from me. I fell over and buried my head in my hands and just lost it.

I felt someone trying to get me to stand up. I heard Brad and Josh telling me to stand up. I could barely stand. Once I got up I saw Ari getting into the jeep and driving off to the deer cabin.

Mother fucker…...not again......she was leaving me......again.

Jeff dropped to his knees in front of me and started to cry.

"Ari *please*, don't do this to me. *Please don't leave me again*....I beg of you!"

Oh Jesus, Mary, and Joseph.........fucking hell! My heart was breaking in two. I loved him so much but I was so fucking pissed right now. I wanted nothing more than to get down on my knees and comfort him. But I couldn't, I just couldn't. He took something away from me tonight. Something I was never ever going to get back. The chance to give him his first child, the thought made me start to cry.

"I love you Jeff, more than anything but I can't handle this right now. I need time......I need to be alone and away from you while you work this out. I'm not leaving you......I just......I just need to be away from you."

"Ari......please tonight was supposed to change everything. Please." Oh god Jeff please stop begging me please!

"I'm going back to the cabin. Please do not come there. I'm going to ride home with Amanda and Brad tomorrow. Please just......just......just leave me alone for awhile Jeff. If you love me you'll just leave me alone."

I turned and walked away from him......again. This time it was so much fucking harder. I knew he never meant for this to happen. It was both of our faults. Well no not really. It was that dickwads fault for not being able to tell me he loved me, and then going on a three month man whore mission.

I can't believe he was going to ask me to marry him tonight. Why didn't my dad just wait to tell me about the fucking restraining order? WHY?

Oh that bitch was smart to get that fucking thing. I so wanted to go right that minute and......and......well I can't say what I wanted to do 'cause the stupid bitch was pregnant!

That stupid mother fucking son of a bitch, stupid ass wipe dumb mother......Oh god......

I cried the whole way to the deer cabin. I almost hit two mother fucking deer on the way. Stupid animals, oh god I didn't mean that! What the hell is wrong with me?

I wish Ellie was here. Oh god how I wish I could call her. I pulled up and saw a few small lights on. I was so tired all of a sudden. All I wanted to do was get into bed and sleep. I sat in the jeep and thought about the first time Jeff and I made love.

It was the night of Brad and Amanda's wedding. They got married at the Driskill hotel and Jeff had booked a room there that night and I didn't know it. The way he couldn't tear his eyes off of me during the whole wedding ceremony should have been my first clue. Of course the slutty dresses Amanda had us all in that showed nothing but our cleavage to the max helped with his lust that night. Talk about not being able to breathe all night in that damn dress.

The room had been perfect. Simple but filled with LED candles and rose petals spread all over the bed. It was on the historical side of the hotel and had a balcony looking down onto Sixth Street. There were massage oils and lotions and chocolate covered strawberries. Oh god......it was magical. It was magical because Jeff was so sweet and gentle. After talking to Ellie I was not so nervous about my first time. She said it had hurt but after awhile it felt wonderful. She was not fucking kidding.

It was amazing.

I sighed as I got out of the jeep. Amanda and Heather would probably be coming to get their stuff. I'm sure once they heard what happened they would want to check in on me. I just really wanted to get out of this dress and these boots and just sleep. I opened up the door and almost fell over.

Oh no! NO! NO! NO! NOOOOOO! The whole room was covered with Stargazer Lilies. I mean the whole room was filled with them. There were bouquets of them in flower vases with blue bonnets mixed in. There were bouquets that had the stems wrapped in a light pink satin. Oh my god. One bouquet was so big......it was sitting in an old bucket with other wild flower bouquets. The smell in the room was unbelievable.

It was......perfect.

It would have been perfect. I was so mad at my father for ruining this for me. OH GOD JEFF! He must have spent a fortune on all of these flowers.

I started to slide down the door and cry. I put my head down on my knees and just sobbed. I slammed my head back into the door and just screamed as loud as I could.

"MOTHER FUCKER!" I ruined everything because I couldn't just let him explain. FUCK! FUCK! FUCK!

I sat there and cried so hard I felt like I couldn't breathe. Oh my god Jeff......Oh god......why did I walk away and tell him not to come here. If I had only known.....ARGH! I'm so stupid!

"Oh god why? Why did this have to happen? WHY!" I screamed out. Then I heard a small knock on the door.

That must be Amanda and Heather. I slowly got up and opened the door.

I sucked in a breath of air as I saw the only man I would ever love standing there. He came for me. He didn't walk away this time.

He came for me..........

A Year and a Half Later

The late afternoon sun felt so good on my face. It was a beautiful December day. There was just enough of a cool breeze coming off the Llano River to make me wish I had grabbed a light sweater. The peacefulness of being out here was so nice and it finally felt like things were starting to settle in. The house was finally done and we were all moved in. I absolutely loved the way it turned out and I loved it even more knowing Gunner designed it from top to bottom.

He worked so hard the last year on that house while also trying to learn everything about running the ranch. Garrett was so wonderful; he never pushed Gunner into it too fast. He knew how important the house was to Gunner and me. Thank god it was finished now and at just the right time.

The firm that Gunner interned for in college, and still did some part time work for, loved the house so much they asked if they could feature it on their website. I was so proud of him. I had to smile thinking about when they called and asked to come out and take pictures of the finished house. He was so proud.

It was a two story ranch style house with a full wraparound porch on the first floor. The kitchen was amazing with tons of cabinet and counter space. Double ovens and a huge six burner range. The breakfast nook was nothing but windows. Hell the whole house was nothing but windows. Gunner insisted it be that way. He wanted to make it seem like when you were standing in the house you felt like you were outside.

We built the house right near our Oak tree that was now in our massive back yard. Gunner had put up a four board black plank fence all around the house and the Oak tree. The front and back yard probably totaled an acre of land. He said he wanted to make sure his kids had a manure free yard to play in someday.

We had a small but functional formal dining room. There was a huge living room for Gunner and Jeff to watch the football games and to entertain. The main living area was all an open floor plan so that if you were in the kitchen you could see into the living room and breakfast nook. The master bedroom was down stairs and 4 bedrooms were upstairs. There was a huge game room also upstairs that was built over the three car garage.

Gunner insisted we needed it. Someday when we had kids he wanted their toys up there and nowhere near his big screen TV.

I had to smile at how much of a kid that man was when it came to boys toys. Tractors or TV's, it didn't matter. He was the only person I knew who had to open the box of something he just bought to start playing with it. Even the new camera we bought yesterday. He made me drive so he could take it out and start seeing how it worked.

Just then I heard his truck. My stomach started doing flip flops. Just the thought of seeing him still had me all giddy after a year and a half of marriage.

I thought about last night and how wonderful it had been. Gunner making such sweet, slow passionate love to me was my favorite thing in the world. I smiled thinking about all the sweet things he whispered in my ear.

I felt his hands wrap around me. He picked me up and spun me around slowly. Then he kissed me.......good god he kissed me with so much passion my knees almost buckled. He kept a strong but gentle grip onto me.

He leaned in and whispered against my ear.

"Shit Sweetheart......you look so fucking sexy walking along this river......I want to make love to you right now Ells. I think we better baby....... I might die right now if I cannot feel myself inside your warm body.

I threw my head back and laughed at him. I turned around to look at him and gasped. He looked amazing. He was taking off his boots. His gray shirt showed off his muscular chest and arms. I smiled at the sight of my husband. He was so damn sexy. He picked up a stick and gave it a toss and Gus took off after it. Crazy dog had been at my side all damn day.

He looked at me and smiled as I smiled back at him. Hmmm......I wonder if we could have sex here?

Why did it feel like I was having a déjà vu?

OH MY GOD......my dream. This was the dream I had that first night I spent with Gunner after the whole Ryan thing! Oh my god......I was trying to remember that fucking dream! Something happened in it that caused me to wake up so upset.

What was it?!

Gunner walked away from me. He left me......

Oh GOD......I couldn't get any air. I bent over and put my hands on my knees. I needed air.

Gunner looked at me and jumped up and ran over to me.

"ELLIE......sweetheart what's wrong? Ellie what is it baby? Talk to me Ellie you're scaring me."

I looked up at him. I couldn't talk......touch me......touch me Gunner I need you! I tried to talk but I couldn't.

Gunner ran back over and threw his boots back on. He picked me up and started walking to his truck. I buried my face into him......oh god it felt so good to be in his arms and his smell just flooded my nose. I took a deep breath in and then another one. Thank god it was passing. This has not happened since the day we got married.

Gunner pulled down his tail gate and set me on it. Gus was now jumping up at me and Gunner yelled for him to get down.

"Baby is something wrong? Are you in pain?"

I started to laugh at his panicked face. He looked so confused.

"I'm okay Gunner. I'm sorry baby; I didn't mean to scare you. It's just I couldn't get any air in and it was just like the day of our wedding. I just needed you to touch me for me to calm down."

Gunner visibly relaxed. He jumped up and sat next to me on the tail gate.

"Fuck Ellie, I thought something was wrong with you or the baby!"

I smiled at him and put my hands on my very big and round nine month pregnant belly. Right then I felt the baby kick. I grabbed Gunner's hand and placed it on my belly.

"WHOA! That was a big kick from little bear."

I just smiled and rolled my eyes at him. Gunner had been calling the baby little bear ever since we argued over buying a bear or a moose for the crib. I wanted the moose and he wanted the bear. I ended up getting my way but ever since then he called the baby little bear. I secretly loved it but rolled my eyes every time he said it.

"Yep, she has been moving around a lot today."

"Oh today it's a she huh? Yesterday it was a he......what will your flavor be tomorrow?"

I hit him in the shoulder. We decided not to find out the sex of the baby. I was counting down until little bear joined us. The baby room was finished and just waiting. Gunner worked so hard on it. Josh made the baby crib and it was breathtaking. His custom furniture business in Austin was a huge success so for him to make such a large and beautiful piece of furniture for little bear meant so much to both Gunner and me.

Gunner placed his hand on my stomach and little bear did a roll and gave a good kick. Gunner leaned down and started to sing to the baby. His voice was beautiful and the baby must have loved it as well because every time he sung to little bear she would go crazy.

Gus started to bark. I let out a laugh as Gunner looked down at Gus.

"What's he barking on about?"

"I'm not sure. He has been by my side all day today. I actually got up and sneaked away from him earlier when he was asleep just to walk around the house without him under my feet!"

Gunner threw his head back and laughed.

OUCH! That one hurt!

"Holy shit! That one was a strong kick," Gunner said with a laugh. "Little bear just might be a boy…...that felt like a pretty hard kick."

"I don't know……could also be a girl….....soccer player maybe?"

"Hmmm, that's true."

"I don't really care if it's a boy or girl……I just want her to be healthy and have my nose."

Gunner laughed and reached over and pulled my mouth to his.

This man's kisses were my weakness. I let out a small moan as I felt the baby move. She sure was active.

"Gunner, do you remember that first night I stayed at y'all's house, the night we watched Cars?"

"KA-CHOW! You bet I do!"

I let out a giggle. "Do you remember when I woke up from a bad dream?"

"Yeah, I do remember that. You were calling out my name."

"Well, that dream…...I remembered it just a little bit ago. In the dream I was walking along a river and you walked up to me. You kissed me but then you dropped my hand and you walked away from me. You were leaving me. I think I just freaked out a little bit. You know, all those old insecurities creeping back."

Gunner jumped off the truck of the bed and grabbed my face and kissed the shit out of me. Holy hell….

"Mrs. Mathews I love you more than life itself and I will *never* leave you. Now let me take you home so I can make love to you."

I smiled at him……. this man has made all of my dreams come true. I loved him so much.

What? What the hell?

"Mr. Mathews, um……I would love for you to take me home and make love to me but……"

Gunner looked at me confused and shook his head.

"BUT? There are no buts Mrs. Mathews. Come on let me help you down sweetheart…….I want to give you at least three orgasms this time."

"I don't think we're going to be able to do that Drew."

Gunner stopped dead in his tracks.

"Why?"

I smiled at him……..

"My water just broke."

Thank You

The first person I have to thank is Arianna Howard. Your input and support meant more to me than you will ever, ever know! Thank you for reading the endless tidbits I sent you and giving me your honest feedback. You are the bestest best friend EVER and Jeff will always be yours! (Insert two girls wearing leotards HERE!)

Gary Taylor, thank you for being such a wonderful friend. You really are one of the most genuine people I've ever know. Your faith and determination are a true inspiration. Thank you for always making me smile. You really are the perfect Gunner.

R.L. Mathewson you are by far one my favorite authors and I admire you so much! You are one very talented woman and I count myself as one lucky bitch to be able to call you my friend. Thank you, for everything!

Molly McAdams you rock! Thank you so much for your support and help and for our weekly lunch dates. You make me laugh my ass off but you still made me ugly cry AND almost break my nook! But I still love ya.

Lynda Ybarra, thank you for answering all my stupid questions and helping me so much. Love ya!

Pat Winn, Ari Howard, Elizabeth Bartell and Susan Sunderlin, thank you so much for taking the time out of your busy lives to read and edit this book! Without your support and help I'd still be doing edits!

Rutheah Rodehorst with Blue House Fotos. Your picture truly made me catch my breath the moment I saw it. You are an amazing photographer and a sweetheart of a lady! Thank you so much for letting me share your talent.

Paige and Drew…. Your picture is breathtaking! Thank you so much for allowing me to use it for the cover of my book.

To all the girls on the BDHM board. OMG…..I love you all and would be lost without you girls. I hope you know that! I wish I could list each of you and tell you why I love you. Thank you for your endless support and posts that make me laugh my ass off every day! I love you girls so much! Ka-Chow!

If it were not for you Darrin I could never have dreamed up Gunner and Jefferson. Thank you for letting me share a little bit of you with the world. They truly broke the mold with you and everyone is right…… you really are different. Thank you so much for your never ending love and support in everything that I do. Oh and thank you for giving me your star wish! I love you Darrin so so very much and yes....I really do love you MORE! HA!

Lauren, first let me just publicly say I'm sorry for the 1 or 2 or maybe 6ish times I pulled your uniform out of the dirty clothes and sprayed it down with perfume and gave it to you to wear to school. Or the few times you might have gone without dinner while I was wrapped up in Gunner and Ellie. Turkey lunch meat and popcorn was a fun dinner thought wasn't it?! Just remember all those trips to Dairy Queen when I gave in and took you! I love you Lauren...... always stay true to yourself and follow your dreams.

Mom.... There's not a day goes by that I do not think about you. I miss you......

Playlist

Christina Aguilera "Fighter" - Ellie's 'song'

Colblie Cailat "Oxygen" - Ari's song (Jeff!!)

Eninem "Til I Collapse" - Gunner's song

Gym Class Heroes "The Fighter" - Jeff's song

Tim McGraw "Truck Yeah" - Jeff's favorite song

Colbie Cailat "Fallin' For You" - Ellie's first "date" with Gunner...she tries hard to deny her feelings for Gunner.

Taylor Swift "Begin Again" - Ellie in the coffee shop with Gunner

Carrie Underwood "Blow Away" - Gunner packing up Ellie to get her away from her mother

Jason Mraz "I Won't Give Up" - Gunner kisses Ellie at Zilker Park for the first time

Ne-Yo "Let Me Love You" - Gunner & Ellie in his truck after their first kiss

Taylor Swifts "Fearless" - Ellie gives her heart to Gunner

Christina Aguilera "Your Body" - Jeff gets angry when Ari is dancing with other guys at the graduation party.

Britney Spears "I'm a Slave For You" - Ari after Jeff makes the comment about her virginity

Brantly Gilbert "Fall Into Me" - First time Gunner dances with Ellie and sings to her.

Christina Aguilera "Shut Up" - Ari dances with Josh next to Jeff at the graduation party

Colbie Cailat " Realize" - Ari in the hospital waiting to hear about Jeff

Nickelback "Trying Not to Love You" - When Jeff finds out Ari "Slept" with Jason

Usher "Hot Tottie" - Gunner dancing with Lori and Ellie gets jealous and leaves

Zac Brwon Band "Goodbye In Her Eyes" - Gunner during his "break" with Ellie

Usher "Yeah" - Jeff watching Ari dance and decides to say he is sorry to her

Rascal Flatts "What Hurts the Most" - Jeff dances with Ari and tell her how sorry he is

Christina Aguilera "Dirrty" - Gunner realizes he love Ellie

Vince Gill "Whenever You Come Around" - Gunner dances with Ellie after he tells Jeff he loves Ellie

Rascal Flatts "Banjo" - Gunner's song when they were heading out to the ranch

Randy Houser "How Country Feels" - Gunner and Ellie in the pasture looking at the stars

Lady Antebellum "Just a Kiss" - Ellie's first orgasm at the ranch

Maroon 5 "One More Night" - Jeff and Ari's song according to Gunner

Luke Bryan "Drunk On You" - At the river on the ranch

Christina Aguilera "Just a Fool" - When Jeff tells Ari he made a mistake at the ranch after Ari tells Jeff she wants and loves him

Colbie Cailat "Fearless" - Ari in her bedroom at the ranch after Jeff broke her heart

Daughtry's "Life After You" - Jeff after he realizes he broke Ari's heart and lost her

Kenny Chesney "You Saved Me" - Ari and Jeff finally are a couple! YEA!!!!!

Daughtry "Septemeber" - Ellie during football season

Flo Rida "I Cry" - Gunner sees Ellie out on a date with Jon

Miranda Lambert "Over You" - Gunner walks away from Ellie after seeing her dancing with Jon

Rascal Flatts "Come Wake Me Up" - Gunner trying to get over Ellie

Blake Shelton "God Gave Me You" - Ellie going after Gunner when she finds out he didn't cheat on her

Colbie Cailat "Magic" - The night Gunner proposed to Ellie and they made love for the first time!! EEEEPPPP!

Colbie Cailat "Stay With Me" - The night Gunner proposed to Ellie

Kenny Chesney "Me and You" - When Gramps is talking to Gunner before the wedding

WANTED

Hunter Hayes "Wanted" - Gunner and Ellie's wedding song

Kenny Chesney "I Lost It" - Jeff after Ari finds out about Rebecca at Gunner and Ellie's wedding

CPSIA information can be obtained at www.ICGtesting.com
Printed in the USA
LVOW05s1915061014

407465LV00017B/1210/P